It Takes A Rogue

Chris Oswald

NEWMORE PUBLISHING

Chris Oswald has lived in America, Scotland and England and is now living in Dorset with his wife, Suzanne, and six children. For many years he was in international business but now has a little more time to follow his love of writing. His books have been described as dystopian but they are more about individual choice, human frailty and how our history influences the decisions we make, also about how quickly things can go so wrong.

"It takes a rogue to know a rogue."

It Takes A Rogue

Chapter 1

Penelope Withers leaned over the body next to her and started stroking his bare back. It had gone well the previous night. Her duty done, she wanted to ensure control was with her.

He groaned, stretched out to grab any part of her he could, and drew that part; her left shoulder, towards him.

"Again," he said, sleep giving way to desire.

"Sir, our agreement..."

"Damn the agreement. That was our parents' doing, not ours. We are free to do as we like."

"Tell me first what you will say to your mother."

"First you tell me what you will say to your father." He was aggressive and on the ball; not bad qualities, but she would need to be careful with him.

"I will say, sir, that you performed and gave me pleasure."

"And I will say the same, provided you do not deny me now."

She did not deny him but her mind screamed caution.

The agreement had been painstakingly slow to negotiate. It had started in the spring of 1687, just after Penelope's twenty-second birthday. It had opened on a brutal note.

"She's old meat," sneered the Dowager Duchess.

"I'll grant you she's mature but that is an advantage to your son," Sir John Withers had replied. "He is young and headstrong. He will benefit from a good wife with a little judgment and maturity."

The negotiations wound on through the summer of that year; long, slow days with constant exchange of letters. Then, in September, the Dowager Duchess halted discussion, announcing that the Duke of Wiltshire had found another wife. They were to be married the following spring.

Two birds with one stone for his intended has both breeding and fortune.

1

It was devastating news for the Withers family. Sir John threw a fit, smashing precious furniture and tableware. Then he collected himself, ordered some things packed and left the house, not saying where he was going or how long he would be.

The two ladies, daughter and mother, were left to console themselves. It had been an ambitious alliance; a far greater prize than Sherborne. With his connections at court, there was every possibility of a position as lady in waiting to Queen Mary, although increasingly her attendants were out-and-out Catholics.

Now they just had dreams of what might have been.

"It's not fair that Father should disappear at such a critical time," Penelope said one morning in October. She had given up looking down the long drive for his return. The same trees; the same fenced parkland; the same stones on the drive. There was no change for the better, nothing ever moved at Withers Court. "It's dull here. Will we go to London for the season?"

"I don't know," her mother replied. "Your father left so suddenly it is hard to be sure what his intentions are."

"I think we should go anyway. We have that great big house sitting on its own. I expect the servants are idling away their time or else taking other jobs and still collecting pay from Father."

So, they went. Lady Withers had not deemed it sensible but Penelope was certain it was.

"Father even took the best carriage," she complained as they bumped along the London road. "This one is much less comfortable."

Lady Withers wanted to tell her daughter to stop complaining and count her blessings but the last time she had reprimanded her she had ended up apologising for several days. Instead, she turned the topic neatly to fashion and diverted her daughter from her woes all the way to Salisbury.

Outside, the brilliant October sun shone on their second-best coach. It shone but imparted little warmth; it seemed all available energy was spent on light, and nothing for heat. The driver and coachman turned up their coat collars until told flatly by Penelope to turn them down again.

"We can't have our servants looking like ragamuffins," she said blankly; no anger, no compassion, just impressions that counted.

"Quite so," her mother hastened to agree but made a note to purchase good new coats for all the staff as soon as she arrived in London.

"Ah, you came to me, I see!" Sir John was in good spirits, meeting them in the hall of their London house, just off Fleet Street, although they were having a new and magnificent house built in the West End.

"We were concerned about you, not having heard a word."

"That's right, Father, we were worried to distraction." Penelope was thinking *He cannot be angry if we express our actions as being prompted by fear for him.*

In truth, she did not feel anything for him, nor for her mother. The only person she wanted to be close to was Sally, her black servant imported from some faraway place and given her freedom so that she could devote herself to her mistress. Sally was the only person she wanted to be close to yet the one person who eluded her.

Sometimes she wondered what it would be like when her father was dead. She would have all the money. She would build a dower house for her mother on the far side of the estate, past the squat village of Winklebury, where the road ran upwards and was impassable in bad winters. She liked bad winters; looking out at the intense cold, with the gardeners struggling to dig frozen ground. Last year she had requested a duck pond at the bottom of the large lawn. She had sat in the window seat in the dining room and watched them work.

In the spring she had changed her mind and had the pond filled in again.

"Well, my dear, no need to worry, for I have news for you. No; all in good time. I have finished my business and was tomorrow leaving to meet you at Withers Court to bring you back here. But first you must change. I took the liberty of purchasing the latest fashions for you. I wanted to surprise you

3

at home but can do so here just as easily. Trot up to your bedrooms now and change. I'll tell Cook that there will be two more to dine tonight."

Both mother and daughter trotted as instructed to their respective bedrooms. There they found several new dresses, exquisitely made in Baroque style, with long, flowing but formed skirts and over- and under-layers in a delightful complication of material.

"Sally, come quickly! Help me change."

"What is your news, Father?" They were sitting in the elegant dining room being served dinner by a host of smart servants; there were more than ever before.

"Wiltshire and his mother are going to a ball." He was going to play with them a little bit.

"Are we invited, sir?" Penelope was thinking, if she could only get in front of this elusive nobleman she would have him eating coal out of her hand in no time.

"Sadly not. In actual fact, I would go so far as to say it would be impossible to invite any of the three of us."

He absorbed their perplexed cries for a few minutes, enjoying their despair.

"Why, Father, why?"

"For the simple reason that we are to host the ball."

Sir John did not tell them exactly how he had restarted negotiations for the marriage of his daughter to young Wiltshire. They did not ask so he chose not to divulge the tactics. But the result was clear and intelligent people like Penelope could easily work out how he had gone about it.

Suffice it to say, there was a young aristocratic lady who had briefly appeared at Wiltshire's side. But she was no longer considered a lady.

The ball was a complete success. Penelope remembered it as a haze of sparkle, lace and silk. Trumpets announced each visitor with nouveau-riche brashness that made the more discerning cringe. "Withers is self-made," they explained amongst themselves. "I hear he made his first fortune in shit,"

4

someone sneered because sneering was all he could offer the world.

"He danced three times with you, my dear," her mother summarised the next morning over a late breakfast. It was an acceptable bare minimum for an intended; society knew this but, thankfully, the Withers ladies knew little of the intricate rules they lived by.

Negotiations continued, dragging through the winter season in London. There were very few invitations to Wiltshire House but many from those who considered themselves to be astute enough to sense the direction of the changing wind. Hence, they kept a busy social life although always at a slight distance from the Wiltshires.

"I want to know the goods work," was the next demand from the Dowager Duchess.

"I assure you…" began Sir John.

"Pooh," she replied, aware of his origins in business. "I don't want your assurances, Sir John." She accentuated the 'Sir' just sufficiently to make it an insult. But Sir John was a businessman and was after the main prize; the aristocracy could play their games all day long provided he got what he wanted.

"I want Wiltshire to inspect the goods," the Duchess replied.

"And if he is satisfied?"

"Then, my dear man, we will have an arrangement."

They considered third party establishments for the trial but none seemed right and, in the end, they settled on the main guest suite at Withers Court. It was grand, expensively furnished and hardly ever used. Penelope thought maybe the last person to have slept there was the old Earl of Sherborne, three years ago. She wondered what life with the current Earl would have been like, living with that huge scar, waking every morning to it. No, they would have to have separate bedrooms, that much was clear.

Henry Sherborne had married some obscure Puritan girl. They had come to the ball at their London home. They had seemed blissfully happy.

But she knew better; happiness had nothing to do with love,

and vice versa.

And, provided she passed the test, it was all set for her to enter the aristocracy right at the top.

The wedding took place in June 1688. It was a glorious affair. The Wiltshires, coming late to the idea of marrying into money rather than breeding, had no qualms about spending a chunk of it on the celebrations. Withers Court was full of activity from the moment the ceremony was firmed up in March; coincidentally, the signatures were set on Penelope's twenty-third birthday. The Dowager Duchess looked at her, remarked that she was older than usual for marriage and she expected a healthy heir within the year.

"Yes, your Grace." Penelope thought it best to appear dutiful. But inside she was in a rebellion of emotion.

For over the last two months, as they had been allowed to spend time together as a couple, she had developed a distinct dislike for the young Duke. It was not his arrogance; that was rather alluring. It was not his cruelty; that was expected. It was more the disdain in which he held his intended. She had overheard a cruel joke between Wiltshire and one of his young friends. The precise form of words mattered not, for the punchline was lost to her. It was the reference to 'marry in shit and stink forever' that got to her.

Sending an ice-cold shiver down her spine.

Chapter 2

Upstream from Sturminster Newton, there is a part of the Divelish, tributary to the Stour, that crosses the road; or more properly, the road, little more than a track, crosses the river. For that road dips down and breaks from rough, compact stone to loose shingle. The waters could be fast or slow but ran with a rush that day, still disposing of the winter snow and spring rains, churning them down to the sea.

Every time Thomas passed this way, he considered how he would build a bridge there. Sometimes it would arch over the river in a glorious span on slender legs, perhaps with elaborate carvings to announce its splendour. At other times, when in more practical state of mind, it would be functional, designed to take the weight of Jim Bigg's heavy carts, all four at once, and laden down with building stone for the next project. With either style, he imagined people coming from miles around to see the bridge Thomas Davenport had built.

But then, as he skipped over the stepping-stones, trying to keep his best leather shoes from getting too wet, he thought, *Why not leave it as is? There is a place for grand building works in the world; many such places.* But there was also room for nature to find its own way and this is exactly what was here on the track to Bagber Manor.

He took this road often; every Wednesday and Sunday at least. He would walk over the Sturminster bridge he had helped build in '85 and '86, then turn right onto Stalbridge Lane to pass the mill. Sometimes trotting from habit, sometimes walking, he left the lane when it met the Divelish, then across the river and six fields further he came to the boundary of the manor. Everything was familiar about this journey but it never failed to calm him when agitated and excite him when bored.

When his father's church had closed and Amelia had turned it into the Luke Davenport Home for the Homeless, there had been no place to worship. He would not consider the Anglican church, St Mary's, mainly because of the memory of his father. He was not so tied to his religion as others in his family but memory of his father made him want to keep the Puritan candle alight.

Plus, of course, he would see Amelia.

Elizabeth had volunteered to organise a suitable church, saying she could find a disused building or barn somewhere.

"Maybe we can have itinerant preachers as they become available?" she had said, not daring to mention her desire to run it herself. Speaking of such thoughts, about a woman preaching in her own church, was not unheard of. But a big part of her religion was about the settled order and knowing one's place before God. She wanted to run her own church but was loathe to break the established structure to make it so.

Lady Merriman, a confirmed Anglican, had stepped in on hearing Elizabeth's suggestion.

"My dear Lizzie," she had adopted her family's name for Elizabeth with ease, "I will not hear of you trying to find a pokey old barn somewhere, full of rats and with leaking roof and the wind blasting through. You shall have use of the Great Hall here at Bagber Manor."

And so it was that every Wednesday evening and Sunday morning, Thomas walked to Bagber Manor to attend his father's resurrected church.

And to see Amelia.

Which was hard to do with heads bowed and facing forwards. But he found a twisted way to marvel at her developing beauty. The transformation over the last few years had been astounding. Slowly but steadily she had grown in quiet confidence, the pudgy, reserved young woman of her early youth unrecognisable now.

"Thomas, you need to talk to her," Elizabeth had finally said on that early summer day at their makeshift church in the Great Hall at Bagber Manor. With no visiting preacher that Sunday, Elizabeth had just filled in with a fine sermon about duty and responsibility.

"Talk to who, Lizzie?"

"Amelia, of course, you idiot!" She scuffed him across the head then withdrew in guilty fashion; tried to hide the offending hand within her skirts but could not find a suitable place.

"What's the matter, Lizzie?"

"It's just that, well, it's wrong to make idle gossip on the Sabbath."

"Lizzie…"

"Elizabeth, if you please. It is the Sabbath and Elizabeth is a fine biblical name."

"And Lizzie is a fine name, too. It is our family name for you and something that should be treasured. Now, Lizzie," he laboured her name, "I declare you are getting more extreme than Father ever was."

"Did you listen to my little sermon, Thomas?"

"Yes, Lizzie, I did and it was hardly 'little'. It lasted over forty minutes." But this was not criticism to Elizabeth; rather praise, and her face showed it. Thomas sighed and moved away towards the larger circle where Amelia was surrounded by half a dozen men, all clamouring for attention. But he stopped short of the group.

It was a wonder to him that Amelia remained unmarried. It seemed she had the attention of every bachelor in the area. Thomas loved to watch the beauty of her animated face; loved to see the occasional arm and hand movements used to reinforce her line of thought; loved to witness that fine mind at work.

"How goes building work, Thomas Davenport?" she asked, her quiet female voice somehow penetrating through the wall of male sound from those gathered about her.

"Very busy indeed, Miss Taylor. We are building a whole row of new cottages behind the meat market." No need to mention it was the last contract to come their way and no more to quote at present.

"Come and join our little circle," she replied. "We are discussing which of the deadly sins is the worst." Because she commanded that circle, was the reason for it, the men around her were forced to make way for Thomas but did so grudgingly, barely moving. "Gentlemen, please allow Mr Davenport to fit in to our group. I'm sure he has something to

9

add to our discussion."

They moved, then, a little more, such that Thomas could turn his body sideways and poke his shoulder through the human wall.

"That is easy," he said, surprising himself with his confidence. "Pride is by far the deadliest of the deadly sins."

"How is that so?" said Lust.

"Yes, how so?" asked Envy. But Wrath just spread his giant shoulders, shoving Thomas into the depths of Gluttony, a great big thirty-year-old man who made one side of the wall all on his own.

"Simple, my friends," Thomas replied, suddenly enjoying being the centre of attention; puffing his chest out so it pushed against the next man, applying pressure to the tight male cordon. "Pride is the sister of arrogance and together they do so much damage to others, whereas gluttony or slothfulness, for instance, mainly harm the perpetrator, dragging them down by their own weakness." He was pleased with his statement, thinking it rather astute.

"So, pride is female, to be the sister of arrogance?" Amelia asked.

"No, not necessarily, Miss Taylor. It was a figure of speech, is all." He felt suddenly foolish, more so when Envy made a snide remark about 'pride before a fall'. He stood a moment longer, just enough for the conversation to drift away, then quietly withdrew. As soon as his shoulder moved out the circle closed up, filling the gap.

Amelia noticed Thomas withdrawing. She also saw his face blush bright red and felt for him. He was out of the main line of sight now but she could see the movement of his green coat, appearing here and there like leaves behind a thick, thorny hedge. She wished he had remained but thought she understood why he had left.

She sighed and one of her male attendants mistook her sigh for tiredness. "See, we have exhausted Miss Taylor with argument and discourse. Let her retire now and rest as this is, after all, the day of rest, so anointed by the Lord." It was pious nonsense but it worked in dispelling the crowd; the men, denied their prize, all drifted out into the pale sunshine.

The row of new cottages was almost complete now. Mr Milligan had left Thomas to the work while he had a prior commission to extend a grand house on the Cranbourne Chase. "You are well up to it," he had said as they went over the plans prior to his departure. "You've managed builds before and I have every confidence that you will do an excellent job with this one."

Four months later, twelve houses stood two meadows behind the meat market, on a long slope rising up towards Hinton St Mary. Each house had been designed with four rooms and a big scullery at the back. The rooms were square, two-up and two-down, with a small hallway carved into the parlour at the front. Their gardens were still fields but the houses themselves were complete.

What made these houses remarkable in a modest way was the beating of every parameter set to Thomas, which he had been determined to achieve. He had made the houses two-feet deeper and two-feet taller, giving far more pleasing proportions than Mr Milligan's original design. Then, into the attic he had squeezed an additional bedroom, reminding him of his own attic bedroom at home. These additional rooms had dormer windows looking over the back gardens and onto the old square tower of St Peter's at Hinton St Mary in the distance, already a quarter of a millennium old. As Thomas stood at those windows, he hoped his cottages would reach that age, remaining under the tower's avuncular gaze.

He had beaten other parameters in their construction, too. Thomas liked to include some stone carving in each project he worked on. With these twelve cottages, there was a series of slightly different pictures carved above the fireplace in the front parlours. These depicted the twelve working hours of the meat market some 600 yards in front of the new houses; starting on the right, nearest the rising sun, each carving detailed an hour further into the working day.

The budget set down by Mr Milligan was another minor achievement for he had spent less than the full amount, despite the increased size of each house.

"This makes a significant difference to me, Thomas," Mr Milligan said as he reviewed both progress and costings during one of his infrequent visits back to Sturminster Newton. "However, I must take you to task on deciding to make the homes bigger than planned. Without this increase, you could have saved even more money. These cottages are to form a large part of my income in my old age and I would have much preferred to have been consulted prior to deciding to spend my money in this way."

"Yes sir, I understand."

It was a lesson learned. In this case, his employer was his customer, as Mr Milligan had used the profits of his firm to buy the land and put up the houses. It was vital to consult with the customer prior to making changes.

"But you have done exceedingly well, my son, and I cannot really fault you. I will be proud to rent out these houses and believe I will be able to charge four shillings a week in rent. Now I want to talk about your future." He put the plans and costings into a neat stack on the table, clearing the way to talk about Thomas taking over the firm.

When he had a little more experience.

"You should know, also, that your brother-in-law has come to me regarding a new wing at Sherborne Hall. I have declined the work."

"What? I mean, I beg your pardon, Mr Milligan, but is it wise to turn away work?"

"Under certain circumstances, yes, it is." Mr Milligan explained that the Sherbornes had no money to pay for the work and it was an unnecessary expense in his opinion. "Let them sort out their finances for a year or two and then I would be happy to do the work."

That left them with little work. There were the final touches to the cottages and a small amount over in Cranbourne Chase but nothing new on the horizon.

"It's the political situation," Mr Milligan explained. "There is so much uncertainty at present."

"You mean the King?"

"Exactly. He pretends at liberty but plays an underhand game to promote Catholics everywhere; in the army, the judiciary, the navy, everywhere."

It was much later on, long into the night, that Thomas realised the truth behind Mr Milligan's refusal to work for the Sherbornes.

"It's because they are Catholics," he said, sitting up in bed, suddenly completely awake. "Mr Milligan refuses to work for Catholics." So much had changed, so much antagonism, because of the actions of the King in preferring Catholics over all others. "He will do them no good in the long run with everybody set against them," he said to himself, speaking into the dark.

He did not blame his employer; a good Anglican, a devout and fair man. But he did blame the King of England for his gross bias. He sat in his bed, long into the night, ranting at the King, who caused his employer to have no work.

For who, other than a Catholic, would risk his capital at times like this?

The answer to that question came even later, when the early summer dawn clattered against his attic window, maybe knocking a code to aid his decision, maybe teasing him with suggestions that made no sense. But he listened with the faith of the young and raised both his hands in fists of joy. "That's it!" he cried.

Mr Milligan was mounting his horse, ready to leave for the Cranbrook Chase and his last real commission. Would he end his days eking out a living as landlord to a bunch of meat workers, earning four shillings a week from each of them? He had designed and built great buildings but was it all to come to nothing at the end?

"Sir! Can you spare a moment?"

"Of course, Thomas." Milligan sensed something in the young man's tone, dismounted and led Thomas back indoors.

It was afternoon before he left for Cranbrook Chase. In that intervening four hours, Thomas had painted a smile on the old man's face that lasted all the way to Stourpaine.

For Mr Milligan had a new commission and, with Thomas working on it, he knew it was going to be a good one.

Thomas had invested every penny of his inheritance in a flamboyant gesture that spoke volumes about the mood of the country.

And which, he hoped, would also delight Amelia.

Chapter 3

Matthew groaned as his stomach churned. A wave broke above him and thrashed down on to the deck, knocking him sideways with its dreadful force. He wished with all his heart for sanctuary, for stillness, but he could not go below; it was far more hellish below, with wooden walls to bounce and bruise against.

And then there was the screaming, rushing noise; all quite natural and not manmade. For centuries the wind had screamed and the waves had crashed, whether there was a boat to throw their weight upon or not. Perhaps the noise was the worst part; hammering at the mind, pounding at the soul.

And adding to the confusion all around.

Why on earth had he agreed to this voyage?

Well, he knew the answers to that. There was the public answer and the private one; both had led him away from the dusty, dry offices and whispered words of the Court of Orange, where he had worked very hard over the last three years to get established, to acquire some respect; the currency of his new trade. Maybe it was a small degree of accumulated respect that had singled him out for this mission; the public answer to his question.

The opportunity to return to England had been sudden and not sought for. Arriving in Holland in late August 1685, he had found employment immediately with the English contingent at the court, led by another new arrival who went by the name of Robert Candles.

The done and dusted joke around the English contingent was that Candles would light the way back to England.

Only, there was nothing jocular about the man. A large, greying shaggy head sat on shoulders clearly used to action. The face was slab-like and hard, as if cut from a quarry and roughly carved into features. He favoured his left shoulder, wincing whenever it was jolted or jarred, cursing under his breath frequently; habits die hard even in strange new places.

He spoke with a neutral accent, which immediately made Matthew suspicious that he was masking some other one; pretending to be someone he was not. At times, particularly of irritation and stress, it slipped and revealed a tongue alien to Matthew; soft yet harsh, grating yet slightly sing-song. When it happened, Matthew would rummage through his mind for a location but it always evaded him.

Matthew disliked his new employer intensely and instantly. Hence a part of the private reason why Matthew was returning to England in June 1688.

He had wanted to go to Poole. He had left from Poole and a part of him wanted to do the journey in reverse; almost an unwinding, to take him back to where he belonged.

But they had him on a ship going to Brixham in Devon. They had been adamant about this and he knew not why.

"Sirs, I am Dorset born and bred..."

"Strong in the arm and thick in the head," Candles interrupted him, reciting the old rhyme whenever Matthew talked of his origins.

"I am from Dorset and have never been to Devon. I would have thought it more sensible for me to concentrate..."

"Don't trouble yourself, Davenport," Candles interrupted again.

The others in the group were mainly Dutch and he warmed more to them for they seemed on his level, appreciative of his efforts.

"Mr Davenport, your insight will be particularly helpful to us in our efforts to restore liberty and true religion to your country. We need a particularly detailed analysis of the mood of the country. Can you manage this for us in the western segment of England while others of our small and select group will tour the other parts?" The speaker was Jacobus Avercamp, a member of the States General. He was a tall and thin man, with a friendly smile sketched permanently onto his angular face, like badly set up rigging on an otherwise sleek sailing ship. The smile tempted Matthew in his uncertainty and swallowed him up completely.

"Of course, Herr Avercamp, I would be delighted to go." It

would mean time away from Robert Candles, who he found to be increasingly aggressive towards him. Matthew sensed some connection from the past but had no idea as to what it might be.

And time, perhaps, to see his family again, which was the majority of the personal reason, for he ached to see them, to be in familiar, easy-going company again.

And these reasons, in total, took him to the swirling storm in the English Channel, with the wind streaming past the minimal rigging, tearing at everything.

Matthew had been allowed to select an assistant from the English contingent but decided to go alone, preferring his own company to that of others thrust upon him. He liked it better to be alone in the world. He was without friends and split from his family. It had been a lonely three years, filled deliberately with unceasing work towards his goal of re-establishing true religion. And that meant ousting the papist King.

Treason.

But at least now he was making progress towards a reunion with those he cared for, even if every yard through the sea was marked with churn and swirl.

The ship was laden with spices. It seemed odd to go most of the way down the channel to a southwestern port like Brixham, where London and the demand for spices was so far away.

"There is a market in Bristol and the rich estates of the southwest. London cannot be the destination for everything," the captain said flatly when Matthew asked. He decided not to raise the subject again. But he would have made a better disguise; thought of something far more convincing to put in the hold.

"How long will this blow last, do you think?" he asked the master's mate, a brusque Dutchman with excellent English.

"Two days, I should think." Matthew had been hoping for a prediction of hours not days.

He made it at last, savoured the first few unstable steps on the dry land of Brixham harbour, praising the Lord for safe deliverance but not falling to his knees; that would have been too dramatic an act for Matthew. Instead, he straightened his hat, felt for his purse, and asked the first person he saw where he might hire a horse. It was a bright, dry day, as if a different weather system worked on land as opposed to at sea. He looked back at the heavy rain clouds hanging over the English Channel, almost losing the ship in soggy, grey mist, and thanked God again that he was on dry land.

The first person he saw to ask for directions was an old lady, who had no hesitation in sending him five miles out of town to her son's inn, where there were always reliable horses that represented excellent value for money.

"Are you foreign?" she asked, barely able to make out his speech.

"I'm from Dorset," he replied, a hint of pride in his voice.

"Ah, foreign then," the old lady said.

"I suppose so," Matthew agreed, although he saw no traces of humour in the wrinkled monkey face.

"Do they have a troublesome king in Dorset too, then?"

"The same king, madam."

"Oh dear, bless you then, youngster."

Matthew, following her directions up and out of the town, considered she had probably never heard of Dorset in her seventy-five-odd years in the very next county.

He walked absent-mindedly past several inns and stables, muttering her directions to keep on track, eventually seeing the Horseshoe Inn after walking an hour and a half. The late June sun beat down on his black hat and black clothes. It had been much colder, with an evil east wind, just five days earlier in Amsterdam. He was over-dressed. There was no one around and it would have been a simple matter to take off his coat, surrendering to the power of the sun. He ached to do it but would not; it somehow felt improper to be half-dressed for his homecoming.

The news in the Horseshoe hit him like a musket ball.

"The queen has given birth," greeted him at the doorway. "A healthy son to be called James."

"Can this be true, landlord?" Matthew asked.

"The source is good, sir, I heard it myself from the mail coach directly come from London. It came in not two hours ago. We had heard rumours before but this was confirmation clear as day."

"It means a Catholic accession." The pregnancy had been worry enough but there was hope it would be a girl, hence falling in line after Mary of Orange and Princess Anne, the two grown-up and protestant daughters of James.

"What was that, sir? Yes, the King and Queen are both Catholic, so it stands to reason the Prince will be so." He would now take precedence over his sisters; perhaps the founding of a new Catholic dynasty.

Matthew took a quart of small beer, watered down drastically, and asked for some lunch. He sat at a table on his own but chair slanted so he could hear the general chatter. It was all about the new-born Prince. There were a lot of hot heads voicing what they would do with a papist monarchy.

But the big question in Matthew's mind was what should he do? He could go straight back. The ship he came on would leave in the morning. He could be with it and, with a reasonable wind, back in Amsterdam in a few days to report his findings. He picked at a well-cooked fish pie while considering his options.

"Sirs," he broke into the conversation at the next table, "do you know when the child was born?"

"It's more than likely be the week afore last," said a reasonably well-educated-sounding man; probably went to the local school until fourteen and now worked as a clerk or under-manager in some establishment. "We first heard rumours ten days ago and it takes a fair few days for the mail coach to come all the way from London." London was pronounced with heavy emphasis, as if it took a great effort to refer to somewhere so far away.

This information helped Matthew make his decision. It was likely that news had already reached Holland and returning now would be a waste of time; besides, he would look foolish rushing back to give news that was already ten days old.

He would go on. He would be home in a few days.

Only there was no horse available at the inn.

"The mail coach took the last we had. There was a big horse sale a few weeks back and we've been short ever since."

"There is nothing at all in the area?"

"You could try Brixham, sir," the landlady volunteered.

"I've just come from Brixham."

"Wait a minute," the clerk or under-manager came up. "I couldn't help but overhear your conversation. You're looking for a horse? I have one that has just become available."

The price was outrageous but Matthew now had a gangly, skinny pony. He set the stirrups high like a jockey to keep his long legs off the ground. The clerk or under-manager bade him a good journey and chuckled as he waved Matthew on his way.

Chapter 4

Matthew's instructions were precise and he had been told to memorise them and throw the paper they were written on overboard, into the sea. He drew out his large notebook as he rode and stopped often to make notes. He added sketches of the towns he passed through, later annotating them before he slept each night. Twice he rode out after breakfast, back the way he had come, because he felt he had not got the layout quite right.

But it was not just a path he was forging. He was charged with fact-finding over many areas. Chief amongst these was 'taking the temperature of the nation', as Jacobus Avercamp put it. "For we need to know how the people feel as well as how the land lies."

More mundane tasks involved noting sources of water and which rivers were hard to cross, and where cannon poked their ugly noses out from stone faces. He stopped and scribbled and sketched, like an itinerant artist seeking the perfect landscape for his next work.

Thus, he made very slow progress up the country. In his imagination, he had seen himself knocking on the front door of his family home within a few days. But after five days he made Exeter; no more than a third of the way to Sturminster Newton.

And in Exeter he purchased four more notebooks and several pencils. He stayed three days in the city, quietly recording everything he thought his masters in Amsterdam might want to know. He went into tiny details; the numbers of soldiers he spotted and how they were armed. Visiting a public house the soldiers frequented, he listened in to their banter to ascertain the mood; their resolve to fight.

Avercamp had insisted he write in some form of code and he had given this a great deal of thought. Instead of some clever system of replacing letters with other letters or numbers, he had the idea to impersonate another profession altogether. That way, if his notes were examined they would look innocent rather than deliberately designed to hide another message.

He learned later that his counterpart in East Anglia had been discovered and heavy questioning had left him severely maimed before he talked. He hobbled to the hangman's noose on broken ankles, half dragged by those who had discovered him.

Matthew thought his sketches quite good and this gave him the idea to be an artist looking for suitable subjects to paint. From there it was quite a game to work out a secret meaning for artistic-sounding descriptions. He did it by use of first letters, hence the 'l' and 's' of 'lovely scene' stood for 'lots of soldiers' while 'rouge tint' meant 'rough track'. He sometimes spent minutes on end deliberating over a particular phrase, trying to find something suitable but also something he would remember.

For nothing of his real purpose could be written down.

As June moved out and July took centre-stage, Matthew continued his steady progress east and slightly north. He went easily and with growing confidence from Exeter to Ottery St Mary and on to Honiton. At Honiton, new news met him at the inn where he was staying.

"The judges have been acquitted, all of them!" came the cries throughout the inn and onto the streets outside. Matthew knew immediately what this was about. He had both read and written reports on this subject back in Amsterdam. It stemmed from King James' insistence that a new Declaration of Indulgence be read on Sundays, from every church in the land.

In theory, the declaration, granting religious liberty to all by suspending the penal laws, was to be welcomed but Matthew, a loyal Presbyterian, was concerned on two fronts.

He had written and re-written these points in reports back in Holland; those reports had seemed dry positions but now he realised he was living them in reality. He recalled the principle arguments against it, wondering why the King kept pushing in this regard.

First was the deeply-held suspicion that James was doing this solely for his own religion, to boost Catholicism and boost its followers too. He had pointed out in his reports that this was backed up by fact.

Many Catholics have been promoted into key positions. My own sister is married to one who, as Earl of Sherborne, has done well out of it, becoming Lord Lieutenant of Dorset. Catholic army officers are everywhere. Even Anglicans increasingly need the patronage of a Catholic notable to maintain office. Yet I am not aware of one Presbyterian, nor Calvinist, nor even Quaker, who has benefitted to the slightest extent.

Second was the political argument addressed by many. The declaration was a suspension of a law passed by Parliament. The monarch was sovereign in Parliament, not despite it. Hence, how could it be right for one man; any man, to suspend the decisions of Parliament?

It was also of note that news of the seven judges' acquittal, including the Archbishop of Canterbury, was met with almost universal acclaim across the whole of the southwest of England. For days afterwards, it was the main subject of conversation wherever he eavesdropped; amongst clergy, soldiers, common folk about their business, and even the few nobles he heard in the inns he frequented. He sensed great joy from so many, tinged only slightly with concern for the future.

It was perfect material for his report on the condition of the southwest for an invasion.

Matthew moved in this way into Somerset and the towns began to become familiar, from previous visits.

It was at Sherborne, getting closer to his home, that the first incident occurred. He was taking a good look at the castle, doing sketch after annotated sketch, when a smart troop of soldiers on horseback stopped by him.

"Sir, can you tell me what you are about?"

"Of course, Colonel." Matthew did not understand the army rank insignia but thought this man probably a colonel; he was young but with great bearing and authority, yet not unfriendly. "My name is Francis Overton and I am an artist looking for suitable landscapes to paint." Francis Overton was the name he had selected from a list Robert Candles had presented him with.

"Colonel Hanson at your service, sir." Matthew had guessed the correct rank.

"I must say, Colonel, there seems to be a lot of military activity around. I was hoping for much quieter scenes for my work!"

"It's the times we live in, Mr Overton. Where do you intend to go next?" The answer came out before Matthew could stop himself.

"Why, Sturminster Newton to visit my…"

"Yes sir?"

"To visit… um… some of my… eh… old acquaintances." He was backpedalling and knew that Colonel Hanson had noticed it.

"Well, that is a sweet coincidence for I am going that way myself," the colonel replied. "Not officially. I am off duty as from ten minutes' time and was planning to ride over there. Perhaps we can go together? I would welcome the company."

Matthew's social skills were not up to a graceful and imaginative refusal. He agreed with a murmur of assent and waited while Hanson led his troop away and handed them over to a sergeant. Ten minutes later, he was back with a saddle bag of spare clothes and a cheery grin.

"I'd love to know more of your painting as we ride. What paint do you use? And do you specialise in landscapes to the exclusion of other subjects?"

Matthew's day went from scary to dangerous when the chatty but watchful colonel told him where he was going in Sturminster Newton.

"My good friends the Davenports," he said, then related a long story about how he had met Grace and Thomas. "Of course, Grace has removed to Sherborne Hall now as the new countess."

"I had heard, sir. Tell me, has she become a Catholic on marrying the Earl?" The letters from his family were strangely silent on this and he burned to know.

"You know her?" Hanson stopped his horse, turned in his

saddle and looked hard at Matthew. "You are not Francis Overton, are you?"

"No."

"You resemble Thomas more than Grace but the family likeness is there. You are Matthew Davenport, are you not, come back from the continent?"

"Yes sir, I am." All his spy-dreams came tumbling down that moment. He had failed at the first hurdle, because of a slip of the tongue; an unguarded response in which he had let his private life get in the way of his mission. He should never have asked about Grace's conversion.

"So why the pretence, Mr Davenport? Why the false name and occupation?"

That was when the inspiration came to him. "I was not sure of my reception, sir. I left in a hurry when Judge Jeffries…"

"Do not mention that name, please."

"Why is that, sir?"

"His name is horror to me, is all."

Matthew had enough tact and understanding not to press the point, although tempted dearly for the sake of clarity; to know where he stood. He felt slightly safer with Hanson's view of Judge Jeffries. He would just have to live with a degree of uncertainty as to whether Hanson disregarded Judge Jeffries, and the Bloody Assizes he had led, sufficiently well to overlook what he had discovered about Matthew.

Sometimes uncertainty is the more certain option, he reflected.

Besides, memories of his secret assignment flashing back at him, here was a chance to determine the attitude of a senior officer in His Majesty's army.

Matthew stepped out of his character then, forcing his natural reticence down like a dog under training. He made light conversation; more than half of it, in fact. Into that light conversation, weather, scenery, trade and farming practices, he threw occasional minor enquiries as to the mood of the nation. He did not realise that Hanson knew exactly what he was doing and replied honestly although carefully and with a polite question of his own thrown in.

Thus, the two men, riding together like the old friends they were not, yet connected through friendship like in-laws, danced around each other; each tried to determine the loyalty of the other; each gaining reassurance but not quite sufficient to declare their own position.

It would take a motherly-type figure to bang their heads together and tell them to stop their silly nonsense.

Lady Merriman came into view in a light carriage, rattling along over the rough road.

"Colonel Hanson, what a pleasure. What brings you here?"

"Visiting the Davenports, Lady Merriman, and, as it happens, bringing a long-lost brother back to them." He introduced Matthew, who tried to bow but his horse shied as he leaned forward, causing Matthew to slide down level with the horse's neck.

"Woah!" cried Lady Merriman. "Careful as you go, Mr Davenport. I would not want to report to your family that I witnessed you being trampled underfoot by the sorriest nag I ever saw. Now, I must go or I shall be all day just getting to Bishops Caundle and no time for my chinwag when I arrive."

Matthew warmed to Lady Merriman immediately. The 'Witch of Bagber', as he had sometimes referred to her in chastising Thomas and Grace about their frequent absences to visit Bagber Manor, was no witch at all. She was charismatic, cheery and fun; all the attributes Matthew would dearly love to own.

And she was beautiful. So beautiful.

Chapter 5

Thomas kept the true nature of his new building secret as long as possible. But it could not be for long; he was a Davenport, and a builder. It stood to reason, therefore, that a speculative build would be a place of worship.

And the secret was out before the first stone was laid.

"I am a builder first," he declared. "I build for profit. Anyone who wants to buy my place of worship is welcome to do so. I care not," he lied, "whether it is Catholic or Puritan."

Yet he shyly asked Amelia Taylor, newly come to Presbyterianism through her friendship with Elizabeth, to lay the first stone.

Which she did in a sweet ceremony on July 15th, the day before Matthew came home.

It seemed a blessed day, much like the bridge-opening ceremony of two years earlier but on a smaller scale. It had rained overnight so that steam rose from the ground all morning, creating a slightly mystical air as a few handfuls of people gathered on Fodrington Field, the newly purchased home of the church-to-be.

Thomas had been awake much of the night rehearsing his speech, learning it by heart yet continually shaping it. When last timed, it was almost exactly nine minutes long; a clever mix of humour and appropriate observations.

"Ladies and Gentlemen," he started. But then all memory failed him. "It… it, I mean, I take great pleasure in asking Miss Taylor to lay the first stone of this new building, which I hope will be a lasting memorial to man's worship of God for many generations to come." He sat down, blushing at the lack of grandeur, of themes and concepts he had planned.

"Thank the Lord for a short and pertinent speech," someone shouted from the crowd, to general laughter. The laughter began its existence as a nervous response to an awkward situation but, after a few 'hear hears' and the odd witty comment, the humour became genuine.

Thomas stood up again hastily. "I forgot to add, refreshments are provided, courtesy of Big Jim's Hauliers." Big Jim, a tiny man, and Plain Jane, his beautiful wife, had done well for themselves since Thomas and Grace had agreed to help them leave Bristol to escape their heavy debts during the Monmouth uprising. Grace had ensured that every penny of those debts had now been repaid, along with interest at six percent.

"Good old Jim and Jane, never miss a chance for a party."

"I thank you, Thomas, for your tact in these difficult times." Mr Jarvis, the butcher, had also done well for himself in a small way since Elizabeth and Amelia had gifted back the share of his business that Simon Taylor had obtained by devious means. Elizabeth had explained carefully that her husband had done no legal wrong but had created a moral position they could not live with. Now, Mr Jarvis was on the Town Council and planned to run for mayor next year or the year after. "In not declaring your intentions with regard to denomination, you have displayed great insight."

"Sir, I…" He was a fraud; he had intended but had forgotten his words.

"Say no more, my lad. There are stresses everywhere in our society and it does you credit that you did not use today to rub up those stresses further."

"But, Mr Jarvis, with the queen giving birth…"

"Hush, Thomas, for something will break soon and there is little point in being at the crack itself. Better to witness it from a short distance and thereby benefit without the attendant risk."

Mr Jarvis was right and wrong. He was right in that something would break soon for there was a curious sense across the land, grown since the announcement of the Prince's birth a month earlier, that change was coming. There was hopelessness in the air; but the strange thing about hopelessness and despair is that they are at the bottom of the barrel. Soon, a new barrel will be opened and each new container has a skim, at least, of hope slid in at the top. Thus, despair and hope are cousins; they have different parents but share the same ancestry.

But Mr Jarvis was wrong in congratulating Thomas for steering a careful course through the troubles to come, for Thomas was soon right in the middle of it.

With no easy way out.

Lady Roakes liked to pack her jewellery herself. All other belongings would be handled by one of the many maids or footmen, but not her jewellery.

And she packed it slowly, savouring each piece in order of when it was received. They told a story she loved to hear again and again, despite the fact that she was both teller and listener.

The early pieces from 1686 were less expensive. That was to be expected. She had been plain Mrs Roakes then, married a week after confirmation of Mr Beatrice's execution. The death of her first husband was not a cause of regret; he had been brought down by his own weakness.

But even in those early days, Roakes had given her the best ornaments he could afford. These earrings, for instance, were not the largest diamonds; probably too small to wear now, but they had been the first gift to her and she remembered them fondly.

The pearl necklace she packed next marked their change of fortunes. And Lady Roakes had to admit that she had been wrong to oppose her new husband in the venture that changed everything. She had wanted to open a brothel in London. "Brothels always make money when run well and, believe me, beloved husband, I mean to run it well."

But he would not hear of it. "Mrs Roakes," he said with a firmness of voice Mr Beatrice had never owned, "if we intend to become very rich then we need to invest in land."

"Pooh to pig farming." Roakes had come from a pig farm in Yorkshire but left it as soon as he could to join the army. Lady Merriman had been held virtual prisoner at that pig farm for many years.

"Did I say farming?"

"No sir, you did not." She called him 'sir' whenever he seemed commanding.

"I refer to land development. What do you see when you look

at this city?"

They had only been in London a few days. It was her first time.

"A great big sprawl, a mass of people."

"Would you say bursting at the seams?"

"I would, sir, yes, about to burst at any moment."

His plan was simple but inspired. They would use their existing capital to buy as much land as possible around London. Then they would build cheap houses on some of the farms; overspills for the London masses. These would go up very quickly, within a matter of weeks, producing a steady income for their everyday needs, and working capital as well. On other purchased lands they would develop grand mansions by the score; all slightly different and all outrageously expensive, with hefty deposits required before a stone was laid.

"We'll collect the rents from the cheap houses while selling the mansions for huge profits, all funded by our customers. We will create whole new fashionable areas."

"With the added benefit that the poor will be out of sight in our tenement slums," she had said, understanding the plan quickly.

With the first deposit from a wealthy aristocrat, Roakes had bought her the pearl necklace.

By Christmas 1686, they were wealthy. By the summer of 1687, Mr Roakes had purchased a seat in Parliament at a discount, for nobody could be sure when it would next be summoned. A few quiet words and a little passing of money and the knighthood followed in March 1688. Mrs Roakes became Lady Roakes.

And Mr Roakes let it be known that he desired to be called Sir Beatrice Roakes.

"In honour of the sad man who is no more but put us together with his demise," he chuckled, adding that he adored her, which she knew to be true.

For the jewellery kept on coming.

She was packing because they were moving. She had been wrong again when guessing where their new house would be.

"It's the one you are building by the river, sir," she had said.

"No, my dear, it is the one Lord Drivers is exchanging for the one we are building by the river."

"But why, Sir Beatrice?" The wealthier they became, the more she respected him.

"Because with a little money spent on it, it will be a magnificent residence. Fit for the Prince himself, I would say."

"Don't mention the Prince, Roakes." Even Lady Roakes was mired in a mix of despair and hope about the new Prince.

"Sorry, my lovely Lady Roakes. If you have time this afternoon, I would like to show you Drivers Court and let you see the possibilities yourself."

She found the time and loved it instantly. Sir Beatrice might have found his business calling but over the next few months Lady Roakes discovered her talent for interior decoration. She turned it into a home of palatial splendour, with room following room of elegant furniture, and elegant guests upon that furniture. The gardens were on a slight bend of the river, looking beyond the huddle of houses on the south bank, to the hills and woods of Kent beyond.

"We will get the pier fixed and a boatman and crew employed," she declared on first seeing the splendid outlook the house had.

Another aspect she loved was that there was always some new discovery. "I think if I live to be a hundred years old, I will still be discovering outhouses and secret walks in the grounds." She skipped ahead of him like she was a young girl again. Then she turned and took his hands in hers.

"Thank you, sir."

"You are most welcome, my dear." He meant it, she could tell.

"And I have a gift for you, sir." It was nearly always 'sir' these days. Her love for him, her respect for him, was mounting like the cash in his chest and the jewellery in her bedroom.

But suddenly she was shy, like a skipping girl stood still.

"What is your gift for me?" He expected a sword or some personal item.

"I am with child." Then she added in a rush of intended reassurance, "I know I am quite old but…"

31

"Old, my foot! What age are you, anyway?"

"I am thirty-six, sir. I will be thirty-seven when our child is born." He liked the sound of those two words; 'our child'. The child he would be having with this sudden-found love of his life.

They were rogues. They knew that about themselves and were all the more honest for it. But even the most desperate rogues can love like romantics; till death do part.

"Well, I always said late thirties is the perfect age," he lied, for it was old enough that the risks were multiplied significantly. His thoughts matched the times. Fear of losing her in childbirth was like the fear of a papist dynasty forming from King James' loin to rule over a Protestant land forever. But then, wonder at fatherhood was like the optimism that pervaded everywhere; that change was upon them and change would be for the good; a catapult into the modern age.

A little later, on their tour of Drivers Court, when obscured from view behind a summer house built out of interweaved slender sticks in the shape of two doves standing together, he stopped and placed his hands around her waist. He could lift her easily and did so now but very gently, conscious of what she carried.

"Either way, I know the baby's name," she said as she was moved through the air towards him, feet dangling twelve inches off the floor.

"What will it be if a girl?" he asked, bringing her to him.

"Beatrice," she laughed, her laughter getting caught in his throat as their lips met.

"And a boy?" he asked a few minutes later.

"Beatrice," she whispered. "The next Sir Beatrice."

And now the day to move into Drivers Court was upon them. Lady Roakes was three months pregnant; over the morning sickness and in perfect health. He insisted on carrying her over the threshold, placing her carefully down in a high-backed chair in the hall.

"Lady Roakes, a letter arrived for you." A footman offered a silver tray, upon which was a single letter sealed with a wax insignia she did not recognise.

"That looks like young Wiltshire," said Sir Beatrice with a knowing air. "Open it, my dear."

"It's an invitation for tomorrow night. Their address is the same as ours. How can this be?"

"Not the same, but the same street. The Duke and Duchess of Wiltshire are our neighbours."

"Oh, the joy of it, the very joy of it." It was all a little too much for Lady Roakes. Sir Beatrice insisted she rest that afternoon in her new bed.

"I'll come and see you later on," he said with a wink.

"We'll have them once and then never have to see them again if you don't like them," Wiltshire explained to his tiresome wife. "But he will be a Member of Parliament and I sense a particularly malleable one. We need a few more like him without confounded principles to consider on every damnable issue."

"If you must," she replied, replicating the haughty tones some of her husband's female friends boasted. "I dare say we will find something to talk about." Then she left the room, calling a host of servants in a loud voice that grated on the Duke.

Their honeymoon over, they now had the reality of life together as a married couple. Penelope had insisted on taking Sally with them to Paris, where they spent a month in a borrowed house with old, heavy furniture and servants that seemed covered in the dust of neglect.

She did not like her husband one bit but liked the connections he brought and loved being referred to as 'Your Grace'. She had to labour the point with Sally, who continued to call her Miss Penelope, seeming not to understand that names will change with circumstances. Clearly, in whatever part of the world this beautiful simpleton came from, this was not standard practice. She would have forgiven much from this dark-skinned beauty, if only Sally would let her touch and caress her as she longed to do.

But referring to her as 'Miss Withers' or 'Miss Penelope'

seemed so utterly ordinary now that she could not bear it. She had insisted on the correct convention, likewise with her mother, who had carried on with 'my dear'.

"Yes, Your Grace, my dear," Lady Withers had flustered.

And now she had to entertain those dreadful jumped-up new neighbours who had the temerity to move in next door to Wiltshire House.

Matthew was welcomed with a scene reminiscent of the father and the prodigal son, yet the welcome came from his younger brother, their father having died in Winchester Jail three years earlier. It was a distortion of the parable; the brother should have scorned the arrival yet made the welcome in place of the father.

Thomas forgot about his church in the excitement of seeing Matthew and they set out for Bagber Manor almost at once.

"Elizabeth will want to see you immediately. And we will send word to Grace." But first, Thomas exchanged Matthew's tired pony for a fine stallion he borrowed from Big Jim, which made snorting noises when Matthew pulled on the reins.

"Give him some head, brother," Thomas advised. "I'll race you across the fields."

"No..." but Thomas was gone, his laughter sailing on the light wind as he streaked ahead. Matthew kicked his horse to catch up and slid off the back when the stallion moved off sharply, landing in the edge of the river by the mill.

However, he mounted again and kicked again, catching Thomas as he cantered across the Divelish, halfway to Bagber Manor.

And with a streak of intense concentration, Matthew drew ahead on the far bank of the Divelish, trepidation at the six hedges to jump diminishing with each one.

He was back home. He was alive again.

But he knew that quite soon he would have to retrace his steps to Brixham, making more notes on the way. Then, he would board the same ship on its next run and hope that going up the channel in August would be better than going down it in June.

34

But there was a lot of hope in the air and he felt new-born. Particularly when, after greeting Elizabeth with a deep hug, he found that Lady Merriman, the owner of Bagber Manor, had returned from her friend in Bishop's Caundle and was walking in the garden with a huge wickerwork basket of picked flowers over her arm.

He was quite sure, as he ventured out into the garden, that she would welcome a hand with that heavy basket.

Chapter 6

Thomas decided at the last minute to use brick instead of stone. Everything substantial he had worked on before had been stone, usually from a quarry near Shaftesbury, digging ever deeper into the hillside.

This time, irrationally, he wanted brick. And he chose one with Big Jim one hot day in early August. He had remembered a building in Dorchester from his stay at school there. They had gone down together, knocking on the door and asking the occupiers if they knew anything of the bricks used in the construction of their beautiful house.

They did not know. They were only tenants and had recently moved in. But they suggested asking at the builders' yard around the corner, for they had recently done some modifications and the landlord had suggested they use them.

"Thank you, sir. Do you mind if I make some sketches of your home? I am a builder in Sturminster Newton and I wish to model a new building on your home."

"Not at all. Do you wish to see inside?" Thomas did, although it was mostly the external construction he was interested in. He had built in brick before but mainly smaller cottages and farm buildings. He wanted his place of worship to have grandeur and proportion. He wanted to build with elegance, using the bricks to add to the sense of God's presence, rather than creating something utilitarian and humdrum. Not that his church would be elaborate at all; it was simple, austere elegance he was after.

Three hours later, Thomas was considerably poorer in terms of cash. But he did not feel the loss, for he was the owner of 50,000 bricks; sufficient for the place of worship he was building and a small house besides. He had also made friends with the tenant of his model house and received an invitation to return at any time to examine both inside and out.

"The name is Browning, sir, James Browning," he had said as he let his two unexpected guests into his home that morning. "I trade in wool and only moved into this house last month, returning from Amsterdam."

"You lived in Amsterdam, Mr Browning?" Big Jim asked, suddenly interested after traipsing around behind Thomas for two hours, making the odd polite observation.

"Yes sir, I was there several years setting up my wool business. Now I have returned to my home town and have taken a lease on this property for my family's enjoyment."

"Did you know Thomas' brother Matthew in Amsterdam, by any chance?"

"It would be Matthew Davenport, would it not? No, I don't think I do, sir. Now, I must be about my business and talking of business reminds me that you wished to visit the builders' yard, which I can take you to as it is on my way." It was a polite rebuff of Big Jim's question, marked by Browning looking away from them, staring pointlessly to the middle distance, view blocked by the large red bricks that made the side of his new home.

"What's your Matthew up to?" Jim asked as the cart rattled along the ridges and fields of middle Dorset. He drove fast and the first load of bricks bumped a little in the back.

"Oh, he's just taking a break from the work he does in Amsterdam."

"What would that be, Thomas?"

"I don't rightly know." Thomas remembered that Jim and Jane were Catholics. "All I know is he works for someone in the government in the Low Countries, or for some high-up official there. I don't pay much attention when he talks about his work."

"You don't have to play safe with me, Thomas." Big Jim flicked at a wasp that would not leave him alone, and clicked to the horses. "I'll try and outrun the pesky thing," he laughed. It lightened the mood but the seriousness was not beaten back. It returned as they crested Okeford Hill and saw again the beautiful panorama below them.

The view sobered them completely. After a moment of complete stillness, Jim released the brake carefully and the cart started easing down to the Stour.

"I'm not a fool, Thomas."

"I know you are not, Jim."

"And your brother does not make a good spy."

"Spy? What on earth…"

"He's always asking questions and scribbling the answers in one of his little books."

"I understand he has an employer with significant mercantile interests, is all. He is a keen worker and wants to find out about these things to aid his employer in Amsterdam."

"So, his master is a supplier to the army, then?"

"Why do you say that, Jim?"

"Because all he ever asks about are the soldiers; what strength they have, what equipment, how organised they are and what their morale is like."

"I know nothing of that. But I have heard him ask on other matters; sheep, for instance, and even building materials." Thomas was half-lying in defence of his brother.

After unloading the bricks on Fodrington Field, both made special reports that evening. Thomas went to seek out Matthew and to relay his conversation with Big Jim as a warning.

"Matthew, you need to be sensible about your many enquiries. You are beginning to raise suspicions with so many questions about soldiers."

"I'm almost done, Thomas." He had always looked at Thomas as a child; found it hard to accept him being a man of twenty-one. "You know what I do is for religion and liberty."

"With Monmouth it was the other way around."

"What do you mean?"

"Liberty came first. His battle cry was 'liberty and religion'; yours is 'religion and liberty'."

"It's not a battle cry. I am no soldier."

"If you are no soldier, why all this interest in the strength and disposition of the army? Oh, and their morale too."

Matthew then told him what he was about. To a certain extent it was obvious. Yet Thomas did not want to hear it.

For then he knew it. And knowing meant he was involved.

Big Jim reported much later into the night, for after unloading the bricks he still had a way to travel. Sensibly, he returned home, ordered his stable lad to rub down and feed the horse then to saddle his riding horse. He went from the stable yard to the kitchen, where Jane was pouring a bottle of red wine into a stew she was preparing. Despite the growing success of the business, they had just a general maid. Jane insisted on cooking and clearing away all the meals, often chiding her husband into helping her.

"A little bit of hard work in the home never hurt anybody," she used to say until Jim commented that it must be that she was getting on a bit, slipping into the language of the elderly.

"There's beer in the pantry," she said, nodding towards the cool room off the kitchen. "It's been a scorcher today and here's me standing over a hot stove just to make my man's dinner."

"If it's your man's dinner, I assume you won't be having any." He got a cuff on the ear for that remark but also a cheery smile.

"Jane, I want to tell you about something." He relayed the conversation with Thomas, then his suspicions about Matthew. "He's not like Thomas and Grace. I mean..."

"Grace is a Catholic now."

"Yes, but is she really, in her heart?" Jim asked. "What I meant is that Thomas and Grace are, well, they're not hung up on any particular religion. What is important to them is the existence of God, not the peculiarities of worship."

"Thomas is building a church for his religion. You went to get the bricks today."

"Yes, but let's be truthful with his motives. He's doing it for a lady he's fond of."

"Who, Jim?"

"For Amelia Taylor, of course. But we're getting off the subject here. Matthew is very different. Matthew is determined to bring about the ascendancy of some form of Puritanical religion. I don't mean he's a bad man; far from it, more that he sees everything very simply; divides the world into right and wrong."

"Very dangerous," Jane poured herself a glass of the same red wine she was cooking with; a second bottle she had opened automatically as she listened to Jim.

"And he's gone away to Holland and come back suddenly, asking a lot of questions."

"Yes, I see. You're going to need to ride to Sherborne tonight." That was exactly why Jim had asked the stable lad to saddle his best horse.

Sir Beatrice watched his hosts very carefully. He noted how assured the Duke of Wiltshire seemed. He commanded easily and with an aloofness that appealed to him. He would practise on his household staff tomorrow. He could see himself issuing orders as if born to it.

"Sir Beatrice, tell me a little of your family if you will?" The Duchess was talking to him.

"Ah, Your Grace, I come from minor gentry in the wilds of Yorkshire." The location was truthful but the assertion of gentility was not.

"And where is your family estate?" she sniffed. The cheek of it; he had done his homework and knew where her father had made his money.

"Ah, Your Grace, it was a modest place which I sold to provide capital when I came to London."

"I suppose in some of the more remote parts of the country it is commonplace to mix the yeomanry with the gentry."

"But, my dear," the Duke intervened, "Sir Beatrice has done wonderfully well since coming to the city. We must acknowledge the improvements he has brought to his station."

Afterwards, as the two men drank brandy in the dining room, the Duke confided that he hated his wife.

"She's an incredible snob," he said, "like most of those who pull themselves out of the gutter." As he spoke this sentence, he looked across at Sir Beatrice with a long, hard and appraising stare. Sir Beatrice did not know whether to be comforted or inflamed, so let it pass.

Better times were just ahead, however. For when the Duke was on his third brandy, he raised a subject that made Sir Beatrice sit up.

"Whose side are you on, my boy?" The Duke was slurring his

words now. Sir Beatrice wanted to point out that the term 'my boy' hardly applied in addressing someone closer to twice his age.

But Lady Roakes had worked on those rougher edges over the last three years, wooing him into less abrupt behaviour and ironing out the aggression. "You can achieve far more with a touch of cunning than a brace of cannon," was one of her favourite sayings.

"Side?" was all he said in reply, furiously thinking ahead. Where was this conversation going? It seemed to be by chance, yet was definitely planned.

"I mean, sir, do you like an orange?" The meaning was suddenly clear to Sir Beatrice. But he could see that the Duke, in his drunken state, was thinking himself rather clever.

"Your Grace, you suspect something, I believe, of the humble origins the Duchess was at pains to expose this evening. They are completely true and I deserved the resulting exposure in every way. I am of poor yeoman stock and I happened to have stumbled on a remarkably good way to make money, is all."

"What's that got to do with my question?" The Duke was descending into a drunken state, pouring himself another brandy. If Sir Beatrice was to get anything out of this he would have to move quickly.

"Simply, Your Grace, that because of my humble origins I admit freely to you in the privacy of your home that I have never tasted an orange."

"Never tasted an orange?" the Duke bellowed in laughter, repeating it several times, as if Sir Beatrice's comment was the height of wit. "Preposterous thought indeed. But, sir, do you see my hidden import?"

"You mean to ask, Your Grace, whether I as a prospective Member of Parliament support the talk of an usurpation of the throne by the Prince of Orange."

"Well, I would not have put it…"

"I do."

"You do?" The Duke sat up straight in his chair, knocking against the brandy glass raised to his lips so the precious cognac splashed on to his face. He looked to Sir Beatrice like a blubbering child, unable to drink without spills.

They talked long into the evening, by which time Wiltshire was banging Sir Beatrice on the back and declaring him to be a fine fellow who said the right things.

While in the drawing room the two ladies sat, daggers drawn, in silence. They had exhausted first their polite chatter then the carefully constructed insults. Now, they chose to sit and glare at each other; two ambitious ladies from similar backgrounds with nothing in common except the reflection each could see of themselves in the other.

Matthew was most concerned that he was leaving soon; he could not justify staying longer and still had to retrace his steps, making further careful notes as he went. He had set himself the additional task of travelling to Bristol, mainly because it might obscure the weeks he had spent with his family. He knew another investigator had been sent out to cover Bristol and the Avon Valley but he reasoned another set of eyes was always to be welcomed.

He would leave on Monday and ask his usual questions along the way to Bristol. After a week in the city, rapidly picking up on the scene there, he would drop down to Exeter, sketchbook in hand. And from there it was a simple trek back to Brixham. Three weeks in total. It was imprinted in him that the latest date for arrival back in Amsterdam was September 15th. Working backwards, if he left on Monday he could be in Brixham on September 5th, allowing ten days for the ship to arrive and give passage to Holland.

He could skip Bristol and stay a few days longer in Sturminster Newton; but his report needed filling out.

He knew this to be the case for he had gone through it in his mind countless times since arriving in his home town. Nothing was committed to paper other than his coded notes but he had recited his findings often enough when travelling alone to Bagber, or in bed at night in his old room in Sturminster Newton.

That was why he knew his report needed something else. Other than his bumping into Colonel Hanson, there had been no direct contact with the military. They were around but not in sufficient force. He needed something else.

"I have to leave tomorrow for Amsterdam," he said after the service at Bagber Manor on Sunday.

"Oh dear, we shall miss you dreadfully," Lady Merriman replied. Was that genuine and particular, or a common phrase used at such times?

"Yes," added Amelia, "your sermons have been most interesting. The one today you did jointly with Elizabeth was so informative. Don't you think, Eliza?" It was the first time Matthew had heard Lady Merriman's first name. He loved it, wanted desperately to be in that circle of first names.

"I really cannot say, silly one, for I was not at your service. I went to St Peter's at Hinton St Mary for my weekly dose of good old Anglicanism. Can you recap it now for me, Mr Davenport? I would be delighted to hear it if you will."

"Well... eh... it was quite ordinary really. I mean..."

"Stuff and nonsense," Amelia interrupted.

"If you insist, Lady Merriman, I will endeavour..."

"I do insist, Mr Davenport."

"Very well." He could not look at her directly, chose instead to study the polished wooden floor that gave great loud clicks and clacks as people walked over it. The others in his group thought he was refiguring his sermon in condensed form. But Thomas knew, for he knew his brother.

"First, let me help set the scene," Thomas spoke to hide his brother's blushes; coming to his aid by aiding him at a different level. "The sermon related to the building of the Tower of Babel, of which everyone is familiar. It was unusual in a number of ways. First, it was conducted by two fine sermon-givers. I present my brother, Mr Matthew Davenport, and my sister, Mrs Elizabeth, 'Lizzie' to her friends, Taylor." Thomas paused to see Elizabeth look sharply at him; the Sabbath was not for joking, yet she enjoyed the promotion to sermoniser her younger brother had given her.

Matthew reflected that he must not be counted one of Elizabeth's friends for he had never known or called her by the diminutive form of her name; never been invited to.

"A second way in which this sermon was such a cut above the rest was the way the two sermon-givers related to each other."

"Go on," said Lady Merriman, when Thomas paused for effect once again. "I am all ears to hear this."

"It was Matthew's idea," said Elizabeth flatly. "I wondered if it was too frivolous for the Sabbath."

"This is the crux of it, Eliza." There was that first name again, this time for Lady Merriman, who smiled sweetly when she caught him looking at her. Matthew wished…

"They spoke as builders speak. They were building the tower high into the sky. They started on the floor of the Great Hall, then progressed onto the dais and finally went to the minstrels' gallery. They gave the impression of gaining enormous height as they spoke their individual words up into the rafters." Thomas looked up into those rafters as he spoke the words. Everyone followed his gaze up, as if drawn by magnets to follow his line of vision. Matthew was one of them; forsaking his examination of the floorboards, he raised up his eyes to the Lord.

But he stopped halfway for Lady Merriman was looking right at him. She gazed at him steadily and seriously. Then the seriousness broke with another sweet smile.

It was clearly meant for him.

"They were very convincing," Thomas continued. "For Matthew came to me beforehand and asked for sufficient building terms to make it so. They conversed between themselves and obviously worked so well together. Then Matthew said, *'I believe, fellow builder, that we build this tower so tall that soon we will be butting into Heaven itself and sharing feasts with our Lord.'*

'What did you say, my man? Do you not like the way I have dressed this stone? Do you think you can do better?' the other replied hotly.

'I mixed the strongest mortar ever seen. How dare you question the strength of my mortar? It is your rotten fault that the splendid tower I built wobbles and shakes as we walk upon it.'"

Thomas achieved a remarkable mimicking of both voices playing outraged builders, before resorting to his own voice to continue the tale of the sermon.

"And so the conversation went on. Or can I call it a conversation, when both proud builders could no longer communicate with each other? Then they paid a servant to make a great crashing sound with pots and pans or something and they simulated the whole tower collapsing around the congregation. It ended with Lizzie going off, shaking her fists at Matthew and Matthew saying simply, *'What have I done to make him so angry with me? He should be pleased I helped him make his wobbly tower stronger. I will make war on him if he does not come and thank me before three days have passed.'*"

"Matthew, that is so powerful yet so sweet and clever," Lady Merriman said.

It was only afterwards, when he had said his goodbyes, that he realised Lady Merriman had called him by his first name.

Chapter 7

Colonel Hanson was not usually clumsy. But the man was diminutive. Add a little distraction and it was not surprising that he bumped into Big Jim just outside the steps of Sherborne Hall. The physics of their clash went like this: Hanson, lean but tall and muscled, had about twice the mass of Big Jim. He also had momentum on his side for he was coming down the steps two at a time, whereas Jim was stationary at the bottom, wondering whether to ask for the Earl or the Countess. There is a formula to calculate the relative actions and reactions but Hanson did not know it, nor was Big Jim concerned about how and why he went flying, whereas Hanson seemed not to move off course at all.

What stopped Hanson in his haste was not the physical encounter but the sight of a fellow human sent sprawling across the ground, ramming into a large stone urn with a sickening thud.

"Are you alright, sir? I am so sorry."

The average gentleman would have made a quick assessment, wondering why a tradesman was using the main entrance. He would have attributed fault to the tradesman on the grounds that he should not have been there at all; should have known his place. He would have moved on, his body swallowing back the initial and natural words of apology as he moved through them.

But Colonel Hanson was not average; he stopped, gave a hand to Jim to help right him. Then he dusted him down and tried to straighten his hat, which seemed to have taken a good deal of damage.

"I think your hat is gone to the great hat-box in the sky," he said, handing it back to Jim. "You will allow me to buy another?"

"No, Colonel, I can afford to lose an old hat." He could afford it; that much was true. But, before he left for Sherborne Hall, he had been sent upstairs by Jane to change into his best clothes. He had liked that hat very much and now it was no more.

"Besides, you are a friend of my dear friend."

"We are acquainted?" Hanson asked, stepping back for a better view of the small man. "Ah, I have it now. The refreshments when we laid the first stone of the new church Mr Davenport is building. So, Mr Davenport is the link of friendship between us?"

"You are quite correct, sir," said with a lack of enthusiasm that could not help to be noticed.

"I am concerned for you, Mr... eh..."

"Mr Bigg, James Bigg."

"Better known as Big Jim; I remember now. You took quite a tumble there, sir, and all due to my clumsiness." Hanson only had a slight acquaintance with Thomas' friend, yet something disturbed him. He seemed, at the laying of the first stone ceremony, to be such a jolly fellow; but was all seriousness and formality now.

"Mr Bigg, please allow me to walk into the house with you and at least obtain a brandy to settle you."

"I shall be quite alright, Colonel Hanson. Thank you for your concern but it is unnecessary, I assure you." He seemed to be shaking the colonel from him and Hanson realised there was nothing he could do about it. He would not try again with such resolute shunning.

"Then I bid you good day, sir. My apologies again for my rude interruption to your peaceful standing at the bottom of these steps." Hanson bowed; Big Jim returned it, turned, and fell again at the first step; blackness closed his mind like the sudden closing of heavy shutters onto the world.

Jim woke, fluttering his eyelids like a butterfly caught in a room. The countess stood over him.

"Grace," he said, forgetting her new rank. Grace was stunning in a shimmering blue dress with white underskirt seen through slits, like thin tendrils of cloud in a summer sky.

"Jim," she replied, also forgetting her rank, "we were so worried about you." As the first-person plural settled in his mind, Jim sat up suddenly. Colonel Hanson was still there, hat off now and placed on an occasional table. He felt a wave of fate rising and taking him head-on.

How could he report with the army in the room? Everyone knew that the army was sharply divided. He could not take the risk. Colonel Hanson could well be a dissenter, annoyed deeply at the birth of the new prince.

A Catholic prince to ensure a Catholic monarchy and a return to the true religion.

For Big Jim had changed as he had grown in wealth. As a poor man, heavily indebted, he had thought of friends first and principles afterwards, with a devil-may-care attitude to life that had given him great popularity and friendships everywhere. But success at his trade had turned this on its head. He felt compelled to aid the Catholic cause; the one steady facet of his rapidly changing world.

"Your Ladyship…" He started to stand but felt gentle fingers, four sets of them, push him back. "I need to get home."

"Jane will be here presently. We sent word that you had taken a tumble. You have been out, Jim, for over six hours. Look," Grace raised his head so he could see the new day through the window, "you have slept like a baby all night long. We were worried about you, dreadfully worried."

He closed his eyes again as new sleep slipped in; matters of state, if they could be described so grandly, could wait a while longer.

When he woke again, Jane was there, chiding and fussing, and nothing else mattered.

Earl Henry of Sherborne put his young head into his hands and wondered what he should do. The country was on a knife-edge; he had known that before Colonel Hanson had come to see him. His own wife's brother was touring the area, asking questions with seemingly casual abandon. Henry knew Matthew would shortly report back to his masters in Amsterdam. Should he prevent him, have him arrested? As a leading Catholic aristocrat, he owed allegiance to King James, who had allowed; no, actively promoted, Catholicism in this country again. Yet, as an Englishman, there was something abhorrent in the perpetual favouritism towards one religion over another, these not even being the religion of the establishment; the watered-down compromise developed under the reign of the great Queen Elizabeth a hundred years earlier.

Now, under King James, barely a day went by without some new announcement involving the departure of someone respected and a relative upstart to replace them. Army officers were being rooted out, to be replaced with Catholics. It was the same with Justices of the Peace and other officials. He knew he owed his recent Lord Lieutenancy of the county to his religion. In turn, Colonel Hanson owed his commission, even his promotion to colonel, to the earl's patronage. If he withdrew that support, Hanson would be gone in an instant; just as would happen to him if he lost the King's favour.

He was Lord Lieutenant of Dorset, a position of power and prestige, simply because he was a Catholic.

There was something distinctly rotten at the core of all this.

"Grandfather, what would you do? Is it to be liberty or religion?" He spoke to a miniature portrait of the old Earl on the mantelpiece in his study. But no answer came back to him; just the gentle sounds of a busy estate on a high summer's day.

Instead, his beloved wife, who had taken his religion when he asked, reversing her true belief in an act of supreme selflessness, knocked on the open door and waited patiently for her husband to give her permission to enter.

"Come my dear, don't stand on ceremony with me."

Perhaps, he reflected, the answers lay with the living rather than the dead.

The recovery in Simon Taylor had not been sudden, or dramatic. He was not a helpless victim of stroke one minute and back to full health the next. Rather, his family noticed good, steady progress, aided by the devotion of his wife, Elizabeth, and his daughter, Amelia. Both carried his family name, for Amelia stubbornly refused to marry one of several suitors.

"I will only marry when Father is well enough to do without me," she had stated many times.

But there comes a crossover time, when a reason loses its power and becomes an excuse. In fact, is not one person's reason or cause just another's excuse or shortcoming? Are right and wrong always known and clear choices easily made? And once made, are choices never varied, or does the landscape itself move with the times, so that what is right today is wrong tomorrow, and what once was wrong is right all of a sudden?

Now twenty-five years old, Amelia, was a remarkable beauty, coupled with an intellect Elizabeth marvelled at.

"Whenever you do marry, Mealy, I shall take your father back to his own house in Sturminster Newton. I think he would actually prefer to be in the hustle of town rather than out here in the country where it is so quiet."

"Eliza will not like that, Mother."

The nomenclature between these two had undergone a quiet revolution. Amelia had gyrated to 'Mealy', being a shortened version of the endearment 'Mealy Mouth', itself no more than a silly distortion of Amelia; for her stepdaughter was far from mealy-mouthed, having the most gorgeous face now that all puppy fat was gone and the woman had come out of the girl.

But the strangest thing about their names for each other was not this twist at all but how it had worked out in reverse. Elizabeth had objected to being called 'Mother' by her stepdaughter, insisting in private, at least, on being addressed as 'Lizzie'. They were of similar age and were growing deeply in friendship after an awkward start.

This had worked for a while. But as they had grown closer, so naturally 'Mother' had returned and was accepted willingly. It underlined the silent but happy accord that, as an unmarried woman and with her father incapacitated, Amelia was under the legal charge of her stepmother.

But that did not stop them sneaking down to the Divelish when their caring duties allowed and throwing off their dresses before jumping into the cooling, swirling water in just their undergarments.

"You know this is most improper for people like us," Elizabeth said on the Monday Matthew was leaving for Bristol.

"What do you mean?"

"I mean, for two founding members of the Presbyterian Church of Bagber Common to be cavorting together in the stream half-naked."

"Is all, Mother, no harm is done." Amelia stretched out on the rock under the willow, where they always went. Elizabeth had put on her petticoats in preparation for dressing; but now she stopped, not wanting to disturb Amelia by asking her to help her into her dress. Instead, she gazed on the dappled-sunlit body of her friend and stepdaughter and, amidst the love that fell out of her, wondered at such perfection. She dearly wanted to touch that beautiful body.

Instead, she fell to her knees, smoothed her petticoats around her in a semblance of properness and clasped her hands in prayer.

And waited for Amelia to come to her. Which she soon did, with all the glory of hateful sin.

And the sun still dappled their bodies as they stroked and sent their fingers dancing upon their half-naked skin.

But no further for, at that moment, came the noise of rustles in the branches behind them.

"Elizabeth?" Matthew called. "Sally said you might be dipping your feet in the stream. I have missed Lady… eh… Eliza and wanted to ask you to pass on a letter to her I have composed." Elizabeth thought that only her brother composed letters; everyone else wrote them.

The voice moved a little further away down the stream. It gave them their chance. Silently as could be, like naughty children sneaking out of sight, Amelia helped Elizabeth into her dress. Then Elizabeth sat and put on her stockings and boots, while Amelia pulled the corset tight and then fastened her dress, bonnet and gloves that fitted snug to the long sleeves of her dress.

"I'll come back to dress you," she whispered, then called to her brother that she was coming and what was this all about?

Twenty minutes later, while Elizabeth, in turn, fastened Amelia's dress, she said, "Perhaps another time, Mealy."

"Yes, perhaps."

But they both knew the time was gone.

Simon Taylor watched them from the window of his bedroom. He saw two demure, neatly dressed ladies walking with their hands clasped before them and their eyes dipped to the ground. It aroused a memory in his mind that played incessantly, like a tune that will not he forgotten. But the memory sang a different song; the two clashing like notes that should never go together. The old tune was all about defiance. He remembered first the saddlebags slung over their shoulders, then the hat ribbons streaming as they almost ran to the woods; as if travelling gypsies or carefree working girls. Yet these were the same two girls he saw now; modestly, no – severely, dressed, walking slowly and steadily, as if they respected everything around them as part of the order they fitted into.

If he had heard the conversation they were having, everything would have been clear to him but, even with the window open to the warm summer air, the distance was too great.

"Mother," started Amelia as they broke from the woods and set off across the lawn, "you should know that I welcome wholeheartedly the religion you have brought to me. However, sometimes I believe you are too strict in it and there is something of merit in the old Lizzie Taylor that teased me so well out of my reticence and showed me the world and some of its wonders. We almost had something of it back just then." She raised her eyes to look at Elizabeth. From the bedroom window, Simon noted the break in posture, bringing some harmony to his thoughts.

"What we almost did was wrong, terribly…"

"Yes, Lizzie, it was wrong. But surely you see why it happened?"

"The devil…"

"The devil, my foot!" Now Amelia stopped altogether and raised Elizabeth's downcast head so they made eye contact. "In some obscure way I expect the devil had a hand in matters by the stream. But what happened was two young women, living by strict rules, had a relapse and felt attraction for each other more than those rules allow for. Now, if those rules were a little more moderate…"

"Amelia, I have to follow my conscience. Look at how Grace is now. Do you want me all finery and silly hats?"

"No, Lizzie; Mother dear, I want you to follow your true conscience, who you really are, and not feel obliged to compensate for your sister's apparent abandoning of hers." She lifted her stepmother's face again, for it had formed a habit of looking downwards, as if her personal gravity was much stronger than all the other gravities around her. She lifted that face and smiled, then leaned forward and kissed her, rubbing bonnets awkwardly to reach her lips. It was an act that meant more than what they might have done on the rock by the Divelish tributary that led speedily down to the pondering Stour.

"Let's wear hats tomorrow," Amelia said with a grin. "These bonnets don't even allow me to kiss my mother."

"I don't know that I can," Elizabeth replied. But the next day she did find a modest one in her wardrobe and presented herself with a little embarrassment to Amelia for their daily walk.

All things in moderation, they remained in the gardens that day, not once looking beyond to the woods and the stream that ran through them.

Chapter 8

Robert Candles struggled to mask his irritation; more so because Avercamp seemed to think highly of the idiotic fellow.

"He's an awkward bundle of principle," Candles said of Matthew Davenport. "The man would not know opportunity if he was invited into bed with it."

"Hush now, Robert, the man means well and will be of use to the cause."

But what was the cause? And whose cause was this strange Dutchman referring to?

One thing Robert Candles was certain about; his cause was his and nobody else's. It was not devoid of principle but his twisted cause was his.

"So, Mr Davenport, this is a very long report. Can you summarise for us in maybe ten minutes or so?"

"Of course, Herr Avercamp. Please give me a moment to compose my thoughts." Matthew stared at the window of Avercamp's vast study, where they had met to consider his report. He had made good progress back to Holland, arriving on September 12th. It was now September 14th and he had worked day and night to produce the 189 pages that formed the report he now had to condense into ten minutes.

What would he say? What would his father have said?

That was easy to answer for Luke Davenport would have treated it as a sermon in the making. Step one: a shocking statement to grab attention. Step two: outline your main points. Step three: back up each main point with summarised arguments. Step four: add a bit of humour; dashes here and there so that they keep listening to catch the next joke. Step five: provide a recap and end on a bang. With some parts still to form in his mind, aware that Candles was drumming his fingers on the long table impatiently, he coughed to clear his throat and began.

"Sirs, the south-west is ripe for invasion." Every head around the table jerked up, eyebrows rising like the tide; nobody else mentioned the planned invasion, although everyone was working towards it.

He had achieved his first objective.

"The West Country has a natural degree of religious toleration with a fairly large bent towards Protestantism in its wider sense, rather than..." No, first mistake. Don't get pedantic, dividing points until, like paper folded, they can be divided no more.

"Carry on, Mr Davenport." Avercamp was a gentleman but even he needed to get to the point and move on.

"Of course, sir. It has both religious toleration and strong Protestantism, although there are particular pockets where Catholicism prevails. But more important than the religious composition is the fact that the people are disillusioned. They feel cheated of their liberties. When I went to Bristol, for instance..."

"You were not supposed to go to Bristol," Candles interjected. "We had our man in Bristol."

"Yes, Herr Candles, you are absolutely right," Herr von Strump spoke up. "However, the deed is done and it is our duty to take whatever information we can get to make the best decisions possible. Herr Candles, have you made a comparison of these two reports on Bristol?" It was a neat turning; taking aggression to the aggressor.

"No, sir, I've had too much to do recently. I will get onto it at first light tomorrow."

"Do so, if you please, Herr Candles," von Strump replied, a degree sharper than Candles would have liked. In the old days he would have reacted immediately and strongly but now he just apologised by collecting together a string of meaningless phrases, until a cough from Avercamp silenced him.

Matthew went on to make his detailed points, finding formulas to put his arguments together while the main part of his mind ranged forwards for a suitable shock to end with. With a start, he realised that he was sermon-writing on the hoof; something he had never done before. That gave him his shock idea.

"Sirs, in conclusion, I give odds of twenty to one as to any other part of England as an invasion point and thee to one with the south-west. It has to be the West Country for any hope of success. Thank you, gentlemen." He sat down, expecting some appreciation, perhaps a polite round of applause.

But Candles got in there first.

"Three to one at best? What prince would risk his entire fortune with odds of three to one?"

"But sir, consider that three to one is just a starting point on the possible locations for the landing. I can guarantee better than evens with the right planning, for which I offer my humble services. In this regard, I would beg the members of this committee to read an additional report I composed concerning an analysis of why James Monmouth failed in his rebellion of three years ago." He handed out eight copies of a nine-page document in his own hand, all the time keeping a fixed smile focused on Robert Candles. It was a bold move against the previously uncontested leader of the English contingent in Holland. It was unplanned; a reaction to three years of contempt and ridicule.

But it worked, for the English in the room were asked to leave, then summoned back twenty minutes later.

"We wish to acquaint you with our decision," Avercamp started the conversation. "Matthew Davenport is to be on staff for advice on the West Country as a possible invasion point. He is to report in this regard directly to me." It was a soft way to sidestep Candles but everyone in the room knew the import behind these words.

The invasion would be from a landing in Brixham. And the first battle between Davenport and Candles was already fought and won; recognised in the uncoupling between Matthew and Robert Candles, or whatever his real name was.

Chapter 9

A whirlwind of activity engulfed Matthew; activity and purpose that took him out of himself. He was consulted on every aspect of Brixham; how big the port was; how many soldiers and where they were garrisoned; what its local government consisted of and where their sympathies lay; where the roads lay out of the town and what condition they were in. Then the questions moved up his suggested path of advance. He found that, if his knowledge of any aspect was wanting, his common sense and confidence could fill the gap. Candles soon gave up trying to undermine him; instead, he ingratiated himself with tight lips.

Matthew had very few quiet moments but when he did, he imagined himself at the head of a great army, soldiers fanning out either side of him, looking to him for direction. Looking to Matthew, who had for so long lived in the shadows of others. He rode up to Bagber Manor many times in those snatched moments here and there. And each time, Eliza Merriman rushed down the steps to welcome him.

He became, in the balance of September, so much at the centre of things that it was a total surprise when Avercamp suggested that he leave immediately for the West Country.

"Your report, Herr Davenport, highlighted great interest in our cause in Bristol and Somerset, and even in Devon, but the map of Dorset was distinctly less orange." Having a prince named as a colour gave plenty of room for little jokes and hidden meanings. "We want you to paint Dorset in the brightest orange."

"Me, sir?"

"Yes, you. May I call you Matthew? Good. Yes, we need you there, Matthew. The work you have done here is excellent but we need quality people in the critical localities and your home county is one such area."

"Yes, of course, of course." Concentrating on Dorset would mean more time to see Lady Merriman. Then he thought of the letter he had written and passed on through his sister. Would she want to see him after his clumsy declarations? "When do I depart?"

"Can you go tomorrow?" It was stated as a request but meant as an instruction. Of course, Matthew could go tomorrow; he had no ties in Amsterdam.

It was a much quicker crossing this time; early autumn being kinder in its coolness than the stormy heat of summer. And the distance to Poole was considerably shorter. Yet he stepped ashore with his stomach churning more than ever. Gone was the pretence of being an artist looking for scenery to paint. He was a soldier in God's grand army, designed to set things right in a world that had gone very wrong. He knew better than to refer to his hastily endowed commission as a major in Orange's army but he was, nevertheless, a soldier simple and pure.

Which meant he would live or die by the sword.

He had learned his instructions by heart and thrown the single piece of paper overboard as soon as they left Dutch waters. They mostly spoke of initiative and preparation for the struggle to come.

"You have no time to lose," Avercamp had said, without needing to state why this was the case. Preparations were going on everywhere in Holland; ships gathering and soldiers and supplies being loaded on.

Matthew had no need to buy a horse this time for he had a fine stallion on board with him; a grudging gift from Candles, who had seen the sudden rise of his underling with despair, then resolved to make the best of it publicly. His time would come again.

He rode fast, not north to Sturminster Newton; that would have to wait. Instead, he rode west to Dorchester and a pre-arranged meeting with a 'gentleman of distinction' as Candles put it, lately come around to assisting Matthew as part of the future. He was to say to the landlord of the White Lion that he was newly come from a far better place. That was the code that would get him in front of the gentleman and create his chance to tip Dorset into rebellion.

It sounded so simple, like an old story out of the bible come to the present. In fact, he felt distinctly biblical as he trotted along the Dorchester Road.

If only it could be that simple.

Thomas was feeling anger like seldom before. It was a different type too, for he could do nothing about matters and frustration lay heavy on him. And he was deeply concerned for Mr Milligan, who had spent decades in his building business, achieving many great things, just to see it come to nothing. There had been no new commissions from customers since the work in Cranborne Chase, now several months complete and all paid for. The twelve cottages had been funded by Mr Milligan and were finished. Even the new church, paid for out of Thomas' capital, was more than halfway to completion.

And Thomas was running out of money. The bricks were paid for and he could just about afford the labour for bricklaying, but that left nothing for the roof. As winter approached, he risked a building open to the elements. He had worked out his cash flow carefully at the beginning but had not allowed for the dreadful business of laying workers off when their tasks were complete.

So, he had kept them on, doing minor decorative works or levelling the land, or even re-stacking the bricks prior to use. And that is why he had no money for the roof.

He rode now in a borrowed cart to pick up the last load of bricks. He could not afford Big Jim's fee to have it done for him but Jim had kindly suggested he borrow his smallest cart for free.

And then, at the last minute, Jim had jumped on the cart and declared he wanted to get away for a day.

"You're not the only one suffering, Thomas, I've had precious little new work these last few months. Most of it has been long-term contracts to move stone from quarries and some of the quarry owners have not been able to pay for there is no demand for stone with no building going on. All we are doing is stockpiling it. I'll drive, Thomas, I am used to it."

It looked to be a gloomy ride to Dorchester. They battled up Okeford Hill against a ferocious, rain-spattered wind that prevented all talk. As they achieved the top and eased the brakes for the downward journey towards Hedge End and Winterbourne Stickland beyond, the trees and rise of land behind gave them some relief.

Thomas knew exactly why Jim had come with him, jumping on at the last minute, too late for counter-reasons why he should stay behind and Thomas go alone.

For the country was alive with rumours; they had been building rapidly since the birth of the Prince a few months earlier.

"I always prefer this way to Dorchester," Big Jim opened the conversation with a general statement. "It's a little longer in time but far more adventurous than going through Kings Stag and Pulham. It seems appropriate, does it not, Thomas, to take the more tricky, demanding route?" He seemed to be moving straight from casual conversation to pointed comments in one opening remark. Perhaps he thought he needed all available time on their journey to get the answers he sought.

"It is the more remarkable route, I grant you, Jim."

"Ah yes, a remarkable route for remarkable times."

"I wish we had more work for these times are certainly remarkable for the lack of building projects." Thomas tried to give the conversation a professional bent, knowing that Jim just wanted to talk politics.

"What is your brother doing?" Jim changed tack completely, throwing Thomas off.

"Matthew? Why? He went back to Amsterdam. He left here, as you know, back in July and travelled a little further on his employer's affairs. These took him to Devon and he got a ship there to Holland."

In response, Jim applied the brakes, calling to the two horses to stop. Then he turned to his friend. Overhead, an early leaf gave up the battle and floated down to land on the empty cart. Thomas reflected that you never saw a leaf actually detach from the branch or twig that had hosted it. They always seemed to be mid-air, trying desperately to stay afloat; neither clinging to the familiar or racing to the unknown.

"He was seen last week in Dorchester."

"Matthew? But that is impossible. I received a letter from him only three or four days ago, saying he was happily back at his demanding work in Amsterdam."

"I expect the same ship that brought that letter also brought Matthew over. In fact, he may even have dispatched it from Poole, where he landed last Thursday. A letter from Poole to Sturminster Newton would be considerably cheaper to send than one all the way from the Low Countries." A flurry of wind brought down two-dozen more leaves into the stationary cart. Thomas tried to count them as they blew in past him but then became aware that Jim was looking at him intently.

"How do you know all this; assuming it to be true, of course?"

"It is true, Thomas, I saw him with my own eyes."

They made ground that day, on their way to Dorchester. Their journey seemed more about honest disclosure than covered miles. Jim clicked to the horses, as if suddenly realising that movement was required to make progress; to break the standstill that existed between them.

At first, there was some more dancing; Jim would profess concern about Matthew's activities and Thomas would blankly deny all knowledge. They wound on in similar fashion through the brick and flint that was Winterbourne Stickland, stopping at the Crown to water the horses and eat a beef pie that Jim had brought with him.

"How come you had a pie in your pocket if you were not coming today and changed your mind at the last minute?" Thomas turned the attack on his friend. But the defence from Jim was another neat movement.

"I always intended to come. I wanted to talk with you."

"Who do you work for?" Thomas could give as well as take.

"Who do you?" Jim replied. Thus, with the cart at rest, they sparred without progress, but as soon as they moved out into the ragged wind that changed its mind as to direction every minute or so, they moved forward in terms of mutual disclosure.

By Winterbourne Whitechurch, Thomas had admitted that he

suspected his brother of inciting rebellion in the cause of the Prince of Orange, married to Mary, King James' own daughter.

In return, Jim had given out that he worked secretly for what he called 'the preservation of order and peace'.

Was it to be 'liberty and religion' against 'order and peace'? In which case, wondered Thomas, why the discord between these aims? Why could they not exist together, picking a combination such as 'liberty and order' or 'religion and peace'? All four were worthy causes to be chased down and harnessed for the common benefit.

"I have sympathy for the cause, Jim, but no actual involvement." This as they pushed through Milborne St Andrew, getting closer to their destination.

"That is not what the establishment thinks, Thomas." Jim decided to trade. He wanted more information to pass on to Sherborne but was desperate not to indicate that his employer in this regard was Thomas' own brother-in-law and dear friend. So what else had he to offer? There was only the offer of what any friend would do for another approaching difficult times. He would have warned Thomas for free, but why not get a little more value if he could? "They see you as a hero against Monmouth, that is true, but a hero of highly questionable principles concerning religion. Don't forget your father, God rest his soul. Moreover, your brother is a wanted man in this country. And you are blatantly building an alternative place of worship and asked a Puritan to lay the founding stone. And then, you have been seen several times in Dorchester, known to be a hotbed of Puritanism and rebellious factions."

"This is preposterous! They are all minor things and not connected. I am building a church to sell to whoever bids the highest; not to use myself or for others to promote sedition from. I go, as well you know, to Dorchester to buy building materials because I did not want to build out of stone this time. You came with me, Jim, when I first went to buy the bricks."

"But why continue to return?"

"Because I remembered the building I had noted from my school days and wanted to study it." Thomas had to admit it did look odd that he had several times returned for the day, sketch book and note book in hand. But he had other points to raise in his defence. "I asked Amelia Taylor to lay the founding stone because, well, because I admire her greatly. Besides, she is hardly a fanatical Puritan like…"

'Like Mrs Taylor has become of recent? Is that what you meant to say?"

"No, you are putting words into my mouth, Jim. It is most unlike you to do so."

"I mean a kindness, Thomas; believe me, I do. You have to see how it looks to others, to those in authority. Now, as a friend, I have a proposition to make to you. Will you listen quietly to the whole idea first and then we can discuss it afterwards? Come now, Thomas, I'll treat you to lunch in the inn around the corner from the brickyard. From there, we can discuss this whole matter and come up with a solution."

The truth was in these words somewhere; just not nothing but the truth. Thomas nodded in assent and the pair of old friends made their way to the Red Lion.

Chapter 10

Lady Roakes disliked leaving London; in particular, her lovely home she had just settled into.

"But, my dear, this is very necessary work for our future security."

"But we have enough money to last us both should we live to 100. You told me that just yesterday. Is it suddenly all gone this morning that we have to earn it all again?"

"No, dearest. We have the money as I said. I'm concerned with other things now; our political connections and our status. I don't see why you should be 'Lady Roakes' forever when there are duchesses rolling around far less competent than you." Lady Roakes thought of Wiltshire's bratty wife and imagined herself looking on the level rather than up at her.

"I see what you mean, sir. I am all yours, sir." She leaned over and kissed him on the tip of his nose. It was something she had learned that he loved. "You are so good to think of me."

"Again," he said, referring to the kissed nose. Behind his back, he waved the servants out of the room.

"Besides, we need to find a country seat." They were in their coach now. Sir Beatrice had had the coach remade by the best coachmaker in London. The man was experimenting with different methods of suspension and had offered the work for nothing, "If Sir Beatrice and Lady Roakes would be so kind as to report back their level of comfort on a long journey."

"A country seat in Dorset, sir?"

"Well you do not want to go back to Bristol, do you?"

"No, sir."

"Then Dorset is as good a place as any, don't you think?" He knew it from his travels in the army but for Lady Roakes it was all new. She cuddled up to him in the back of the plush coach and smiled, closing her eyes, remarking on the smoothness of the ride, then drifting into imaginings of grand country estates. She had certainly left the laundry business far behind.

The truth was Sir Beatrice did not need her on this trip as it was entirely the business of dangerous politics he was engaged in. But he could not bear to be parted from her longer than a few hours. She made him what he had become. She was the left hand while he was the right. And he knew his feelings for her were returned with interest.

They were a couple of downright crooks but even the most reprehensible can love like the angels.

When they find the right partner.

Three days later, the coach came to their destination in Dorchester. They had sent a servant ahead on horseback to locate the best accommodation available. The servant had returned to them at Southampton and declared his mission accomplished. Before tethering his tired horse to the back of the coach and climbing up beside the footmen, he whispered some words in Sir Beatrice's ear.

"What did that man say in your ear, sir?"

"Just something on the fellow I am due to meet, my dear." He could not and would not lie to her. There was no point, for she would know anyway the moment the false words left his lips. "He is arrived and waiting for me. But that need not concern you, for I think you will be much occupied looking at houses in the area and then, when my work is complete, we will visit together the ones you approve of. With luck, we will make a purchase on this excursion; if not, we can return again."

"Am I to go alone initially, sir?" She looked at him; needing him, willing him to be available; wishing for the politics to suddenly go away, dispersed like the sound of the horses' hooves on the long journey.

But she knew all the rumours, just like everyone else. She felt the same tension; a curious mixture of fear and hope; fear of dreadful reprisals and further government oppression and hope for change; indeed, expectation that it was inevitable. Sir Beatrice had once said to her, "Sometimes things have to get very bad before they get better." She had thought of her despair when Arkwright had disappeared and her previous husband had killed Parchman in defence of her then become blind-drunk in the Earl of Sherborne's tent while the Battle of

Sedgewick raged a mile away. She had felt terrible despair then but to think of the improvements now; the leaps she had made with her dear Sergeant Roakes.

"No, my dear, you will not be alone. Although I cannot be with you for a few days, I have hired the services of the most pre-eminent land agent in Dorset. He has come all the way from Shaftesbury and will stay in Dorchester to help and advise us for as long as it takes."

The servant had done his job well, demanding the best rooms available and being directed where the coach now went, to the White Lion. There they had a suite of rooms on the first floor, while their four servants shared a room at the back. The whispering from servant to master at Southampton had informed them that the man they had come to meet was waiting impatiently at the same inn.

For Matthew it had been six days of wasted time. He had expected his associate to be there for him, not having to do the waiting himself. But then he knew little of the workings of government and the precedence of rank and station; nor of the frantic manoeuvres behind closed doors to get preparations in place for the invasion.

Sir Beatrice and Lady Roakes were met by the landlord, cringing in his gratefulness for the hefty bill he had negotiated with the servant. People were not spending money at the moment and this fee would allow him to do the urgent roof repairs his builder said was needed before winter hit in its fury.

"I am come from a far better place," Roakes said while Lady Roakes looked around the spacious rooms; spacious for an inn, at least.

The landlord looked blankly at Sir Beatrice, then it twigged. Mr Davenport had said the same thing to him when he had arrived six days ago. Then, absurdly, he had said the same thing each day with the hopeful look of a boy expecting a surprise birthday present that was sadly delayed, giving rise to the question as to whether it would ever come.

"I see, Sir Beatrice, you'll be wanting the gentleman staying upstairs, no doubt. Shall I send him down, sir? I believe he is most anxious to meet with you."

"I don't know what you mean, landlord." Sir Beatrice was too wily to allude to knowledge of a planned meeting. "But if some gentleman is anxious to meet with me then I am happy to oblige. Let us say tomorrow at nine o'clock. Lady Roakes will be gone house-hunting by then. Please tell him to present himself here at nine sharp."

The landlord left to convey the message, new coins clinking in his pocket. He went straight to Matthew's room, managing to secure a few more coins by pretending sympathy at Matthew's extended wait, now dragged on another half a day.

He had already made more money this week than the whole of the month before. He shuddered in excitement as he took the back stairs to the kitchen to chide the women into attending on the Roakes' needs; a light supper, wine, and warming pans.

Plus, he sent a boy with a note to Mr Partridge, the land agent, staying at the rival Red Lion at the other end of the High Street. The message asked him to attend on the Roakes at half past eight in the morning. The landlord added a piece on his own initiative, suggesting that if Mr Partridge desired to be under the same roof as his clients for his and their convenience, he could squeeze him into some nice rooms at the White Lion and would send someone around for his luggage in the morning on his confirmation by return.

That confirmation came within twenty minutes. It was worth an extra penny to the boy who had run all the way there and back in the dark, for things were definitely looking up for the landlord of the White Lion.

Not so for Penelope, Duchess of Wiltshire, who regularly now threw tantrums in response to the deep frustration she felt.

The cause of that frustration was not that there was no child, for time was still hers at twenty-three. It was not even her husband's infidelity, for she cared not one bit for him and preferred remoteness from him. But she needed company, needed to be touched and caressed, and to touch and caress in return.

And Sally, her black servant girl, neatly dodged her every move. It was as if she held herself out for something better. But two points rubbed at her. What was there better than a duchess? And Sally was her servant so how could the wispy, chocolate-brown figure; so slender with glowing skin and pert features, hold out for something else?

Another irritant plagued her life. With Wiltshire's endless discussions in private with Sir Beatrice, she had been forced more and more into the company of the upstart, Lady Roakes. Their silences together were interrupted only with barbed comments from each side; carefully manufactured during those silent periods, the poison wrapped in extreme politeness.

And now she was ordered to manufacture a reason to visit Sherborne, who she had once planned to marry. She had done much better, nominally, with Wiltshire; being a duchess was infinitely better than life as a mere countess. But Sherborne had married for love and that irked her. She had seen the new countess at the ball they had held to reinstate matrimonial negotiations with the Wiltshire family. She was attractive, with ringlets of strawberry blonde hair and a dress sense that rivalled her own.

"Just make the introductions, arrange the visit, and leave everything else to me." Wiltshire would not answer any of her questions as to why.

"But, husband, if I know something of your aims in securing this relationship, I might be able to help in some way."

"I require you as my wife to follow my instructions without questioning them. Is that understood?"

"Yes, husband dear." Said with as much acid as she could summon.

But the question remained; how was she to perform her duty and arrange a visit by the Wiltshires to Sherborne Hall?

Mr Milligan answered that question for her. For he came to her and asked for the possibility of work, citing what he had done five years earlier at Sherborne Hall as a reference to his suitability. She wrote immediately to the Countess, requesting a visit. *We are serious about some additions to our home and are considering the firm of Milligan for a role in these plans. Would you*

*be so gracious as to honour us with an invitation, such that we may
inspect the works Milligan has done at your seat and enquire as to his
suitability?'*

The answer came by return that they were most welcome.
And would a visit that very week be an inconvenience?

"You have done well, wife. I would not have suspected a visit
could be obtained so soon. I am pleased with your
endeavours."

"Do you wonder, sir, why they are so keen to receive you as
a visitor?"

"That is not your concern."

"But, sir, whatever your motive in seeking such a visit, do
you not consider that perhaps they too have a reason to want
you to visit? They replied very promptly and made themselves
available immediately. Might it not be worth considering such
matters?"

"Your job is to obey and produce an heir, woman. Do not
presume to question me on matters that are the sole concern of
men." He raised his arm and Penelope shrank back. Then he
softened and she relaxed a little.

"Will you come to bed with me now and allow me to perform
my duties as a husband?"

"I fear not, husband dear, for my time of month is upon me."
He sighed, wondering how it really could be coming around
again. Then he left her to the fire and her thoughts while he
rode out, seeking a woman to satisfy him.

Afterwards, when alone, she considered that she was no
different to Sally; reacting with revulsion to his aggressive
approaches, just as Sally did with her. It was a hard lesson to
learn.

But, she reflected, the harder the lesson, the more ingrained
it becomes.

Now she was supervising the packing for their visit to
Sherborne. Wiltshire had been much absorbed in his state
work, leaving her to make the arrangements. She planned a
great progress; like royalty of old, long baggage trains filling
her mind, with scores of attendants for every purpose. But the

reality was that her great progress was isolated to a single section that dealt with a visit to Sherborne Hall; that was all her husband wanted from her.

The Duke played big politics on a national stage, while his Duchess was involved in much more supportive roles.

If only she had been born a man.

Then, perhaps, Sally would show some interest in her. And provide the physical contact she ached for.

She could do something, of course. Not with Sally but with Wiltshire. She could find out something of his business at Sherborne Hall; why he wanted to meet with him so urgently.

Then she would at least be armed for the future.

Chapter 11

When Henry, the new Earl, was a boy at Sherborne Hall, he had played behind the deep red curtains in the Great Hall. There were six sets of luscious velvet hanging from way above his head to the floor, each one framing or hiding, depending on whether opened or closed, a large leaded-light window. The top panes were multi-coloured, depicting scenes from the gospels of the Life of Christ. Five of them were obvious: the birth in Bethlehem; the flight to Egypt pursued by wicked-looking soldiers; the sermon on the mount; the feeding of the 5000; and the crucifix itself, with one large cross for Jesus and two hopelessly subordinated ones for the thieves, such that they could not hope to fit on their crosses without major distortion of bodily dimensions.

The sixth window faced east to the morning sun and was his favourite, although he was never quite certain whether it depicted the trial and condemning to death of Jesus Christ or him sweeping aside the market stalls in the temple. It had been repaired many times over the last few hundred years. It would seem the east window took the main force of the weather, or perhaps this window was a century older than the others. The carved stone that contained the glass was certainly different, lacking the smooth fluidity of the other windows.

Each window was played at in turn. When Henry, a solitary child by circumstances rather than inclination, wrapped himself in each set of heavy curtains, he entered a different world; not, strangely, inhabited by Jesus who threw his multi-coloured images out across the scene, but the type of world that a ten-year-old boy loves to inhabit; full of pirates and soldiers fighting against the odds, rescue missions and daring adventures.

The east window was his favourite, for the many glass repairs in different colours and thicknesses magnified the sunlight and sent distorted bends of colour against the white lining of the curtains, transporting him to a truly wonderful world of make-believe.

It was in the east window that he was a spy, travelling through Europe and beyond in desperate times. The long, broad window seat made a tiny stage, converted in his imagination into a ship, a lavish palace, or a bawdy drinking hall; all places full of intrigue and adventure.

Now, as a grown man, the reality of subterfuge was both more mundane and more thrilling; more ordinary yet somehow hopelessly exciting.

"We need to contain Matthew Davenport before he does any real damage," he said into the Great Hall, which contained only four other people, standing grouped around the east window. But there were no curtains; he had learned on enquiry that they were being cleaned for winter use. Hence, the window seat he sat upon was exposed to the whole room.

Still, he did not need his childhood props, for this was the real thing.

"We could arrest him. You have the authority, My Lord."

"No." Sherborne was sure of that. "I said contain, not detain. We must be subtler in our methods."

He looked around the four in the room, fanned like a theatre audience around the window seat stage. Were they expecting some grand speech from him? A composition worthy of Shakespeare? He had nothing to offer in that line.

"Lady and Gentlemen," he started. Big Jim and Plain Jane he knew quite well through his wife, Grace; not as friends so much as acquaintances. The other two were new to him completely. Franshaw was an athletic-looking man in his mid-thirties. He bore a remarkable likeness to the portraits Henry had seen of the Tudor King Henry VIII; large but still slender, like the King in his early years; red hair thinning above a broad and smiling face. Franshaw had drawn the comparison with King Harry to the earl's attention on first meeting him half an hour earlier. "Everyone thinks I must be related but I am not; in fact, have no Welsh blood in me at all. My family are from Lincolnshire and have been there since 1066. May I introduce my superior, Mr Cartwright?"

Cartwright could not be more different. Three-quarters of the height of Franshaw, he was probably less than half the mass, and a quarter the muscle. He had greasy, slicked-back hair that was jet-black and shiny. He looked to be sixty-five but had the dark, still vibrant, hair of a thirty-year-old.

But it was his eyes that struck Henry. They never stood still. And not only did the pupils dart around within their yellow-white frames like rats in a cage but it seemed the whole eyes and sockets changed shape, minute by minute, as if he were a dressmaker holding up new patterns for his customers' examination.

"My Lord, will you hear out a plan I have constructed and give me the benefit of your opinion on it?" Cartwright's voice was surprisingly mild; cajoling and reasonable. It made a contrast with his appearance that surprised Henry.

"The floor is all yours, Mr Cartwright." Henry felt that they were a troop of travelling actors, five in total, presenting whatever play was in season at the time and often improvising when their repertoire fell short.

Cartwright made a small bow to Henry then turned and did the same to Plain Jane, who nodded back but did not curtsey.

"Fellows, this is the idea I have. It is far from perfect but with your assistance I feel it might bear out."

They argued long into the morning after the plan was laid out before them. They argued so long that the sun moved away from the east window and stood, briefly, overhead before descending the other side. Because there were no curtains and the early October day was bright, the western window then tried to lend its light to the east. But it fell short in this task, never achieving more than strange moving patterns that spilled across the polished stone floor.

And Cartwright's reasonable voice droned on, a ready answer to each point raised, showing an incredible patience and a logical, step-by-step mind. Henry suddenly realised that Cartwright did not need the others' approval. This was all about gaining sanction to proceed from the Lord Lieutenant of Dorset. It would be Henry, Earl of Sherborne, who would be ultimately responsible either way; backing a foolish plan or refusing to back a brilliant plan.

But there was, of course, the option that he backed it and it was brilliant. The simplicity of this thought pleased him enormously for it did not involve blame or intrigue at all.

It was the simple stuff that boys were made for.

"That is quite enough debate. We will hold a vote. I retain my casting vote in case it is a tie."

And it was a tie, despite the fact that Henry had said four rapid Hail Marys; praying that this situation, this campaign, these antics would be worth it, and four more, to keep it uneven between the two sides, that he would not be called upon to make the final decision. Big Jim and Plain Jane voted against, the two newcomers for.

It all came down to Henry. Should he vote to embroil his friend, his wife's own brother, in such a dangerous confrontation with the enemy of the established order? Was it so established, this sudden Catholic ascendancy, wrought through the King? King James had been clever. By promoting general religious freedom, whatever Christian denomination, he ensured Catholics were included. His numerous dispensations from the Test Act, passed just a decade ago, meant that the law was bypassed and Catholics; in theory, all Christian religions, could hold office, whether political or military. In reality, however, only Catholics were appointed; a stream of them to the expanded army; expanded because outside wartime there had been no army before.

And it was not just the army. He knew that, as a leading Catholic nobleman, he had benefited from the dispensations. He should not, under the Test Act, hold any office, yet he had been appointed Lord Lieutenant of Dorset the previous year.

There was more to consider. There had been no parliament since 1685; three years without the supreme law-making body. Was that a violation of the individual's rights or just a normal part of government? King James' father had gone eleven years without a parliament and then had followed civil war. Were they headed that way again? He had often heard his grandparents talking of those terrible times. Was it his duty to act to prevent such a calamitous time again? Where did individual liberty cross over with the collective good? He was no philosopher, no political manoeuvrer and these questions seemed dreadful circles with no way to cut through to answers.

Cartwright was talking again; silky words that interrupted his thoughts. He wanted a private audience. The two left the Great Hall.

When Sherborne returned a few minutes later, ashen-faced, it was to vote in favour of the plan. The course was set.

Franshaw took his broad, smiling countenance straight to Sturminster Newton. They had decided that he was more likely to persuade Thomas than Cartwright. Big Jim had tried over lunch at the White Lion in Dorchester but failed completely.

"Jim, I am not going to play false with my own brother."

"But, Thomas, think of the consequences. I do not know Matthew well but he seems much frailer, gentler, less worldly, than the other Davenports. He is walking blindly into a very dangerous situation. If he is caught, the consequences will be truly awful for him."

"I will warn him, is all I will do." That was a concession but did not meet what they wanted. Jim needed Thomas to play a part in neutralising Matthew's efforts to incite uprising in Dorset, not just warn him of the dangers. He had had to report failure to Sherborne and then stand back for the two obnoxious government agents from London to make their devious proposals.

And the worst was that Jim and Jane were given other tasks to take them away from Sturminster Newton, so they could not even temper the message to Thomas with friendly words.

Franshaw wasted no time. It was not that he was rude or aggressive, rather that he knew exactly what he wanted and was ruthless about achieving it.

"It's kind of you to see me," he started. They were in the parlour of the Davenport family home, occupied by just Thomas these days, with a cook, a maid and a housekeeper. "As I mentioned on site, where you are putting up that fine church, I am sent by His Majesty to make certain enquiries and points concerning the security of his realm in these parts." He made it sound as if the King had personally drawn up his instructions and sent him on his way with a hand on the shoulder and the other patting his back. In reality, Franshaw had only once met the King during a ship's inspection when he had tried his hand in the Royal Navy and the King, at that time, had been commander in chief of the navy as the Duke of York. He had stood in a line and they had been congratulated as a group for displaying some obscure bit of seamanship. This was the first mistruth uttered that day.

"If this is about my brother…"

"It is, sir."

"Mr Franshaw, you should know that my brother is his own man. I have not seen him since I heard he returned from Holland a second time. The last time I saw him was at church in August in Bagber, close to here. I thought he had returned to Holland for the longer term but a friend of mine informed me he was back here again. I have not seen him on his return."

"Your friend is James Bigg, am I correct?"

"Yes, sir. Big Jim, as he is known."

"Well, Big Jim works for me." That was closer to an outright lie and certainly the second mistruth that morning. Jim was not employed by the Government; merely, his Catholicism drove him to support the King.

"What do you want of me, sir?"

"I need your assistance in a matter of security. Your brother, Matthew, is in serious danger and is, by all accounts, behaving very stupidly. I was instructed to arrest him and take him to the Tower of London for questioning." That was the third mistruth; nobody had ordered Matthew's arrest; in fact, Henry had specifically ruled it out. "But I wish to try another method first. I want you to do two things for me."

Franshaw desired Thomas to align himself with Matthew; be a soldier in his cause, or whatever it took to become established in his inner circle.

"Then I want information fed to my people as to his activities."

Thomas stood up, obviously angry. "Why should I deceive my own brother?"

"That is an easy question to answer, Thomas. If you do not,

76

Matthew will be arrested and, after our questioning, will no doubt implicate you and your sister, Elizabeth Taylor. The wheels of the law are relentless, my friend. Sooner or later they will come for you, as they will for Elizabeth, too. And others associated with your church. Is there not an Amelia Taylor also?"

Thomas argued for twenty minutes but to no avail. This was the same plan that Jim had outlined, only put more crudely by a stranger who kept smiling as he brought bad news for Thomas. There were subsidiary arguments also. His new church building was not licensed, nor was the temporary use of the Great Hall at Bagber Manor. They would be closed for sure, the new building pulled down and the foundations dug up and scattered across the field.

There were some details to cover, mainly when and how he would report. Then, business concluded, Franshaw, his three mistruths spent on the project, retired the victor to report his achievement back to Sherborne Hall, where Henry Sherborne was hoping for failure, for he had never wanted to vote for the plan in the first place.

And when he heard the news, given by the jubilant team of Franshaw and Cartwright, he feigned delight, smiling at the pair as if he was a key contributor.

For he was caught in a deadly trap with only one way out.

Cartwright had enjoyed playing his ace; watching pride and authority crumple on Sherborne's face. He felt he had played it neatly, employing tactics he had learned long ago when in the theatre. He always said he was one generation removed from Shakespeare, claiming to have been taught the trade by an old man who had, in his youth, acted alongside the great playwright and actor.

He had taken Sherborne out of the Great Hall that early October day when the afternoon sun tried to stretch across the width of the hall from west to east, creating unusual patterns that moved on the pale grey stone floor. They had gone to an anteroom, the ground floor of an octagonal tower that stuck like a growth on the side of the Great Hall. It contained a sweeping staircase that wound up several flights to give access to the minstrels' gallery above. He had used the broad bottom steps as his stage. By standing on the third step, he achieved a little height over the Earl. With a deep breath, he launched into his often-rehearsed lines.

"Sire, I wish to impress upon you the seriousness of this situation."

"I know that, Mr Cartwright."

"But do you, My Lord? I am charged with maintaining order in Dorset."

"As am I, as the King's representative for this county." It seemed the Earl had learned the lines of the same play Cartwright was performing. Cartwright smiled but kept it swallowed; gave instead a picture of considerate concern.

"What the King gives, so the King can take away." That was a bit corny; taken from somewhere else. In slight panic, he tried to focus on the lines he had learned.

"Is that a threat, sir? Either I bend to your will and act against my friend and conscience or I will have the Lord Lieutenancy taken from me?"

"No, My Lord, it is no more than a practical statement of the politically obvious." There, he was back on track. Now the time for the killing blow. This time he could not keep down his smile, which came out as a smirk; somewhere between a smile and a sneer.

And Sherborne saw it and a premonition hit him. This vile man had something on him. But what could it be?

"Then, why do you seek to persuade me, sir?" he said, playing for time; brain churning through the possibilities but nothing rising to the top.

"Sire, I work for one of the highest authorities in the land." Now was time for that killing blow. Cartwright was all eyes; as if he was determined to remember the changing expressions on the earl's face in order to record them for prosperity; to tell his grandchildren, except he had none, no children to continue the line, no wife to produce an heir to follow after him.

"And who might that be?" *Perfect lines*, thought Cartwright.

"My employer, sir, is none other than Parchman."

And it worked. Henry Sherborne took a full minute to

register and then his face crumpled.

"You know?"

"Yes, My Lord, we know your secret."

"And?"

"And, Sire, we require complete obedience to our cause or you will not only lose the Lord Lieutenancy but your very earldom."

There it was, said as plain as day. Parchman was the only other person who might have known Henry's true parentage; that he was born out of wedlock to the then heir of the earldom and his lover, Lady Merriman. They had never married. They had been prevented from marrying by Henry's grandfather, the earl, acting through Parchman. Parchman had clearly gone on to much greater things but had kept his memory of past happenings in case they were useful one day.

And clearly this memory was of utmost usefulness.

Henry agreed to the plan at that moment. Perhaps he could have forgone the earldom, he told himself, but the dishonour on his mother, Lady Merriman, would have been too much. And then there was Grace, his wife, to consider. She had taken to being a countess as if born to the role.

What else could he do?

Chapter 12

The Duchess of Wiltshire did the best she could but was limited by her husband's parsimony; increasingly so, with everything connected to her, and very irritating when she wished desperately to make an impression on the man she once had wanted to marry.

And now wanted again, on the broad steps to Sherborne Hall, for the livid scar of three years earlier was much faded, although still clearly visible; it no longer looked loathsome but somehow interesting. She wanted to trace her long fingers over it, feeling the ridges jut out from the centre like a mountain range turned to the horizontal, such was her desire to caress human flesh.

Any flesh other than that of her husband.

Despite his evident health, the words 'frailty' and 'vulnerability' went through her mind the moment she had time to study him. Was she noting that responsibility had added shades to a character that had been largely unformed when they were betrothed three years earlier, before his face was slashed in battle and she had been obliged to walk away? Or was something troubling him? Perhaps that trouble was why Wiltshire was so keen to visit?

She would love to know but would not lower herself to ask her husband again. She would find out some other way.

"How nice that you were able to come," Grace was saying to both of them. "When you have settled in you must see around the wing that Mr Milligan built in the old earl's time. It is quite remarkable, in that it connects so many ground-floor rooms together. It starts with an octagonal tower next to the Great Hall and stretches around to the library." Grace pointed with her arm to the left, where the complicated array of rooflines and walls dipped to meet some ancient spreading cedar trees on the lawn. "That's where Henry's father had a fantastic treehouse when he was a boy. I grew up in a town and none of the trees were big enough for a treehouse but we used to go and play at Bagber where they had some lovely ones."

"There was a witch at Bagber," said Penelope. "My mother used to tell me the story when I was a child."

"That was make-believe," Grace replied, then changed the subject. "I've put you in the queen's suite, so named because Queen Mary visited in 1556 and they refurbished the rooms for her."

The rooms indeed looked like a century or more had passed since major work was done. They were large, with faded rugs on faded floorboards and washed-out tapestries covering almost every inch of wall space. There was a bedroom, two dressing rooms and a solar with rounded walls looking boldly out over a formal garden of roses still blooming and pear trees bound like prisoners to a warm brick wall. Sally found a bath and asked for hot water from the kitchen, then helped the Duchess to undress. The Duke drank brandy, sprawling on an easy chair, his right boot kicking at the tassels of a patterned carpet. He stood suddenly and moved his chair a quarter-turn so that he could look through the door to her dressing room where she was in the bath, attended by Sally.

Penelope noticed immediately, felt the eyes boring into her, and slunk down in the bath, trying to hide. At first, Sally did not see the Duke shift his chair and wondered why her mistress was making it hard for her to be washed. But their eyes met and the Duchess flicked her head towards the Duke. Sally understood in an instant, stood up and pushed the door, saying, "Please excuse me, Your Grace," as the door swung on its hinges.

"Thank you, Sally."

"That's fine, My Lady, I mean, Your Grace."

"Call me 'My Lady' if you prefer."

"Thank you, Your Grace." Their eyes met a second time and they smiled at each other for the first time ever. Then Sally lost herself in wringing out the cloth and scrubbing her mistress' back.

She wore a black satin dress with silver moons and golden stars. Immediately, she wished she had not, for Grace was dressed in an almost match; a deeply navy-blue gown that flared at the same point as Penelope's but lacked the celestial decoration. Instead, it had slits running the length of the dress and revealing a pale-yellow underskirt, like rays of real moonshine spilling into the night sky. Beside Grace, Penelope felt expensively foolish and unnecessarily flamboyant. True, Penelope was three inches taller, but the elegance of Grace's dress gave her a height that the Duchess could not match.

"Who makes your dresses?" the Duchess asked in a smaller version of her own voice. "They are wonderful."

"Thank you, Your Grace."

"Please call me Penelope."

"And I am Grace," she smiled awkwardly about her name and Penelope picked up on her embarrassment.

"So, if you became a duchess, your name would have a double meaning."

"I suppose so, Penelope," she laughed. "I have a lady in the village who makes all my dresses. I could send her to you if you like."

It was an unlikely friendship that spawned that day. They shared a love of fashion but little else. Grace's stories of life on the estate bored Penelope, as Penelope's tales of London bored Grace. Yet there was some connection that could not be ignored.

But friendship is not something we buy in the market from a carefully prepared list. It is a gift of God, springing on us in the most unlikely times. It jumps across fences and walls with ease, then settles, enveloping its target in the warm glow of amity; a little like the pear trees strapped to the sunny wall.

Friendships come directed from God but it is man that breaks them up time and time again.

"What's the matter, my dear?" Grace asked Henry as they retired to bed that night.

"Nothing, Grace dearest." He ached to confide in her but was sworn to secrecy twice over. First to his real mother, Lady Merriman, for if it was known that his birth was out of wedlock, he would be disinherited from the earldom. And that grand earldom would be no more, for he was the end of the line. History would pay lip-service to the Sherbornes, then tidy them away in a few short paragraphs and a note at the bottom of a page. He owed something to his forefathers; to his grandfather, who had also known this secret and kept it so for the sake of the succession.

Second, and more recently and unfairly, he was sworn to Parchman, the agent of his grandfather who had acted viciously against his mother. Cartwright had extracted an oath from the Earl, promising on what Cartwright said was a Bible, but Henry had suspected it to be something else altogether. But an oath is an oath; just as blackmail is blackmail and consequences are consequences. Thus, he could not share his most fearful secrets with his own wife, for fear that it would be his undoing.

And the undoing of both wife and mother he loved so dearly.

"It is just that you appear distracted." She came over to him and stretched up to put her arms around his neck. They kissed. Suddenly, she withdrew and stepped backwards so that she could see every feature of his anguished face pretending, really, to be at ease. "It's not that you wish to be away playing the soldier again, is it? I could not stand us to be apart unless it were very necessary."

He assured her it was not the case; putting on his truthful face once more and delighting in the sensation of honesty pouring forth. There was nothing wholly dishonest in their marriage but some parts troubled him deeply because he had been forced to set the truth a little to one side.

And secrets creep into the gaps truth leaves behind.

But that evening, he could justly say he had no wish to be a soldier again; no desire to inflict and receive such pain at the tip of a sword.

"The Duke was strange," he said, pleased to have an observation to make that was permitted by Parchman.

Through his henchman, Peter Cartwright.

"In what way?" she asked.

"He seemed in two minds, like there were two people questioning me at the same time."

"Questioning you?"

"Yes, questioning me for certain." Henry took Grace to sit

83

side by side on the bed, Grace's head resting on his broad shoulders, or so they seemed to Grace for she loved every bit of him, whether physical or otherwise. Talking quietly, he explained how his evening had been with the Duke of Wiltshire.

"Most of the time, certainly when you and the Duchess were present, he was cordial enough, although he seemed tight-lipped…"

"I observed that," Grace interrupted. "It was as if he was forcing himself to be pleasant against his natural countenance."

"Exactly. But when we were alone together he was quite different and changeable, too." Henry described the peculiar mixture of aggression and pointed affability he had encountered. "I believe he was trying to find out if I had any connection to the Crown, such that I was active in pursuance of the interests of the King. I sensed that he was either seeking reassurance that I was not involved or that he was hoping to persuade me to come in with him. Hence the changeable nature of his questioning; when he wanted to persuade he displayed a friendly front but when he was quizzing me as to involvement, the gloves were off."

"Do you think he is involved with planning the rebellion everyone is talking about? And with Matthew, too?"

"I think he is on the winning side and is trying to work out which side that will be, although I doubt very much that Wiltshire gets involved in the everyday affairs, more that he directs things through others." That was as close as he could go with the oaths he had given to keep things from his darling wife. "We know Matthew, your brother, is involved in the rebellion, for Jim Bigg has told us directly. But, of course, it goes much higher than Matthew's level. I should think half the aristocracy are involved in these plans. There may well be several plans going off in all directions. But as to what side Wiltshire is on, I really cannot tell." He thought of Cartwright grinning at him as he turned the screw, enjoying the victory he had won over Henry. People were taking sides and his wife knew he was involved on the fringes; reporting back local intelligence to the authorities. But she knew nothing of the fact that he had been pressganged into wholehearted support of the crown in its preparations against invasion. What would his beautiful wife do if she found out about Henry's true involvement? Would it matter that he was forced or would she see his betrayal as exactly that? Or would her own natural feelings for liberty rise up and overwhelm the loyalty she had promised him on their wedding day? It would make a tidal wave of common sense to sweep away the traditions of centuries in the Sherborne family.

"Poor Matthew. I support the King because you want me to, dear husband. But my natural feelings are with Matthew and the others who stand up to the tyranny we are living through." There was his answer, at least in part.

"I know, my dearest and I love you all the more for subordinating your feelings to mine and my family's." He lifted her face, snuggled into his shoulder, so that he could kiss her warmly on the lips.

Whatever happened, he could not let her down. She was the Countess of Sherborne and, because she loved being so, he would do whatever possible to keep it that way.

On the floor above, Penelope was thinking hard. Sally was working quietly in the room, tidying and folding clothes. Wiltshire was somewhere else, drinking or whatever he got up to when away from her.

"Sally?" Her servant straightened her body.

"Yes, Your Grace." Penelope noted that Sally was getting her address right but somehow it did not matter much anymore.

"Have you been much in the kitchens?"

"Yes, Your Grace. I eat my meals there in the big servants' hall."

"Is there any talk, I mean, do you know why we are here?"

"No, Your Grace, other than that the Earl is being tested."

"Tested? How so?"

But Sally did not know or would not say more. Penelope watched her turn down the bed and wondered suddenly what it would be like to lie in bed with Sally.

But it would never happen for Sally despised her and kept

right away from her mistress whenever possible.

"There is one thing, Your Grace." Sally cut across Penelope's thoughts but then looked shy when Penelope pressed her.

"Well, I could go and see his manservant in the morning, after his Grace has risen and Cummings has attended to him. He might impart some knowledge."

"Yes, do that for me please, Sally."

It was much later that night in her small crib in the dressing room that Sally awoke suddenly; the Duchess had said please for the first time to her.

And when she had said please there was a look about her that Sally rather liked.

Chapter 13

"Sir Beatrice, this is my brother, who I've been telling you about. Thomas, please meet Sir Beatrice Roakes." Matthew pronounced the name with an evident degree of awe but, like so much Matthew did, it came across wrong; more as a circus announcement than respect for an aristocrat. Sir Beatrice winced at the tone.

"Good day to you, sir." Sir Beatrice made a gesture towards standing by placing both elbows upon the table and using them as leverage to raise his bottom briefly from the chair. When that bottom hit the chair again, it had done a neat shift through forty or fifty degrees so that Roakes could see Thomas side-on for examination and was facing away from Matthew.

"Glad to meet you, Sir Beatrice," Thomas replied, taking the seat immediately in front of him and subconsciously adjusting his own chair so that he was directly facing Sir Beatrice. Now Matthew appeared more like an attendant, waiting on the pleasure of two great men sat across the table from each other. He blushed at his ancillary position, looked at his barely-touched ale on the table in front of him. "Roakes, is it?" Thomas continued. "No relationship to a Sergeant Roakes who was in the army during the Monmouth uprising?"

"No sir, not to my knowledge," he lied, then justified it to himself that no man could be related to himself. "In fact, I am an orphan." This bit was fanciful, in suggesting he had grown up on his own. His parents were dead now, allowing him to dispose of the hated pig farm where Lady Merriman had been imprisoned in her misery for so long, but he had grown up with them. He also had plenty of cousins back at home.

"This man was from Yorkshire."

"I believe, Sir Beatrice, that is where you are from, is it not?" Matthew piped in.

"No sir, I said I hailed from Yorkshire as a convenience because we did not know each other well and security in espionage is all important. I actually come from Bristol."

"That is strange. I knew a Beatrice in Bristol. It must be

coincidence because Beatrice was their surname. I only knew the wife but found her a thoroughly dishonest and unsavoury character. Are you married, Sir Beatrice?"

"He is, Thomas, and Lady Roakes is here at the inn."

"Matthew Davenport, you really must learn some discretion if you are to remain working in subterfuge. And I am quite capable of answering to my own circumstances." This was getting dangerous. Roakes had not made the connection to Grace when he first met Matthew, but the likeness with Thomas was unmistakeable. As Sergeant Roakes, he had led the gang-rape of Grace Davenport as she rode through the countryside to try and free her brother, Thomas. And he had got away with it due to his connections with the old earl, the current earl's grandfather.

Now he had met Thomas here in the White Lion in Dorchester and knew the young man would kill him if the connection was made.

He would have to take some precautionary steps.

"But, Sir Beatrice, please tell me how my inn has caused you upset?"

"It is not me but Lady Roakes. Your clientele is too rude and vulgar for someone of such delicate countenance."

"Then I will clear the rooms and, for a small extra fee, the whole place can be yours, Sir Beatrice. I can't say fairer than that, can I, sir?"

"It's too late, landlord, we are quitting this place. My wife will have nothing more to do with your inn, whatever you promise to remedy."

"I see, Sir Beatrice." The landlord switched his tone suddenly as another idea came into his mind. "Where shall I send on your luggage, Sir Beatrice?" he asked obsequiously, wiping his hands on his apron as he imagined good landlords did.

"The Red Lion. We are departing for there this minute." Lady Roakes came down the stairs and, ignoring the landlord, took her husband's arm, expressing her own desire to be somewhere else as soon as possible.

"Yes, Sir Beatrice. I'll get them sent over immediately." The landlord backed out, willing them to be gone; for once not even displaying his palm in the hope of a few coins clunking in. He did not want these people to think of money at all.

"Are we ready, Sir Beatrice?"

"Yes, dear. But I am sure there is something else to do. Well, never mind. Let us walk up the High Street as it is such a pleasant day. Now, you must tell me how you have been getting on with the house hunting. Landlord, is there anything else to take care of? Oh, it seems he has gone to attend to our luggage. You know he is not such a bad fellow; I have stayed in much worse places."

The landlord went up the stairs to the first-floor rooms the Roakes had just vacated, jumping three steps at a time and calling to his underlings to collect the trunks and maids to clean the rooms.

He had got away with it. The Roakes' servant had paid for his best rooms for a month and they had stayed just four days, without claiming any of the money back. Now he could rent the rooms out again; offer someone a bargain and still make pots more money.

He would send a message for the builder to attend that very afternoon.

Parchman crossed the street, swore at the east wind that tried to blow in the new day, and kicked at a beggar for satisfaction.

"Have a care, sir. Can you spare a coin?" There was no coin forthcoming but Parchman gave a second kick; this one was well aimed and with force so the beggar went sprawling; yelping in pain like a dog.

Parchman was late, hurrying; then thought, *No, let them wait.* He stopped within sight of the beggar and pulled out a flask, drinking deeply of the strong, rich brandy. Then he did an uncharacteristic thing and held the flask for the beggar.

The old man scrambled up, scraping his shins badly on the rough stone that made the road; the thought of that delicious brandy roaring down his throat and swirling around his stomach, sending fire into each and every organ and limb, made caution stand aside.

Back in character now, Parchman took his time to make his third kick right in the guts. There was a loud crack as head hit stone, then the beggar was still and Parchman had to step over him to continue on his way.

He placed the flask back carefully in an inner pocket and went about his business. He detested the two men he was meeting; the smug, oily Cartwright and the bluff, round-faced Franshaw. The former was sickly sycophantic, the latter too wholesome to bear.

But they had their uses.

Parchman was less than a mile from his home off the Strand but it was a very different world down where the river ran its slothful way though Westminster. If truth was known, at least at night, he preferred the seedy street life, where strength and brutality replaced manners and gentility. It was closer to nature with its cunning, survival ways.

Cartwright was getting to know his employer, Parchman considered as he walked, all senses joyfully alert for danger. Why else would he recommend a street corner down here at a quarter to seven on a late October morning, when the sun lacked whatever it needed to push night out? Parchman loved both time and place; he practised walking from shadow to shadow, silently creeping, gaining ground on his employees without them being aware he was there. But his shadow had its own shadow, which moved as he moved. It was even quieter than Parchman, like a soundless echo. But the shape of a man following Parchman could just be made out by the serious observer of this scene.

"Sir, you scared me," said Franshaw, jumping high so that he brushed that low-level sun trying to shine around the corners of buildings.

Parchman was always just Parchman, or sir to those who worked for him. Cartwright had tried calling him 'My Lord' in an attempt to gain favour but was frozen into correcting his ways.

"You found us, sir," he said now, his wet eyes shining like lanterns on puddles.

"Of course I found you. Why would I not? I am experienced

90

in such things," he said proudly. But Parchman did not elaborate; did not let these two into his life at all. "I wanted to see you and sent a messenger to Dorset. Then I find you are come to London already and have left your station. Why is that?"

They had left Dorset for a simple reason. They were making no progress with Thomas spying on Matthew.

"He's giving us little snippets of information but never any names or anything else useful."

"What do you propose?"

"That's why we came to see you, sir," Franshaw offered. It was the last thing Parchman wanted to hear. And he exploded in ice-cold anger.

"Never approach your employer with no suggestions," he roared. "You need to come up with something and then approach me."

"I fear you misunderstood my colleague, sir," Cartwright said, with a kick to Franshaw's shins to silence him. "Or rather, he expressed himself inadequately." In the gloom of early morning, reds and yellows trying valiantly to make themselves known, Cartwright used the shadows like an expert, moving his rounded shoulders to block a clear view between Parchman and Franshaw. "Sir, what Mr Franshaw meant was we came to you to discuss the problems but we have our ideas as to how to solve them."

"Fire away, Cartwright. I have not got all day."

Now Cartwright was on the spot. He had seconds to come up with at least two suggestions.

"Sir, can I tempt you with some breakfast while we discuss this?" A good move but Parchman was having none of it. He liked his food but did not relish the company.

"Get on with your suggestions, man."

"Sir, the first idea we had was... to... carry on as we have been doing. The argument goes that we need to exhibit patience and consistently apply pressure on Thomas Davenport." His voice picked up speed as he moved into his first suggestion.

"And the alternative?"

There was no alternative at present but Cartwright found a

little hope in Parchman's dismissive statement. If he was seeking 'an alternative', then there was no third or fourth option to find. He only needed one more.

"Sir," it suddenly came to him, "we take the opposite approach."

"And what might that be?"

"Just that we come down hard on the Davenports."

"Meaning?" Parchman was beginning to listen, sensing a solution.

"We arrest the Davenport brothers and everyone else we can associate with these traitors. Then we use tried and practised methods to extract the truth from them." Cartwright's grin shone through the grey, inferior light, like a bright star piercing an overcast night-time sky.

Parchman's lopsided smirk met the grin midway and the policy was set. All that was needed now was the detailed planning; who did what and when.

"You have a week," Parchman concluded. "Continue with your current approach for a week longer but, if nothing is achieved by then, you have my sanction on arrest and what follows from that. Now get back to Dorset this instant."

Franshaw wanted to shake hands to mark the decision but Cartwright still shielded him from full view, and by the time he had moved around his much smaller colleague, Parchman was gone; back to the gradually fading shadows from where he had come. What Parchman did not see was the shadow in the shadows; stealth on stealth. Franshaw saw something; made to move against it but Cartwright held him back.

'Get back to Dorset this instant' were Parchman's parting words. And Franshaw and Cartwright did exactly that.

But after they had rewarded themselves with breakfast. And Cartwright was determined it would be appropriate for two highly important agents in the employ of the crown.

The bill would be submitted along with their other expenses, which were mounting nicely.

The shape behind Parchman moved as he moved, all the way back to the Strand. It moderated by degrees, becoming bolder as a mix of other people entered the scene. Finally, at the end, close to Parchman's home, the bulk of Robert Candles strode right past Parchman, as if he had no interest in the man at all.

Chapter 14

The arrests came four days later, on November 1st.

They were led by Franshaw, ever the public face of secret agency. He looked honest and straightforward; hence made the perfect front man.

Cartwright decided after four days that they were getting nowhere with Thomas spying on Matthew. He silenced Franshaw's protests that four days did not make a week in anyone's eyes.

"It is more than half, is it not, Mr Franshaw? Who is going to quibble about a fraction of a week, man?"

"But he told us to carry on trying for a full week."

"Mr Franshaw, am I not senior to you in every regard? Have I not worked longer at the business? Am I not older and wiser? Did I not save you from a tongue-lashing when we last met our employer?"

"You are and you did."

"Precisely, so trust me if you will. I want you to arrest Matthew and Thomas Davenport. Round up anyone else you come across, if you suspect them to be associated with the Davenport boys." It came across like a campaign to stop children scrumping for apples; so reasonably put, so many words manipulated, that Franshaw found himself agreeing.

They got Matthew first, starting with the easiest, as Franshaw said. Eight soldiers were all it required; eight redcoats and a green one with gold trim for Franshaw. They burst in on Matthew as he sat down to a bowl of porridge, as he had every morning since before he could remember.

"Hands up, in the King's name," Franshaw shouted into the bustle of the early-morning inn. But Matthew, spoon to mouth and back to bowl with thirty years' practise and muscle memory, was not in this world at all. He did not react, for in his world there was only Eliza Merriman declaring her love for him. There was his family, of course, including his father, who had died three years ago in Winchester Jail. Then the door opened and a fan of angels dressed, peculiarly in red, entered. At the centre of the spearhead of scarlet was his mother, long dead but resurrected for this scene. She wore a dress of luscious green, trimmed in gold. She was clad like Mother Nature in high summer; the vibrant green turning to golden yellow with the beating sun.

"Hands out, my son. I want to see that they are clean before you eat." It was said so gently but it was a command and Matthew obeyed. He was sitting but she was standing; floating above the ground, even, so he raised them up in the air for her inspection.

"You are under arrest," Franshaw chimed, his voice an octave above normal, adrenalin causing the words to jumble out together in excitement; the excitement of mother for child; the churning of emotion that flows down the generations.

"Yes, Mother, I shall take a rest for I am tired after eating my porridge."

"What did you say, my man?" Franshaw was suddenly at his most serious; trying to cut into a room of make-believe.

It was the click of the handcuffs that brought an end to the daydream. First the right wrist then, a second later, the left. Matthew was swirled around to face the person in green with gold trim.

And it most certainly was not his mother.

"Who... what... are... why?" he spluttered, weakness at the knees.

"Silence, prisoner!" one of the redcoats roared, raising the butt of his musket in a threatening gesture.

"You have no..." that same musket-butt struck and Matthew doubled over in pain. Pain is so real. There is no daydreaming about pain and no pain in daydreaming. This was harsh, cold, forceful pain.

"You are under arrest," repeated the green-coated one, clearly in charge. Matthew saw a big man with an open, round face; an exact lookalike for old King Harry, with his red hair and speckled face.

Matthew suddenly thought of his history lessons as a child. King Harry had looked bluff and handsome but it hid a cruel character within. Not just resolute like monarchs would have to be; not overly sadistic, either, just cruel.

The memory of King Harry's treatment of rebels washed over him with its icy fingers clawing at his nerves.

Matthew was in deep trouble.

They led him away, or rather jerked at the chains attached to his handcuffs to lead him like a beast. He followed, a running stumble, keeping balance as best he could.

"Sirs," called the landlord, "this fellow might be a traitor but even traitors need to pay their bills. He owes me for the last three weeks."

"I do not," said Matthew, outraged at this minor deception.

"Silence." The butt was raised and served its purpose. "How much has he about his person?" They searched him and found several sovereigns and some smaller change. "Here, landlord, is this sufficient?" The green-coat asked, flicking the sovereigns into the landlord's open hands, then passing the smaller coins to the redcoat with the raised musket.

"Just about, sir, although not full compensation for the loss of business and for the disruption this arrest has caused me and my reputation."

"It will have to do, sir," interjected the raised musket.

But it had been another good day. Double rent and the second payment way over the going rate. Perhaps he could invest in a second inn alongside the White Lion. He had heard the landlord of the Red Lion moaning about trade. Perhaps he could buy him out? Of course, he would need a few more windfalls to make that happen, but he seemed to be on a roll.

Matthew was bundled into the back of a large cart with a heavy canvas cover. He was not maltreated; it was more like someone would swing a sack of clothes up and over the backboard.

The man in green and gold leaned over that backboard for a word in his ear.

"I'm sure this is all a dreadful mistake, sir," he started. "We will be able to sort it out in a moment once we get the paperwork underway. Ah, paperwork, bureaucracy; the bane of my life."

"Why am I being arrested?"

"Hush now, sir, don't fret. I'll get a written apology for you in two shakes. But orders are orders, sir, and its more than my job's worth to disobey them." He did not stop to consider he was disobeying orders; direct orders from Parchman that said to maintain the current methods for a week before resorting to arrests.

He was disobeying his ultimate superior by obeying his immediate superior. He shrugged, did not care much, as long as the coins clinked in his hand every so often, he did not care.

"I was paid up with the landlord, you know." Matthew seemed as incensed about the claim of being behind with his lodging money as with his arrest.

"In all likelihood we'll get that back for you, sir. Now, where is your brother?" Franshaw made to shake Matthew's manacled hand in a gesture of conviviality.

"He's in St…" Matthew stopped mid-declaration, recognising the trap. "I'll not say more." He had already given it away by telling the truth.

He had opened his mouth to tell the truth because that is what he had always done throughout his thirty-three years on this earth.

"More's the pity, you imbecile." Similar to King Harry, Franshaw had a temper that flipped like yacht tacking. He slammed the upper part of the backboard shut, catching Matthew's ring finger and thumb between the metal bracket. "Serve you right," he shouted. "Driver, to Sturminster Newton and you'll get a flogging if we're not there by the middle of the afternoon. We have unfinished business to attend to."

Thank the Lord, thought Matthew, as he settled back in the cart, nursing the torn skin and rising bruises on his right hand; the hand he had stretched out in friendship only to have anger thrust back at him.

Thank the Lord, for Thomas was not in Sturminster Newton at all; rather, he was in Stallbridge, investigating the only new enquiry to come to the building business in quite a while.

They would not find him in the elegant short streets of

Sturminster Newton, perched on its hill like he imagined Bethlehem to be. They might tear the Davenport home down, ransack the unfinished church Thomas was building, terrorise his neighbours and friends.

But they could not arrest someone they could not find.

The day for Matthew was long and slow, punctuated by a mixture from Franshaw of false bonhomie and livid anger, in roughly equal doses. On balance, Matthew preferred the anger, for it was honest and bare for all to see. But it was painful to Matthew for he was struck often and hard; the soldiers took their cue from Franshaw and inflated their first acts of cruelty as the day went on and their frustration at not finding Thomas increased.

Thus, by evening, Matthew had many bruises and he suspected a finger was broken. It sent a piercing, pulsating pain up his arm to dominate his mind and prevent clear-thinking. In his daydreams, he had remained cool when pressed; the reality was very different. He was numb by evening and the negatives kept working at him: pain soaring; hunger making him want to vomit; fear playing games with him. The cart jolted back and forth across the town of Sturminster Newton, seeking out Thomas Davenport in ever less likely places and with each disappointment came another step of retribution against Matthew, the brother.

But he kept his silence, glorying in it. It salved his cuts and bruises and fortified the soul. He reasoned that the day could not go on forever so he broke it down into little segments, settling on 100 sections of ten minutes each. That would cover from the breakfast arrest to midnight and the blessed end of the day.

He tried to pray by closing his eyes but fear drove them open to see and guard against the next strike from Franshaw or the soldiers. And when he forced his eyes closed, their red coats became a sea of blood, threatening to wash him away and drown him. "I am holding out," he said to himself, muttering it repeatedly like a priest at his rosary.

And then they found Thomas.

He was walking home late in the day. It had been a promising meeting in Stallbridge and he felt positive about business matters for the first time in months. He whistled silly tunes in the dark as he walked home, his mind on how he would tell Mr Milligan. He did not want to give false hope but he did want to buck up the spirits of his elderly employer.

It was Matthew who gave him away. Into his gloomy thoughts came the distinctive whistling and he could not help himself from crying out his brother's name. Too late, he tried to gobble the words back up but they were out for all around to hear.

The difference between Matthew's arrest and that of Thomas is that Thomas put up a fierce fight. He possessed a looping, bendy stick, which he had been attempting to twirl in his fingers as he strode along. This became his weapon, both sword and shield. It fared badly against the butt of eight muskets but it did make a fight.

And Matthew, with the advantage of height from the back of the cart, saw an opportunity and gave a vicious kick to one of the soldiers as they streamed down the side to attack Thomas. His boot caught the red-coat on the left temple and downed him instantly.

It added assault to the charges Franshaw brought before them when, now severely trussed, the Davenport brothers were both carted to Shaftesbury Jail and their grim future.

Cartwright had a role to play while Franshaw was out and about that day. He sent early for Big Jim and Plain Jane, who came immediately, arriving at Sherborne Hall mid-afternoon to a fierce wind that drove every sensible person inside. They were kept waiting together another hour in a freezing anteroom. It had a large fireplace but lacked a fire. Bizarrely, they stood in front of the fireplace, as if the memory of a once-upon-a-time fire would warm their shivering bones.

Then Big Jim was summoned but not Plain Jane. The servant was emphatic on this point.

"Come anyway," growled Big Jim.

"No, I'll stay away if I'm not wanted. Heaven knows why

they wanted me to traipse all the way over here if they don't want to see me."

The 'they' of Jane's sentence was singular and male so 'he' would have been more appropriate. Cartwright would have loved an audience for what he was about to do. But he could not justify it and audiences also meant evidence. Plus, hearsay would lead to wild rumours and he certainly did not need those.

The dismissal of Big Jim and Plain Jane was a simple affair. Perhaps Jane would have had a better response and that is why Jim was summoned alone. As it was, Jim grunted, scowled, bit back some swear words and then shrugged his shoulders and stood to leave.

He had acted to protect his religion. If they did not want his help, so be it. Roman Catholicism had seen many worse crises and survived; indeed, been strengthened by them. He and Jane had been volunteers so there was no need to discuss money. He was in and out in five minutes.

"Come," he said to his wife. "I'll tell you about it on the way home. I want to be shut of this place now."

They left immediately, seemed to be bowled down the drive by the fiercest wind since spring blew in warmth. But this wind promised just dead coldness.

And they left behind a disheartened Cartwright. He had expected to enjoy the dismissal process far more than he had.

He blamed Jim Bigg for that; clearly, he was not committed to the cause to accept dismissal so easily.

The second task for Cartwright to perform started later that day and went on into the night. It was more substantial, held more promise of satisfaction.

He would start his questioning with Matthew first and then alternate between the two brothers. Separate cells, separate questioning times. The Davenport brothers would be kept apart.

He rubbed his hands together and did a little jig so that his slick hair fell into his eyes and had to be plastered back. He was going to enjoy this task.

Chapter 15

Sally left the room as quietly as she could; creeping out like a parent who has finally got an unsleeping child to lay down its head.

She wanted nothing more than to put her feet up for half an hour before bed, sipping on a little wine in the kitchen, talking to peace and discussing the day with solitude.

If she could just get to the bedroom door, open it and close it silently behind her, she would be free.

She knew the door creaked. But it only started its creak at the one-third-open point. She was thin and could slip through; it was a slender but safe gap, low odds for being heard. The real problem was closing the bedroom door, for it was heavy with a loud thud as it shut. She considered leaving it ajar but the cold air blowing through would wake her mistress. She had to risk closing it.

She was on the other side of the door now, drawing it carefully shut. She thought about locking it and running away. She had long and powerful legs and knew she could run a long way, fast. She could run the sixty miles to London. She would take a little satchel with bread, cheese and water; plus, the beautiful silk shawl Lady Withers had given her for her birthday. It was decorated with butterflies, making an intricate 'W' for Withers, "So you may know where you belong, Sally dear."

She knew it was meant kindly but did she truly belong to the Withers; hence, by gift, to Penelope, their only child? Or had they stolen her, making the shawl no more than a delicate branding iron to stake out property they had no right to claim?

There were plenty of questions inside Sally, but right now she had to steady her mind to get the door closed with herself on the outside. The door was shut now, just the lock to fall into place; a series of minute turns until she could sense the weight of the door knob resting in place.

"Sally, my dear?" The voice was sleepy but Sally froze for several minutes, hand still on lock, hoping her rapidly beating heart would not vibrate through the door and awaken the Duchess.

It did not, for there was no more calling for Sally. Eventually, she released the lock and slipped away, only allowing her clogs to tap on the wooden floor when she was down a whole flight of stairs.

She had her half-hour. She would use it wisely. After pouring a cup of wine, she pulled out an alphabet book and started studying her letters. She was already on M and hoped to do several more that evening before she took herself to bed.

She sat and studied by the light of a small fire in a servants' parlour off the kitchen. She was alone after a 'goodnight' was called from the cook's first assistant as he made his way up the stairs to bed. She was quickly lost in her letters; seeking out words that began with 'O', then 'P' and 'Q'.

She did not hear the door open and a figure float in.

"What are you doing?" It might well have been a lightning storm centred directly above her. She jumped in shock.

"Oh, Lady Penelope, you surprised me." She put both hands over the book in a ridiculous attempt to hide it.

"What are you doing?" she repeated.

"It's just a book, My Lady."

"I didn't know you could read."

"I'm learning, My Lady."

"How far have you got?" Penelope drew up a chair. Sally had seldom sat in her presence and made to rise.

"No, sit down, Sally." Penelope waved her back into her seat. "Let me see if I can help you." They went through the book. Penelope's interest was mainly in testing her, expressing delight when she got the letter sound right, as if it were her own personal achievement. Then she had Sally make out simple words. She quickly tired of the usual 'cat' and 'dog' and moved on to more interesting words:

L-O-V-E spells love. H-A-T-E spells the opposite of love; hate. See, it is easy when you get down to it. Now, what does this spell? B-E-A-U-T-Y, see it spells your name because you are beautiful.

The words rushed out of her. A moment later, realisation of what she had said made her stand, mumble something awkward in place of explanation.

"That's alright, Your Grace," Sally reassured but was severely shocked. She had thought the Duchess incapable of feeling. She tried to right the upturned apple cart. "I am your servant, Your Grace, you may say as you please to me. I am here to be of service to you." But Sally's eyes belied the subservience of her tongue. They dared Penelope to sit next to a servant girl with chocolate-brown skin and a long, lithe body.

And Penelope listened to the eyes not the tongue; she used her own eyes and

forgot to hear. She sat back down, next to Sally.

And they finished from 'Q' to 'Z' without stopping once.

When they exhausted the alphabet book and both had grown tired of Penelope's rigorous testing methods, Penelope sat and looked at Sally, who kept her eyes fixed deferentially on the floor but wanted to look up at her mistress.

"What did Hummings say?" Penelope asked.

"Who, Your Grace?"

"Wiltshire's man, of course." Usually when Penelope added 'of course' to a statement, it grated badly with Sally but not this time.

"Oh, you mean Cummings," she replied, forgetting to look down. "He did say that the Duke spoke about his meetings with the Earl of Sherborne; not that night, for he was too drunk, but the next morning, Your Grace."

"What did he say?"

"Just that when the rebels were beaten back into the sea, the King would have a lot to thank the Duke for. And it was worth a bit of underhand dealings to achieve the objectives."

"Did you ask him anymore?"

"Yes, I did, Your Grace but he told me to mind my own business and politics was not the province of women, still less coloured bastards like myself."

"I'll have him dismissed for that."

"No, please do not, Your Grace." She looked so earnest with her plea that Penelope thought she would do anything to please her. "It's no more than most people think, even if they are too polite to say it."

For her turn, Sally looked at Penelope and saw for the first time the straightforward honesty that ran through her. She lifted her hand, made to touch her mistress' arm, then thought better of it and instead stood, saying it was late and she needed to get to bed.

"I'll see you first thing in the morning, Sally."

"Yes, Your Grace. I'll bring the tray as usual." She curtsied in the doorway and left Penelope with her many thoughts.

The trouble with house hunting, Lady Roakes soon appreciated, was that nothing quite matched the image in your head. Lazenby Court had perfect grounds, with beautiful lawns dotted with elderly spreading cedars and giant oaks; each one, it seemed, sufficient to build a man-of-war. Even the building exterior offered some grandeur, with its turrets and battlements. But the inside was dreadful. The main rooms looked east and north and the occupants seemed in perpetual deep-freeze. Those rooms were dark and poky and completely unfit for entertaining. Barrington Hall, on the other hand, had beautiful interiors, touched by someone with a real eye for features that pleased. But the garden ended abruptly at the churchyard, giving the owners no privacy at all.

"I quite despair of finding the right house, my dearest. I fear we will end our days in this miserable inn, looking forlornly for what does not exist." The Red Lion was not as spacious or grand as the White Lion and Lady Roakes did not understand why they had moved; less so why Sir Beatrice had said it was she who had insisted on quitting it.

"We must look a little longer," Sir Beatrice replied; his work in Dorset was far from done. Besides, he liked the simple ruggedness of the Dorset countryside. The land was wild but within a civilised framework; so different to his native and elemental Yorkshire, where the rocks rose above the surface, declaring their contempt for the humankind that lived upon them. Here, in Dorset, similar skylines spoke of man's cohabitation with nature, not its surrender to it.

"But you have not visited one of these dreadful little houses, sir." This was said with mixed tones. The main thrust was complaint; even outrage, that he had left her to hunt alone for their country residence. But in the mixture were wavering chords that sang of a plea. Sir Beatrice recognised this instinctively; they were, after all, two of a kind.

"My dear, please do not be upset. My business is very pressing suddenly and I am much preoccupied with how to deal with it. I hope to be able to attend to your needs; indeed, to our needs, shortly. In the meantime, I beg you to keep searching and make a list for those we can visit together. You will do this for me, will you not?"

"I will, sir." Put this way, and accompanied with a squeeze of her delicate fingers, followed by his hand lightly on her long white neck, she could refuse him nothing; he had become everything to her. "And I hope that your business does not cause you too much aggravation. It worries me to see you in distress, sir."

"I will make it through," he replied, but already distant; his thoughts returning to his problems as soon as they were able to.

The arrest of Matthew Davenport two days earlier, followed later that same day by his brother, had given him both problems and comfort. Assured in his seedy business environment, he was struggling with this new world of subterfuge. How could he continue his role of co-ordination with the main players behind bars? And why was the younger brother suddenly involved? Was it from a fit of Puritan zeal or something more sinister? Thomas had asked a lot of questions, not only about Matthew's activities but also about Roakes and the name Beatrice.

And therein lay the comfort. For with both Davenport brothers in custody, there was no one to lead that questioning as to the Roakes' murky past and, specifically, the rape of Grace Davenport three years earlier.

In fact, it was probably quite safe to move back to the White Lion and raise their comfort level considerably after the cramped rooms at the Red Lion. He would walk there now and arrange it as a surprise for his wife.

An hour later the delighted landlord of the White Lion was

at the Red Lion to supervise the removal of the Roakes' luggage and take it to an extended set of rooms at the White Lion. He had dared to ask for twice the money as last time, arguing that all the best rooms were now at the Roakes' disposal, "with your gentleman friend now gone away so suddenly." Sir Beatrice had negotiated on the fringe but seemed disinterested and paid most of what the landlord had demanded.

In advance, too.

The arrest of the Davenports created a problem of co-ordination and solved a problem of personal comfort. However, one other problem gnawed at Sir Beatrice as he pondered what to do. He dispatched many reports to Wiltshire, often with interesting facts from Matthew. Yet not one report had received a reply from the man. He could picture the report arriving, nobody knowing what to do about it until some underling filed it in a pending box that never saw light again.

Elizabeth Taylor cried when she first heard of the arrest of her two brothers. Then she tried to draw herself together, admonishing the weakness she had displayed. "They need strength now rather than emotion," she told herself over and over again.

"What is the matter, Mother?" Amelia asked, looking up from her sewing as Elizabeth walked into the sitting room they used. Seeing her friend and stepmother back in her strict Puritan dress, Amelia despaired at the reversion. The more flamboyant Grace Sherborne became, the more severe her sister; as if the scales had to be continually redressed. At Amelia's request, immediately after the day by the stream that summer, Elizabeth had dallied with a hat, wearing it on three occasions but confessing she felt a flirt. Now she was back to the bonnets she always wore; only, Amelia noticed the bonnets getting longer, making dear Lizzie's face more and more withdrawn within a severe linen enclosure. Likewise, Amelia had briefly coaxed her out of grey into a tolerable sky-blue dress for a day or two but only to see her slip right back into that miserable attempt at colour. She yearned for the Lizzie of old; carefree yet responsible, fun-loving yet God-loving; a mixture that had attracted Amelia to follow her religion in a moderate way.

Regret lay heavily on Amelia; the feeling that she had played an indirect part in encouraging Elizabeth in her newfound zeal of Puritanism. She was partly responsible for the severe woman standing before her. She was Elizabeth's friend and had sat with her needlework while her friend became entangled in extremism.

"They have arrested them." The tears were back in flood; had been held only by the flimsiest of resolve.

"Arrested who?"

It took several minutes for Amelia to get the full details from Elizabeth; several more for it to sink in.

Elizabeth stood to lose two of her three siblings in one death blow; one figurative strike of the axe or two nooses hanging from the one beam. The third sibling was lost to her already; gone on a path she could never go down. The pain of impending loneliness drove her to despair.

And, thought Amelia, if they had arrested both the Davenport men, they would, for certain, soon be after Elizabeth. Even if they did not talk under questioning, her views, her stance on God, were well known. The same soldiers would soon be knocking on the door of Bagber Manor and Lady Merriman, for all her popularity and connections, would not be able to save her friend.

"You must go and see your sister," Amelia said.

"I can't, she's…"

"For goodness' sake, Lizzie, you must go and see Grace. I'll come with you. Let's get changed and…"

"Changed?" Elizabeth looked down at her clothes, wondering why there was the need to change. Then she turned and looked in the mirror, just as Amelia explained.

"Yes, Mother, you must change. And I will choose your attire for it is done with purpose. You must go and see your Catholic sister, the Countess of Sherborne and you will play the part." She rang the bell and gave Kitty instructions to send for the buggy and then for both her and her sister to attend on them in her bedroom. Elizabeth followed Amelia along the broad passageway at the front of the house to the bedroom. Lady Merriman arrived a few minutes later, breathless from running up the stairs.

"I heard from Kitty," she gasped. "I'm so sorry, Lizzie dear. Give me ten minutes and I will come with you. No, I insist. I have some influence with Grace as you well know and in the hour of need we must all turn to what strengths we have."

They left within the hour. Three ladies in their finery, squashed slightly inelegantly onto the narrow seat that was built for two in comfort. Amelia clicked once to the horses, speeding the trio on the way to Sherborne Hall.

Chapter 16

Let us step aside a moment and examine what emotions course through the heart following an arrest. The first has to be shock. Whatever the circumstances. Even if expected, it comes as a total surprise. The loss of freedom is something no human can get used to.

The second is usually outrage. With Matthew, there was right on Franshaw's side; legal right, if not morally so. The only serious wrong by Franshaw, and, really, he was only obeying Cartwright's instructions, was pre-empting the end of the week, thus breaking Parchman's ruling on the matter. In all other regards, Matthew was in the wrong as a willing rebel agent. He was playing a deadly game and should have expected to be tracked down at some stage. Outrage in Matthew's case should, therefore, have been muted; still present but not in powerful form.

But Thomas was a different case. He had unwillingly become an accomplice against his own brother, acting the counter-spy role forced upon him. Then, as soon as he started co-operating in the game of double dealing, albeit half-heartedly, the same people flung the handcuffs on his wrists and the shackles on his legs. By rights, Thomas should have felt that outrage far more keenly than Matthew. Yet it was Matthew who was shouting for justice through the narrow spaces between the bars on the door that made the only light into the cells. Thomas, in contrast, seemed resigned to his capture. He kept his eyes roving while they were moving about but as soon as his cell door slammed, he put head in hands with eyes closed. He could hear Matthew shouting in the distance but could not raise himself to call back. He seemed strangely settled to his fate.

But that is where the next emotion comes in and here paths differ significantly. With Matthew, the outrage turned to anger; useless anger, like a troubled child banging his head against the wall. But to Thomas, all such activities were a waste of energy.

And he needed every ounce he had if he was to make his escape.

"The older brother is a bundle of trouble," the jailer said to his assistant, resigned to a noisy night.

"Yes, but at least the other is quiet as a mouse."

"They're the dangerous ones. They seem obedient and docile and then they suddenly spring when you're least expecting it. I've been in this occupation for over thirty years and I can tell you some stories. For instance, the time when…" But the assistant had closed down for the night. He had not quite completed thirty months, to stand beside the thirty years of the jailer, but knew exactly how to block out all unwelcome sounds, whether coming from prisoners or staff. He could sleep with his eyes open, seemingly alert but out like a snuffed candle.

Several days passed, with a tiresome routine developing. Bread and water in a little churn was pushed through a hatch in the door every twelve hours. The prisoners would receive one curt reminder for 'pots'. If they were not quick enough with their chamber pot, the hatch would slam closed and the pot would remain unemptied for another half-day. Matthew kept getting the timing wrong; he would wake to see the bread and water on the floor, scrabble to get it and eat it all out of hunger. Then he would use that energy to raise hell for a while; beating against the door and shouting to anyone who could hear. There was never a response, except a yell back when the jailer, despite his experience, let the noise get to him. His assistant never let it trouble him and stayed cheerful through all.

Then exhaustion would take hold of Matthew and he would sleep through the next pot time, waking to see the bread and the water churn on the floor again. And the next cycle of mistiming was upon him. He tried notching the pot and food times on the wall, using his shoe buckle. But he did not always remember and mistakenly thought each pot change marked a full day rather than a half. And then there were several notches in several places on several walls.

His existence was a muddle of misplaced resolve, of anger and confusion, of regret and despair; these last two emotions, in particular, marching in time to the broken rhythm of his days.

Let us not dwell too long on the comparison between Matthew and Thomas. Suffice it to say, Thomas coped a lot better than Matthew, although inside he was racked with anger at his treatment and determined to seek retribution.

My God is an angry God.

We do not dwell on the comparison because far more pressing is what interspersed the dreadful monotony of solitary confinement. At irregular intervals for both brothers, the door would suddenly clank open and the prisoner would be expected to step into the corridor; dimly lit yet blinkingly-bright compared to the cell. The guards all wore felt slippers so as to give no warning of their approach. The first sign was the clank of the door and a flood of pale lamplight.

They were taken to a large room at the end of the corridor. In there sat Cartwright, in a high-set chair against the back wall. There was no door to this room, the jailer claimed it was so that the screams of pain would traverse the length of the prison, sending shivers down the spines of the other prisoners. The room was well-equipped for torture, with thumbscrews and hammers in one rack, pincers in another.

Yet neither Matthew or Thomas had any pain inflicted on them during their several sessions in the questioning room. Cartwright was clearly itching to have a go. He would often walk over to a particular instrument of torture and pick it up, almost caressing it with fondness. Then he would place it back again, turn around in frustration and start another line of questioning altogether.

There was no need for another team member with Cartwright in charge. He could play both Mr Nice and Mr Nasty, fluidly swapping between the two roles. His movements, his hand gestures, even his outline against the dim lamplight, would transform to meet the requirements of each character he took on. Thomas noticed a trick he had of using his shadow to enhance his bulk when Mr Nasty entered the room, then stepping sideways when Mr Nice took over so that the bulk shrank, resuming a more friendly, homely, shape and size.

Even Matthew noticed that Cartwright was not trying very hard. It seemed as if he wanted this tamer version to fail so the real fun could start. Sometimes, as Cartwright wrote on the paper in front of him, he sensed he was not writing a record of the interrogation but a critique of the techniques employed. He seemed to be carefully cataloguing the failure of the 'no-torture' technique that had been forced upon him.

But by whom? Who was in authority sufficient to demand no torture of the Davenport brothers?

And why would that person want to spare them?

On November 4th, Big Jim won the contract to supply bread to the prison. He offered also to take the chamber pots away for free and replace them with new, clean ones in a rotating cycle. The incumbent contractor wanted extra for this and Big Jim was certain this is why he had managed to steal the contract.

He made the first delivery and collection himself the next day, explaining that it was his policy to get new contracts established before handing over to one of his workers. His contact was the assistant jailer, who had, up until then, the responsibility for emptying the pots and rinsing them out.

"Hello, Mr Bigg," he said on the morning of November 5th.

"Call me Big Jim, everyone does."

"Hardly appropriate," the assistant jailer replied, chuckling. It was the oddest nickname for Big Jim was tiny; just as his wife, Plain Jane, was the prettiest girl most people ever saw.

"Maybe not, but at least people remember my name. Now, can you run me through my duties so I don't run the risk of letting you down?"

The duties involved bringing a large basket of bread twice a day.

"You can get the bread from these bakers towards the end of the day. That

way, we keep the cost right down." He then whispered the next sentence with hand over mouth, as if imparting state secrets. "It's two days old at least, you see. The bakers sell what they can of the old bread by discounting it. Then, at the end of the day, they throw it on your cart and it comes up here." He clearly wanted applause so Big Jim commented on the ingenuity of it all.

"Waste not, want not, I always say."

Once the bread was settled, he had to incorporate the chamber pot part. This was not as well thought-through as the assistant jailer had been doing it himself until good fortune had offered up the new haulier, who was happy to take it on.

They talked about it for a few minutes. Jim asked several questions, seemingly trying to understand how to make life as easy as possible for the prison and their staff.

"I don't see any need why you should touch them at all," Jim finally declared.

"Well, we have to get them to the gate so you can pick them up."

"Not necessarily."

"What do you mean?"

"I mean, let me and my team handle everything. We'll collect the used pots and shove in the old ones. All you need to do is throw the bread in later." It was a clever move to allude to 'throwing' in the bread, for it made Big Jim a colluder in their poor practices and, hence, one of them.

"I don't know, Big Jim, I'll have to talk it over with the jailer, see what he thinks of your scheme. I like it though," he added quickly, in case Jim dismissed his own proposal on first rejection.

The thought of someone else doing the dirty work was appealing.

Jim was about to accept this as a reasonable step forward when something made him stop. What if the jailer could not care less because he never sullied his hands with the chamber pots?

"I assume, being a team, you share the unwelcome duties," he said.

"What, the jailer get his hands dirty? You certainly don't know the hierarchy of prison life, my boy. He sets strategy and general principles and leaves the details to me. The dirtier the details, the more he leaves them to me." This was Big Jim's chance.

"I see, sir." It was time for a little flattery in his address. "Well, sir, if he leaves the details to you and the dirtier the details the more so, there is nothing quite as filthy as this particular subject."

"Meaning?"

"Meaning, sir, he clearly expects you to handle such matters and not trouble him on it. Besides, you will get a great increase in efficiency by following the proposal we've discussed." It was important to take this from being his idea through to a joint idea and then on to the assistant jailer's proposal altogether. "After all, sir, good ideas like this one you've had through discussion with me will save a lot of working hours. Think how much time is wasted by your staff collecting the pots and washing them out. Now all that will be handled by my firm for no more than you were paying before for the bread alone." He had jumped several steps at once but knew he had won; was just wrapping things up now.

He started his new duties that afternoon, again reminding the assistant jailer that he would run the contract until familiar with the processes and then train up his staff.

"Can you tell me the occupant of each cell so I know who I'm talking to?" Jim asked.

"No talking allowed, my lad. Just say 'pots' and if they don't bring it in thirty seconds slam the hatch shut."

"But…"

"No buts, son; those are the rules. I'll have guards watching you so don't get any ideas of chatting to the prisoners. They're all in solitary confinement and that means silence. Do you understand, my lad?"

"Yes, sir. Can you tell me how many cells there are?"

"Twenty-four, with three on the top floor vacant, so twenty-one prisoners. That's the most we've had since Judge Jeffries' time, just before I started in this job. We got two new ones this very week."

"Who would they be?"

"The Davenport brothers, filthy spies, the pair of them. They'll hang soon enough and reduce the jail population to a more tolerable level. Mr Cartwright is questioning them right

114

now." The assistant jailer gave him a knowing look, as if everybody ought to know what questioning by Mr Cartwright entailed, despite the fact that torture was evidently banned in this instance; at least for the time being. Big Jim forced a smirk in reply, as if he shared in the pleasure of inflicting pain on others.

As he picked up the stale, sometimes mouldy, bread, he laid the whole problem out in his mind. There were four floors; presumably six cells on each floor to make a total of twenty-four. The ground floor housed an armoury and a refectory, where the guards could relax when not on duty. In total, it was a compact, stubby building of five floors of dirty stone under a slate roof. A short passageway at ground-floor level connected to the chief jailer's house that came with the job. This was two floors and the stone was washed regularly by trustee prisoners so it seemed a brighter, more wholesome place than its neighbour.

How to find Thomas and Matthew was the question. He could not risk talking at each door for there would still be a guard roaming around the floors. He did not want to end up the other side of the bars.

He had a few ideas but no plan. It was only when the coffin-maker turned up on his second day that he started to get something together. He hung around, slowing down his work, until the body had been removed.

"Sir…"

"You still here, Big Jim?"

"Yes, sir. I wondered if you wanted me to clean out the cell. There is blood everywhere. I'll give it a quick washdown for sixpence." They settled on four pennies, promised for when he had done the job. The assistant jailer left for some paperwork concerning the dead body, wondering why anyone would volunteer for such grizzly tasks.

He should have wondered a bit harder as he was soon to learn.

Jim managed to drag out the job for several hours; long enough for him to see first Matthew and then Thomas being taken to separate questioning. He heard Matthew before he saw him; berating the guard for the lack of justice, shouting at the top of his voice about *habeas corpus*. But he spotted Thomas shuffling along an hour later. He coughed and clanged his pail against the wall. When the guard looked up he saw a tiny man working his mop on the filthy cell floor. When Thomas looked up he saw his good friend winking at him.

Thomas winked back.

Chapter 17

Parchman heard the news, he imagined, before anyone else in London. He had a network of agents like Franshaw and Cartwright across the country. Some were highly competent, most were average. But all understood that information was power and that their positions relied on Parchman receiving information before anyone else.

This is how the news travelled from Brixham to London. Fitler was the local agent. He was the son of a prosperous wool merchant, acting for Parchman because of a promise of a knighthood for his father that always seemed just a short distance away. He was based in Paignton and the news was received by him within an hour. Ten minutes later, he was riding out on his main indulgence; a beautiful palomino stallion of tremendous spirit. He made the fifty-mile stretch to Lyme Regis in fourteen hours by cantering, trotting and walking in stages and only stopping to water and feed the horse. At Lyme Regis, he passed the baton to the local agent, Alastair Brown, and then collapsed in an inn for the sleep of someone who knows they have done their duty.

Brown handled his challenge differently. He also had fifty miles to cover to get to Poole but he changed horses and galloped wherever he could. Accordingly, Brown covered the same distance in under ten hours.

Thereafter, the distances were shorter, as the agents became more plentiful. Franshaw did a reasonable stretch, coming in at thirty miles in five hours. Each agent passed on the same message to the next:

Orange – Brixham – Sizeable force

Thus, forty-one hours after the Prince of Orange's landing, Parchman was in receipt of the information and was hurrying to Whitehall to tell the King, confident that he was the first to bring the news.

He was dismayed to find the Duke of Wiltshire in there first. He could not have received the news earlier than Parchman? It had to be a coincidence, especially as Wiltshire was only on the fringes of government.

He kicked his heels in the King's anteroom, with a half-dozen others, while the evening of November 6th turned into a black, cloud-filled night of drizzle.

"At least it is warm for the time of year," some other waiter-for-the-king tried to make conversation but was frozen into silence by Parchman.

"Hardly a night for bonfires," ventured another, partially sighted, hence unable to discern Parchman's looks.

"But they served their purpose, just like the Armada."

"What do you mean?" Parchman growled.

"Why, Orange's arrival would be signalled in the orange of flame, just like the Armada's sighting 100 years ago. Wiltshire organised a chain of bonfires up the country. He's in with the King right now. We're waiting for our orders when he comes out."

"Everyone knows?"

"For the last day and a half, yes. Everyone knows, sir."

Parchman's ignorance, his lack of any education, had let him down. Some men learn everything the hard way, while others sit down and read the exploits of their forefathers.

But this was not Parchman's main concern right then; time enough for bitter contemplation later. His heart was beating at twice the normal rate because of the King's evident choice of Wiltshire to play a prominent role in the response.

Parchman's spies had identified him as a dangerous man who erred on the side of rebellion; not from principle or love of liberty, as so many did, but for the sheer joy and excitement of it.

And because authority is an insatiable quality, sucking in more at every moment like a drunk for the next drink.

Parchman settled down to a long wait to see the King, only to be surprised again when summoned shortly afterwards.

He was with the King and Wiltshire over two hours; left in quiet determination, making his rapid steps count on the stone and wooden floors of the Palace of Whitehall. Thirty minutes later, he was on his best horse, riding fast for his native Dorset. But hard riding, like any exercise, rubs the edge off emotion; in

118

this case surprise, rubbing it down like a stone on the seashore. Reporting to Roakes to manage the defence of Dorset seemed a clear demotion but the King and Wiltshire had both been emphatic that it was anything but.

"Dorset is fast becoming a hotbed of radicals," Wiltshire had said. "I need you to report to Sir Beatrice Roakes. Nominally, he is loyal but we have suspicions about him. The King wants you to act under his orders and determine where his loyalty lies. Do nothing to make him suspicious, obey his every command, but report your findings back to me. Is that clear?"

'"Perfectly clear, Your Majesty and Your Grace." Parchman's bow gave emphasis to his understanding.

"Together we will see off these rebels and send them packing," the King added, as if he needed to convince himself of his own policy.

It was a fight between order and liberty, the King's rights against the people's. Parchman knew which side he was on; not from loyalty; rather, an assessment of who would prevail.

It seemed that Wiltshire was on the same side; catapulted by his title into the highest ranks of Government. Yet there were all the rumours about his siding with the rebels.

"Parchman, you might express astonishment at my place here," he whispered during a particular rant of the King. "I know the talk is about me being a rebel for I have deliberately cultivated it. Clever, eh?"

"Yes, very clever, Your Grace." If it was to be believed.

And then there was the strange conversation he had had with the King while Wiltshire briefed others from the anteroom. The King, a man of fifty-five, was behaving oddly. He had conferenced with him many times over the last three years, both with others and alone. He could not say he liked the King, finding him arrogant and stunted in imagination and intuition; these limitations gave him a stubbornness that looked down on everyone around them.

Take away this man's birth right and there would be nothing left. Yet he was an enigma; a brave fighter and able commander, yet flustering over his future and the future of his dynasty.

He could not be more opposite to his brother, the dead King Charles. Nobody would have found him tedious or patronising.

But the King's character was known to Parchman. It was not his personality that had struck him. It was something else. He had seemed to cling to Wiltshire; seeking reassurance at every step.

"You will deal with these rebels in Dorset and return to defend the King in London?" he had asked, rather than ordered, looking over Parchman's head to Wiltshire at the end of the room.

But even his search for reassurance was not everything.

"I have lost the south-west to vile rebellion," he said, then a little later he had declared a resolve to crush it in time. Then, only two minutes later, he was asking Wiltshire what concessions he should make to calm the people.

He was all over the place. The only certain thing was he looked to Wiltshire for guidance. And Parchman wanted to be in that position. Well, a resoundingly good job in Dorset and he might be so.

Sally trembled as she dropped her dress and stepped out of it. She turned as instructed so that her corset could be loosened and taken off altogether. Then she turned again to face her mistress.

Quite when she fell in love with Her Grace, Penelope, the Duchess of Wiltshire, she did not know. She thought it was maybe the third session they spent together at the alphabet, late at night when secret meetings are at their most romantic. Penelope had been sketching the letter 'P' to make a comical figure of a stick-thin man with an enormous head. Sally had laughed when she realised it was an accurate depiction of Wiltshire, the Duchess' husband. She had leaned over and made to pick the pencil from the Duchess' hand, stopping herself at the last moment; realising how forward she was. Their hands had not quite touched skin on skin but she had felt the fine hairs on the side of her mistress' hand.

And she would never forget the sensation arising; she

imagined like lightning running through her.

After that, she could not get the Duchess and her commanding ways out of her mind.

"Your Grace," she had said when attending to her the next morning after a sleepless night.

"Yes, Sally?"

"Your Grace," she said again, getting the address right through long night-time rehearsal. "Your Grace." But the lines left her, wafting into the heavily scented air that inhabited the Duchess' dressing room.

"You've said that three times and each time I know what you are trying to say."

"You do? I mean, Your Grace."

Penelope did not reply, instead she took Sally's hand in hers and held those long, brown fingers; wondering at the beauty of them. She held the hand loosely, not wanting to exert pressure for a response.

The response came and Penelope watched it in her dressing table mirror. Sally slowly bent over her mistress from behind and kissed her on her exposed neck. Penelope was proud of her elegant, slender neck; prouder now that it sang with the joy of those lips upon it.

They did not take it further that morning. It was too much for either to bear.

"Dear Sally," said the Duchess.

"Your Grace." It seemed that Sally could not get past the opening lines.

"Call me Penelope when we are alone," the prompter said from the side of the stage.

"Dear Penelo... Dear Penny." Suddenly, they were Sally and Penny; two beautiful girls in love; each pushing their long fingers in exploratory traces across the body of the other. Penelope moved over on the dressing table stool so that Sally could sit. Together, they stared at each other in the mirror as if each body was a gateway to a magnificent garden beyond.

Then Penelope stood, walked around the stool to the back of Sally and began brushing her jet-black hair.

"I wish I had your hair," she said to Sally.

"I wish I had your whole body, Penny. You are so beautiful."

"You are far more beautiful." As they spoke, their eyes never left each other's, reflecting back from the mirror. Penelope was brushing Sally's curls almost absent-mindedly. Then she removed Sally's cap and pulled her hair loose. "There, that is better."

All too soon, they had to move back into the real world. Wiltshire had asked several of the leading families in the area to lunch and they would soon be arriving. Sally dressed Penelope in fits of giggles; completely unable to understand what had changed between mistress and servant; such a leveller was love.

But Sally put extra into her preparations, such that the Duchess was stunning by the time Wiltshire barged in through the door.

"The guests will be arriving soon, Penelope. What's been keeping you up here? Oh my, you look ravishing this morning. I may even have to take you myself tonight."

"Thank you, husband." The thought of Wiltshire coming to her bed was not bearable; especially when she had been hoping for Sally in his place. She walked out of the door, head high without a backward glance. Sally followed her to the landing; wanting to see her for as long as possible. She was walking down the main staircase like a queen about to meet her court.

"Sally, dear," she said in her best patronising voice from the last flight of stairs. "While I am occupied, please be so good as to take my old red dress and make what you will of it for yourself. Attend on me when I retire."

"Yes, Your Grace," she made a deep curtsey and her heart banged against its walls when Penelope gave her a double wink as she reached the bottom stair.

Penelope was the centre of attention from the moment she moved into the Great Hall, where the guests were gathered.

"You look delectable... ravishing... quite beautiful..." The platitudes poured out everywhere she turned. Eventually, Penelope realised that there was a difference. She looked into the mirror that dominated the north wall of the Great Hall and, for the first time, appreciated how she could look.

With the care and love of a good woman behind her.

Amelia led as they entered Sherborne Hall. Elizabeth was there, of course, but a pace and a half behind her stepdaughter; it made Amelia realise how much she had to thrust herself forwards.

For the sake of those she loved.

Grace, wearing a luscious pink dress with a low neckline yet high, stiff collar standing alone for effect, rushed into the room.

"My dear sister, you've heard the news?"

"Yes, that is why we are here. What can we do to help them?"

They were dismayed to find that Grace had no idea as to how to help.

"You mean it was not Henry who ordered the arrests?"

"No, sister, he is as anxious as you. This is some other power."

"He did not carry it out for this other power?"

"Lizzie, could you really think Henry would do this to his good friend? He has risen far under King James but he would never stoop this low."

"No, you are right, Grace. I am sorry, I am lost to reason with the stress of their arrests."

"Listen, ladies, we need to concentrate on freeing them," Amelia put in. "Grace, can you talk to Henry and get some more information; anything that might help us free them?"

"Of course I can, Amelia. But we also need to look beyond what my husband can do and decide whether there is any direct action we can take ourselves. Do you know where they are being held?"

"I assume in Shaftesbury Jail. There is nowhere else around here secure enough."

"We need to find this out. We can't do it as sisters of the prisoners. Amelia and Lady Merriman, you two could visit, if you will be so good as to do it. There is a good chance they will not connect you to the Davenports."

Amelia and Lady Merriman agreed. That meant Grace had something to do in quizzing her husband as to what might have happened and who was involved. Likewise, Amelia and Lady Merriman were scheduled to make a trip to Shaftesbury Jail, by far the more dangerous assignment. But Elizabeth had nothing to do.

"I'll call on all their friends and come up with a plan to rescue them as soon as we know where they are," she added as a postscript, the idea suddenly coming to her. "Don't worry, you three. We will get them out if it is the last thing we ever do." It was a rousing finale but a lot of bluff for Elizabeth had no idea as to what to do next.

But, somehow, she felt she was on the right road.

It was as they were leaving that Grace took Amelia to one side.

"What has happened with Lizzie?" she asked. "She is much changed."

"What do you mean, Grace?"

"I mean, she has not been here for three years. She has barely talked to me in that time."

"You know why; she is upset about you turning Catholic. Now she is come to see you from concern for your two brothers. It does not change how she feels about you, Grace." They were harsh words to hear but Amelia did not see any point in speaking anything but the truth to her aunt.

"Yes, but she is so changed in appearance. Gone is the drab…"

"Don't go on any further, Grace. Her drabness has been a direct response to your gaiety. The more flamboyant you have become in dress and appearance, the more conservative she has moved. It is, in her eyes, a balancing before God. She is doing it to save your soul, Grace. And, on balance, I have to say I agree with her. I am as one with her on faith; it is just that she feels compelled to take it to extremes."

"But now, the change right now? I have not suddenly become drab to allow her freedom of dress?" Grace ignored the comments about her conversion and concentrated on the immediate.

"No, that is my influence. I believe as she does, Grace, but feel she interprets too extreme a response. I forced her to dress as you see her today in order not to offend you and to be ready as a beautiful woman to play her part in gaining freedom for Thomas and Matthew. I do not need a lady in sackcloth and ashes, Aunt, but looking her very best for the world so that we might have some influence on how it works out for the ones we love."

"You would whore her then?" Grace stepped back, as if suddenly aware of the dangerous capacity contained within her step-niece.

"It is you who selects those words but words are just breezes that blow to buffet us here and there. We know the weather is extreme at present and we must react accordingly. Yes, if you prefer to say it so; I am whoring your sister as I whore myself and would have you whore yourself for the safety and security of your dear brothers."

It was a point well taken by Grace, who left them then, seeking Henry to accomplish her task and bidding them well in theirs. "We will meet again here tomorrow morning and make a plan," she said as the footmen held the door for them to leave.

Chapter 18

Parchman's instructions were clear; given verbally by the Duke of Wiltshire while quick copies were being made by the clerks. He was to ride to Dorchester and make his services available to Sir Beatrice Roakes.

"I will stop at Sherborne Hall on the way and…"

"You will do no such thing, Parchman." Wiltshire seemed determined to get Parchman in front of Sir Beatrice as quickly as possible. "Sherborne is not to be trusted," he added. His visit to Sherborne Hall, orchestrated so cleverly by his wife, but his idea in the first place, had produced this conclusion. He was a papist and had declared loyalty to the Crown, but in a wooden fashion, as if reading a poorly written poem and determined to get to the end of it. Wiltshire's report to His Majesty had said as much, in a complicated game where he saw his cleverness as a key ingredient.

Or, considered Parchman as he rode south and west at speed, perhaps Sherborne was to be trusted and Wiltshire held in suspicion. What were the Duke's motives in swinging behind the Crown? Or was it a façade? The Duke was capable of any amount of double-dealing.

King James would have done well to consider amongst the myriad that made his court, who was a true friend and who posed as such, seeking advice solely from the former.

Beware the false friend, I say.

Or perhaps the King was playing a double game himself; pretending devotion to, and dependence on, Wiltshire while really undermining him; turning the game back on the originator.

Beware the false friend, I say.

There was much to occupy Parchman as he travelled. Wiltshire's shortcomings occupied much of his journey, as would most when consumed by the rapid rise of another.

Step back a moment while Parchman rides like fury to do his new master's bidding. Stop while others do the work and consider those shortcomings. Consider, for instance, that a little more adept application during Wiltshire's visit with Sherborne, would have determined that the Earl was no different to thousands of other Englishmen; putting the liberty gained and established over countless centuries above a modern religious rivalry. But, like thousands of other Englishmen, the Earl was hesitating; not knowing which way to turn. A little more expertise from Wiltshire in double-dealing and he could have recruited the confused Sherborne to his cause; to any cause, in fact, placing hints like stepping stones to lead the Earl along the path he wanted.

But where Wiltshire had been quite clever, possibly by design although some later argued by accident, was in sending Parchman to work for Roakes, thus placing an arch-establishment figure under the direction of someone who sided naturally with Orange; for, as Roakes had said to Wiltshire when recruited, "Change brings opportunity and I am all for opportunity."

His cleverness was that he caused confusion and upset, which are constituent parts of the change Roakes had linked to opportunity.

And also taking Parchman right away from Westminster and the centre of things.

"My instructions will be in writing and will be clear in this regard. You are not to stop for any reason, other than a change of horse, until you have found Roakes. You will transfer your obedience to Sir Beatrice; do you understand?" This was said too loudly for comfort. Several courtiers looked around in surprise. Wiltshire lowered his voice to a whisper. "But ensure you monitor Roakes carefully and report back to me. Do you understand? You ultimately work for me and, if you want to rise in Government service, you will remember that well."

"Yes, Your Grace." But said with little intention of keeping the instruction if something better came along. Loyalty, to Parchman, was like an equation that balanced perfectly but would never be solved. He could only give loyalty when he received something in return.

Besides, something struck him about the name 'Sir Beatrice

Roakes'. Could it just be a coincidental combination of 'Beatrice', responsible for the terrible hurt in his side, and 'Roakes', the sergeant who had conspired with him to hold Lady Merriman in captivity and confusion, all for the sake of the old Earl and his precious inheritance? He would have time enough to ponder it as he rode through the night.

But, like many men of the world, he did not believe in coincidence.

Thomas had taken all he could of the four grey walls enclosing him. They may have originally been painted white, or even pale blue or green, but time had rubbed its grime into them, such that any bright colour faded to grey. He tried examining them to see specks of an earlier colour scheme but the dim light from two lanterns in the corridor outside the cell door was insufficient for that purpose.

By November 8th, entering into the third day of captivity and questioning, Thomas' stomach was churning. He felt his forehead and, like a child playing with fire, quickly withdrew it. He was raging hot; could imagine himself so hot that he was the cause of the condensation on the grimy walls. He tried praying on November 9th but his mind kept wandering so that any listener, were there any, would have heard the Lord's Prayer become, in mid-course, instructions to the roofers or the wood-carvers.

Thy Kingdom come, Thy will be done and then the battens should go, lengthwise first, across the roof trusses.

Give us this day a good carving of the Sherborne coat of arms above the door. There's the daily bread and the pot must go out, or is the pot coming in?

And deliver us from rain so that the slate can go on.

For Thine is the Kingdom, the Power and the Glory of a building put up well to last forever.

On November 10th, he had a brief interlude when the fever dropped and kept dropping. He went through a zone where everything made sense for a short while. He wondered how Matthew was doing. He thought Matthew far less likely to cope, being infinitely more highly-strung, also so straightforward as a person. For a moment, he imagined he was witnessing not his own life rushing past before death, but that of his brother. He saw Matthew's lost childhood; lost when their mother died and their father turned to drink. He saw in one still picture the pathetic attempt of Matthew trying to be like their father; a great preacher known across the country, with sermons published in several bestselling volumes. Matthew had written many of those sermons, or rather threaded together the inspirational thoughts of their father into a coherent lesson on morals.

The picture faded as soon as it had appeared, replaced by Matthew fleeing to Holland; alone, dejected, demoralised, yet trying to do what he thought was right. He imagined for a second how it had been in the Netherlands; some junior position, pushing paper from point to point.

He came to with a start, imagining Matthew dead, brains bashed out against the grey walls, spilling down to make the next occupant of his cell wonder what had gone on there before his time. And what might happen to him.

Then his temperature fell further and reason was frozen out. His teeth chattered and his body shivered. Then into that block of ice that was his cell came a piercing hot iron of a voice.

It was Matthew's voice come from beyond the hastily dug grave; come to welcome him, to take him to the afterlife; to be his companion for eternity.

"But I don't want to die!" he screeched, breaking his rule to keep his silence.

"No one is going to die, brother dear." Matthew's voice was much closer now. His touch was a firebrand on Thomas' arm. "But we do need to move quickly."

Hell could not be this hot and cold at the same time. It was against the natural law for hot and cold to co-exist; they must merge into warmth, like the raging hot sun dispelling its heat through the universe so that we are warm in our beds at night and at our work by day. Summer and winter do not happen at the same time; they transpose slowly through spring and autumn. That is how God set the world up; how everything runs.

So, how was it that he was freezing and burning at the same time?

"The lad is in the throes of a fever." That was another voice, not Matthew's. It made Thomas scrabble from his sunken, crumpled position. If someone had a fever, he had to help, especially in this inferno of ice.

"Can you walk? Here, lean on me." Thomas offered himself on hearing these words, felt a body crush close to him. He would guide the sick man out to warmth, plain and simple. All they needed was for the extremes to merge and everything would be alright.

It made for an awkward movement across the cell floor to the cell door; Thomas desperate to help the man who was helping him. That man was so familiar. His name was...

"Big Jim," he said suddenly into the November night. "Are you alright, Jim?"

"He is delusional," said Matthew, his voice so close now so that his breath disturbed some of the icicles surrounding Thomas' face, breaking them to the cell floor. He had to make more effort because his good friend, Big Jim, was delusional as well as sick.

"One more effort and we will be out into the passageway," Matthew seemed in command and Thomas was in support of him.

One more effort.

Thomas slumped in the back of the cart on a makeshift bed, tended by Plain Jane, who knew exactly what to do. They did not rush at first, for no cart on prison business ever rushes. They had a way to go to safety but did not want to alert anyone on the way.

The outline of the plan had been Big Jim's. Amelia and Lady Merriman had reported back excitedly that they were being held in Shaftesbury Jail and that Big Jim had just won a contract there to supply produce to the prison. Elizabeth had left immediately, tracking Big Jim down on his way to Shaftesbury and his new duties at the prison. She had tethered her horse to his cart and ridden with him.

She had taken Jim's outline and made a detailed plan of it. He put the wedge in the log but it was Elizabeth that delivered the blow that split it.

"We need a diversion," she had said. "I will do that if Jane will help me dress the part."

"The part, Mrs Taylor?'

"I will be the type of girl that attracts every man's attention. I believe from what you describe of the internal layout, that such a diversion will give you the fifteen minutes you need."

"But we will have to break down two cell doors. I will have to do the first one myself. I've seen those doors and it will take considerably longer than fifteen minutes."

"Well, Jim Bigg, have you never heard of such a thing as a key?"

"But we have no key. If we try and steal one we'll…"

"I shall provide a key but I shall require help from Amelia, Eliza Merriman and Grace Sherborne. Also, from your wife. We will need all day tomorrow to get ready and then we will lay our plan tomorrow evening. I will leave you now as we are close to the prison I will scout the area myself on horseback and then we can meet at your house tomorrow morning at ten o'clock."

Big Jim stopped the cart, assisted her down and helped her onto her side-saddle.

"Until tomorrow, then."

"Until tomorrow."

The diversion was a classic. And it came in two parts. They drew lots for who would have the more intricate role. Elizabeth cheated by secreting a short straw in her palm and claiming it was the one left after the others had drawn theirs. Nobody believed her but everybody saw how desperately she wanted the role. They spent the morning and early afternoon getting ready. Plain Jane had once run a brothel before she had met Big Jim in Bristol. She knew exactly what to do.

By two o'clock they were ready and jumped into a covered cart for the journey to Shaftesbury. They rolled and shunted with the rough road for three hours, until the cart drew to a halt. Jim called to them through the canvas that all was in place and Elizabeth slid down from the back of the cart, straightening her bright red dress and gaudy hat with two large black feathers making off at forty-five degrees from the vertical. She was ready. She whispered the instructions once again.

"My target is the assistant jailer and two things we need from him. First, I need to get my hands on his keys without him realising. Second, I aim to get permission for all of us to visit the prison later this evening, when the chief jailer has gone home for the night. Yours and my job, then, is to keep the guards distracted while Big Jim frees Matthew and Thomas. Right, any questions? Then wish me luck!"

She disappeared into the November night. Within seconds, there was nothing to be seen of her; red is swallowed by black every time. Big Jim did not mention the dash of spice he planned for the end of the evening; his little contribution to the plan.

It was a long wait for there was nothing to do but wait. They played a game in the back of the cart, telling exaggerated stories of their most embarrassing experiences and then voting on them. Plain Jane won hands-down and with little exaggeration as well. Not yet thirty, she seemed to have led a full life. "I started as an orphan on the streets of Bristol. I stole food and picked pockets for a living. Then I was caught; I must have been fourteen or fifteen, and spent four months in prison before they forgot there was a case to answer and let me go. Actually, I think it was an administrative error that saw me released. Then I got in with this lovely older lady who had a growth on her neck the size of a small saucepan." Jane used her two fists to demonstrate the extent of the cancer. "The lady ran an upmarket brothel in Clifton and I moved in with her; ran it when she was too sick to do so. I spent two happy years with her until she died. I organised her funeral and that's how I met Jim. He was the young man who marched at the head of the funeral procession, solemn as anything. As soon as I saw him, I knew he was the one for me. We got chatting and before you could say 'how do you do' we were married! Mrs Farringdon, the brothel lady, she left me an old horse and cart we used for deliveries from time to time and we set up as hauliers together and you know the rest of the story. Now, Amelia, it's time to hear from you."

But there was no time for that, for Elizabeth came back at that moment.

"All on," she cried. She had run back and was breathless. "I've got the key." She handed it solemnly to Big Jim, who slipped it into his pocket. "And the assistant jailer wants us there at seven o'clock. We're going to earn half a crown each tonight. I negotiated very hard for he wanted to pay a shilling a girl."

"So, you more than doubled our fee," Amelia responded. "We're going to make a woman of business out of you yet."

From this point of advantage, it was an easy run. The guards were all in their refectory on the ground floor, where Plain Jane led the others in entertaining sufficiently well to keep their attentions focused on the five ladies. That left a clear run for all four storeys above that made up the cells. Big Jim seemed to be going about his business, making quite a bit of noise delivering bread and water and exchanging chamber pots. He knew from observation which cells Matthew and Thomas were in. Matthew was second-left on the third floor and Thomas directly above him but one cell further down.

Jim went to Matthew's cell first, imagining him in greater need of rescue. The key grated horribly in the lock. He grabbed one of the lanterns from the passage and creaked the door open. Matthew was sitting calmly on the narrow bed.

"Who are you?" he said. "You're not one of the usual guards."

"I'm a friend of your brother and sister, Grace. I met them in Bristol but now live in Sturminster Newton and run a haulier business." He tried hard to sound reassuring. "I've come to get you out of here."

"And Thomas?"

"Yes, he's next."

"Good, let's go. Do you know which cell he is in? Good, well there is certainly nothing here for me to delay my departure."

Big Jim was speechless. Could this be the awkward, often tongue-tied brother they had all talked about?

"I've gone through panic and out the other side," Matthew explained, as if he could see, even in the dim light, the thoughts working through Jim's mind.

Thus, Matthew had displayed the full set of emotions on being arrested. To recap, first shock and outrage, then anger in short order. After that came panic and then the beautiful calm of courage rediscovered; calm from the knowledge that whatever they do to the body and mind, they can never touch the soul.

And Matthew's soul had grown over the six days in captivity, such that it had outgrown his body and become a bigger thing than his physical being.

They went up the stairs to Thomas' floor. Again, the key grated and the door creaked. And they were in to Thomas' cell. Expecting it to be easy, Jim was taken aback by the state of his friend.

"We need to help him stand up," Matthew said, understanding the situation immediately. He had been there himself, of course.

They steadied Thomas and got him to the door of the cell, then out into the short corridor. Jim led the way down the stairs, with Matthew keeping a tight grip on Thomas right behind. Suddenly, Jim stopped a half-flight and three steps from the ground. He signalled frantically with his arms behind his back. Matthew almost collided with him but just managed to stop himself in time, teetering on the step above Jim, swaying with the motion of his downward movement set against the will to stop.

Below, two guards left the refectory and banged into the end block containing the staircase and the door to outside.

"They're going to relieve themselves," Jim whispered as the outside door swung behind them. "We'll have to stay here until they've gone back in. Back up to the next flight so they don't see us when they come in."

Matthew did not try and turn Thomas; instead, he backed up the stairs one at a time, taking great care not to make a sound.

"The cart's just outside the door so we can make a run for it as soon as those guards get back in."

Only the guards took their time, evidently enjoying a bottle of something as they anticipated the pleasures to come.

Then Big Jim remembered his surprise and disappeared up the steps. He went first to the fourth floor and turned the locks of every single cell, swinging the doors open before moving on to the next one. Some creaked like Thomas' and Matthew's; others were silent, as if offering no resistance. Then the third floor and the second, and finally the first. The prisoners were generally too stunned to respond to their doors opening but gradually they started moving out of their cells; treading cautiously as if expecting some sick trap.

Matthew understood now what Jim was up to. But did he have his timing out by a minute or so? Would the guards return just as a stream of liberated prisoners rushed down the stairs to freedom? He left Thomas gripping the stair rail and went up a few steps to slow the downward movement.

Then the door opened from the refectory. Were more coming out to relieve themselves?

"Come on, Joe and Bill, you don't know what you're missing."

"Coming," replied the two from outside and the door banged open. It was a matter of split timing. Jim raced down the last steps to the first floor and skidded to a stop right behind Matthew.

"Sshh," whispered Matthew. "Just a second longer. Now we go." Matthew grabbed Thomas on the way down and hurtled for the door, Big Jim just behind them.

Then they were through the door but Jim paused at the door and shouted, "Fire! Fire! Fire!" as loudly as he could. The single word was quickly picked up by others and a great screaming sound filled the air: "Fire! Fire! Fire!"

Jim propelled the two brothers into the cart, already turned to make a quick escape down the hill. But he did not move off as the other prisoners and guards came out of the building. Everywhere was panic, as flames shot out of a first-floor corridor window.

"I lit it," Jim grinned, his face distorted by the tall orange flames.

"Why? Why not just slip away quietly?" Matthew shouted above the pandemonium.

"For the girls," Jim replied. And seconds later, all five ladies ran from the door and made for the cart. Jim jumped down to help them. Matthew followed suit, not understanding at all what was going on. Then, they were away, rattling slowly down the hill on official prison business, heading in the dark for sanctuary. And behind them, on the hill, the orange flames took hold and flickered to red and yellow and then back to orange again. Small, dark figures ran around the place and the cries came down the hill, as if cries alone were what pursued them.

In the back, Thomas was slowly coming round, confused at first as to why they were moving. Surely prisons were static objects? Then he recognised Matthew and Elizabeth and Grace; Lady Merriman, too. There were Plain Jane and Big Jim, driving the horses at the front. And here was Amelia, looking into his face with a strange expression all over hers.

He had never seen love of this type in a woman pointed directly towards him; now he drank it in in great big restorative gulps.

Chapter 19

She had found the perfect house.

And it came with such a strange name. At first, she had not believed it when Mr Blake, the estate agent, had said he had another house for Lady Roakes to see.

The Great Little Manor had been the seat of the Little family for 400 years, since Sir Jacob Little had done some great service in helping to crush the Welsh. The Great came from a need to distinguish the manor he built from several others the family owned following the same grant of land from Edward I.

"You see on this map," Mr Blake said, spreading a map of the area on the dining room table in Great Little, "Sir Jacob drew together several manors into one great one."

"Here we have Winterbourne Little and even King's Little, reflecting their donor, I suppose," Lady Roakes replied, fascinated and charmed at the same time. "And Sir Jacob built this house after the Welsh Wars?"

"That is correct, Lady Roakes. It is brick and flint construction, although you will note that the west wing is stone from a quarry nearby, just north of the quaint town of Blandford Forum, situated, as you know…"

"Please, Mr Blake, less of the estate agent's talk. I can make my own opinion as to whether I would count Blandford Forum quaint or not," she laughed and caught a twinkle of amusement back. "Let us talk plainly about Great Little, all its good points and bad. I am considerably impressed by what I have seen so far."

Despite her request for less talk to sell the property, Lady Roakes showed a tendency to negotiate every point she could. She adored the house from first sighting, yet the drawing room was too small, the staircase long neglected, various roofs needed replacing. But even she could not find fault with the gardens. They extended over fifteen acres and opened onto a parkland of 300. Beyond that was the home farm and then, fanning each side of the Stour southwards, the tenanted lands.

"The estate will need considerable work to bring it up to

condition," she said as they retired to a country inn near Winterbourne Stickland for refreshments.

"That is the tack I intend to take in negotiations," Mr Blake replied, glad to sit with a pint pot after four hours traipsing around the house and grounds.

"Tomorrow, I desire to see the home farm but first walk the parkland to get to the farm. We will need to start early, I think." There was something delightful in her imperiousness. He had heard a rumour that she had run a laundry before marrying into money. Yet she seemed born to it.

"Yes, of course, Lady Roakes. We could even stay here and have the coach go back for luggage and to give a message to Sir Beatrice. That way, we could make an early start tomorrow."

It was arranged. Lady Roakes had a small suite of rooms on the first floor while Mr Blake had to take an attic room, quickly vacated by the landlord's son. The coachman was despatched for luggage and with a hastily written note that simply said, 'Darling, I have found the house for us. Staying overnight in an inn to view again tomorrow. I'll tell all when I see you tomorrow evening.'

Then she sent a briefer still message to Mr Blake, asking him to come for an early supper so they could discuss again the merits and demerits of Great Little Manor.

It was as well that Lady Roakes was away that night for Sir Beatrice was interviewing Parchman, sent down to assist him by Wiltshire.

"So, it is you," Parchman had said on entering Sir Beatrice's private sitting room at the inn. "What have you done with your stripes, man?" It was a feeble joke; there was nothing jocular about Parchman at the best of times.

"Exchanged them for a knighthood, dear boy." Sir Beatrice found it natural to be patronising following his elevation. It created distance between those he had left behind during his meteoric rise.

And he certainly intended leaving Parchman well behind.

Parchman had recruited Roakes years earlier; not into the army, for he was already in uniform, rather to the service of the

138

old Earl of Sherborne. Private Roakes had been before the magistrate in Sherborne for drunken fighting when Parchman happened to be in the court on other business. Something had made him stop and listen to the hearing. Roakes had weaselled out of the charges easily; clearly, he had attributes that could be useful to Parchman and to the earl.

On impulse, Parchman had invited the private for a drink. Roakes, without any cash and believing in the hair of the dog, had welcomed the offer but had the sense to choose a different inn to that of the previous night.

And when Parchman heard about the pig farm in North Yorkshire, occupied by Roakes' very elderly parents, he connected it immediately with Lady Merriman.

"It is the perfect location to stow her away," he had reported to the Earl that afternoon.

"Except for one problem," the Earl had replied. "It is occupied by this soldier's parents."

"I can manage that in a few weeks," Parchman had replied. "But I need to boost this fellow Roakes, in order to use the farm for our purposes."

"Well, I can manage that in return," said the earl, pleased to have the less direct involvement.

And two weeks later, Sergeant Roakes came to tell Parchman; just returned himself from a hurried trip north, that he was obliged to go away for ten days, to the funeral of his parents back in Yorkshire.

Parchman had condoled with him on his loss, congratulated him on his promotion, and suggested he may have a buyer for the pig farm, willing to pay a handsome price.

"Thank you, sir," Roakes had replied in his deep Yorkshire accent. And Parchman had done him another favour as the newly promoted sergeant left to lay his parents in the ground, suggesting he lose his regional accent as Parchman himself had done with his native Dorset tone.

"You don't want to be limited by a parochial pattern of speech, dear fellow."

Now it was a very different Parchman standing before him; his employer become his employee, at least for the time being.

There was one element of the change that involved both knowledge and emotion, separately and together. Parchman did not know of the connection with Mrs Beatrice, now his wife. She had confessed to Sir Beatrice that her first husband, Mr Beatrice, had killed Parchman in a fight in their Bristol home before fleeing to the battle site of Sedgemoor, where they had met. Parchman had just informed them that the subsidies for holding Arkwright in captivity were stopping because they had let her escape. As soon as Sir Beatrice heard her description of the man, he knew that it was the same Parchman he had reported to for two decades.

But he was not dead. And, therefore, Lady Roakes was not an accomplice to murder.

That was the knowledge, now for the emotion. Sir Beatrice had never liked Parchman; nobody could like the man. But in place of general dislike was pure hatred for the animal who would turn on his beloved wife with a knife in his hand.

Then to the combination of knowledge and emotion, for he knew that the whole episode troubled his wife enormously; not because she had volunteered any more about it but because of her sleep-talking, where she often re-enacted the terrible scenes.

And anyone who troubled his beautiful wife troubled him.

"So Parchman, you are from this area?" he started, wondering what on earth to do with the man. The note from Wiltshire just said to use him in whatever capacity he thought best, plus a warning that he was a vicious and ruthless man. Well, Sir Beatrice knew that from first-hand experience, starting with his parents; he had no doubts about their sudden accident when their heavy cart had overturned and pinned them to the ground. They had died slowly, squealing in pain like the pigs that surrounded them.

But the man now opposite him looked apologetic; almost embarrassed to be reporting to Roakes. Yet, if he knew of his connection with Lady Roakes, he did not doubt that Parchman would happily snap his bones, and those of his wife.

But the question that worried at him most was why Wiltshire, who had introduced him to the cause of rebellion, had sent someone from the establishment to assist him in the defence of an order he wished to bring down? And, if this man was a spymaster close to the King, as he claimed to be, he must know where Sir Beatrice's inclinations lay.

It smelt like a trap. Wiltshire was a cold fish. Was he playing both sides, hedging his bets for the future? But why, then, go out of his way to court and woo Sir Beatrice to the cause of rebellion?

Not for the first time, Roakes considered that business was a lot simpler than politics. Soldiering was as well. Why had he chosen to enter the political world just when he had everything he could ever want?

Hence, so much to lose.

It had been a fast-moving few days. First, Sir Beatrice's links to the rebel underground movement were rudely broken through the arrest of Matthew and Thomas. Sir Beatrice had been responsible for co-ordinating the rebel strength in Dorset and both passing good information back to Wiltshire and then spreading bad information wherever possible to confuse the Government side. He had a particular success with a man called Cartwright, who he had fed a string of false information, suggesting that any landing by Orange would be in the north, perhaps even Scotland. It had been a joy to watch Cartwright pretending casual interest out of politeness, knowing he was lapping up every bit of information he could get hold of and feeding it back up the chain.

But the success of this whole ploy rested, crucially, on the honesty of Wiltshire. Sir Beatrice shuddered at the thought; he had placed his trust in one of the least trustworthy creatures in England.

Then, as expected, had come the news of the landing in Brixham, far from the north and Scotland as Sir Beatrice had carefully indicated, although not promised, in discussions with Cartwright. Matthew Davenport had confided in him as to the location but not the date because he had not known it. In his view it was a naïve act for Matthew to disclose anything because Roakes could have been playing double on him.

Just as Wiltshire was surely doing with him.

In fact, as Sir Beatrice would be the first to acknowledge, he most certainly would have double-crossed the rebellion, had he imagined the government of King James had any chance of being in power much longer. But instinct told him that the English people would always side with liberty; it was in their nature.

He was convinced he was on the winning side and working hard to bring complete success to Orange, painted as the liberator of Englishmen; though Roakes suspected he cared nothing for the English and just saw an opportunity to pursue his war against the French.

But the questions he faced now were what to do with Parchman and how to keep the man away from his wife, the love of his life.

And what game was Wiltshire up to?

"Landlord, find a bed for this man in the common room; make sure it is a clean bed, mind you." There was no point in making out they were on equal terms. "Have some supper, Parchman, and report to me in the morning." He enjoyed the red of embarrassment that spread across Parchman's face. This was the man who had thrust a knife at his beloved wife. If nothing else, he would revel in this man's humiliation.

Provided he could keep him away from Lady Roakes.

The morning was red and raw; a beautiful morning for an estate inspection. Lady Roakes was up and ready, tutting impatiently for Mr Blake.

"There you are, Mr Blake. I declare the day is half gone already. We must be away quickly, sir. No, there is no time for breakfast. We must be away and I am too anxious to eat a thing anyway."

Mr Blake had a curious impression that morning. It was something like a duck in water or a bird in the tree. Lady Roakes belonged at Great Little and he saw his mission to ensure she became its next mistress.

He had arranged two horses rather than the carriage. He was

a little old to ride comfortably but was happy to see the estate this way. He kept up a chatter as they rode along the lanes back to Great Little; fact upon fact about the area, the principal families, the annual income from the estate.

"Tell me the history of the place," she interrupted the flow of information.

"Well, as you know, the Little family were granted the…"

"No, Mr Blake, go back much further and start at the beginning. What people, for instance, made those rings around the hill there and why?"

He described what he knew of the iron age forts but it was scant.

"You mean people lived there and made it their home? And those mounds are where the kings and chieftains are buried? We must find out more about these strange people from so long ago. What were they like? What did they eat and what were their pastimes?"

Then, when they moved through the parkland that straddled the highest hill for miles around, dotted with ancient barrows and topped with the iron age rings she had noticed, she saw below the home farm. It lay like the skirts of a fine dress, spreading out along the river with its patchwork of reds, browns and greens; ripples in the land looked like folds in those skirts.

In the centre of the panorama was a stubby white two-storey house, with a series of barns and outbuildings stretching back to a tumble-down beech wood; the whole seemed like a toy farm-set left outside, exposed to the elements. As they rode closer, she noticed the roses rising up the white stone walls, climbing ever higher to reach the black painted gutters and spilling out over the grey slate roof.

"Now that is what you call quaint," she said, completely forgetting herself in her wonder.

They had their breakfast after all. They sat, lady and old professional, in the farmhouse kitchen while the farmer's wife cooked eggs and bacon and made hot chocolate, served in chipped white dishes with mismatching saucers. She was Mrs Harris, from Lancashire, but the Harris family had managed the home farm since before the Littles.

"And, if I have anything to do with it, you shall farm here after the Littles, too."

The Harris couple knew the Littles were selling up. The Littles were ancient and the only heir had died over forty years earlier, in the civil war. They had never recovered from the death of their son and had lost all interest in the estate.

"You see, ma'am, nothing lasts for ever."

"Quite right, Mrs Harris. I suppose their sad loss and consequent disinterest is why the estate is so run down," Lady Roakes replied.

Mr Blake thought that Lady Roakes never missed a thing but turned the most everyday event to her advantage. He was impressed.

But Mrs Harris was embarrassed. She wanted to be loyal to the Littles but also wanted this evidently wealthy and forthright lady to be the next owner of Great Little. She wanted the estate sold before it became even more rundown so that nobody would ever want it. She covered her embarrassment with a compliment.

"If you were to take over the estate, ma'am, I don't doubt you will be a power of good to it and all who make their livings out of it."

"Well thank you, Mrs Harris. Now we must be on our way. We have much to see. If you have a lad who could spare an hour, we would welcome a local guide."

Mrs Harris supplied her thirteen-year-old son, Fred, who knew the farm and the whole estate inside out.

Consequently, it was quite some time before Mr Blake got a break from riding and touring that day.

And there was another chapter in his day yet to come.

But first we must go south and west a dozen miles, to examine how Sir Beatrice was getting on with his new subordinate.

Parchman, once used to mucking in where necessary, had spent too many years recently in comfort and seclusion in his large house just off the Strand. He did not enjoy sharing the snorts and snores and restless moves of the common sleeping room. His pallet was clean, he granted the landlord that, but it was just a thin straw mattress on the floor in a row with a dozen others and a dozen against the far wall, too. Supper was stew and bread, washed down with beer at a long table with benches either side. Breakfast was the same setting, only the food was now cold mutton and eggs, again taken with a pint of beer.

Parchman spent most of breakfast shunning conversation and wondering when best to report to Roakes. The man had just said, "In the morning." Should he go straight after breakfast, or make the conceited man wait for him? He summed up the options before deciding; he would go for a walk to discover Dorchester before returning to Roakes when the morning was well into its late middle-age.

He had suspected that Sir Beatrice was the man he had known as Private and then Sergeant Roakes, recruited to the old earl's retainer over twenty years earlier. His suspicions were confirmed the moment he entered the sitting room at the White Lion. Yet the man was changed. There was no semblance of the old deference for Parchman, the old collusion of rogues together in some form of harmony. Instead, there was just a haughty arrogance, as if he had just been acting as a soldier, as a subordinate, and now the real Roakes was there for all to see.

And he was lording it over him as if Parchman had not been responsible for bringing him up from nothing, setting him on a course for greater things.

Perhaps if Parchman's espionage ring had been a modicum better, he would have tracked down Mrs Beatrice and then made the connection with Roakes. But he did not, remaining puzzled in the extreme as to the change of attitude towards him.

And what Parchman did not understand, he liked to eliminate.

Like a wild animal.

He did not enjoy his walk. It was not the crowds; he was used to bigger and busier in London. It was not the noise; same or greater in London again. Dorchester, the White Lion in particular, was the scene of his humiliation yesterday evening.

Could it be that? No, he should not judge a whole town on the evidence of one snippet in time and place.

It came to him as he walked, head down, as if unable to meet the level gaze of the people of Dorchester.

For there was an insolence about the place; as if every last man, woman and child was confident that liberty would prevail. It unsettled him greatly so he cut his walk short and returned to the White Lion to place himself in front of Roakes again, a full hour earlier than he had planned.

"Ah, Parchman, there you are. I first require a report as to the strength of support in London. I need to know what is behind us should Dorset and other counties of the south-west fall to the rebels. You will write that during the course of today. Then, when complete, I want you to take horse again immediately and visit the western extremes of our county in order to determine the detailed defences against rebellion in that area. I imagine it will take you three or four days to visit each area to the west and compile a full report. Send a message back to me when you are near complete and I might come out to tour with you. Do you understand?"

"Of course I do. What could be simpler?" He wanted to say he had been used, these last three years, to dealing with complex matters of state; of spying at the highest level. How could compiling a simple report compare to that?

"Less of your insolence, my man, especially around your superiors," Sir Beatrice snapped back, just loud enough for several others, including the landlord, to hear the rebuke. "Make settlement for your stay before you leave today. I know not when you will be back here." He was not even, therefore, to have his expenses paid. And the landlord's ears had pricked up at mention of payment. He turned to seek a table or desk at which to write and Sir Beatrice smiled at his back as he left the room, his shoulders an inch and a half lower than they had been the previous evening.

Outside, in the common area, Parchman found a table, ink and paper and settled down. He would write the report for Roakes, full of fiction of course, then another for Wiltshire, detailing just how unreliable Roakes was to the cause of order, of established government. As he put pen to paper, an idea came to him which he rather liked. But he would not risk it on paper, rather go to see Wiltshire himself. Roakes' survey of West Dorset could wait.

This is a good morning's work, thought Sir Beatrice as the door closed behind Parchman; a good morning against the man who would wield a knife against the lovely Lady Roakes.

Who, at that moment, was cantering across the home farm without a care in the world.

"Lady Roakes, will we away to the inn now? Have you seen enough?" Mr Blake was exhilarated by the ride, yet clearly tired. "I believe it is the first time this year I've been on horseback."

"Then relish it, sir. I wish to go to the house again."

"For what purpose, Lady Roakes?" He had a premonition, whatever the purpose, it was going to be awkward.

"Why, to negotiate, of course."

Mr Blake pulled his horse up to a stop, grabbed the reins to pull up her horse as well.

"But Sir Beatrice…"

"Sir Beatrice will still love me was I to pay top price," she declared, taking the reins back, then adding, "which I have no intention of doing, Mr Blake."

He tried a few minutes longer to persuade her, both sitting tall on their mounts like twin trees growing alone in the middle of a ploughed field. She imagined that every year the farmer's wife, more practical than the farmer, would demand the two trees come down and the farmer would find some excuse why they should stay, carefully steering the plough around them and noting the new growth each time.

She had the time for such imaginings because she was not listening to Mr Blake's pleas for moderation in approach. She, Lady Roakes, was going to get what she wanted.

That was the only way, she had found, over the thirty-six years of her life. Slowly, she turned her horse towards the manor house and urged it on to a trot.

"Lady Roakes, please at least walk the horses so that we

147

might decide on our strategy as we ride."

She looked back, drew gently on her reins and said, "Walk, my beauty, walk." This last suggestion from Mr Blake made eminent sense.

Chapter 20

Every male firstborn Little since time began had been called Sir Jacob. The current incumbent, a bent man of well over eighty, was no different. His wife, Lady Little, was stick-thin and upright. She had started their married life six inches the junior in height but was now the taller of the pair. He was crooked from arthritis while she stood upright but hid in the folds of her clothes a nasty growth on her stomach that caused her constant pain. Both wished for nothing but release from this world; their only pleasure for years now had been reminiscing about their son, who had died fighting for King Charles I in 1644. They cherished every moment of his twenty-two years on this earth; asking God daily why it was him taken and not them.

They had tried for a new son but Lady Little, actually a few years older than Sir Jacob, had been past child-bearing and the years slipped by in fruitless endeavour. When the cancer first came, Sir Jacob had briefly hoped that a quick and merciless death for his wife would free him to marry again and produce an heir. But she hung on and he forgot the idea in the solace of looking after the only other person he cared for in the world.

For he certainly did not care for himself.

And into this bitter world where there was nothing to do but wait for death, came a forceful woman, quite suddenly, with an elderly man in tow.

"I am interested in buying the estate," she said after the briefest of introductions. "Provided the price is right."

The Littles could not believe their luck. They had been trying to sell for more than ten years but no one had seen beyond the leaking roofs and rundown barns. Here was someone actually starting with the intention to purchase.

"The asking price is twenty thousand guineas."

"Nonsense, I'll give you ten thousand… pounds."

They moved slightly closer over the next twenty minutes. Lady Roakes stuck obstinately to pounds but increased her offer to eleven thousand once the Littles had come down to eighteen thousand and agreed to negotiate in pounds rather than guineas; a significant concession as a guinea was worth more than twenty-four shillings. But now they were at a stalemate and it seemed the only thing for Lady Roakes to do was retire with dignity.

"May I interject a moment?" Mr Blake spoke into the silence. "I know I represent the purchasers in this potential deal but sometimes it pays to have someone, at least somewhat impartial, to make a few observations." He received three nods so carried on. "Lady Roakes, I believe it is fair to say that eleven thousand is a ridiculously low price for the Great Little Estate." His attack on his client's position made all three sit up.

"What do you…"

"Hush, I beg you, Lady Roakes." His expression to her said 'trust me' and she let it go. "May I suggest that Lady Roakes retires to some other room and perhaps is served a dish of tea or chocolate while I go over a few matters with the Littles?"

"Of course. Would you care to come this way, Lady Roakes?" Lady Little led Lady Roakes to the library and pulled the bell for tea.

"Why do you want to leave this house, Lady Little?" she asked, instinct telling her this was a double opportunity. She could delay Lady Little while Mr Blake worked on Sir Jacob and she could find out more about their circumstances, maybe probe into any weaknesses she discovered.

Lady Little had been turning to go. Suddenly, her thin body unravelled as she plumped onto a leather chair, the same as the one offered to Lady Roakes.

"It's all too much," she said, hanging her head deep into her hands. "Since little Jacob died, we've hated the place that was to be his. We tried for years to make a success of it but our hearts were not in it. We had heavy debts from the interregnum period and from our contributions to the royalist cause during the war. Those debts have mounted and are threatening to place us in debtors' prison for what months remain of our lives. It is all too much."

"May I ask how much the loans come to?"

"Ten thousand pounds. And they seem to add a thousand

every year."

"Where will you live if you sell?" That was the other important ingredient to the mix.

"Ah," she brightened, "that is a bit easier. When we married, my father gave us a house in Salisbury in the cathedral cloisters and right by the river. It is small but perfect for us and two maids. It is rented to a stonemason doing repairs on the cathedral but he will move to make way for us; that was the condition of the lease. We would very much like to live there, for in our indulgence years ago we had a memorial stone to our son put in the cathedral. We have yet to pay for that stone, I regret to say. We would like to visit him every day that remains to us if we can. But we dare not while the debt hangs over us."

"Would you consider an idea if I am bold enough to propose it?"

"You mean with regard to the sale? Yes, but bear in mind that we must have some hundreds each year to live off; otherwise we will be straight back into debt again."

"Yes, I see the problem," Lady Roakes replied, genuinely touched by the frankness of disclosure. "Here is my proposal and afterwards you shall judge whether it serves your needs."

Mr Blake was making some progress but had started at the other end to the approach by Lady Roakes.

"It's clear, Sir Jacob, that in tiptop condition the Great Little Estate would be worth in excess of your asking price."

"That is flattering to hear, sir."

"It's a potentially attractive property but I have here a list of works to be done, in rough format obviously, to both the house and the farms. Would you care to examine it?"

"Read it to me, my man. My eyesight is not so good anymore."

Mr Blake started with the house. He read out the obvious first, picking smaller items that could not sensibly be disputed. Sir Jacob acceded these points with a murmur or two.

"That brings the total so far to two thousand four hundred pounds. Now, I move on to the roof."

"There is nothing too much wrong with the roof." That was

an outrageous statement but Mr Blake kept calm and put the roof condition over the next few minutes into several different categories; breaking it down into indisputable pieces.

"So, we are agreed, Sir Jacob, that the house requires between six and seven thousand guineas spent on it."

Mr Blake did a similar process on the parkland and the farms, producing another deficit of five or six thousand, all agreed in little stages.

"But, Mr Blake, you forget that with all this money spent, the estate would be worth in excess of twenty thousand."

"Quite so, Sir Jacob, you are good to remind me. What value do you think it would have?"

"Nearer thirty, I would say." That was a preposterous valuation but again Mr Blake kept calm.

"Shall we settle on twenty-six thousand guineas? Good, then we deduct the investment need of, let's be generous and say twelve thousand and arrive at a valuation of fourteen thousand."

Mr Blake sat back and waited for Sir Jacob to do the final calculation. Fourteen thousand guineas less ten thousand and climbing of debt, did not give them enough to pay for the memorial stone and provide for their expenses in Salisbury. "It will not work," he said finally. "We need to have more."

The door opened just then and the two ladies returned.

"I think we have a deal," Lady Little said. "Lady Roakes has offered twelve thousand…"

"That is certainly not enough." Sir Jacob made to rise from his chair but lacked the energy and sank back in despair.

"Please do not interrupt, husband. The price agreed between us is twelve thousand plus five hundred pounds a year, quarterly in advance, for as long as either of us live."

The deal was done on a handshake and celebrated with the dregs of a bottle of madeira. Then Lady Roakes and Mr Blake left for the inn and their coach to take them straight back to the White Lion in Dorchester.

Chapter 21

The only safe place Big Jim could think of to hide Matthew and Thomas was Sherborne Hall. He reasoned no one would think to look in the home of the leading Catholic in the county, even if he was their brother-in-law and a good friend. Jim considered Bagber Manor but ruled it out immediately for it was the first place they would look for the fugitives. For the same reason, his own home was out of the question; he was a suspect now, or would be as soon as he did not turn up for his duties in the morning.

He even considered taking them to the Red Lion in Dorchester; the landlord was a sympathiser, but it was too close to the old haunt of Matthew at the White Lion, the other end of the High Street. And the landlord at the White Lion would sell them straight back to the authorities for a pocket full of pennies if ever he found out where they were. Big Jim knew this because he had been paying him for information about Matthew's activities.

There was nowhere to go except Sherborne Hall and that meant a journey of over twenty miles or much of the night. He would go by Bagber and drop off Amelia, Lady Merriman, Elizabeth and Jane, his wife. Then they would keep going the twelve or thirteen miles to Sherborne Hall.

They got all the way down St John's Hill and were halfway to Guy's Marsh without incident. Cries and fire from the burning prison died away, leaving a damp stillness that was pitch-black as well as slippery under hoof. They had to go slowly and, once, they all had to get out and push.

"We could throw out these smelly chamber pots," Jane half-joked and half-hoped.

"No," said Lady Merriman. "The smashed-up pieces would leave a trail like Hansel and Gretel."

Then, when rattling along between rough pasture either side of the road, they saw flashes of new light above and behind them. They appeared and disappeared, as if the light was playing hide and seek with them. But each time it was a little

153

bolder; a little closer; like a child gradually colouring in a drawing in her sketchbook. Then there were cries of men and the sound of hooves cantering, to give life to the light.

Thomas was steadily coming back to himself with the soothing attention of all four females in the back of the cart. He felt the fresh breeze created by their progress and it seemed so sweet; so succulent and restorative. He breathed deeply; then watched the lights flashing on the hill behind the cart. He knew now that he and Matthew had been sprung from the prison; did not understand the role the girls had played.

"We won't make it," he said suddenly to whoever was listening. "We'll be caught at this rate." He spoke louder this time so that Jim turned from the driver's seat and asked him what else they could do.

"You have to drop Matthew and me at the next stream. We'll head west, running upstream in case they have dogs. But I suspect these are just the guards and are not used to chasing escaped convicts. They'll have sent someone for the militia and as soon as it's light they'll have the dogs out."

Matthew considered the problem as the cart rolled on and the guards drew closer. He thought Thomas right.

"It might work," he said. "Jim, when they catch you up, just say you went about your normal duties this evening but also you provided the prostitutes for the off-duty guards' entertainment. Then, when the cries of fire came out, you gathered them up and ran. You wanted to get the girls safely home. It might just work." As he spoke, he squeezed Thomas' hand. It was a warning to be quiet. "I'll explain later," he whispered.

They were dropped at a sharp bend in the road, where a small bridge carried them over a stream. The cart did not stop but slowed sufficiently for both to jump. To the guards, now just 200 yards behind, it would look like they were slowing to negotiate the bend. The two brothers landed in two feet of water, just sufficient to break their fall. Their legs were in running mode as they hit the stream. It was a beautifully co-ordinated jump and move-off, as if rehearsed over and over

154

again.

But one thing broke the perfect synchrony; there was a third splash, this extra splash not nearly so elegantly done. Lady Merriman struggled in the water; Matthew stared as if he suspected something but could not be sure. Thomas went to her aid.

"Did you fall out of the cart, Eliza?"

"No, Thomas." She sounded surprised.

"Then you jumped?"

"Yes, Thomas, I'm coming with you and Matthew." The way she said 'Matthew' made it obvious what she meant.

When they next looked back, at the turn of the stream to head due west instead of south-west, they saw the lights were blazing; torches held high to light the way. And they were still now, not moving. And the cart was there with them, 100 yards from the bridge. The three of them kept moving, for fear of being caught, so they lost sight of the cart. But ten minutes later they caught the yellow ring of torches blazoned against the darkened sky. They were moving south towards Manston and Sturminster Newton beyond. With luck, the girls and Big Jim were safe.

All they had to do was find their way across country to the Sherborne road. Luckily, Thomas had roamed the countryside with Grace throughout their childhood. He knew his way without thinking about it. In addition, Lady Merriman's extensive lands were all about and it seemed she knew them intimately as well; especially how to avoid any houses.

Soon there was nothing but darkness all around them, punctuated very occasionally by a lonely farmhouse with a spear of light from under a door or a loosely pulled curtain. In time, as they walked, even those lights were snuffed out for bedtime and they walked in absolute darkness.

"It's not long now, Matthew. Four miles to Sherborne but we turn south before that and then it's a couple to the hall. What happened to me in the prison, Matthew?"

"You were delusional, brother. I believe the confinement got to you in the last twelve or twenty-four hours of our captivity.

It is not surprising that happened with us being in solitary."

"But I always thought… well…"

"You thought I would crack first, is that what you wanted to say?"

"Yes, Matthew." Somehow it was easier to speak the truth into the dark; when your confidant's gaze back could not be discerned; the anonymity of the curtained confessional. "You were ranting in the first hours and days, Matthew. I heard you from my cell. How did you end up so calm?"

"Easy," Matthew replied. "I had a shaky conversation with Our Lord, it must have been about the third day. I started it by bargaining with Him, would you believe it? My freedom for a life's devotion, but there was no taking me up on the offer. When I opened my eyes again, the bars were still there."

"I tried the Lord's Prayer but got it confused with other things," Thomas replied. "I remember that much and then I think a fever got hold of me. So, if the Grand Bargain with God did not work, what did for you?"

"I used just one part of the Lord's Prayer, over and over again.

"*Thy will be done. Thy will be done. Thy will be done. Thy…*

"And eventually I grew calm and incredibly clear-headed. I realised that the only thing that mattered was God's will and I was genuinely pleased to be a part of his version of events. Then, the next thing was the scraping of the key in the lock and Big Jim standing there with a great big grin on his face."

"So, faith saved you, Matthew."

"Yes, it did, it certainly did," Matthew concluded, then added, "only not in the way I was expecting it."

It was then that Thomas saw his two companions were walking arm in arm in the dark.

A little later, Thomas asked the other question that had been on his mind.

"What role did the girls have in this? And why were they so gaudily dressed?"

Matthew replied with a question. "You did not hear when they told me in the back of the cart?"

"No, brother, I must have been recovering from the delusions then, for the first thing I remember is seeing the orange lights of the guards behind us."

Matthew chuckled as he remembered being told of their role. Thomas gave him a dig with his elbow, missed him and stumbled in a ditch in the dark.

"Tell me, Matthew, or I swear I shall never speak to you again," he said from the ditch.

"They were dressed as ladies of the night in order to distract the guards while Jim released us."

Matthew had to say it again before it got through to Thomas. Then Thomas laughed a long and infectious laugh, caring nothing for who might hear. Matthew added his chuckles to the mix and it was five minutes before they could move again.

"Apparently, they earned twelve shillings and sixpence between them tonight but have not yet been paid."

This caused another bout of laughter, although at least they were moving now. Then Lady Merriman said, "It is a strange debt for we gave nothing for it but a half-hour of good humour and play-acting the whore!"

"I expect it is a debt that will never be collected, my dear Eliza. But the real payment from them is our freedom."

"And to all involved, we owe a great debt indeed, Lady Merriman," Matthew replied, looking at her, wanting desperately to call her Eliza. There was no laughter now; just the solemnity of the presence of their Creator as His will was done in the strangest of ways.

Lady Merriman gave no permission to Matthew that night. It was too dark to see his expression and she mistook the tone of his voice for wonder at the Lord. But she did take his arm and lean upon it, declaring the ground a little hard-going at present.

They reached Sherborne Hall in the early hours of the morning and bedded down in the stables for a few hours, Lady Merriman declaring it was the greatest adventure since her escape from Bristol three years earlier. They were woken by a stable lad going about his duties and then running off in alarm when he found three warm bodies, fully clothed, in the straw. Entering the house an hour after sunrise, they found the household staff in turmoil and Henry frantic with worry.

"Grace is gone and nowhere to be seen," he shouted in place of a greeting.

"Calm yourself, Henry. She was fine when we last saw her seven hours or so ago."

"You've seen her? Where is she? Is she alright?"

Thomas ordered a brandy for Henry and told the staff to resume normal duties. Then he and Matthew led Henry to his study and told him all they knew.

"She was in good spirits," Thomas concluded. "The more I think about it, the more I believe they will be fine. No, I am not just convincing myself. Big Jim had legitimate business at the prison with some new delivery contract and no one could suggest he had done anything other than his duties. They were seeking escaped prisoners. Jim let every prisoner out. There must have been fifteen or more besides ourselves. I doubt they were even looking specifically for us."

"I must go to Bagber immediately. She told me nothing of this plan." Thomas noted the disappointment in his voice.

"Yes, but can we stay here in hiding?"

"They will search here for certain," Lady Merriman said. "All of Dorset is in turmoil. We will need to hide somewhere safe within the grounds; an attic or some such place."

"I know exactly where to hide," Lady Merriman said after a minute's thought, standing up as if she were going there at that moment. "Go now to Bagber, Henry, and return as soon as you can. We want news of them all as much as you do."

"Oh, Thomas, Eliza; Matthew, too, there is so much to tell you and no time. I must go to Grace. But there is a great need for me to be frank with you on my return."

"Whatever did Henry mean?" Thomas asked as soon as Henry had left, shouting for his horse.

"I think, like so many these days, he has a confession to make," Lady Merriman observed. She hoped a full confession would not include the fact that she was Henry's mother. That was a secret they had sworn to take to the grave as the earldom was at stake. If Henry was found to be illegitimate, he would not inherit and the earldom would revert to the Crown, probably passed out again to some vile sycophant who agreed with everything the monarch said.

"I don't understand."

"Thomas, everyone seems to have worked against everyone else; friends set against friends; workmates against workmates, and…"

"You think it was Henry behind our arrests?"

"No, not for one moment, but I think he either knew of it coming or had some suspicions. I do not know exactly how but I think he has as good as admitted it to you, his dear friend." Lady Merriman seemed preoccupied but Thomas was too rushed to take it in; something would trigger later but not now.

"Thomas, we have a day in hiding ahead of us; at least until Henry returns," Matthew said. "Let us wash and change clothes and then secrete ourselves away with a pie or two and a flask; anything but bread and water. We have time a plenty to talk amongst ourselves and get everything as straight as we can."

"You were ever the bossy one, Matthew Davenport." For which Thomas got a playful bash on the ear. But, as Thomas hurriedly washed, he reflected that something serious had occurred with Matthew, such that now he could joke with Thomas and tease him; two things that were completely new to his brother. And in the presence of Lady Merriman, who would normally put Matthew in a spin.

He dressed quickly and ran down to the kitchens to organise some supplies.

Lady Merriman was much longer getting changed, borrowing clothes from Grace and requiring a couple of maids to fasten dresses, corsets and stays, such that the two brothers wondered whether she was coming at all.

But she did eventually and looked heavenly as she walked into the kitchen basement. She had selected a lilac dress with dark red and purple brambles climbing up the skirts. Her hair was in ringlets that spilled over her shoulders and concentrated one's vision on her beautiful face. Lady Merriman would turn forty next year but she looked barely thirty. Matthew could not stop looking at her and she was immediately conscious of his attention. She blushed, adding to the makeup the maids had used to add delectable hints of colour to her eyes and cheeks. And suddenly, as she swayed her skirts in ever-so-slight embarrassment, she seemed a decade younger than thirty; much as she would have been all those years ago when Henry's father had loved her.

Then the three of them went the kitchen way out of the house, across the lawn and into the thick bank of trees that bound-in Sherborne Hall. From there, they doubled back, darting from tree to tree, seeking the right one, but to Thomas they all looked the same.

"It's this one," Lady Merriman said and she was right.

"I'll give you both a leg up," Thomas said, clasping both hands together to make a stirrup. "And then you can haul me up from above. This is the treehouse that Henry's father had as a child. I spent many... well, no matter; I know of it. From below, even with the leaves falling, you would never know it was there."

Chapter 22

When the soldiers came, they found three young ladies at their needlework in the upstairs sitting room at Bagber Manor. Colonel Hanson, the leader of the militia, knew them all. He was a professional who would do his duty but did not enjoy it. The sergeant who accompanied him into the sitting room stood religiously to attention, as if frightened that any other pose would reveal a personality.

"My dear ladies, we seek Thomas and Matthew Davenport. Do you know anything of their whereabouts?"

Grace was about to say 'no' when Elizabeth spoke first.

"Yes, Colonel Hanson, we are much distressed about our brothers."

"Where are they, madam?" His voice sounded like a mallet on wood; or a grocer reading back the long list of a customer.

"Why," she declared with the hint of a smile, "they are both under arrest. I believe they are being held in Shaftesbury."

"There was a fire at the jail last night and..."

"Are they alright, sir?" Amelia interrupted, her voice rising with concern.

"All the prisoners escaped; every single one of them. It seems the jailers were otherwise occupied with some, ehm, ladies who tease and provide comfort." Hanson was fighting to hold back some emotion; the three ladies were doing exactly the same. If no prisoners had been recaptured then Thomas and Matthew must have got away to safety. They were probably safely hidden at Sherborne Hall right now.

"I have orders to search the house and grounds. Would you mind if I instructed my men?"

"Strictly, Lady Merriman should give permission, as it is her house and we only live here as her guests." Elizabeth indicated herself and Amelia, her stepdaughter. "However, in the interests of justice, I am sure she would give her permission in absentia." The stress Elizabeth gave to the word 'justice' was met with a level gaze from Hanson; the type that says many things in a moment.

"Thank you, madam. Sergeant, be so good as to give my compliments to the captain and he is to commence a thorough search of house and grounds. He is to report to me when finished. In the meantime, do not disturb the ladies unless it is absolutely necessary."

"Sir." The sergeant managed to come to attention, salute and about turn in one fluid movement. It reminded Grace of an elaborate piece of fairground machinery she had seen once; turning one handle produced multiple dispersed happenings at the same time.

The door closed and Colonel Hanson was alone with the three ladies.

"Oh Grace," he said, for she was the closest to him of all the Davenports. He had protected her and nourished her after she had been raped and left for dead in the woods, during her valiant mission to track down Thomas and free him during the Monmouth rebellion. That had been three years earlier, before she had married Henry and become the Countess. The Duke of Monmouth had been making his bid for the throne, as Orange was now. Monmouth's bid had been selfish and badly planned and had led the Duke straight to the executioner's block. Most people were of the opinion that Orange would fare better.

It seemed to Grace right now, as she gave her hand to her dear friend, Colonel Hanson, that it was always the Davenport girls getting the Davenport boys out of trouble.

Hanson was invited to sit and refreshments were called for. It was awkward for a moment because officialdom was in the way. The colonel was an officer of the crown; it was his duty to maintain the peace and bring criminals to justice.

Escaped prisoners were, de facto, criminals.

As were those who aided their escape.

"Who were the fourth and fifth ladies?" he asked suddenly over his hot chocolate.

"Jane Bigg and Lady Merriman," replied Grace without thinking, then, "Oh, I mean…"

"You are very clever, sir," said Amelia.

"Not really, Miss Taylor. One of the guards in the refectory must take the credit. He came to me this morning and said he had his suspicions about the ladies of entertainment who were suddenly provided last night. He told me he noticed a slipping from time to time of coarse accents to something far more refined, like true refinement 'escaping' from a prison of crudeness; I believe those were his actual words. And then, he embarrassingly told me that none of the girls actually did anything for their money. He went on to explain in some detail that real women who earned their keep in that manner would be far more forward. It seems you ladies broke your contract." He smiled as he uttered these last words, wanting everyone to know the lightness with which they were meant.

"We were not actually paid," Elizabeth pointed out. "So, there was strictly no contract in place."

"Hark the lawyer's wife speaks," Hanson replied good-naturedly to general soothing, relieving laughter. This moment had played on all their nerves and was better out. But what would the colonel do about it?

Amelia had another thought on her mind.

"Do you know the guard's name, sir? Was it Jennings? It was as I suspected then. He and I spoke last night and, I'm afraid my accent did 'slip'. He is an intelligent man, wasted as a guard."

"How so?" Grace asked, relieved for any diversion that postponed the reckoning with her friend, the colonel.

"Such a bright mind dedicated to clanking doors shut and passing out measly bits of stale bread. It seems a terrible waste."

"Probably his father was a prison guard before him. He is only following what is natural." Elizabeth was ever the more conservative, although once Amelia had filled that slot; before Elizabeth had opened Amelia's eyes to the world and then closed her own.

"Ladies, I have a confession to make." This got everyone's attention. The colonel had slipped from seeking confession to making one. "My heart is not in these proceedings one jot."

"You have a leaning, sir, towards another view?" It was Amelia who got the meaning first; ever the dullard at school, she had evidently saved her brilliance for post-school life.

"I have, Mealy, and that is my confession in the round." Using her nickname brought him into their conspiracy.

There was no going back.

"More than half of England thinks the same, sir." By which she meant to impart the approval of the majority as reassurance for his stand.

"And Orange is on Dorset's doorstep," Grace said, adding that her husband was in turmoil over it. "He, as a Catholic, has risen so far under King James, yet his stomach is for liberty over oppression. And now he stands to lose so much."

"He should not concern himself," said Elizabeth.

"Why so, sister?"

"Because I have learned something these last two days. I was filled with anger at you becoming Catholic just to marry Henry, as I saw it. The infidelity of turning your back on Father's religion twisted my soul and blinkered my vision." She put down the needlework she had been holding; stood up. She took off her new bonnet with its starched deep sides and folded it clumsily in two. Then she walked to the fire and threw it in. "No more will I be blinkered. I see now that goodness is not the property of one sect to be wielded against another. Instead, it is the rightful aspiration of all. Grace, your husband is a good man and you should rest assured that his goodness will shine through." She loosened her hair, letting it tumble down her back; rich and bouncy, like life itself.

Or like it should be.

Henry arrived shortly afterwards. His anxiety doubled when he saw the soldiers criss-crossing the grounds. It was only assuaged when he held his darling wife in his arms and kissed her over and again.

For the benefit of both men, the girls now told their story from the beginning. Elizabeth excused herself halfway through and returned twenty minutes later. She had changed her drab grey dress for a shimmering green one, with a necklace of emeralds to match. Her hair had been piled high on her head, its blackness revealing her slender, white neck and making the dress dance to her tune as she wheeled in her husband in his specially-made chair.

"I think Simon should be a part of this conversation," she said. "His mind is perfectly sound, he just has difficulty in speaking and is confined to his chair, for he cannot easily walk." She further explained to Colonel Hanson that Simon had been helping Lady Merriman buy many blocks of land over the last three years, such that she had become a considerably wealthy person.

"He finds it and agrees the price and she manages it. They work superbly together. Now I feel he will be able to help us with decisions we all need to take."

Elizabeth used the plural in referring to what they had to decide. In reality, it was just one decision as to allegiance. Moreover, when she considered the issue, the ladies were all decided for liberty. It was the men that still had to make their minds up.

And all three; Henry Sherborne, Colonel Hanson and Simon Taylor, did exactly that.

Chapter 23

For once, Penelope listened carefully to her husband. He was talking intricacies that normally would take her back into another daydream; Sally filled almost her every waking moment with her beautiful curves and soft brown skin.

But not now; for Wiltshire was talking rebellion, and rebellion was exciting.

"Penelope, so you see why I have to go to Dorset to see Roakes and I want you to come with me."

"Yes, of course I will come. When do we leave?" Her compliance made him take note; he had expected a fight.

"You and I will leave tonight in the light carriage. Just the two of us."

"And Sally, I can't do without my Sally."

"Just the three of us then, but be ready to go in two hours, and not excessive luggage. We might be away for two weeks but not too much stuff, do you hear?"

"Yes sir, I hear you."

Not only was it an adventure but she would share it with Sally. Wiltshire was bound to take himself off into clandestine meetings. That would leave Penny and Sally to please themselves.

But the Duke had omitted one key fact; they were to be the first guests at Great Little, the house now occupied by Sir Beatrice and Lady Roakes. The conveyancing was ongoing but it suited both parties to sign a lease giving immediate access. The Littles were now comfortably situated in an inn in Salisbury, awaiting vacant access to their cloisters house.

It would have mattered little for an adventure was an adventure; except that Lady Roakes and the Duchess of Wiltshire detested each other. Wiltshire, on the other hand, stated often; perhaps too often, that he admired Sir Beatrice and believed he could have learned some clever business practices from him.

He could have, but would not know, for he had received his new instructions that morning.

"Sally, where are you?" Penelope rang the bell several times. "Ah, there you are. Sally, pack immediately, for you and me for two weeks but mind the total volume of luggage. We leave in two hours." She repeated his instructions faithfully, then added, "I will come up to assist you."

"Yes, Your Grace."

Penelope went to her bedroom suite up the main stairs while Sally took the longer route by the back stairs. She was waiting for her servant just inside the bedroom door, breathless with anticipation.

"Sally."

"Penny."

They kissed; silk rubbing with muslin, golden ringlets knocking against her black frizz, tied back neatly but nevertheless escaping here and there. Penny laughed when she saw the hair askew and made to straighten it.

"Leave it, Penny. We don't have much time."

"Yes, Sally. I'll help you pack, of course, afterwards."

"Good girl, Pen." Sally turned the key in the bedroom lock.

Afterwards, as they packed together, Penelope carefully folding her dresses as Sally had shown her, their conversation turned to their intended trip.

"I don't understand," Sally said.

"What is that, Sal? What don't you understand?"

"Why we are going to see Sir Beatrice Roakes if he is a known supporter of Orange and your husband has definitely switched to the other side. No, Pen, if you throw your petticoats in like that, I shall spend the entire trip ironing them. You have to fold them as if a dress, see?"

"Sorry, Sally." She took it out and folded it neatly. "Is that acceptable, dearest?" For her efforts, Sally came around from the other side of the bed and kissed her on the lips, then hissed that they did not have time when Penelope wanted to lie down together again.

They resumed their packing after Sally slipped from Penelope's grip and skipped away; the pillow Penelope swung at her new lover just missed her and they laughed, their eyes

167

locked onto each other's.

"The Duke had a messenger this morning," Sally continued. "He had ridden hard all the way from London."

"How do you find out these things?"

"It was I who brought him food and drink in the servants' hall. I was… sort of… around at just the right time to carry it in."

"And what did you find out, Sal?" Penelope had not continued with the packing, sitting on the bed instead, such was her concentration.

"Just that he carried a message from the King himself. He was that proud of the connection that he blurted it out."

"Wiltshire reads the message from the King and suddenly we are away to visit one of the King's enemies in great haste. What can he be up to?"

"I do not know, Pen, but I am so glad you insisted I accompany you. I think there is danger ahead. It seems your husband plays the rebel when it suits him but acts in the interest of King James underneath it all."

"What are you saying, husband? Our first guests are to be that brat of a duchess and her husband?"

"Needs must, my dear. I report to him in my other work and it is necessary to me that you are civil with his wife."

"But I can't stand her, and to think she will be the first person we welcome at Great Little, our lovely home."

"Do this for me, my dear. It will bring us something else altogether if we persist a little longer in these distasteful tasks."

"I will, sir, if you ask it. And I will try again with the Duchess."

A month ago, a week ago, Lady Roakes would have brightened at her husband's comment about future rewards. She had loved the idea of advancement; the possibility one day of being a duchess herself. But that was somehow so unimportant now. Three things had happened in the last three days.

First, she had felt her baby kick inside her for the first time. And then a second time, and again. It was such a joy to feel the offspring of the man she adored inside her. Whether boy or girl, she would love it endlessly and devotedly as a miniature version of Sir Beatrice; her husband born again.

The second thing to happen was also to do with Sir Beatrice. When she and Mr Blake had passed on the news of the sudden purchase of Great Little, she had feared he may be angry; may have wanted to do the negotiating himself. But he had smiled and said how wonderfully she, they both in fact, had negotiated. It was Sir Beatrice who then decided to move immediately to Great Little and got a lawyer out of bed that night to draw up a temporary lease while the purchase went ahead. It was signed by Sir Jacob and back in their possession by the next afternoon. They had fixed the date of their move for November 12th, the same day Sir Beatrice had received a short note from Parchman saying he was finished with his survey of the Dorset defences and would Sir Beatrice like him to come down to Dorchester to present it?

But the third reason had nothing to do with Sir Beatrice and everything to do with her past; a past they did not share, for they had only met in the loyalist camp behind the lines at the Battle of Sedgemoor three years earlier. Mr Blake had come out to say goodbye and to wish Lady Roakes the best for the future. He was going to retire.

"Your commission was the last in a long line and certainly the most dramatic in its earning," he said as they walked in the beautiful gardens that surrounded Great Little.

"Thank you, Mr Blake, I enjoyed working with you. Do you know why the gardens are so well kept when the house is so neglected? I will tell you. The gardeners have not been paid for nine months but they have come in to work each day regardless, taking produce from the kitchen garden in partial payment. Is that not wonderful loyalty, Mr Blake?"

He agreed and then asked whether she would pay the back wages.

"It is not my responsibility, sir," she had said, a little hotly.

"Yes, Lady Roakes, but in every step we take on this earth we have the capacity to do good or to do nothing. With so much good fortune come to you recently, I simply imagined you might want to give a little back to others. But please do not bother with my silly talk, Lady Roakes. Now, I must be on my way."

"A minute or two longer please, Mr Blake. Let me ask you something, for I grew up in my parents' house but received little by way of guidance in these matters. Sir, if I did a great wrong in the past, can I atone for it with good deeds in the future?" She seemed to Mr Blake like a young girl eager to learn from her tutor.

"Lady Roakes, good deeds should be done for the love of others, even strangers; not to atone for past misdeeds. They should be given freely, not reckoned up in advance." He looked across at her as they walked in the gardens, saw the internal struggle and voluntarily gave more to this strange woman who seemed everything but nothing; cut out from a single piece of paper yet with shades and shadows that stretched back in time and space. "Lady Roakes, is there something you wish to tell me? Something you did and now regret?"

All of a sudden, her backbone was gone. He saw a lady, taller than him and proud with it, shrink in height, in size, in stature. Thirty years rolled back and she was a six-year-old girl, unformed and uncertain.

She told him then about Arkwright and Parchman and the first Mr Beatrice. She told him in a quiet but wavering voice as she laboured to control the flow of words. She pulled out everything until the cupboard was bare.

It made sense to him as she went through the words for he knew who Arkwright was; he knew Lady Merriman well, for he had worked for her over the last three years, acquiring land in and around Bagber.

Mr Blake was a man and a man feels emotion as a story is told. He moved in quick order from sympathy to incredulity to anger and outrage. He struggled with those emotions for he was also a good man and he had always liked this strange woman who seemed wound up to be something she was not and was now rapidly unravelling herself into broken pieces of spring and apparatus.

He could not leave her in bits on the ground of her new

garden. The garden of the estate he had taken great joy and pride in helping her acquire. And noted the fierce intensity with which she had gone about the task of acquiring; admiring the way she had sought and found a solution to the obstacles put in her way. And the simple, loving joy with which she had hurried off to stand in front of Sir Beatrice and report on what they had achieved.

There was something in her that toned the revulsion he felt for her past for, he realised; none of us are wholly bad, just as none are wholly good. There was, he was sure, something in the Bible on this but his senses were honed to the girl in front of him and he wanted to live in the present, not drag himself back to long ago and deaden those senses with something tried and tested and written down centuries before.

All this in half an hour and now he saw Sir Beatrice leave the house and start to walk towards them. If he was to help, he had to help now.

"My dear," he started. "My dear girl, you have told me of terrible things but, however bad, no person is lost and damned forever. You can redeem yourself and if you stay open in your heart, the way forward will become clear to you. God will talk to an open heart." It was inadequate but what else could he say with Sir Beatrice almost within hearing distance, bearing down on them like a ship of the line? "You have much to give to this world, much to offer to others. Do not harden your heart again. Stay true and open and you will find a way."

"What was that, Blake?" Sir Beatrice called from across a bed of roses with pinks and yellows brightening the grey day.

"I said, Sir Beatrice, that I must be on my way. I hope to get back to Shaftesbury tonight."

"Yes, sir. We must not detain you, just thank you again for all your help and for leading us to this wonderful home. I see Lady Roakes is quite overwhelmed by it all and, being with child, she should come inside and rest."

"Sir Beatrice and Lady Roakes, it has been a pleasure to work for you and coming to know you just a little has been reward enough, despite the handsome fee you have paid me." He shook Sir Beatrice's hand and kissed the hand she offered then turned away to seek his horse.

"Kind words from a good man," Sir Beatrice said. "Now, let us get you inside to rest, my dear."

"Yes sir," she said and leaned into his broad shoulder all the way back to the house.

Afterwards, she realised that was the moment when most of her earthly ambition left her, swarming up amongst the bare tree tops and up to the rafters of Great Little, to leave her forever. She would never be a duchess, not even a countess, but these things mattered not one jot. She would find a new way and take her wonderful husband with her on that path.

Thus, the devil left her on the early afternoon of November 13th 1688, her second day in residence at Great Little. He regretted his expulsion briefly but he saw too many other opportunities in this crazy world that his one-time master had made for his entertainment.

And on the third day, the Duke and Duchess of Wiltshire came to stay.

Chapter 24

Thomas, Matthew and Lady Merriman spent a day in the treehouse. At first, it was like a game. They had some supplies they stored in a hole in the tree trunk; a cold ham cut into thin slices by the cook's assistant, some beer, and two loaves of bread. The boys explored the tree, climbing to the very top and out to some of the extreme positions so they perched at silly angles to look down on the world below them.

Thomas then put down a rota by carving 'T' or 'M' on one of the planks that made up the main platform.

"It's a watch rota," he said. "Two hours on and two hours off. When you hand over you scratch out your name. I'm down first so Matthew is on duty in two hours' time."

"But I should take a turn at keeping watch," Lady Merriman complained so he re-scratched with 'LM' in third position.

Thomas went back to the very top of the tree to start his watch but found the wind had picked up considerably and blew him like a sailor in a storm. He came down about ten feet and found a depression where the main trunk went off at an angle and a large branch had broken completely. It made a kind of chair and he settled in. It had the advantages of being out of the wind and also masked from view. For several minutes, he looked keenly around. Then a heaviness came upon him and forced his eyes closed. "Just for a moment," he told himself.

The cold woke him. It was a damp cold that settled on the skin and worked its way deeper, to spread across tissue and into bone. He woke with a shudder. The day was almost spent; dark invading the lawn below. He remembered why he was here and saw the mounted soldiers riding down the drive. He almost shouted when he recognised Colonel Hanson at their head.

They were leaving and had not found the fugitives. Then he recognised his sister, Grace, standing on the steps and waving to the colonel. Henry stood by her side like a statue of a god in some pose that the sculptor thought appropriate but no one could remember why.

Grace was safe, which meant the others must be as well. And the soldiers were leaving. He stood, finding it harder to balance through sleepiness and the gloom descending out of the sky. It denied him sight of good foot- and hand-holds. But he made his way down slowly to the main platform where he found the other two stretched out on the boards like drunks asleep in the street. They were sleeping apart, a satchel they had used to bring the food making a token barrier between them but, through this division, their arms were stretched and met in the middle so that Lady Merriman's hand was neatly cradled in Mathew's.

"Matthew, wake up." He did not know why he whispered. The soldiers were now through the gate, over half a mile away. With the creak of saddles and the clang of horseshoes on the stone road, they would not have been alerted had Thomas gone back to the top of the tree and shouted with all his might.

Matthew woke and blinked at his younger brother crouching over him.

"Is it my turn already to stand watch?" He did not move, hoped Thomas would say "No, you still have an hour so, go back to sleep."

"You've slept all day, Matthew," he said instead.

"Oh, my goodness!" He sat up and banged his large forehead against an overhanging branch. His foot scrabbled on the edge of the board and went over the side so that the loose-fitting shoe Henry's servants had found for him went knocking down through the lower branches to land with a thud on the ground.

"Oh, dear," he said, thinking this a bad dream. He looked over the edge but could see nothing. Then he looked for Thomas, could just make out his grinning face. Lady Merriman stirred, stretched like a lion and turned over. When she opened her eyes, she saw Matthew a foot away from her, looking back at her like a cat can look at a king.

"You both slept the day right through," Thomas repeated. "But you know what, so did I."

After Thomas, still bizarrely whispering, had told Matthew and Lady Merriman what he had seen from the crow's nest he had found near the very top of their mast, they clambered down the remaining rigging and felt the deck, solid and sure, beneath their feet. It took them too long to find Matthew's shoe so they set off without it, Matthew doing a curious lope, as if one leg was longer than the other.

It occurred to Thomas, as he walked behind the others that dusk, that Lady Merriman had never been a suspect. The other ladies had returned to Bagber Manor and waited, presumably knowing the soldiers would arrive at some point. Why, then, had Lady Merriman clambered into the tree and slept all day long on the hard boards of a boy's old treehouse? Moreover, she had known exactly where the treehouse was; as if she had been there before.

It was quite a mystery and he did not know where to start in unravelling it all.

Grace was overjoyed to see them, spreading her arms, somehow, around both her brothers and Lady Merriman, causing an unbalanced quartet of human life that almost toppled into the fire in the drawing room.

"Steady there," said Henry, smiling as broadly as his wife. He had made his decision back at Bagber Manor, with Colonel Hanson sitting in an easy chair, waiting for his soldiers to search house and grounds.

"I'll have to do the same at Sherborne Hall," Hanson had said when the captain finally reported nothing found.

"We'll ride back with you," Henry had replied. "Unless Grace is too tired to travel and wishes to stay the night here?"

"No, I will come with you, husband."

Henry had wisely put his horse alongside the young captain's, sensing that Grace and Hanson needed to talk. He found the captain tolerable company, with a knowledge of politics and farming and not much else. He, like all the militia, was a part-time soldier, and his main occupation was to run a 200-acre dairy farm he rented from Lady Merriman.

"Was, it strange, sir, to be searching your landlady's house?"

"These are the strangest of times, My Lord." Which answer amounted to the most depth Henry got from him throughout the twelve-mile ride.

He noted, however, that his wife and Hanson were completely absorbed in conversation the whole three hours it took them to Sherborne Hall. A lesser man might have objected but Henry's love for Grace was unshakeable and she loved him just as much in return.

Besides, he knew that Colonel Hanson was happily married with seven children and a rambling home in Bishops Caundle, where they stopped, mid-journey, for refreshments.

"You know he saw you," Henry said into the melée of Davenports, laced with a splash of Merriman.

"What?" said both Matthew and Thomas together.

"He did not say as much, but he detached himself from his soldiers and went to stand under the treehouse. I saw him raise his face up into the tree and stay that way for the longest time, as if he were studying the way the branches met the trunk or some such thing."

"What did he do then?"

"Nothing. He never mentioned it to me. It was like his own secret thing."

"I sensed something different in him towards the end," Grace said. "And he was suddenly in a dreadful hurry to leave off the search and get away."

"I think he has made a decision," Thomas said, hoping now that they had a convert to the cause in the shape of a real-life colonel and their friend.

But what cause was this? For, true to Elizabeth's silent observation in her upstairs sitting room, some of the men had yet to make their decision. Thomas had been roped into the arena as a double agent, working against his own brother. He had been suspected and arrested because of who he was, not what he had done. He had never chosen a course in this matter; rather, courses had been forced on him.

Until now when, as a fugitive from the law, an escaped prisoner, he finally had the freedom to make his own choice.

And he knew now what that would be.

"The question is what to do now," Henry said. "Everyone is

coming down on the side of liberty and I made a great mistake going against it. I need to prove myself now before it is too late, for fear, otherwise, of losing everything." They were sobering words from the Earl to his closest friends.

"We go to Dorchester and see my agent there. He will know what to do." Matthew spoke into the silence of indecision. It was obvious once it was said. The three men would go together.

"Grace will go to Bagber to stay with Lady Merriman," Henry decided, ignoring her protestations that she wanted to be with him. "I need you to keep them safe and together. I would feel much easier if all the ladies were together safe and sound." He did not add, did not need to, that Bagber was capable of defence with its walls around and two high towers way above the roofline. "I will organise a detachment of men from the estate to stay with you."

Lady Merriman had one more thing to offer. "Take Big Jim with you," she said. "He probably needs to be out of the area for a few days in case he also is a suspect."

We can make a safe assumption that Colonel Hanson, Thomas Davenport and Henry, Earl of Sherborne had all made their decisions concerning the subject of liberty; the recurring theme of much of history in the known world. That left only one male member of the party in Elizabeth's upstairs sitting room still to decide. Simon Taylor may have struggled a little to communicate any decision but he had every capability of making up his mind.

Strange things had happened to him over the last three years since his stroke in that very same sitting room upstairs at Bagber Manor. He had met with extraordinary compassion and love from those he had treated with disdain. He had found a way to make an excellent living. He did not know where Lady Merriman's capital had come from; that remained a mystery. But he was more than happy to share in it and, in the process, multiply it many times. He had previously relied for the bulk of his income on the old Earl of Sherborne's methods to undermine his rivals for his own ends. He had taken large commissions, setting up expensive loans, and this had given him the capital to make other loans to small-time local businessmen. By 1685, he owned several of these businesses and also their homes. But Amelia, his daughter, and Elizabeth, his second wife, had returned all this wealth to the individuals he had taken it from, reverting it back so that he owned nothing but the Sherborne commission and the proceeds from selling his law firm, which they had carried out on his behalf, without even telling him.

But he had made more than ever now with a good salary from Lady Merriman, who also covered every household need, insisting on them staying on at Bagber Manor. And from the commission he received on every land deal he brought to her attention.

He had been a crooked and ineffective lawyer but he became an excellent land agent.

Quite how he did the research, nobody knew except Simon himself. For he had a closely guarded secret which he would spring on everyone at just the right time.

His stroke had been real enough and dramatic enough, although quite minor in damage done. But he had faked his recovery so that it appeared painfully slow. He could walk and he could talk. He just chose to keep this to himself. And so, he bided his time, feigned remorse and plotted his next move while his capital was growing again.

The decision in Simon Taylor's head was different to those the others had faced. It was not the choice between liberty or oppression. Rather, it was whether now was the right time to make his break from the prison he was surrounded by; the prison whose walls were built of love, with gates of compassion and locks that opened outwards rather than in.

And he yearned to be free; to live dangerously and make his own way in the world.

Cartwright and Franshaw arrived at the White Lion at the very moment that Henry Sherborne and his three companions drew up and dismounted. Cartwright saw Sherborne in the stable yard and walked up to him, then shrank back when Franshaw yanked at him urgently.

"That's the Davenport brothers he's with," he whispered urgently.

"Are you sure?"

"I arrested them, didn't I, Mr Cartwright? I think I would know."

But it was too late to slink away.

"Mr Cartwright, good afternoon to you," Henry said, his voice sailing over the various saddled horses between them. "What brings you here?"

"Good day to you, My Lord. I could ask you the same question."

"Oh, just to visit an old friend I heard was staying here."

"You mean Sir Beatrice, I presume."

Henry did not answer but his face coloured red as a sunset.

"Well, on with work. Duty calls as always. No peace for the wicked," Cartwright resumed with a jaunty air. If Henry had known Cartwright a little better, he would have recognised the joviality that preceded action. Cartwright whispered to Franshaw then wheeled his horse around and made for the exit. Franshaw stood stock-still, an inane grin on his broad face. His was the public face of subterfuge.

"We've got to move out," Henry whispered. "I know enough of Cartwright to know he's a highly dangerous man."

"No," Thomas whispered back. "They'll be doubly suspicious if they see us leave now. Let's go through with it, have a drink, something to eat, then find out if your contact is here."

The four of them could never earn a living as actors, for their collective performance that afternoon was appalling. They made exaggerated moves to the bar, declaring in loud, toneless voices how tired they were after a hard day looking for fugitives. Franshaw stuck with them, grin pasted on his face, like you would struggle to remove with a scrubbing brush.

They found Franshaw's weakness by accident but, once found, they jumped on the opportunity. Matthew was delayed by some instructions to the stableman about diet for his horse. The three of them went to the bar, Franshaw hovering.

"Shall we get an extra beer?" Big Jim asked, not sure if

Matthew would take beer.

"Thank you, kind sirs," Franshaw spoke, thinking the extra was for him.

"No, you are..." began Jim.

"No, you are so welcome," interrupted Thomas, seeing the opportunity. He slid the ale along the counter and Franshaw accepted it eagerly.

"You are very good, sir." He drank the beer in one, then tried to be friendly with his enemies. "That went down very well," he said, smacking his lips and wiping his mouth on his sleeve, offering the glass forward for a refill.

By the fifth beer in rapid succession, he was useless, sitting wide-eyed and slurring his words. Thomas slipped out first, caught Matthew coming from the stables and turned him around. "We're riding out. Our contact is not here. And this place is crawling with Government agents." He thought this last comment an exaggeration but needed to make his point. Matthew turned without breaking his momentum, back to the stables.

Chapter 25

"You are most welcome to our house, Your Graces. Things are a little awry as we have only just moved in but we have given you our rooms at the front of the house as the more bearable. I hope you will not be too uncomfortable." Lady Roakes curtsied, deeper than politeness dictated, causing the Duchess to look sharply at her. "I would be happy to show you the rooms now, if you like. We are still discovering much ourselves about the place."

"That would be kind, Lady Roakes. Sally, bring my bags up."

"I will see the rooms later," Wiltshire said. "There is pressing business to discuss with Sir Beatrice."

Lady Roakes led the way up the broad central stairs, flanked all the way up by a large window depicting a medieval banquet the Littles had hosted generations ago. She could tell it was the Little family for there were little scrolls beneath the key two-dimensional figures, with heads twice the proper size and long arms that reached across the tilted table. She could read 'Little' on several of them, including a beautiful woman with a long, tall wimple that seemed to rise out of the scene to hook passers-by. Penelope imagined a sinister trap whereby Lady Roakes used the depiction to catch those guests she did not like and condemn them to a life in the banquet, standing stock-still in some silly pose forever. Behind the window was the Great Hall so the guests and hosts at the feast looked out to both rooms, turned around to face left instead of right.

"You have an interesting house," said the Duchess civilly enough. It was as if it was the first day of a truce after a long war; each army waiting to see who would break it first.

"Thank you, Your Grace. Here are your rooms now."

The allocated rooms occupied just about the whole front of the first floor at the front.

"We did not know your sleeping preferences so have allocated two main bedrooms, an additional one for your maid, a sitting room, and two dressing rooms. I very much hope this will suffice, Your Grace." This last 'Your Grace' made the

Duchess suddenly stop her visual tour of the rooms and look at Lady Roakes. It was almost said with reverence; like someone testing the carpet before the important visitor stepped onto it. Penelope felt uneasy. She would have preferred the hostility they had always shown each other; it was more comfortable to hate and be hated in return.

"You are very kind, Lady Roakes," said in a neutral tone to be safe.

"Is nothing, Your Grace." The same intonation of deference. Penelope shook herself; was there something political going on she did not know about? It would be typical of Wiltshire to leave her in the dark.

"The rooms all have interconnecting doors so you have flexibility as to how you may use them," Lady Roakes continued.

"They can be locked from my side?" Penelope asked a little too shrilly. Also, Sally stopped her meanderings through the chain of rooms and went to stand very close to her mistress. There must have been a finger's width between their two arms. She suddenly knew about them, imagined little sharp rays darting between them.

"You mean to ensure female privacy?" It was a gentle way to ask the question and both Sally and Penelope breathed out with relief. "I suggest, Your Grace, that we lock this door here so you have three rooms that are private. You can open the door at any time and have use of the central sitting room. Would that meet your needs?"

It would do very well indeed. Sally walked over and locked the door and slipped the key up the starched sleeve of her dress. "As I shall always be in attendance, Your Grace, shall I take ownership of the key?"

In return for Lady Roakes' evident kindness, Penelope asked the obvious question as the baby was evident now at almost four months.

"Yes, Your Grace, I am with child, much to my joy and to Sir Beatrice's. The baby is due in April, I am told. Now I must leave you to unpack and sort out your things. I will be in the library, to the right as you come down the stairs and into the entrance hall. Please come as soon as you are ready, Your Grace." Another deep curtsey and the door closed behind her.

"Well, I declare," said Sally. "I thought you said she was awful."

"I don't understand it, Sal. She is much changed, it seems. Now what shall we do for the next hour?"

"First, you will help me unpack and then we shall see what time is left. Come now, Pen, the quicker we get it done the more time we have afterwards."

Lady Roakes just heard this interchange as she closed the door and paused outside. It confirmed her suspicions. She smiled a new smile to herself; perhaps these two were almost as happy as she was.

She went down the main stairs to the large entrance hall, hands on belly as she descended, trying to discern a kick or two. At the bottom, she turned right for the library, under the banquet window where the food never ran out and the people never tired. She reached out to turn the library door handle and push it open.

Then she froze, for at the far end of the long, thin room; more like a portrait gallery than a library, came loud voices, two voices directing their anger at each other.

One was her husband and the other was Wiltshire. It was too far to hear all the words but snippets of anger ran the whole length of the room:

Arrest... no progress... lack of co-ordination... a child could do better... running rings around you, Roakes... gallivanting around looking at houses when there is work to be done.

My God, Wiltshire was berating her husband and he was fighting back:

No action from my reports... indecision... lack of information... my wife did every part of the house hunting, not I... you won't get away with blaming me... with blaming me... blaming me... blaming me... me... me... me.

"My God," said Sir Beatrice, attracted by the thud as Lady Roakes slid to the ground. He covered the distance to her in seconds, slid to the floor beside her and felt her pulse.

"She's fainted."

"So I see. What of it?" Wiltshire had not moved from his position. "Roakes, this is exactly what I mean." The foolish man was playing right into his hands. "We have matters of high importance to resolve and you spend your time chasing after your wife."

But Sir Beatrice just snorted and turned back to his wife. Wiltshire felt suddenly foolish himself, then anger built up in him like the flames of a mighty bonfire reaching ever higher into the night-time sky.

"You'll pay for this, man."

"Help me, someone, Lady Roakes has fainted."

"You are a fool, Roakes."

"Good," two servants had entered the library, "help me get her up to bed."

"No one lets me down and gets away with it."

"Be careful now, remember she is with child. Smith, go for the doctor, run now."

The doctor pronounced that woman and child were fine.

"She fell in a relaxed pose because she was unconscious as she fell. That meant she offered no resistance and just slid to the ground. It is the best way in these cases. It could have been much worse."

Sir Beatrice would not leave the room. Indeed, it became his room, for he crawled into bed next to her and felt her warm, pulsating body. He was rewarded for this attendance for in the early morning she opened her eyes, smiled at her husband and found his hand with hers. He returned the smile happily. After a little while, with him sitting on the side of the bed, she invited him to lie with her. He stood up, locked the door and came back to the bed.

When he came downstairs later that day, he found Wiltshire gone and an embarrassed Duchess filling her days with nothing much to do.

"Can I see her, Sir Beatrice?"

"Is that wise, Your Grace?" He was aware that they disliked each other intensely.

"She was kind to me when we first came. I would like to see how she is."

"No more than five minutes please, Your Grace."

"Thank you, Sir Beatrice, and my name is Penelope if you would prefer to use that."

"Penelope," he said, but the single word said so much.

A few minutes later, Penelope went through the whole name thing again.

"Please call me Penelope," she said to Lady Roakes after enquiring as to how she was and receiving a "Quite a lot better, thank you, Your Grace."

It made Lady Roakes sit up suddenly, as if Penelope had drawn the strings sharply on a puppet that was her.

"Are you sure, Your... Penelope?"

"Of course, Lady Roakes, but it would help if it was reciprocated." There was just a hint of the old acerbity but dressed now as humour and it went down well. Just to be sure, however, she added an explanation. "I could sense something was different with you when we arrived. You seemed gentler; kinder. It has made me think that we should be friends." Penelope drew breath and continued, "I would like very much to count you as my friend, especially as I do not have many at all." She did not count a lover as a friend because they were different; friendship may develop from love but it is not the same thing.

"Me too," laughed Lady Roakes. "Oh, and my name is Alice."

The murder happened that night. It was vicious, it was ruthless. It was Parchman at his very best.

And Wiltshire, returned from his urgent business, let him into the house. They knew this for Sally saw him open the French window that led from drawing room to lawn. She saw the dark shape that was Parchman enter the room, a look of no nonsense about him; a man set on a purpose.

"What is this, sirs?" she asked of the two big figures before him. Wiltshire spun around in response, lifted a poker from the fire and raised it high.

"Hush, black slut. Forget you ever saw anything, do you hear?"

But Sally was not the type.

"Sirs, this does not seem right to be sneaking around at the dead of night."

"I could say the same of you, slut."

"I was getting a warming pan for my mistress, Your Grace. And I cannot forget what I have seen, sir, for I have seen it and that is a fact." She turned at the drawing room door to leave. Parchman grabbed the poker, still raised above Wiltshire's head as if he were a native frozen in a ritual dance. No such problem for Parchman, who strode across the room and took aim.

The blow from the poker would have hit Sally on the back of the head, quite probably killing her. But she heard Parchman approach and turned back as the poker came down. It glanced across her face, tearing into her right cheek and saving her life.

Blood poured and she crumpled to the floor. Parchman stepped over her, as he had the beggar in the Westminster street. He went about his business, leaving the room.

Wiltshire stooped, felt for a pulse; she was alive. He lifted her brown head; the blood was flowing freely but the wound looked superficial. He set it down gently; it was the best he could do. He left the room and went to bed.

Sally was found early the next morning by a servant girl coming in to clean and lay the fire for a new day. She whistled a favourite tune while she went about her work, knowing her supervisor, who forbade whistling on duty, would be below stairs enjoying the cup of tea she had just made her.

That whistling stopped and a soundless cry came to her lips. Then she found voice and the scream woke the whole household.

Penelope was beside herself. She dropped to the floor, shouted for a doctor to be fetched, praying that her Sally should be alive. The body was so still, so peaceful; just like she imagined death when all the troubles pass out of you to land upon another poor, helpless soul.

"She can't be, she can't be. Pray God she is not."

"Hush, Penelope." Lady Roakes was down beside her. "She

is not dead. See, she is stirring." Penelope looked and saw her Sally move, just as Lady Roakes had said. Sally opened her eyes, closed them again.

"Keep back, everyone. She needs peace and air," Lady Roakes used her free hand to wave the onlookers back; her other hand was tight around Penelope, her new friend.

"Can she... can she talk?" Penelope looked to Lady Roakes as if she was an authority; she needed someone else in charge; someone to tell her repeatedly that it was not so bad.

"My dear Penny," Sally whispered three words that only her mistress could hear, then closed her eyes to find that peaceful place again. Those three words rose, almost silently, into a room full of noisy people: servants, guests, mistress but no master. But Penelope heard them.

The doctor bandaged Sally's face under the close supervision of Penelope, who then organised her to be carried upstairs to her own bedroom. Other than her trio of words; a great effort to demonstrate to her lover that she was able to speak and issue coherent thoughts, she spoke no more. Instead, she just opened her eyes from time to time, to seek reassurance that Penelope was still close by.

"She is evidently traumatised," Lady Roakes said, her arm around Penelope's shoulders. Penelope's arms, in turn, were entirely devoted to Sally; one stroked her hair in what she hoped was a soothing motion, the other held her firmly on the bed, as if she imagined Sally had lost all sense of position in the world and would roll off at any moment. "She needs to rest," continued Lady Roakes. She was, as far as she knew, the only person in the house who knew just how dear Sally was to Penelope.

"You will be fine, Sal," Penelope spoke through her tears, sniffing them back up as if she was in command of all emotions in the world but the machinery of control had temporarily broken down and flooding resulted.

Sally raised her right hand to her bandaged face, looked in horror at Penelope and said one more word that hung in the air forever.

"Sherborne," she said and this time all in the room heard it.

Lady Roakes shooed them out but it was too late; rumours could spread from a single word, like bluebells in the wood. Penelope knew immediately what Sally meant; she had walked away from the Earl three years ago when he had been struck by a sword while fighting against Monmouth's hotch-potch army. The livid scar on his face had been too much for her. But now Sally would have something similar. The girl was frightened that Penelope would walk away from her, too. All she could do was squeeze her hand in hers and look earnestly at her, mouthing 'No' because she could not speak right then.

"I'll go for Sir Beatrice," Lady Roakes said, standing up and giving Penelope another hug before leaving the bedroom. "He'll know what to do about Sherborne." With a start, Penelope realised that Lady Roakes had taken Sally's single word to be a naming of the perpetrator of the attack against her. She turned to deny it but Lady Roakes, her new friend, was out of the room with the door closed behind her.

It was Lady Roakes, on entering the study downstairs, who found the second victim of Parchman that night.

At first, she thought Sir Beatrice was resting at his desk. "Sir," she said, "please come quickly. There is such a calamity in our house this morning. Penelope's little black servant has been attacked. She has named the Earl of Sherborne, although he must have done it through an intermediary."

"Sir, please do come. Sir?"

Twenty minutes later, the same servant girl who had found Sally entered Sir Beatrice's study to find Lady Roakes talking sweetly to a dead body. At first, she did not take it in, thinking they were having some conflab, and quickly curtseying and murmuring an apology. Then she noticed the blood everywhere; thick and brown from drying overnight, it had reached everywhere like ink shaken from a quill.

The servant wanted to talk and move; her instinct was to take Lady Roakes away from the blood and say some soothing words. But all she could manage was a single piercing scream and the household; what was left of it, came running again.

Chapter 26

Wiltshire believed you make your own luck in this world. And he had made a bundle of it recently. Not only had he got away with the murder of Sir Beatrice, carried out by Parchman, but he had silenced, or virtually so, that dark-skinned brat of a maid to his wife. She had said one word, which was the joy of it all. For that one word had been 'Sherborne' and now they all blamed the Earl of Sherborne for the death of Roakes and the attack on Sally. That much was unplanned and amounted to a distinct bonus.

For Sherborne had been next on Parchman's list and now there was no need; the authorities would take care of that particular problem in due course.

True, he had first cursed the stumbling interference that brought Sally into the drawing room at just the wrong moment. But it had worked out so well in casting blame in Sherborne's direction. The moral, it seemed, was to take the long view; everything worked out in the long run, provided one stayed calm.

With Sherborne out of the way… no, best to deal with one stage at a time.

First, he had to make sure that the Sally-brat did not recover so that she could squeal what she knew. The question was how.

"Wife, you need to take some rest. Let me take a spell at the bedside." He had tried the pleasant, caring approach but was met with, "I wish to stay by her side, sir. I am fine to do so and feel the responsibility. She is my maid and received her injury going about my business."

Next, he explored the firm husband approach; much closer to his true nature.

"If you think, madam, I'm going to hang around on my own while you while away your days playing nursemaid to your maid, you have another think coming."

"Sir, if you think I'm going to cavort downstairs, playing cards and indulging in idle chatter, while my maid lies unconscious up here, then you have another think coming."

She almost jabbed at him as she spoke over the bed where Sally lay, just managing to stop her hand movement at the last moment, sweeping that hand down to straighten Sally's sheets instead.

"And what if I want you tonight? Am I supposed to share your bed with that?" His hands moved in Sally's direction to make his point, causing Penelope to grab him by the arm lest he disturb the sleeping woman.

"Sir, it is my time of month. You cannot come tonight."

"Let go of me, wife. I will not be restrained by a woman." His voice was sharp with anger, sending a steel blade into Penelope, who shuddered and let go of him.

But the moment passed, for Wiltshire kicked back the chair and left the bedroom without another word or gesture.

On both sides of the closed door there was jubilation. Inside, Penelope was delighted just to have dispensed with her vile husband and to have managed to stay with her beloved Sally.

On the outside, Wiltshire was equally content with developments on two fronts. First was the confirmed knowledge that Sally had slipped back into unconsciousness, making his plans that much easier. Second, he had used his time in the bedroom wisely, staying longer than his temper allowed him for a singular purpose; to gain the key to the interlocking door.

That key was on a brass ring, which he twirled around his fingers as he walked down the staircase, past the Littles in the window, being as they always were.

Penelope's weakness was her new friendship. It sounds like the world turned upside-down for friendship to weaken a person but it did. As soon as Penelope heard of Sir Beatrice's murder, she left Sally, locking the door behind her.

"I'll be back, my love," she whispered before closing the door.

She found Alice Roakes on the terrace overlooking the rose garden. She sat alone, no shawl against the rising and biting wind. She had sat on the first thing she had come across; an old iron roller the gardeners sometimes used to level the lawn. It made a damp and uncomfortable seat.

"Oh Alice, I am so sorry," Penelope cried out and meant it, possibly for the first time in the twenty-three years of her life. There was no response from Lady Roakes, just a dull stare sent somewhere in the middle distance; from where it dispersed itself into God's creation.

Penelope tried three different poses. At first, she knelt down in front of Alice, looking back up at her, like a child looks at their mother. Then, when this did not work, she sat beside her as her friend. Finally, she stood and looked down on her; a benevolent aunt on a mission of concern.

None of them worked in that not one of them got a flicker of response.

Penelope tried words too but realised soon that words were inappropriate; there was nothing to say that could reduce the pain in the slightest. Later, there might be. Tomorrow or some day after that, it might be right to put words into a conversation; to talk about Sir Beatrice, perhaps, and how much he loved her. Soft words, words of love; then, a day or two later, a tentative joke, even, in the hope of a faint smile.

But not today. Penelope felt hopelessly inadequate as she went back to the friend's pose and sat again on the roller, taking Alice's hand in hers loosely as the minutes went by.

Penelope was perpendicular to religion; her religion, if any, had been about herself. But she prayed now, like someone suddenly introduced to a much higher society than they were used to. Her prayers were stumbling and self-conscious.

God, who others call dear but I know not, come now to Great Little for you are needed. Great Little is near a place called Winterbourne Stickland and has lots of hillocks in the ground, where old people from long ago are buried. There is another person to be buried now for my friend, my only friend, has had her husband snatched from her by some cruel devil of a man. I need you to comfort her and to repair my Sally, who was hit by the same devil and lies unconscious in her bed upstairs.

Come quickly, Jesus, or God the Father, or even send the Holy Ghost; I care not which one comes as each of you can provide the hope and the strength my friend needs; to teach her that there is life after death for the living as well as the dead.

Then, when you come, you can next go upstairs to my bedroom and make my Sally better.

It never occurred to Penelope to bargain with God as so many do in times of stress, promising better behaviour and a reformed life if only a certain wish is granted. It did not occur to her because she did not have God in her life at all and, other than the prayers her nanny made her recite as a child, had never prayed before.

Her prayer was more of a command to come, as if to a servant rather than the Lord; dealing with precise instructions laid down clearly.

But if Alice had heard that silent prayer right then she would have smiled through her grief, recognising immediately the fragile imperiousness that was her new friend.

Prayer over, Penelope sat and wondered why it was that she had gone twenty-three years not caring about a living soul other than herself. Then, in the space of two weeks, she had two people she loved; a dear friend in Alice and the dearest lover in her Sal.

It never occurred to her that God may have had a hand in it; as noted before, she was perpendicular to religion. Instead, she took a firmer grip on Alice's listless hand and said under her breath, "I'll get Sally better and Alice on an even keel and then I'll get my revenge. Three things to do; perhaps that is what they mean by the Holy Trinity."

Her firming of her friend's hand presently got a reaction. Alice Roakes turned to look at her, as if not knowing previously who had sat beside her. Her head of beautiful hair and fine features swung out of sorrow and asked how Sally was doing.

"She is unconscious, Alice. I am worried about her."

"Go to her, then. She needs you." There was a way about these words that made Penelope sit bolt-upright.

"You know, then? You know about us?"

"Yes, I do. Now go to her." The beautiful hair and fine features sank again, its duty done.

"I'll go then." But no response.

Penelope went quickly upstairs, suddenly aware how long she had left Sally. As she went past the Littles at their perpetual feast, she thought she heard cries from her bedroom half a flight up. She quickened, running up the stairs as the cries became a muffled scream. She fumbled with the key in the bedroom door, panicking at the sudden silence. Why would Sally scream then go quiet? But the key was stuck in the lock, would not turn all the way around. She banged it, rattling the door knob in frustration.

It turned and she was in. Sally lay on the bed quite still, eyes open to the ceiling; pillows and sheets around were in disarray. A struggle or a fit? Whatever, it was the last thing her dear Sally had experienced. Penelope was sure of that and did not want to approach the still, staring body with one leg bare from the blankets and parked awkwardly so that it might snap with any pressure on it.

She circled around, cautiously checking the wardrobe and the dressing room, even Sally's little tiny room. There was no one there; it must have been a fit then and not a second attempt on her life.

Only then did she approach her lover's body, noticing the torn nightgown that sat incongruously with her fit theory. As she got closer, her spirits awakened from the deadened state of Alice on the terrace below. She thought she heard ragged breathing. She stopped and held her breath lest it be hers she was hearing. The breathing continued.

Sally was not dead. Penelope rushed to her and was welcomed with a turn of the head.

"Pen, my love, I was worried about you."

"Sally, dearest." She sat on the edge of the bed and leaned over and they kissed. It was the kiss of life; breathing fresh, warm, pulsating air into Sally's lungs.

When they had finished, Penelope stood and remade the bed. She puffed up the pillows and turned down the sheets like any good maid or nurse would do, hoisting Sally's body into a comfortable position.

She liked doing these things for Sally, who even made a joke about always wanting a maid for herself. In response, Penelope stood back and gave a pretty curtsey before returning to the bed and kissing her all over again.

"What happened, Sal? You were screaming."

"It was your husband, my love. He tried to kill me." The words were out, standing like a thorny hedge between them. But Penelope did not hesitate from chopping down the hedge to reach the other side.

"How did he get in?"

"I know not, Pen." She shifted herself higher in the bed. Penelope went to help her but she did not need it. Instead, Penelope straightened the sheets where Sally had disturbed them. "I was sleeping…"

"You were unconscious, in a coma."

"I was unconscious, then, nit-picker. And the next thing I knew was a pillow pressed against my face. I struggled and fought…"

"So, his attack gained you your facilities back again."

"Stop interrupting, woman or, as my maid, I'll have you beaten." Sally was in high spirits and Penelope loved it; too much to concern herself with relative status. She would happily be Sal's maid forever just to see her each day.

"Sorry, miss." Another pretty curtsey and they both laughed. It was the laughter of the warrior after battle; wounded, maybe, but alive.

"I quite like you this way," Sally said.

"Whatever, I'm just happy that you are alive. But how did you know it was my husband that came to finish the job?"

"Because I saw him, just like I saw him with that henchman he let in before. I only saw him this time when he heard the key turning in the lock and rushed away, dropping the pillow."

Penelope sat on the edge of the bed, borrowing a little bit of pillow from Sally for a few moments, deep in thought.

"Where's the key?" she asked suddenly.

"What key?"

"The interconnecting door, that door." She pointed at her suspicion, confirmed when neither she nor Sally could find the key anywhere.

"You must tell all this," Penelope said. "At the moment they think it is Sherborne behind this, trying to get rid of anti-Government agents."

"What is the point? It will be a duke's word against a servant girl; a black one at that."

"I will speak also."

"Don't be silly, Pen, for if you do so, it will all come out about us. What we do is a mortal sin, you know."

"He does not know, surely?"

"Surely, he does, Pen. But, anyway, it is not worth the risk. Instead, we have to lay a trap for him with me as the bait."

Penelope was full of admiration for her lover. At first, it had been physical attraction but this marvellous, intelligent and wise girl was rapidly becoming so much more in her life. Half an hour ago, Sally had been struggling for that life against a big man determined to kill her. Now, she was plotting a trap to snare both poacher and gamekeeper, they being the same person, in the form of her husband.

There was something wonderful about being in love. And when it was your maid, it added a dose of secrecy as spice. And when you threw adventure in to the pot, all sorts of bubbling creations came out.

Except they were dealing with murder; the end of a fantastic being on this earth, as Alice had found out to her terrible cost. All ideas of fun suddenly gone, Penelope drew Sally to her and cried as she clung to happiness.

Chapter 27

Somehow, the authorities moved quickly rather than grinding through the paperwork at the normal pace. With a delightful sense of unsuspecting irony, Colonel Hanson was despatched by a magistrate, woken at night, to arrest the Earl of Sherborne.

Hanson knew exactly where the Earl was so did not trouble himself going to Sherborne Hall or Bagber Manor. Instead, he rode hard and alone to Dorchester, swinging into the much smaller yard at the White Lion three evenings after the death of Sir Beatrice.

Henry was not there. He, Thomas and Matthew were out riding across the countryside, in search of Sir Beatrice Roakes, Matthew's contact for developing support for Orange. They had first ridden west, thinking him likely to have gone that way. Also, the landlord at the White Lion had informed them, after quite a few coins had changed hands, that he believed Sir Beatrice had moved his centre of operations to the west of Dorchester. They did not know that Sir Beatrice had paid him liberally to send any enquirers in the wrong direction; he had most certainly not wanted Parchman to meet his wife. He had ached to tell her she could no longer be a murder suspect for Parchman was alive and well. But he would bide his time and tell her the news when Parchman was no longer around to threaten her.

It had all backfired, of course, because of Wiltshire. And Parchman, without knowing it, had happened upon the prefect revenge for the one he blamed for wounding him viciously in her house in Bristol three years earlier. It had been her first husband who had turned the knife back onto Parchman but Mr Beatrice had been hanged by the old Earl for petty theft, leaving her free to marry again. Moreover, Mr Beatrice had only acted to defend Mrs Beatrice. In Parchman's twisted mind, it mattered not that he had been trying to kill her, just that her husband inflicted the wound on him.

But then Mrs Beatrice had disappeared. As Parchman had

established himself at the centre of several spy rings over the next three years, he had many times sent people out to search for the woman but every man drew a blank.

The landlord of the White Lion had been unable to resist the coins Henry flipped as they talked. But he had stayed true to Sir Beatrice, knowing him to be richer, therefore a better man. He had sent the three men westwards and had not mentioned that Sir Beatrice was now basing himself at a country house. Hence the two days of fruitless searches, seeking out every inn across the southern half of the county, even stopping overnight at the inn that Lady Roakes and Mr Blake had stayed at when visiting Great Little.

But their lack of success in finding Sir Beatrice also proved Henry's saviour. For, if he could not find the man, he could hardly murder him. Hanson saw this straight away; he, anyway, knew the charges to be false, regardless of hearsay, because it was not in Henry's character to murder anyone.

"They are at an estate north of Dorchester," Hanson told them when he finally tracked them down at the Fox and Hounds in Cattistock. "I know because of the news that Sir Beatrice was murdered there four days ago."

"What?"

"He was struck down from behind while he sat at his desk late at night. Then the murderer made sure by stabbing him repeatedly and kicking his head so that his skull broke open. It was a vicious and cold-hearted killing by someone who does such for a living, I've no doubt."

"This is the man I met?" Thomas asked. "The agent of…" He stopped mid-sentence, remembering that Hanson was an army officer.

"No matter, Thomas, you may say it freely to me. He was Matthew's agent in gaining support for Orange in Dorset. I have known as much for several days now."

"How did you find out about Matthew?"

"The landlord at the White Lion was very helpful, especially when I emptied my purse and laid its contents on the table."

It was a hard twenty miles' ride from Cattistock to Great Little and it was already late in the evening. Rain was driving sideways, whipped by a wind that would not lay down and be quiet. They debated delaying to the morning but then Hanson informed them that Henry was currently the prime suspect.

"I know it to be fanciful," he said. "But despite the lateness of the hour, I deem it best to be there rather than here. If you agree, I'll see the landlord about fresh horses and we should be on our way."

They agreed and Hanson left to see the landlord while Thomas went to the kitchen for some supper to take with them; cold beef, bread and cheese, and tasty apples from the recent harvest. Matthew was alone suddenly with Hanson; someone he did not know well.

"Sir," began Hanson, not one to hide away if something needed to be said, "know please that I have struggled with my conscience on this matter."

"I can imagine, sir." But Matthew could not for he had always known right from wrong, never had to deliberate for long. He had been born with right and wrong burned into his conscience.

"And have decided... may I call you Matthew?"

"Please do, and your name is?"

"James." The tiniest of bows to formalise the informal address. "Matthew, I am firmly on the side of the liberating force of Orange. I see the obstinacy of King James as an oppression on the people, just as in King John's day. I believe the people, Parliament, must make a stand and enshrine our basic liberties in a new charter to stop corrupt kings from ever again wielding excessive power."

Matthew was about to say, "Amen to that," but suddenly thought this was not a religious conversion but something secular.

"I'm glad to hear it, James. And welcome to the cause."

Penelope spent half her waking day and all her nights closeted with Sally; the other half of daytime was devoted to Alice and her recovery from the dreadful loss.

Except that there was no recovery; Penelope in her hopeless superficiality imagined it would come any day now and puzzled as to why she was not mending.

"Am I treating her wrong?" she asked Sally.

"No Pen, dear, but think on it. When I was taken away from my family and sold to be a slave, my family became dead to me. It took more than a few days for that pain to mellow."

"Do you mean it hurt, like a wound, like your face hurts?"

"Oh Pen, you are so adorable in your ignorance. Of course, it hurt. It still hurts now but has eased with so much time passing. It is like a piece of you, your very self, is wrenched out of you."

"I would not mind if my parents were dead. It would not bother me at all."

"But if I had died? If your husband had succeeded in his attempt?"

There was no answer Penelope could give to this. She saw it now, as clear as day. If you care for someone, you become joined to them; like a freak mythological animal that is part this and part that. Then, when one of the species dies, it tears you in half.

"Talking of your husband's attempt on me, we need to lay our trap," Sally said.

But Penelope, having considered Sally's idea carefully, would not hear of it; she would not risk losing Sally for anything.

"He will get away with it and another innocent man will suffer in his place."

"I care not for any man. I need to keep you safe."

"But, Penny my darling, you like the Sherbornes. You told me so yourself."

"Sal, the Sherbornes can roast on the flames of hell for all I care. Yes, I like them, but I need you." There was something deliciously honest about Penelope; she broke every convention yet was a duchess.

Penelope sought to avoid danger for Sally and herself but that same danger came to find them.

For Wiltshire, while frightened by his close escape, had not given up; especially as reports were that the slut of a maid was making a good recovery. She might, even now, be talking about what she had seen.

But Wiltshire saw too much risk in entering again the bedroom where Sally lay. So, he decided to send Parchman to do the job for him.

"You understand, Parchman, that she is the one person who can set you swinging on the end of a rope?"

"I understand, leave it to me." Parchman shuddered, reference to hanging was one thing he could not stand.

"What will you do?"

"Don't ask because you don't really want to know," Parchman said, then relented and outlined his emerging plan and Wiltshire's role in it before leaving to make his preparations. "I'll be there tomorrow night, Your Grace. Can you let me in as before?"

Wiltshire rode back to Great Little, wondering when he would finally be rid of these people and on to his own glorious future. He had a feeling whatever Parchman was planning would be dramatic but the killer's words remained with him throughout the ride from the White Lion to Dorchester; taken at night as a further security measure.

Nobody must ever link him to Parchman.

He was lucky that the black brat had been unconscious when he had made the attempt on her life. If she had seen him, he would be in serious trouble. He shivered as he thought how close he had come to killing her. He wondered whether it was as he had read; that the first time is always the most thrilling. Well, because the attempt had failed, he still had that to look forward to.

To pass the time as he rode through the wet, windy night, he went through the attempt again. He had steeled his nerves in the sitting room, just through the locked door from where Sally lay unconscious and unmoving. He had thought to check on Penelope; she had just moved her position on the old roller on the terrace, was now sitting next to Lady Roakes, holding her hand. It seemed the coast was clear.

He pulled the key out of his pocket and automatically swung

the key ring around his ring finger, catching it in his palm after three swings so that it stopped dead. He remembered being pleased that he had managed to catch it in a directly usable position; a minor skill but it added to the air of nonchalance, as if he were playing with a ball rather than with someone's life.

The door opened silently. He crossed the room, equally silent, and stood at sleeping Sally's side a moment. She was so ugly with her dark brown skin and frizzy, uncontrolled hair spread out on the pillow like a damn peacock sketched in black and white only.

The pillow; that was his instrument of death. But first he would have to take it from underneath her head. He bent, not wanting to touch her but having no choice. The skin on the back of her head, as he got a grip, felt like any other skin he had touched; soft and delectable; pity she was so damnable ugly or he would have taken her first. He slid his hand up her neck to the head of tight wiry hair splayed across the pillow; shuddered at the strangeness of it. He lifted her at the top of her head, not thinking to support her back and neck so her head seemed like a toy duck he had had as a child. When you lifted the head back, the duck gave a miraculous 'quack'.

There was no quack this time. Just a flutter of the eyes but they essentially remained closed. Then they flashed open but, surely, not long enough for the brain to register the snatch of sight?

"Penny," she had said, as if she were on intimate terms with her mistress. Perhaps she was or perhaps her long-lost mother was another Penny. He hated that name, used it as little as possible.

Then, as he levered out the pillow from underneath her, he made his mistake. It was the only mistake in an otherwise faultless exercise. He let go of the head and it fell from its hinge at the neck, down eight inches to hit the mattress with a dull thump. She opened her eyes but Wiltshire cleverly moved back into a shadow; instrument of death whipped from beneath her and held in both hands.

When she closed her eyes again, he moved the pillow into place. Then the cries happened and the struggle for air. He had thought, somehow, it would be soundless, the brat just drifting off to a more permanent sleep. But she fought the murder, struggling with all her might so that Wiltshire had to lean over her and hold down her arms and legs.

Then the hurried steps outside and the key fumbled in the lock. Wiltshire thought only of escape. That was all that was important now. He would have other chances. As he released the pillow, Sally screamed but he was halfway to the interconnecting door and to sanctuary. A second later, he was through that door and the lock turned smoothly and easily.

He was back in his private sitting room, where he poured himself a large brandy and considered what to do next.

He would go and see Parchman and let him sort it out.

Chapter 28

Seven people rode towards Great Little that night, in three distinct parties. The biggest was led by Colonel Hanson, with Thomas, Matthew, Big Jim and Henry making up the five. That meant the other two were solo efforts. Wiltshire went a longer way around than Parchman, who had lived as a child in the area and knew it well. Parchman also travelled with a greater sense of urgency, for he had a plan; one that he was pleased with.

He arrived a good hour before Wiltshire and was gone again before his new employer rode into the courtyard and shouted for someone to take care of his horse. Parchman would be back but he had finished making his preparations; all that remained now was to execute them.

Wiltshire was second to arrive, into a house quietened for the midnight-to-dawn spell. He went first to the drawing room, leaving a door to the garden unlocked as he had said he would do, to facilitate Parchman's return in the dead of night. But he did not remain there as last time. Instead, he poured a brandy, thought better of it and took the whole decanter to his bedroom where, as was custom, another decanter lay waiting for him. He was on the cusp of something truly great and he felt it in his waterlogged bones. Swinging the bedroom door closed behind him, he started to pull off his boots and then stopped and rang the bell for a maid; any female maid would do.

And as luck was following the Duke around these days, the maid who answered was stunning.

"Pour me a brandy." She poured him a brandy, wondering why he could not lean over the side table and pour his own.

"Pull my boots off." She did as instructed, wondering how it was that a statesman could not even pull his own boots off. Sir Beatrice had done so in his brief time as lord of Great Little. She had pulled off Sir Jacob's but then the man had been over eighty. The Duke looked a quarter of that age, although she knew from kitchen-gossip that he was nearly thirty.

"Open the window."

"Your Grace, it is fearsome wet and windy out there."

"Do as I say." Parchman had told him he would give a whistle, going up the scale from low to high and then back again, when he was ready to deal with the brat. He would need to vacate his rooms at that time and repair to the drawing room or library in order to be away from danger. "Then pour me another drink and have one yourself. What's your name? Ah, yes, Betty, such a pretty name."

The maid opened the window slightly, aware that the Duke was watching her as she crossed the room. It flattered her to have the attention of a duke.

But she hated the cold, damp weather that was often Dorset in winter. She had to obey him so she pulled the heavy curtain almost across the window to block the drafts, checking first that he was still looking at her and not at the window.

"What's it like out there?"

"Normal night, Your Grace." She had taken in what he wanted from her and was prepared to give it, for a price.

"No unusual noises?"

"Just the foxes and owls. Nothing unusual. Were you expecting something, Your Grace?"

"No, thought I heard something, is all."

"Well, if that is all, Your Grace, I have a lot to be getting on with. My sister is getting married next week and we can't afford a seamstress so I've got to do it all."

"How much does a seamstress cost?"

"A guinea, Your Grace."

"A guinea! She must be seamstress to the queen for that price." He reached into his purse and casually flicked a gold coin to her. "If I paid for the seamstress, could you find time to stay a while?"

"I could for a short while, Your Grace." She gave Wiltshire a little curtsey and slipped off her apron and cap. "I take it, Your Grace, I'm off duty now?"

"You're off that kind of duty, my gorgeous."

The larger party, led by Hanson, arrived, exhausted and cold, as Parchman was approaching the house to kick off stage two of his plan. He withdrew immediately into some shadows, crouching down below an old lawn roller that was rusting on the terrace, cursing silently when he cut his finger on the flaky metal and felt the blood seep. He put his finger into his mouth; it reminded him how much he liked the taste of blood.

It was not a setback for a patient man like Parchman. He withdrew quietly and would be back in an hour.

"Can we stay here?" Thomas asked, as they were let into the house by an elderly servant who had one leg longer than the other so stood with one leg bent backward at the knee and the other propped up on tiptoes.

"We will sleep in the Great Hall," Henry replied. "My man, can you bring some blankets and perhaps a cup of wine each? I know it is asking a lot but we have come a long way and will make our peace with Lady Roakes in the morning rather than disturbing her now in her grief."

"Sir, are you not the Earl of Sherborne?"

"I am, and these are dear friends of mine."

"My Lord, I will send for those things immediately. My name is Tomkins." When Henry heard this, it meant nothing to him. Then something came back from his lonely childhood.

"The under-steward from Sherborne Hall? You left when I was a child. But I remember you well. You were kind to me when I was alone."

"That was I, My Lord," Tomkins replied, delighted in a way only a subordinate can be at being remembered. "Sadly, My Lord, we have no rooms to spare and it will have to be the Great Hall. The house is almost derelict and very few bedrooms are habitable. I was only called back to work four days ago. We are trying to do what we can."

"You are the steward now?"

"Yes, My Lord." His chest moved out as if driven by a pump. "We will get the place sorted out, provided Lady Roakes decides to stay."

"Do you think she will leave?" Matthew asked.

"I think most women would, My Lord. It puzzles me how she can associate this lovely house with anything but the loss of her husband now. I suspect she will move back to London and

Great Little will be left to gradually decline. Come this way please, My Lord and gentlemen, and we will make you as comfortable as we can." He led the way through a door carved out of the giant painting of the Little family feasting; the door when closed forming a fat minstrel playing a fiddle.

"Truth is, my love, you need to face other people and I need to go and seek out Lady Roakes and check on her." The doctor had come that afternoon and taken the bandage off Sally's face, leaving a livid scar the shape of a taut longbow, where the poker had sliced into the skin. The doctor had sewn it but advised it would be an eyesore forever.

"It's far worse than Sherborne's," had been Penelope's first comment.

"Well, thank you for nothing." Sally replied, hoping for reassurance, for a recommitment to her.

"Well, it is, no point in denying it." Then she said something as profound as Penelope could get. "At first, I just wanted you because I desired to touch your skin and stroke your hair and because you always rejected my approaches. But now it's different."

"How is it different, Pen?"

"Oh, I don't know. You should not task your mistress so! It's just a sort of feeling deep inside."

That was when Penelope made the suggestion that Sally go down to the kitchens and spend an hour or two with her own kind.

"They'll be no one up at this time of night."

"There always is someone. I rang for some tea yesterday much later than this and one footman answered the bell and another footman brought the tea up. He saw my bed in there," she pointed to Sally's tiny bed in the servant's annex, which Penelope had used sometimes when Sally had been especially restless in her sleep. "He remarked that it was not turned down and sent two maids to sort it out. Never mind for I slept in here with you last night, in case you had forgotten, but it shows the untruth to your words. There are plenty of servants around all through the night."

In actual fact, Penelope had made a tremendous fuss to get any service during the night. She had learned the lesson and went down to the kitchen the following afternoon with a purse half-full of coppers and silver. She had arranged for several staff members to be up all night long.

For she had a terrible fear that her husband would come again for Sally in the night. And, she reasoned, the more people awake, the more to catch and restrain him.

"I'll go then for an hour," Sally said, seeing that Penelope really wanted her to. "I hope they don't make any remarks about my scar."

Sherborne's scar had been quite different. It had been long and deep, a single sword-point ripping through his face to the bone. Sally's scar was like someone had set out to skin her alive and then lost interest after the first few jagged cuts. Penelope could not take her eyes from it, which was another reason for seeking the blessing of a silent, blank hour with Alice Roakes.

"If they do, let me know and I'll make them wish they had not. I'll just make the bed now so it is fresh when we get back."

"You really are turning into quite the maid, Penny."

"Stop teasing me or I'll withdraw my love," she replied, then stopped to think that, yes, she did love Sally. And could she actually withdraw it when she had so little control over it?

Parchman's plan involved fire so he carried a small lantern with him. Ostensibly, it made him look like the night watchman, now lying trussed up and suffocating slowly in a ditch beyond the stables. In actual fact, it served two purposes. It lit his way, slightly, in a dark house he did not know well.

And soon it would light the fire under her bed.

Wiltshire had told him there would be one, maybe two, figures in the bed, depending on whether his wife slept there also. He had hinted that Parchman's plans should go ahead regardless of whether his wife was there or not.

"Make sure you mask the lantern in the bedroom," Wiltshire warned, thinking of the attempt he had been forced to abandon. It would be too much to fail again.

Parchman was a logical person. On reaching the top of the

main stairs in the dead of the night, he had a choice of several doors to try. He had been told it was straight ahead. He easily picked the lock and the door opened with a creek that made him stop still for a full minute. But nobody stirred inside.

That was because nobody was inside to stir. He could see the bed clearly from the doorway. It was made beautifully for someone but clearly not for his target, because she would be sleeping there. He quickly checked the ancillary rooms; all were deserted. But one door to the right was locked without a key. He would have to go in the other side and go around, through the chain of rooms that made up the suite the Wiltshires were occupying.

He went back onto the landing, listening carefully for anybody about. It was deathly quiet; well, it would be deathly soon, but hardly quiet.

His breathing stopped on entering the next door. There was a large four-poster bed straight ahead. That must have been what Wiltshire meant in saying 'straight ahead' for the bed contained two people asleep. It took just a few minutes to collect and crumple papers from the desk, pour oil from his lantern, then kneel like a soldier on camp and flick flames from the wick across to the papers soaked in oil. He stayed long enough for the flames to take hold of the bedding and left as quietly as he had entered. Six minutes later, he was trotting his horse down the long drive that separated Great Little from the rest of the world. He turned to see long flames coming out of an upstairs window. He watched backwards, while his horse continued forwards until the drive ended at the road. The flames were surging now, like shimmering towers in the night sky. He turned back to the road with a sigh of satisfaction for a job well done.

Parchman's timing had been either perfect or terrible, depending on your perspective. True to say, had it been a minute either way there would have been a very different outcome. If he had walked down the main stairs a minute earlier, he would have stumbled into Tomkins greeting Henry and his people. None of them knew him by sight, although Henry had known him as a boy, but they would have been suspicious of his presence in the house. Questions would have prodded at him like arrowheads and the answers he gave would eventually weave a cordon around him. Maybe it would be too late to save the dark brat upstairs but Parchman would swing for the crime without a doubt.

And if he went down, he would take Wiltshire with him.

If, on the other hand, he had delayed a minute or two, he would have had to skip back behind the curtains when he heard female shoes on the stairs. He would have watched as a beautiful aristocratic woman and Lady Roakes came up the stairs and kissed each other warmly before going to their bedrooms. Perhaps the astonishment at seeing Lady Roakes, who to Parchman would for ever be plain Mrs Beatrice, the cause of the agony in his side; perhaps that astonishment would have made him gasp and be discovered hiding behind the curtains.

But this is unlikely, for Parchman had an iron will. Despite the shock, he would have stayed stock-still until all risk of discovery was gone. He would have wondered who the woman was, and why she went into the deserted room. Would she discover the fire through the locked door and raise the alarm too early?

The strange woman was Penelope, come to make ready for bed. She changed into a nightgown then laid out her prettiest for Sally, stretching it out on Sally's side of the bed. Then she filled a china basin with water and laid out a towel for her maid. She stood back to check her preparations, twitched the nightgown so it was symmetrical on the bed, then sat on a chair to wait for her lover.

To recap, on our alternative timing, Parchman is standing completely still behind the heavy curtains that made a stage of the giant Little painting on the wall that ran up the staircase. He waits there a moment longer to ensure no risk of discovery. He waits a little longer for he then hears more female footsteps on the stairs. He peeks out and sees the dark brat, the one who should be burning in the bed upstairs.

In this scenario, would Parchman feel the ache of terrible regret? The guilt weighing in on him that two innocents were upstairs being roasted as they lay in bed together?

No, he would have cared only that he had failed in his mission. And that would have eaten at him sorely.

Chapter 29

What alerts sleeping people to a fire in the house? Is it the reek of burning, the roaring of the flames, or the way the smoke twists its way under doors and across rooms to break sleep with fits of violent coughing?

It matters not, for fire cannot creep; rather, it creates havoc as it spreads and the only blessing is that it then gives warning of itself as part of the terror with which it moves.

Thomas, asleep on the floor in the Great Hall, was first to wake. For those who are interested, it was none of the options above that woke him but a heavy timber that made the elaborate mahogany canopy of the bed crash down to break the burned bodies of Wiltshire and Betty.

Thomas was almost instantly alert; the cry of "Fire!" from Tomkins, still awake after settling his unexpected guests, brought him to all his senses.

"Where is it?"

"The bedrooms above!" Tomkins cried.

Thomas streamed up the stairs, followed by Tomkins, Hanson, Henry, Matthew and Big Jim, in that order. The air was full of smoke so that Thomas could not see.

"There's a door to a bedroom straight ahead," Tomkins roared above the spitting and crashing all around. "And another one just over there. I'm going to check on Lady Roakes." He was gone into the thick grey swirl.

Thomas tried the door ahead of him. It was locked. There were cries from inside.

"Can you open the door?" he yelled but his voice was ripped out of him by the noise all around. He stepped back, saw Hanson on the top step, roared, "Bedroom to the right, then get help to Tomkins, he's gone after Lady Roakes." Then Thomas charged at the door and it gave way at the hinges. Another charge and he could fight his way through the broken door. Instead, thinking of an exit route, he smashed through the door with a fist and turned the key from the inside. The door swung open as if it had never intended any resistance at all.

211

Inside, he saw nothing but colours. He saw grey against black, mostly, but then there were the great big stabs of orange flame; spreading from the right where there was another closed door. The bed was covered in short baby-blue flames, as if a nursery for the real fire to come.

And there in the centre of the room were two ladies, one stark-naked, the other in a flimsy nightgown. They were clutching at each other as if they had just been sentenced to eternity in hell together; terror was jerking their faces in vivid movements, distorted by the flickering light that played across the grey and black background.

And the grey was the smoke; the worst component of fire. It seemed the easier to cope with, for smoke cannot hurt; surely not?

Only it can, for the two ladies were now bending double, choking and retching.

Thomas did not think. He strode to the middle of the room, grabbed the first woman and slung her over his shoulders. She would not let go of her companion so it became like the clumsiness of a three-legged race as they stumbled and staggered across the room.

He got them out to find Henry at the top of the stairs. He was about to ask him what he was doing when Hanson's voice rang across the crashing timbers.

"Henry, take both girls downstairs then come back." He turned to Thomas, so much in command of the situation that he had time for explanations. "Tomkins got Lady Roakes out. Matthew and I dragged two very burnt corpses from the bedroom over there. All the servants sleeping on the top floor have made their way down the back stairs, guided by Henry and Tomkins. They've gone for the fire pump and the others are organising a water chain. Big Jim has just been helping me rig a pulley system so we can get water up here quickly. With any luck we will save some of the house."

"I'll check the other rooms to the left," Thomas answered.

"Quick check, Thomas, I don't want you taking unnecessary risks. Everybody known is accounted for; Tomkins has done well on that score."

Time and fire get on well together, like two sides of the same square or lines on a single graph; as time goes on so fire grows bolder. But man can take time and turn it against fire and that is exactly what they did at Great Little, under the leadership of Colonel James Hanson. Big Jim, under his direction, had climbed from the top floor into the attic and smashed the ceiling so that a large rope could hang from a main roof beam all the way to the ground. Hanson seemed everywhere; one minute in the attic, the next at ground level, directing Tomkins in setting up the pulley.

"They used something similar at Shaftesbury Jail," he said, knowing exactly who had started that fire.

He had all the servants who had their wits about them tie short ropes to the main rope that hung from the beam on a makeshift pulley made from several saucepans with their wooden handles torn off. To each baby rope was hung a pail. Then they formed a human chain of more pails from the kitchen well to the entrance hall, where the main staircase made a vault to the top floor and the pulley system hung.

It worked. By pulling on the main rope, it turned in a giant loop and the buckets moved around that loop; full buckets rose on one side and empty dropped on the other. Three people; Thomas, Matthew and Henry, were stationed at the top; one to detach each bucket, a second to throw the water on the flames and a third to hook the empty bucket back into the system. At peak rate, they could dump a bucketful of water every four seconds.

At first, Thomas did the discharging of water. He aimed for the base of the flames on the landing, stilling inches of space at a time with a fierce hissing of quenched flames. Where once flames had quivered and danced, they were replaced with black and red smouldering embers. The fire was retreating.

Matthew took over on the buckets, to give Thomas a rest. It was Matthew who took on the fire in Penelope's bedroom; it had clearly spread there from the rooms to the right, where the burning was fiercest. Matthew felt like an early Christian spreading the faith through heathen territory. In his imagination, a minute was a year of endeavour, and he battled

213

over half a generation to clear Penelope's bedroom of non-believers.

Then Henry took the fight to the sitting room between the two bedrooms. Soon, it was Thomas' turn again, this time at the centre of the fire in Wiltshire's room.

"If we can bring this room under control, I believe we have it beaten," Hanson said as Thomas took up the water-throwing again.

There came a time when all activity was over. November rain added a force against the flames and a little afterwards there were no more jets of orange and red. People stumbled over the ruins; masters and servants alike, all in a daze after the intense activity of the last few hours. Daylight gave a new vista; a roofless house standing like a shipwreck on the rocks. Steam rose from beams and scorched window frames, hollow like sightless eyes.

Hanson never tired, it seemed. When the pulley had done its work, he and Tomkins toured the survivors, listing names and checking for injury. There were four bodies lying under two rugs taken from the drawing room.

"We have the Duke and whoever he was sleeping with."

"My niece," said Tomkins, distraught. "She only started working here a few days ago. I got her the position when I came back. What will I say to her parents?"

"I will help you," Lady Roakes replied, forgetting her own loss for a moment. Thomas turned to see the owner, Lady Roakes, for the first time. She was dreadfully familiar but he could not place her. She looked at him with gratitude for what he had done but no other recognition; perhaps it was the type of face he had seen before, and not the particular one. "Who are the others?" Lady Roakes asked. Again the voice struck something with Thomas but he could not recall it precisely.

Two other servants had lost their lives. One had been helping Tomkins rescue Lady Roakes when the roof had collapsed on him. The other had been rummaging through Wiltshire's bedroom, presumably looking for valuables.

The collection of burns amongst everyone was varied, as to

214

both location and intensity. Three servants, including Tomkins, had serious burns to legs and arms. Matthew had a nasty burn where a beam had fallen on his neck, knocking him over so the flames could feed on his feet while he lay helplessly stuck. Henry had rescued him, looking to take his turn at the pails.

Thomas had a dozen minor burns, similar to Henry. Neither would suffer badly but their skin stung against the cool air outside. Hanson, however, was almost untouched.

"I believe I never stayed still long enough for any flames to take hold," he joked but did not smile.

Surprisingly, neither Penelope nor Sally were badly hurt; a few nasty burns on fingers and feet, a corresponding number of bruises from their escape. They were clothed in curtains torn from the windows of Sir Beatrice's study and wrapped around their naked bodies, for Penelope's skimpy nightgown had given up in the struggle. The curtains were secured around waist and neck by curtain cords and rope from the pulley. They moved together, as if needing to be constantly assured of the survival of the other. But they moved often amongst the wounded, pouring cold water on burns and tearing sheets into rough bandages.

Thomas stopped a moment and watched them. Sally took the lead on every decision, every movement. She directed and the Duchess rushed to do her bidding. Then, task complete, she looked back into the face of her maid for further direction.

If it was not for the colour of Sally's skin, it would appear that Sally was the Duchess and Penelope her maid.

Fire and danger, he concluded, were great levellers.

Mr and Mrs Harris came from the Home Farm, along with a cohort of workers; more came from Winterbourne Stickland, from where the flames had been plainly visible. They brought more pails but these remained on the carts for they were no longer needed. But they also brought food and beer, gin and blankets. It looked, by noon, like a large family picnic, with groups of five or six scattered across the grounds.

Mrs Harris took in the scene with Sally and Penelope at once. She tried to persuade them to come away so they could wash and change at her house. But Sally would not leave the burn victims and Penelope would not leave Sally. So, Mrs Harris went off in her cart and returned an hour later with clean, plain clothes donated by her maid at the farmhouse.

"I'm far too large for any of my clothes to fit but I think Sarah's might do," she said. "Now, go to the drawing room and get changed." Fire, again, seen as the great leveller as Penelope, Duchess of Wiltshire, picked up a bundle of brown and black coarse clothing and followed her maid to the drawing room. At the main entrance, the ground floor being largely intact structurally although a mess decoratively, the Duchess paused. But she did not look back for reassurance as to entering the building again. Instead, she looked to Sally, who understood her need and gave her hand to lead Penelope over to the drawing room.

One thing amongst all this disaster gave Alice Roakes a little kernel of hope as she surveyed her ruined house. The painting of the Little family at feast was completely untouched, other than a brown tinge to the white table cloths, and Lady Little's wimple had a round scorch mark through it. The staircase that rose beside it was severely damaged; steps gave way as the adventurous tried to climb it, but the painting looked almost as new as the day it was complete.

As Great Little had burnt around them, the Littles had carried on with their feasting; eating and drinking as if merriment would never end. Lady Roakes looked at the picture intently for several minutes, wondering what happenings there had been in that extraordinary house while the painted figures had made repast.

"I'll rebuild the house to make it bigger and better than ever before," she told the Littles, who did not move but the raised cups dotted around the picture may have been in acknowledgement of her commitment. "And I'll make it a fit memorial for my wonderful husband, who would have been so happy here. I will live for him."

"What did you say, Alice?" For a moment she thought the picture was talking to her. But the direction was wrong. She turned to see Penelope behind her, dressed in a drab brown dress, with black stockings and short, stubby working boots. The brown dress had a high neckline for modesty and a pretence of elegance with a minimal white lace collar.

"I said I am going to rebuild this house so that it is bigger and better than ever, if it's the last thing I do. But I see we need first to visit a good dressmaker."

"That would be a fine idea, Alice, in fact both ideas are in order." Penelope smiled at her little joke; then realised that Sally was not with her. She turned to look for her, then shrugged. She would be about somewhere and surely the death of Lady Roakes' husband meant the danger was gone away now?

Chapter 30

Things returned to how they had been, which meant rumours abounded and new stories came every day about Orange's advance across the West Country. He seemed in no great hurry; perhaps predicting that the longer he remained outside London, the greater his strength would accumulate and the more likely his uncle and father-in-law, the King, would panic.

It seemed a completely different progress to the constant and insecure wanderings of Monmouth three years earlier.

Penelope did not go to the dressmaker with Alice. She was summoned back to Wiltshire House by the new Duke; an elderly second cousin of her dead husband, who sent a messenger with orders not to return without her. She and Sally left a week after the fire. They had turned ground floor rooms into bedrooms and camped out in the Great Hall by day. It had been fun to do things differently and Penelope, not wanting to leave at all, was not in good humour as the carriage rolled into Wiltshire House.

"This is all mine now," the new Duke declared, his eyes roving and cataloguing his new possessions. "I never expected it to come to me but there it is."

"You are welcome to it, Your Grace." It was the first time she had used this expression to a man. It felt strange, like a separation of the ways, like a goodbye and good riddance.

For the new Duke, come suddenly into his good fortune, took Penelope's word for it and made no provision for her.

"You have your own money, I assume."

"It is customary…"

"I find customs so tiresome," he interrupted. "Of course, you must stay as long as you need to make your other arrangements."

But Penelope was roused by this cut-off. She would happily have walked away and thrown herself back on her parents' generosity but for the Duke's avarice.

"As I was saying, sir, it is customary to provide for the

218

Dowager Duchess. I think there is the matter of a country estate and a London home, a clutch of servants at each establishment and an annual income that will not see me a beggar, thus maintaining the dignity of the Wiltshire name."

They settled on no real estate, no ongoing servants, or bills paid for stockings or candles. Instead, she left Wiltshire House for the last time with three trunks of clothes, a small amount of pretty jewellery, the carriage and horses they rode in, and ten thousand pounds in silver and gold.

She had another possession she had negotiated for but hesitated to share this with Sally just then. It was something the new Duke threw on the table in despair at Penelope's persistence.

"Is this worth nothing to you, then, cousin dear?"

Penelope opened the document to find a deed of ownership for one negro who went by the name of Sally Black. It had been signed over on Penelope's marriage date from her father to her husband.

Sally and her mother had always declared her to be a free woman but all along she had been a slave.

And now she belonged to Penelope.

Alone in the carriage with Sally, she folded the paper and put it away. Then she swapped to the same seat as Sally and snuggled down into her.

She was in the enormously privileged position of owning the thing she cared for most in all the world.

What else could a girl want?

Henry Sherborne had to go through the ignominy of arrest; a warrant had been issued by the magistrate in Dorchester and could not be reversed. He was held in the foyer of the court for ten minutes by Hanson, chatting easily to his friend until called to stand before the judge.

Thomas and Matthew could not be witnesses for they were fugitives themselves, although nobody in the whole of Dorset was still looking for them. Instead, Hanson, the arresting officer, rode along the roads Henry had travelled with the Davenport brothers when they had searched for Sir Beatrice.

He collected together eight men and two women who swore to the Earl's being to the west of Dorchester nearly the entire time.

"So, My Lord, there is no possible way the suspect could be causing trouble at Great Little when he was at least twenty miles away during this time. Indeed, I took him to Great Little and he has sworn to you that was the first time he had come to that place. Moreover, the single word of an injured maid saying 'Sherborne' can be explained." Hanson went on to relate how Henry, at the age of nineteen, had been wounded when fighting against Monmouth. "He has a wound on his face that ended the engagement he had with a young lady, who happens to be the employer of this maid. The maid's injuries are remarkably similar to the Earl's in that both have led to a disfigurement of the right cheek. It is clear to me, My Lord, that the injured girl was concerned the Dowager Duchess of Wiltshire would despatch her as she despatched Sherborne three years prior." This was met with amused chuckles around the courtroom. The judge had the sense to let it die down before speaking.

"Colonel, you make a good case and I am persuaded by the thoroughness of your investigation and by your conviction. Case dismissed. However, you are to continue the search for the murderer, Colonel, and submit your expenses to me."

"Thank you, My Lord."

There was one person in the crowded courtroom who was displeased with this ruling. Parchman, dressed as a parson for a disguise, shuffled out of his bench seat, making sure he knocked into Henry on his way out.

"Have a care, sir."

He kept on walking, disgusted with the verdict, for now there was a chance he would be discovered during the ongoing investigation.

But wait, he thought; surely the unfortunate death of Wiltshire meant he was in the clear. And he could, in all likelihood, reclaim his position at court now for it was Wiltshire who had taken him away for his own underhand purposes.

Provided this upstart Orange did not get his way. Perhaps there was something he could do about that.

Thomas and Matthew, technically fugitives but with no will

behind the status, left Great Little a few days after Penelope and rode the eight miles north to their home in Sturminster Newton. Professionally, Matthew felt like an extra place set at a dinner, upsetting the smooth symmetry of the supper table. His contacts had died with Sir Beatrice and he had nothing to do; no way to build up the support the Prince of Orange was counting on in Dorset.

"I could go to him. I know the way well."

"And be caught and thrown back in prison?" Thomas replied, for the blind eye turned towards them would be opened again as soon as he became active. "Leave it a few days and then see how you feel." What he meant was to see how matters develop for Lord Churchill had already gone over to Orange and the whole country, especially the west, seemed on a knife-edge. "Besides," Thomas decided to play his ace, "I intend soon to go to Bagber and hoped you might accompany me there."

They went that afternoon to inspect the building works at Fodrington Field. It was late November and the sun was masked by heavy clouds; every hour or so the sky sent down a shower of sharp rain that blew this way and that in the wind, knocking the leaves from the trees and sending slabs of sodden browns and yellows skidding before them. The church looked forlorn; a little like Great Little, with no roof to keep the rain out.

The difference was that Great Little was already recovering. Lady Roakes had cleared much of the rubble and was asking Mr Milligan's firm to quote to rebuild.

"There is no other firm in contention," she had told Thomas the morning he left her home. "You have earned the distinction to rebuild my house through your bravery and kindness." Every time they had talked over the past week, he felt that he knew her but she did not know him. She was innocent of knowledge while he was guilty; doubly guilty, for she was a fine-looking lady and he just could not place her. The voice; that was the key thing. It was gentler now than it had been before but where was that, and who was she?

"The profits from Great Little should enable us to finish your church, Thomas," Mr Milligan had said on his trip to Great Little to survey and start plans. "Lady Roakes has already made over to us a thousand pounds. She wants an extra floor, with more bedrooms for guests. She says it is to be a happy house, full of laughter."

"She is a good woman," Thomas replied. But something was there, like a nail in a shoe. Whenever he had known this woman before, she had been harsher than now; stressed, perhaps? Yes, incredibly stressed.

He shrugged; mysteries had a way of solving themselves. In the meantime, he had to plan remedial work on his church. Could they get the roof on over winter? Or should they use great tarpaulins to safeguard the bricks until spring? He wanted the former but suspected the latter would be safer.

Matthew did not sleep that night; in his half-dreams he kept proposing to Eliza Merriman. She was older than him by six years but what did that matter? She was so much more accomplished than him, so connected to the world and not at odds to it.

That did matter. In one scenario around three in the morning, he was turned down in his proposal of marriage. She suddenly grew much larger than him; as if standing in the world dictated physical size. She looked down at him; her head as big as the whole of Matthew. She laughed; no, that was not fair and gave the falsehood to his imaginings; she would never laugh at him.

He tried then to re-run the scene, amending her behaviour as patently ridiculous. But it would not go right; things became twisted and distorted as the night-time daydream moved towards nightmare. Finally, he shook himself awake, rose from his bed, knelt in prayer for thirty minutes. The cold in his bedroom braced him, finally defeating him so he stopped praying and got dressed.

He went to their father's old study; swept the cobwebs and dust from his desk and sat down. Luke Davenport, their father, had been a man of action. Yes, in latter days he was a country town preacher with a reputation as a firebrand, but in the first half of his life he had been an adventurer. He had switched sides in the Civil War; first for the King but changing to parliament as their cause became understood; it was liberty over oppression, just as today. The Stuarts had much to answer for in many ways. Charles II, the King he had grown up with, had been different; a manipulator of every situation in order to survive, but done in a jovial way. He had been cynically sincere in a strange way; driven by pleasure but fundamentally right in his approach to the country. His father before him and his brother after him – the current King – had been plain wrong, undermining the ancient rights of the English people. He was right in standing up against King James, even if he was more involved in subterfuge and planning than fighting in the open.

But his father had been a man of action and Matthew seemed to himself no more than a pale reflection of his father.

Father had more about him in his little finger than I have in my whole body.

What would his father have done about Eliza Merriman? She was so beautiful, so alluring.

He drifted off to sleep in his father's study. Thomas found him early the next morning; head on the desk, like a drunk man sleeping; like the drunk their father had become before reforming towards the end of his life.

There are many quarters in a man's life so perhaps dividing them continually is not a good idea.

Lady Merriman spent an extra half-hour getting dressed that morning. She told Kitty, her maid that it was because she was ageing and needed the extra time to cover the blemishes. But Kitty knew better.

"Who's coming today, milady?"

"Just the Davenport boys, I believe." When you demote someone in a sentence by putting 'just' in front of their name, it stands to reason, to the test of time, that you think highly of that person.

As was the case with Matthew Davenport. Lady Merriman could not get him out of her mind. Would he ask her today? Did he ever intend asking her?

He was so shy; his shyness made a blessing and a curse;

adorable but intensely frustrating.

"Is that right, now, milady?" Kitty had brushed Lady Merriman's hair until it shone, then put it up in a great big bundle of top of her head. It showed her neck to perfection.

"Thank you, Kitty, you have done fine work today."

"We've been together a long time," Kitty replied absent-mindedly.

"Don't say that. It makes me seem old!" But Lady Merriman was laughing.

Matthew and Thomas set off late in the morning, intending to walk the few miles to Bagber Manor. They walked down the hill and over the bridge Thomas had helped to build as his introduction to the trade. His head was full of plans for Great Little that morning. Matthew listened patiently, hoping for a pause so he could ask his brother, younger by a dozen years, for his advice.

Should I ask her to marry me today? He had to be content with rehearsals in his mind for Thomas would not stop talking about his plans.

They reached the mill, now run by old Mr Hunt's son. He was unmarried, far brusquer than his parents, and did not bake cakes so they did not stop.

But then they did stop, for galloping along the road from Stallbridge was Big Jim on a horse so big he must have needed a mechanical device to get onto its back.

"I thought I saw you from the other road," he gasped, more out of breath than his horse. "I have news. Orange is at Sherborne, visiting with the earl. His army is encamped on Sherborne's estate, not twelve miles from where we now stand."

There was nothing for it but to go to Sherborne.

Lady Merriman would have to wait until another time.

Chapter 31

"Will you take the news to Bagber and pass on our excuses?" Thomas asked.

"I will divert that way now then go on to Sturminster Newton." Big Jim was all helpfulness. "I did wrong, Thomas, in putting my religion before anything else because it led me to support a constitution that is rotten to the core."

"You put it before friendship, Jim."

"I know, then I saw what wrong I had done and tried to atone."

Thomas knew that Big Jim was right in his wrongness; paths of right and wrong seemed to him to cross and re-cross countless times, causing a web of confusing ways for man to walk down.

I say unto you, that likewise joy shall be in heaven over one sinner that repenteth, more than over ninety and nine just persons, which need no repentance.

"You certainly did right at the end," Thomas said, thinking of the prison break. And not much more needed to be said for friendship shines through the darkest nights and some of the loneliest roads have friends posted along the way.

If only we knew at the time.

They made Sherborne estate before dark, after doubling back to Sturminster Newton for two horses. A sheet of rain followed them down, making the road slippery and reducing vision to fifty yards at times. It felt like running uphill but they made progress steadily.

Then they were stopped by a group of soldiers. They were clearly foreign, with little ability to talk in English. Matthew spoke Dutch and they became animated, hearing their native tongue so far from home.

"What are they saying?" Thomas asked.

"So far, just that my accent is almost perfect."

"I did not know that you were so able, Matthew." To which Matthew commented that he found languages quite easy and had picked up French and German over the last three years, plus a little Spanish.

"So, what do they want?"

"They are a picket post for Orange's army. They want to know what our business is and where we want to go. I suppose it is normal security. They see that we are unarmed and I have told them a little of my work in Holland."

"Will they let us through?"

"Yes, but they are sending a runner to their headquarters first, just to be sure. In the meantime, they are asking us to dismount and say we can shelter in the trees."

They dismounted, led their horses under the trees, and picketed them by tying the reins onto a fallen tree that also made a seat for them. The runner, a boy of about fifteen, quickly disappeared into the gloom. Presently, the sergeant came over to them, pleased to find a Dutch speaker. He brought with him a bottle of jenever and offered it to the two brothers. Matthew translated between Thomas and the sergeant.

"It's a strong drink, Thomas, be careful." Thomas took a tentative mouthful, rather liking the malty taste.

"It's not bad at all," he said. "What's the flavouring?"

"Junipers, mostly."

"But it's not gin? It has a completely different taste."

The sergeant smiled as Thomas took a second mouthful. "You like?" he said in his halting English.

"Yes," he replied. "I like."

The sergeant left the bottle and went about his duties. Thomas and Matthew watched him efficiently dispatch soldiers; always at least two at a time, in different directions. They patrolled in such a way that someone trying to sneak in could see no pattern to their movements.

"No wonder the Dutch are so powerful," Thomas commented. "They certainly know their business. Nobody is going to get along this road unless they allow it."

Their wait was long; several hours. To pass the time, Thomas started asking Matthew about his work in Amsterdam.

"A lot of planning," he replied, taking the tiniest sip of jenever before passing the bottle to Thomas.

"What sort of planning?"

"Endless invasion scenarios, and then reviewing reports about the state of this country, summarising them, breaking them down, discussing them in committees and then seeking more information. Every question answered seems to bring two new questions at least."

"So, the work kept expanding? A perfect situation for the wage-earner. How many Englishmen were there out there?"

"It varied. I was part of an influx after Monmouth. We must have been sixty or seventy in total at some times. We were led by a very difficult man called Robert Candles. I disliked him intensely."

"An unlikely name, I would say," Thomas replied, suddenly a bit more thoughtful as he considered the complex world of subterfuge that his brother had plodded away in.

"Earlier this year, I was taken from his team and put directly under a senior Dutch man called Jacobus Avercamp. He was much more a gentleman, although probably even more determined and thorough than Candles. It was Herr Avercamp who sent me back here the second time."

"No doubt Mr Candles was displeased at this diminishment of his power?"

"Yes, I am in no doubt that I have an enemy there, Thomas, should I ever come across him again. I hope very much that I never do."

Prophetic words, perhaps, for Robert Candles was, at that very moment, enjoying a bath at Sherborne Hall, less than a mile from the log that Matthew and Thomas sat upon, waiting for permission to proceed.

"There's a messenger, sir, saying a Matthew Davenport and his brother, Thomas, have approached the picket line north of us."

"Matthew Davenport, you say? How interesting. Keep this news to yourself, Simms. Do you hear?"

"Yes, sir."

"Send the messenger back with an instruction to arrest them both and bring them to me; only to me. Make sure they are well tied up, do you hear?"

"Yes, sir."

"And if they are a little, shall we say, inconvenienced in the process, I shall most definitely not hold it against you, Simms."

"I understand, sir." Simms left the room with a short, business-like bow. Robert Candles, his superior, claimed to be an Englishman from some northern part, but when he became excited Simms heard distinct Scottish tones to his voice. Simms, like most who worked for him, disliked the man but he was powerful, especially since the excellent work he had done tracking key establishment figures in London. It was Candles who had discovered Wiltshire's duplicity; Wiltshire had pretended to be pro-Orange, while secretly undermining the cause and leaking information back to the Westminster authorities. It was as well that Wiltshire was no more following a fire somewhere in Dorset, for he would have met a short and painful end once Orange was King.

It was Candles, too, who had tracked this man called Parchman, becoming fascinated by him in the process. Candles had reported that Parchman was responsible for the death of Sir Beatrice Roakes; a recent and powerful convert to the Orange cause. Had not Sir Beatrice been the main link with Davenport's efforts to rouse Dorset? And now, here was Davenport, come to the Orange encampment and being arrested for his trouble.

Simms shrugged his heavy shoulders and thanked the Lord that he was only a middle person. He could not cope with the decisions at the top but, equally, would not want to be at the bottom doing the dirty work.

The middle was fine for him; instructing others to arrest the Davenports rather than doing it himself; following orders from above without having to worry as to their consequences. At the end of all this, when Orange was King, he would get a pleasant manor somewhere as recompense and would be highly satisfied with his lot. Perhaps he would even find a cheery wife.

Not much longer now.

Every time Matthew took a sip of jenever, Thomas took a mouthful, relishing the unusual taste as it swilled around his mouth, becoming light-headed by degrees as the afternoon turned to evening and the lit world shrank around them.

"How much longer do we have to wait?" Matthew asked the Dutch sergeant. "He says not long now," he reported back to Thomas.

It was not long but was not as expected. There were hushed words between the soldiers, just beyond their limited range of vision. Matthew listened keenly but could not make out the words. Then a group of soldiers moved towards them. Thomas thought it mildly unusual that there should be so many, presumably to provide safe passage to Sherborne Hall.

Thirty seconds later, the handcuffs clicked on Matthew's wrists. Thomas saw his brother's face go white, then he rolled back off the tree trunk, tried to complete a neat somersault to take him to his feet but fell instead, down a long slope. He scrambled to his feet at the bottom, ran blindly into the dark night and hit his head on a low-level branch after fifty yards. He went down and the dark became darker; much darker still.

He woke to broad daylight; the rain had petered out during the night, replaced with a sunny stillness that filtered through the bare branches. He was lying on the ground and, as the trees above came into focus, he noticed flocks of birds moving south in a pale blue sky. Everything was at peace, except his head ached between the eyes. He raised his hand to it and felt crusty, dried blood; traced a segment that ran down his cheek to the corner of his mouth. What had happened? Another battle?

He stood up suddenly, just missing the branch that had taken him down the night before.

Matthew! They had taken Matthew last night; arresting him with a click of the handcuffs. He saw Matthew's horror-stricken face before him and everything turned dark like the night before.

But now was not the time for running away. Matthew was in trouble. And Thomas had to do something about it.

Chapter 32

William, Prince of Orange, was pleased with his progress. It was a progress measured not in miles but in support. If it had been a race to London, with the finish line the Palace at Whitehall or the coronation chair at Westminster Abbey, he would have lost badly. But he was in no hurry. Every day for almost four weeks now, he had received a boost from some worthy nobleman or official coming over to his cause. The most significant had been Lord Churchill; undoubtedly the finest general in England, and perhaps even across the continent. He had planned his route, or rather others had planned it for him, in order to pick up such support along the way.

He disliked Robert Candles intensely, often asking Avercamp if he was necessary but clearly he was, for their apparent meanderings across south-west England had been his design.

"Sire, if we can pull in the Earl of Sherborne, I believe the whole south-west will be secure."

"You have not mentioned him before, Mr Candles. What is it with him now?"

"Much has changed, Sire, with recent developments. Wiltshire is, as you know, dead; killed in a fire at some remote Dorset house. Some other woman was in his bed…"

"I don't want to hear of adultery, Candles."

"Pray suffer me for it has significance, Sire. The magistrate in Dorset believes the fire to be deliberate. Wiltshire's body was burned horribly. If he was murdered and his own wife was not in his bed, Sire, his wife has to be a suspect."

"What sort of woman would burn her own husband?"

"I don't mean she would carry the torch herself, Sire, more that she would pay some devil to do the nasty work for her."

"And why does this matter to us and our cause?"

There were two reasons why it mattered but Robert Candles concentrated on the one. Wiltshire had been a powerhouse in the eastern half of the West Country, extending influence and control from his seat north of Salisbury into Dorset and parts of

Somerset, and even Hampshire. His successor, his second cousin, had nothing to recommend him.

"With him gone there is a huge power vacuum in these parts."

"And you think Sherborne is the best replacement?"

"He is the only one, Sire, but he will be nothing like as powerful as Wiltshire had been."

"Sherborne is questionable, Candles. He is a Catholic."

"He comes from a long line of ardent Catholics, certainly. And he has met with agents of your uncle, King James. But I sense something else in the man. His Catholicism is not so strong as previous earls and, of course, there is his wife."

"His wife, the Countess?"

"Grace Sherborne, née Davenport. She is the daughter of Luke Davenport, the Presbyterian preacher." Candles had known Luke Davenport well, had been envious of his success. "And the sister of Matthew Davenport."

"Who you currently have in custody, here in the tower?"

"Yes, Sire, exactly. But, we should test out Sherborne first, see what he is made of."

"I take it you have an idea for that as well?"

"Certainly, Sire. I will tell you about it if you like."

"I have a meeting now but come back to me at two o'clock."

The second reason, Robert Candles kept to himself, as it negated the first. Dorset was already secure; it mattered not whether Sherborne was for their cause or against it. But Candles was sure the Earl would fail at the task he would later plant in Orange's mind. Then, he would be free to deal with the detestable Matthew Davenport who, like his father before him, had ever usurped him.

He did a few dance steps on tiptoes as he went along the passageway; dancing to an old Scottish tune from his childhood.

He was well on the way to killing two birds with one stone. It had been a Davenport brat who had struck him down at Sedgemoor. He was convinced Monmouth would have won the battle if he, Robert Fergusson, had been able to fight longer with his new-found love of war.

231

He ached to throw off the name he had taken on arriving in Holland three years ago; he had looked around wildly for inspiration as Avercamp and his lackeys had demanded his name.

"Robert... Candles," he had said, his eyes focusing on the candles that lit the room.

His other grudge was against the earldom of Sherborne for they had led the charge against him at Sedgemoor and done so well from the victory while he had been forced to flee for his life to Holland.

Thomas could hear his best friend talking from the hiding place he had selected. Henry was uncharacteristically hesitant in his address to the Prince of Orange.

"You went against me, Sherborne."

"Yes, Sire, but I saw the error of my ways. I am a convert to liberty and they say converts are the most ardent of all believers."

Thomas, no more than eight feet from the talkers, could hear the tremors in Henry's voice. He remembered a famous passage from one of his father's published sermons.

Give me ten converts and I will return ten thousand back to you. Give me twenty such converts and I shall return twenty thousand back to you.

They had, as children, mimicked their father with a silly chant:

Give me ten hundred thousand million converts and I will return...

He could only think of two converts other than his sister, Grace, who he was convinced did it for her love of Henry. Plain Jane had converted to Catholicism on marrying Big Jim, yet she was not as ardent as Jim had been. Then there was Amelia. She had converted to Lizzie's form of Presbyterianism, yet she knew her own mind better than anybody he knew. He drifted off, thinking of Amelia. Then realised that someone was moving towards the heavy curtains he hid behind.

It had been the only place he could find; the window seat behind the east curtain in the Great Hall. The servants had pulled the heavy velvet curtains as dusk had fallen that afternoon. He doubted they would be pulled back before morning. That gave him twelve or fourteen hours to come up with a plan.

He had carefully worked his way through the deer park all day, arriving at Sherborne Hall in the late afternoon. Getting into the house had been easy. He had simply put on a butcher's apron found hanging on a washing line and walked in through the kitchen door. Once inside, he changed disguises, discarding the apron and picking up some books and papers he found in the butler's pantry. He was no longer the butcher's assistant but a minor official amongst the hundreds hurrying here and there across the house. He hurried as they hurried, giving good effect to his disguise.

He remembered Henry talking about his solitary games behind the heavy curtains of the Great Hall and went there automatically, slipping behind them when no one was looking.

His mind tried to work on a plan as he sat on the deep window seat, hunger rumbling in his stomach. The jenever and the blow to his head both contributed to aches in the forehead and around the temples. He had drunk deeply at a stream in the deer park but now wanted nothing more than a hot meal and a bed.

He had imagined having until morning to work out a plan but now he heard the heavy steps of inevitability walking towards the curtains he sat by, knees bent to put his legs upon the stage.

The man was talking. It was Henry. Relief washed over him; followed immediately by concern that he might give Thomas away through sheer surprise.

How often do you draw back curtains to examine the weather outside and find your best friend crouched behind them? Could he warn Henry to stifle his cry? How much presence of mind did Henry have? He was stressed, judging by his voice; both on edge and distracted, that much was clear.

It was hard for Thomas to concentrate on how Henry would react, for fatigue and hunger had worn at Thomas, breaking into his thought patterns and disturbing him with constant visions of stew and clean sheets. This was why no plan had come to him; why he was now about to be caught.

He heard the click of the handcuffs; louder and harsher indoors compared to under the trees with the rain falling. Or was it a triumphalism that echoed across the Great Hall stating, "We've got both the Davenport boys now"?

The curtains moved as Henry was talking urgently, repeating mantras over again but Thomas only heard the sharp metal of chains and clicks as muskets cocked.

He looked up at his friend's face, urging him to be silent.

It was as Thomas had supposed in one regard but not in another. Henry was stressed. In fact, he was fighting for his future, for his earldom, for his wife and mother. Cartwright had made it clear that all would be revealed about his illegitimacy if Henry did not do exactly as told. And Henry had broken that obedience almost immediately. And now he was tainted on both sides: as a disobedient bastard son with no inheritance rights on the loyalist side and as an unbelievable and suspect Catholic nobleman on the other. There seemed little chance that he would still be in Sherborne Hall next year; next month, even.

But Thomas had supposed these problems would damage Henry's presence of mind. And this did not happen. He opened the curtains halfway, saw Thomas, gave a half-muted squeal of surprise; the type that is swallowed back into the mouth that gave force to it before it escapes around the room.

"What was that, Sherborne?"

"Nothing, Sire, just that the rain has started again, even heavier than before." He knew why Thomas was there; had heard from Simms that Candles had arrested a Mr Davenport and Simms knew not why. Except Simms did know how to play both sides exceedingly well. If Orange failed, perhaps the Earl would be kind to him.

Either Thomas had been arrested and had escaped or, more likely, for he had not heard of an escape, Matthew had been arrested and Thomas was come about rescuing him.

"I'll close the curtains again, Sire, for it is becoming a nasty night outside." A little wink gave Thomas a thousand reassurances that he was in good hands; the presence of mind was still present.

Then Henry took the fight to the enemy; except nobody really knew who the enemy was anymore.

"Sire, on another matter, we fight for liberty, do we not?"

"I stand for liberty. I know not what motivates you." The tone of voice seemed to Thomas slightly wrong; a touch too imperious. Henry had a way in because of it.

"Sire, the English have a deep-rooted love of liberty that will not be masked, nor caged. My family came with the Normans 600 years ago. We have married in to the Anglo-Saxon culture a hundred times over."

"Your point, man?"

"My point, Sire, is that we together represent a stand for liberty."

"I am in full agreement... so far."

"Yet in this house; my house, that has represented freedom for six centuries, we have a man held captive on as yet unsubstantiated charges; in fact, the charges have not yet been laid before him yet he has been detained for over twenty-four hours."

"What do you know of this man? How come you know of him?"

"Sire, this is my house. More fool me if I did not know everything that goes on in my own house. What respect would you have for me then? How then could you consider me for great office, were I to remain ignorant of events under my own roof? I know his name is Matthew Davenport and that he is held in the North Tower and that Mr Candles has detailed two guards outside the door day and night. I know that he has received neither food nor water since his incarceration in the North Tower on the top floor." This last bit was invention; Simms had reported only once to Sherborne and that had been a few hurried words. Sherborne had ordered Simms to ensure the prisoner was taken care of and Simms had shrugged, as if to say it was out of his hands. "Moreover, I know something else of this Davenport character. I know that he has done your cause considerable service in Holland, working tirelessly to plan and execute your... accepting the crown of England when it is offered to you by Parliament."

"How do you know such things?"

"I admit I was tempted by the other side, Sire; tempted by promise of further rank and privilege. But I have come down firmly on the side of liberty. I heard these things when working for King James and bring them now to your attention."

"This Davenport man, I am told he is a traitor."

But Henry had moved beyond his spirited but doomed defence of Matthew Davenport. He seemed to go back to his general plea.

"Sire, please know that I am behind you. I keep my sword and a brace of pistols in my bedroom to fight for you when and if it is required of me."

"If you are so much behind me, sir, I have in mind a task for you. If you will undertake it faithfully, it will persuade me of your loyalty. Does this sound like a reasonable proposition?"

"Yes, Sire, I am all ears."

"Well, Sherborne, we need to eat and rest, unless we are to wear ourselves out with hunger and fatigue. I will tell you as we walk towards our supper." The voices continued in discussion as they left the room, fading gently. Thomas could not hear of Orange's plan for his friend.

But, thanks to Henry, Thomas now had his own plan. It was to be an armed assault for nothing else would work. Thomas was advised as to where to find the weapons he needed and it had been suggested also to consider food and drink for Matthew, as it may have been denied him in his prison tower.

"I've been sent to bring bread and water for the prisoner and a delicious stew and some beer for his guards, courtesy of the management of this fine inn." Both guards, bored of their task and even more bored of each other's company, looked down at the sumptuous smelling stew. They looked up to see two handguns pointing at their chests. "It's a great pity you will not be eating the stew. Still, I expect the bread will be sufficient for your needs."

The beauty of depositing the guards in the room they have just unlocked to allow the prisoner out is that, whatever racket they put up to gain attention, everyone hearing it will assume the prisoner is the cause. They might swear and curse at their disturbed sleep but they will not get out of bed in the cold night and seek to end the ranting.

With the door locked behind them, Matthew and Thomas sat on the top step of the tower staircase and ate the rich stew and drank the beer.

"I knew you would come," Matthew said. "I just thought it might have been quicker than it was." For which comment, Thomas gave him a thump that almost pushed him off the steps. "Take a care, Thomas, why rescue me just to throw me down the stairs?"

In fact, as Matthew admitted later, his soul had been crushed when he had felt the handcuffs grip his wrists. He had not tried to pray or to think; had just wallowed in the depths, slowly sinking, like being pulled into a marsh.

"You came when the water was up to my chin and threatening to enter through my mouth. A little later and I would be food for the fishes or frogs, or whatever it is that make the wastelands their home. Thank you, brother."

"That's what brothers are for, brother."

Chapter 33

Lady Merriman sat before the mirror in her bedroom, quite alone. Except for her reflection.

"What am I to say?" she asked her reflection. "How do I organise my emotions when there are so many of them?" The face in the mirror stared back at her, twitching as she twitched; arching her neck as she arched hers. It was like the copy game that children played; an irritating child would mimic the exact movements of another to drive them to distraction.

She opened a drawer in her elaborate dressing table, drew out a small notebook with a silver cover and 'E.M.' engraved on it. Her mother had been Eliza, too. It came with a tiny pencil, which she remembered her mother using to jot notes and reminders. She turned to a clean page then glanced up to see that her double in the mirror had also gone to a drawer to extract a silver notebook.

She wrote on the new page under a heading of 'Concerns and Worries':

1. For the safety and security of my dear son, Henry.
2. For Elizabeth's husband that he might continue to recover.
3. For Grace, that she will support her husband, my dear son.

She stopped to reflect that she liked writing 'my dear son' so, for a moment, she turned the page and drew out the letters in several different ways: large and small; looping and plain; bold and faint; masculine and... She turned back a page and continued her list.

4. That Matthew and I may...
5. That Amelia may be happy as she deserves.
6. That Matthew and I...
7. That the country be settled with little fuss and no loss of life.
8. That Matthew may...

This time, she wrote over the name 'Matthew', adding little embellishments to the long strokes and making cute faces out of the round ones. Then she drew a picture of him at the bottom of the page; a pensive, severe face. No, not severe; he was never severe. Rather, it was contemplative. No, not that either. She asked the person in the mirror what the word was.

"Serious," came the answer back to her.

And then she threw back her head and laughed.

And the lady in the mirror did just the same. But there was no sound from the mirror so no way of detecting whether the lady in the mirror was laughing because she was scared.

For Lady Merriman most certainly was.

Lady Roakes woke each morning to the absence of Sir Beatrice. It hit her every day, a second after she opened her eyes and became aware of the world around her.

She had hated and conspired all her life until he, a crook every bit as much as she, had come into her life. They had made a lot of money very quickly but, crucially, they had been happy together; blissfully happy.

And now he was gone and she was alone.

The days were like yoyos, springing from despair to hope and back to despair again.

"But, I was good with a yoyo as a child so I will manage again."

She rode every morning, mounted on a beautiful brown stallion with two white socks. He was tall and proud and would have jumped the fences around the park and farms with ease. But Alice was aware of the baby growing inside her and would not risk its well-being in any way.

She was not riding for pleasure but for purpose. For Great Little had become her purpose and she was tireless at it.

"Mr Carter, I will repair your barns and reduce your back rent but in return I require you to clear the ditches on all the land you rent from me."

"Mr Hampton, you have suffered great misfortune with the loss of your son. I understand you had hoped to have him take over from you at Mossdown Farm one day. I would have you consider an option I have thought about these last few days. Thank you, I will take a glass of milk at your table."

Her idea was to terminate the lease on Mossdown and add it to the Home Farm. The Harrises were fine farm managers and easily able to handle more land. Lady Roakes understood that Mr Hampton, an old man now, sought security for him and his wife. She proposed that they move into a small cottage in the deer park and help with maintenance of the fences and other such work. She discussed it first with Tomkins, her steward and right-hand man in matters of the estate.

"You may have the cottage as long as you live and will earn a good wage while you can. If you save well, you should have enough to see you by in some comfort."

Alice was riding that day to check on the Hamptons in their tiny cottage. They had moved a few days prior, packing a lifetime onto a medium-sized cart lent to them by Mr Harris.

Today, as she rode through the slanted sunlight, she saw a carriage approach across the park. She went over, inquisitive as to who was visiting.

"Penelope, my dear."

"Alice, we have come to seek shelter. We are homeless and destitute, candidates for the workhouse unless you will accommodate us." Penelope spoke with false embellishment; the only way she could ask a favour.

"Come with me to Baynard's Cottage first, I need to check on some new tenants. Then you can tell me all."

Afterwards, when back at Great Little, Alice took Penelope to an old, tired summerhouse that had become her office. Sally followed at a distance, not sure whether she was included or not. Alice decided to make a point; to get to the bottom of this strange situation.

"Sally, are you still with us? Are you not to take your mistress's bags indoors while we ladies have discussions?" She played it absolutely straight, hoping for straightness back.

"Please have her stay. We can take the bags up later," Penelope said.

"Why so, Penelope? Are you to be managed by your servants now? Has the world gone completely upside-down?"

"Yes, Alice, the world is upside-down. I am a shit-shoveller's daughter, nothing more and nothing less. I don't deserve to be so happy."

The discussion in the summerhouse lasted an hour. Tomkins passed by, thought better of disturbing them, and took his sheaf of papers back to his own makeshift office.

They emerged partners in Great Little, not because Alice Roakes lacked the capital to rebuild the estate but because she lacked the companionship she so desired.

To get there had involved a confession from Penelope.

"We are lovers, Alice. It just happened. At first, Sally loathed the sight of me, much as you did, but something changed a few weeks back and we fell in love, hopelessly and absolutely."

"I could see it," Alice replied. "And for both Sally and I to change our view of you so drastically is quite a coincidence, don't you think? Yes, we may have changed, circumstances may have changed, but it is clear as a summer's day that you have changed. But how will you appear to the world at large?"

"I don't care about the world at large. The world at large can go and drown themselves for all I care."

"Vintage Penelope! But, my dear, you have to see it from Sally's point of view."

Sally had remained very quiet during this conversation but now she spoke, a tremor in her voice. Everything could so easily go backwards and she was so much in love, which meant she had so much to lose.

"Lady Roakes, I love Pen… I mean the Dowager Duchess just as much as she loves me. That is without question. I want her happiness more than I want mine. I understand that I am a servant girl. Moreover, I am black and disfigured now." Her hand went involuntarily to her cheek, rubbed the wound which itched constantly. "I want to be whatever will guarantee her the respectability and status she deserves."

"You will be her maid, then, Sally. Whenever there is risk of exposure, you are to play the right part. Do you understand? We will maintain the façade in public at all times. There should be nothing that detracts from this presentation." She turned to Penelope. "You have been far too comfortable with your lover,

241

Penelope. You must maintain your distance at all times when in public. You are a Dowager Duchess and not a shit-shoveller's daughter; remember that always. Please adopt the arrogance you had cultivated so magnificently before when I disliked you intensely. It is your security in the world. In private, we can be ourselves and I care not how you are with Sally." Behind Alice's words were the weight of the law and of public opinion. If it were generally known what they felt for each other, they would be torn apart. Sally would be taken away to work in some meaningless position of drudgery while Penelope would never surface from some ghastly sanatorium.

As her friend digested this thought, Alice suddenly thought of Arkwright.

Repent ye therefore, and be converted, that your sins may be blotted out, when the times of refreshing shall come from the presence of the Lord.

She thought of the terrible things she had done and then she thought of Mr Blake and his thoughtful words; his advice to her to keep an open heart.

To do some good in this terrible world.

Penelope was talking but Alice was not taking it in, distracted by Arkwright and Blake.

"Say that again, Penelope, please."

"I said, Alice, I will happily play the part of imperious Dowager Duchess when in public and Sally will be the dutiful servant."

"Good, it is certainly for the best. Already, there is talk, and talk is dangerous."

"But in private, when just the three of us, Sally is at least my equal in every way. I will not have her play my maid when the door is closed and the curtains drawn. We will either share the work or get others to do it for us." She turned to Sally and asked if that was not plain and fair.

"It is, Pen, it certainly is."

"All agreed then," Penelope said. She thought about the deed of ownership she had for Sally. She would deal with that another day. It was too complicated for now.

From there it was a simple step to a partnership concerning Great Little. Alice positively wanted to share the burdens and the joys and had only the one, wonderful but unusual, friend to share them with. Penelope wanted nothing more than to live with the only two in the world she cared for. They would still go to London for the season each year. But Great Little would be their home and the centre of their operations.

And from the partnership agreement it was another simple step to the blossoming of Sally Black, for as her status was clarified, albeit with the duplicity of her remaining the maid to all other sets of eyes, so her mind and soul were liberated to fly all over Great Little. While Penelope was full of ideas but lacked the resolve to see them through, Sally was all resolve and had a brilliant business mind to distil the best ideas and see them to completion.

But to all and sundry, she was the strange, quiet, black maid who had been wrenched from her family at some time in her childhood and sent to this cold, northern land where the rain fell constantly. She was the one with the nasty scar on her right cheek, sitting proud in its ugliness; becoming, at least to Penelope, beautiful in its ugliness.

For the world was turned upside-down.

Chapter 34

Henry, Earl of Sherborne, rode alone and rode hard. His mission, given to him by the Prince of Orange, was surprisingly simple.

As most doomed missions are.

"Henry, I want you to find out who killed the Duke of Wiltshire and Sir Beatrice Roakes; presumably the same killer for both."

"They thought, for a short while, that it was me, Sire."

"I want you to find the real killer. Bring him to me in chains and I will believe in you as my supporter. Fail and do not expect office when I am crowned King. Do you understand?"

"Yes, Sire."

He had then been sent by Orange for a briefing with Robert Candles, who seemed confused and at odds with himself. At one point, Candles was determined that it was an accident; the next, that it was a deep and complex plot. Wiltshire's wife, Henry's old fiancée, was to blame first, fourth and ninth. But in between it was a wide range of loyalist and counter-loyalist elements.

But he seemed to Henry a little too confused; too wild in placing blame.

"I'll find the culprit, Candles." *Or whatever your real name is.*

You won't, thought Candles, smiling with his best sycophantic grin, *for I have already led you on a merry dance.*

Besides, Candles knew exactly who was behind the murders and considered that, if Henry ever confronted Parchman, he would come off the worse by a mile.

I'm sure you were somehow behind Davenport's escape and you will pay well for that, my friend. The two guards had been put on short rations and perpetual latrine duties. He would not tolerate spikes in his plans; not again, not after last time.

But his plan would work almost as well whether Matthew Davenport was in custody or not. You needed a lot of resolve and cunning to disappear as he himself had done three years ago. Nothing about Matthew spoke of him having the necessary qualities. At the right time, he would be rounded up again with ease and his clever escapes would just add to his evident guilt; moreover, as Davenports stuck together, he would catch a handful at the same time.

"Godspeed," he said, wishing Henry a slow and troublesome journey. "Report back in three days." He knew it was the best part of a day's travel to Great Little, the scene of the crimes, from where the Earl would start his investigation.

"Three days? That is impossible, sir."

"Are the Prince's wishes to be deemed impossible, My Lord?"

"No, Candles. I will report as the Prince requires."

Hence, he was riding hard, to cover the distance as soon as possible.

But Henry, Earl of Sherborne was not riding to Great Little for he had deemed that to be pointless. Instead, he was going a much shorter distance to the long, low house in Bishops Caundle where Colonel James Hanson lived.

"Welcome, friend," Hanson greeted him in the hallway. "Let Stevens take your coat and come and take a glass with me. I want to hear all your news. You know that I have declared for Orange? I am not an important conquest but I believe that a thousand such people like me add up to one Lord Churchill and therefore we count a little in the whole."

"I too have declared for him and the Prince is right now at my house. But, James, you come very quickly to the crux of the matter and for that I am grateful. I am not trusted and am tasked with a test." Henry accepted the cup of wine and settled down to tell his friend what was required of him. "So, in conclusion, I am tasked with discovering who it was killed the Duke of Wiltshire and Sir Beatrice Roakes. Furthermore, I have to bring him, assuming it is one man, to Orange in chains. Success in these tasks will mean I am accepted and failure will mean... well, the opposite."

Hanson thought for some time, going through each possibility in order but not seeming to move the discussion on. Mrs Hanson came in and drank a glass of wine while her husband asked questions. She then asked a few herself, about the strange man called Candles.

"It's clear to me," she said suddenly.

"What do you mean?" Henry asked.

"I mean it is clear to me who Robert Candles really is, not who killed the Duke."

"Well, I have an idea as to who killed the Duke but not one clue as to who Candles is," Hanson put in. "So, it seems like you may have come to the right place, my friend; a husband and wife service to solve all mysteries!"

Henry could not agree more after hearing what they had said. Mrs Hanson went first.

"My Lord," she began.

"Please call me Henry."

"Henry," she began again. "You don't know this Robert Candles, do you?"

"No, I don't believe I have ever seen him before."

"But he has a wound on his shoulder that bothers him considerably?"

"He does but he will not talk about it."

"And a Scottish accent he works hard to disguise?"

"Exactly, you evidently know this man."

"Only by reputation, Henry. His name is indeed Robert but I believe him to be Robert Ferguson, not Robert Candles."

"You mean the famous preacher? The one who completely disappeared after Sedgemoor?"

"I do, Henry. He evidently went straight to Holland and quickly became established as a key figure there."

"How do you know this?" It made absolute sense but the powers of deduction seemed incredible.

"Simple, Henry, but I am no great detective. The answer is right in front of you." She looked at her husband as she spoke these last words.

"You mean James?"

"Exactly. My husband, God bless him, has bored me silly with relating what happened at Sedgemoor three years ago. It was his first and, thankfully, only battle and his success in it put him on path for his promotion to Colonel. It has been a major defining experience for him and countless times he has told me of every detail of what happened."

"I'm sorry to so bore you, dear wife," Hanson joked in reply; the joke seemed momentarily to drag him from his private thoughts. Falling to his knees in comical fashion, he added, "Will you forgive your tongue-wagging husband? But how did you deduce that Candles was Ferguson?"

"It came to me when Henry described him; especially the wound on his shoulder that obviously troubles him so much. But, also, the attempt to hide his Scottish accent. That meant he was attempting to disguise who he was. Therefore, something had happened in his past which he wished to keep from those he works with now. I was racking my brain, thinking of who might wish to present themselves as more conservative and law-abiding that they really were; a man with a bad wound and a Scottish accent. There has only been one battle in a generation, else you as a soldier would have more things to talk about. And then I thought of Ferguson's rabble-rousing as a preacher and how that would not appeal to a would-be-king. Suddenly, I made the connection."

"This is brilliant deduction, Jane," Henry said, to which she blushed and lowered her head, fidgeting to straighten her skirts, especially when she peeked up and saw her husband's look of intense admiration, as if first seeing some new vista after twenty years travelling the same road each day.

"Now, as to who killed the Duke and Sir Beatrice," Hanson started. "You have to take the story back a way to understand what has happened here. On one side, cleverly worked out by the brilliant detective, Jane Hanson, we have a rabble-rousing Scottish Presbyterian preacher called Robert Ferguson, who miraculously escapes from the Battle of Sedgemoor and turns up in Holland under the alias Robert Candles. There, he leads the British contingent for three years until an innocent young man called Matthew Davenport steals some of his thunder. He knows, also, that it was another Davenport who struck him down at Sedgemoor, ending his promising military career, for I remember him well, fighting like a madman and enjoying it, too. So, we have an unprincipled man of God, who has grown to hate the Davenports. This much we all know and I apologise for repeating it so soon after my wife's brilliant exposition of the facts."

"It is supper time, dearest. We should discuss it further over supper, as well as where you are going to sleep tonight."

"What do you mean, my love?"

"I mean my head has grown so large with praise from you both that there will be no room for you in our bed tonight."

"Don't worry, Janey, we will prick that inflated balloon of a head for sure over supper. There is a particularly sharp carving knife I could use."

"Just try," she laughed. "And see what is coming to you."

Hanson did not rib his wife at all over supper. Instead, he remained thoughtful as Jane and Henry tried to tie up each aspect of the correlation between the two Roberts: Candles and Ferguson.

"Why else would he have ordered the arrest of Matthew? Matthew is an exemplary agent in the cause and too straight to ever be fickle, that much is certain."

"Candles or Ferguson certainly hates the Davenports. It might go back longer than '85 and Monmouth's attempt on the throne. Luke was probably the pre-eminent Presbyterian preacher of his time; he had several volumes of sermons published and they sold well," Jane Hanson replied.

"You think everything might stem from jealousy; one preacher jealous of the renown of another?"

"Exactly, and, of course you, Henry, married a Davenport."

"Yes, and she converted to Catholicism to please me. Another source of hatred for this man, whatever name he goes by."

Jane then turned to the head of the table and addressed her husband.

"Sir, you are withdrawn, something is taking up your mind." Behind her, the maid took away the fish plates and brought out the roast beef.

"Yes, dear. There is much going through that department at present."

Hanson carved and they ate in silence.

"There is one thing I don't understand," Hanson said as the maid returned at the end of the meal and Jane stood to leave the room. "No, don't leave us, dear. We will need your input."

"What is it you don't understand?" Henry asked, feeling his solution dissolving as the long, thin dining table was cleared. He would pick out the pieces and return to Orange with half-answers wrapped in the failure the Prince had warned him about.

"Better to tell you what I do understand first," Hanson replied. "I know that there was a killer despatched to Dorset from London and now, by all accounts, returned to London. This much I learned when Orange first landed in Brixham and I was briefed by Mr Cartwright. I thought Cartwright an unsavoury fellow but the killer is clearly much worse. They briefed me because they did not know of my wavering conviction towards the establishment and thought I remained loyal to the Government."

"I know Cartwright, and agree with your opinion. He left a cold shiver down my spine when I met with him." Henry's mind was suddenly sick with concern. Cartwright knew the secret of his illegitimacy; if that came out, Henry would be reduced to nothing. "Was his sidekick the killer? Franshaw, I believe it was."

"No, Henry. Franshaw was described to me as the public face of subterfuge; like the front man, the one everyone sees and trusts because he is good-looking and seemingly good-natured. The killer is a man born and bred in Dorset, one who was well known to your grandfather. I believe he is the man Cartwright reports to in London."

"Parchman," said Henry in a low voice, as if the man might be listening from outside the window; his fear was complete, rising above him like the walls of a well he was thrust down. Cartwright had been clear during his private discussion with Henry at Sherborne Hall as to whose authority he carried behind his threats.

"Yes, Parchman," Hanson replied. "But the question now is how to put the devil in chains."

Chapter 35

Henry, Earl of Sherborne, rode alone and rode hard. He rode into driving rain from the west, his direction of travel. He had five miles to cover and spent the time in grim contemplation, jerking at his mind to force concentration on the task ahead of him. That same mind kept slipping into despair.

"I will be found out," he cried out loud and the wind took his words and splintered them into tiny bits and sent them on the back of raindrops driving down the road behind him.

He brought his mind back to the task. He had to get in front of Orange without Candles being present. Candles would reduce his interim report to shreds in an instant.

The Hansons had helped with a plan over the bare supper table, hosting just three glasses and a decanter, but the stopper had stayed on the decanter and the maid had put three clean glasses back in the cabinet, thankful not to have to wash them up.

"What are Orange's habits, compared to that of Candles?" Jane had asked.

"Orange rises early and works all day with meetings and reports then retires after dining. Some people come and go into his bedchamber; actually our bedchamber we vacated for him, but I have never been invited."

"And Candles?" Jane asked. Henry had to stop and think a moment.

"I've never seen him before ten in the morning but he has only been four days at my house."

"Then that is your window. If you sleep now for a few hours we will wake you early enough to ride back and see the Prince well before Candles emerges from his slumber."

He had not slept, despite a comfortable bed in a spacious but crooked room with a low ceiling; everything seemed low about the Hanson home, yet Hanson and his wife were above average height and had to stoop in various parts of the house. Henry went over and over in his mind what he had to report, finally slipping off to sleep it seemed just as a maid knocked on the door.

"Time to get up, My Lord."

"Thank you." He washed and put on his clothes. Downstairs, both his hosts were waiting for him in the dining room, a bowl of steaming porridge on the table with a tankard of small beer.

"We thought porridge appropriate as you are going into battle against a Scotchman," Jane joked. The room was warm, like the porridge. In a moment he would have to go outside into the cold and wet night.

He wanted to go back upstairs and get into bed again; he felt sure he would sleep this time around.

"You must be off," Jane said, as if she were the colonel issuing the orders. "I've allowed an hour and a half for the journey and an hour to get through the pickets, even though you will probably go straight through due to your rank."

"They are stopping everyone but I do have a letter of safe conduct." He patted his pocket as he talked, then looked at the clock on the sideboard. "So, following your timing, I should be coming to my home by seven o'clock, hopefully a full three hours before Candles surfaces.

Now, he was out on the road and approaching his own estate in the dark of an early December morning. Just around the next corner he would slow from a fast trot to a steady walk. Then, at the next corner, it would be a cry of "Man approaching!" to warn the soldiers on guard duty.

It went very easily and by twenty past six he was riding up to his own front door. He dismounted just as a tiny groom came running up to take his horse.

"Treat him well, Jim. It's been a gruelling ride. Saddle my bay just in case I need to go out again."

"Yes, My Lord," the boy raised his cap and trotted beside the horse around the side of the building, the Sherborne home. Henry went up the steps to the front door and nodded at the footman, who opened it at exactly the right moment and headed straight for the main staircase.

"My Lord, you can't go in there." The two guards at the bedchamber barred his way.

"Of course, I forgot I had given up my rooms for the Prince." He backed away, spun on his heels and went up to the floor above, where he and Grace had decamped. A moment later, he was in her arms, kissing her passionately.

"You are back so soon. Is everything alright, my darling?"

He told her quickly where he had been and what he had found out. "I had intended to stop there and exchange views on the situation before riding on to Great Little but it proved unnecessary; everything I sought except Parchman himself was waiting for me at Bishops Caundle."

"Goodness, husband, so much discovery in such a short period of time. What should we do now?"

"I have to see the Prince without Candles, which means right now, before Candles wakes up. But the guards at the door to our rooms turned me away."

"That's easy," Grace replied. "Come this way." She pulled him out of their temporary bedroom and onto the main landing.

"They won't let us in," Henry said.

"They can't stop us if they don't see us." She turned left instead of right for the main staircase, went to the end of the landing and through a small door that Henry had not noticed before. He had to duck to go through it. "It's a service staircase built behind the new staircase in the new wing. It goes all the way down to the Great Hall on the ground floor and then the kitchens and storerooms in the basement. But on the way down you can get across to our rooms. It just takes a little agility to get there."

He followed Grace down the narrow steps until they reached an equally narrow landing.

"Through there is the new staircase rising from the Great Hall up to the East Tower, where they kept poor Matthew. These steps mirror it and are used by the servants."

"I never knew it was here."

"I think when this wing was built by Mr Milligan's firm you were away in Oxfordshire. It was twelve or thirteen years ago, when you would have been nine or ten."

"I spent the whole of that year in Oxfordshire because the work here was extensive. But how do we get into our rooms from here?"

"Simple, my love, look above your head." Henry looked up. Squinting hard, he managed to make out a tiny trapdoor in the landing ceiling.

"I don't know if I can get through that."

"You don't need to."

"If I don't need to, who will? No, not you. I won't have it."

"I've done it before, just for a dare with my maid, but I know that I fit. I'll go in because they are never going to see me as a threat. I'll get the Prince to allow you in and then you can have your say."

"I will not allow it, my dearest," he repeated adamantly.

Five minutes later, the main door to the Prince's suite opened and the Countess came out with a sweep of her skirts, climbed the stairs and winked at the man sitting on the ornate chair studying a dull portrait of the first earl. It closed and then opened again for a secretary. He came out in search of the Earl, which was an easy task for he was sitting on that ornate chair that provided an eye on the portrait and an eye on the Prince's door below.

Two minutes after that, he was bowing to the Prince of Orange, who every day was looking more like the next King.

And Candles was nowhere in sight.

Chapter 36

The carriage left Sherborne Hall at ten minutes to ten. Robert Candles, rising from his bed, saw it disappear over the ridge that marked the halfway point through the park.

"Who is leaving us?" he asked Simms as he stretched at the window.

"The Earl, sir, with the Countess."

"What? The Earl is back and gone again? Why did you not wake me?" His stretch stopped with his hands held above his head. Simms thought he might be readying to strike him and shrunk back against the tapestry opposite the window.

"You said, sir, not to disturb you, sir. It was the last thing you said last night, sir." To which Candles grunted and demanded Simms seek an audience for him with the Prince immediately.

"I will be available in ten minutes," he said, splashing water on his face in a token effort at washing. Simms scurried out.

But it was another two hours before Candles could see William of Orange. He was at prayers and then in meetings. At midday, he found a few minutes for Candles.

"What is it, man?" There was respect for his capabilities but clear dislike for Candles' personality.

"Sire, the Earl, what was he about?"

"Oh, Candles, he has found his murderer, is all. Now, I have a meeting, so if there is nothing else?" Orange swept out of the room as Robert Candles spluttered for more information. He would have followed but the door swung firmly behind the Prince and he did not want to risk disfavour by following him.

The carriage Candles had spotted contained two people for the first leg of its journey and four for the second. Henry intended to drop one for the final leg in the morning but a little patience is needed to see how that works out. To mark leg one from leg two, Henry and Grace Sherborne stopped at Sturminster Newton for their two additional passengers.

"Where are we going?" asked Thomas.

"First to Great Little," Henry replied. "I'll tell you all about it in the coach."

The messenger covered the distance to Bishops Caundle in record time, pushing his horse dangerously on the slippery roads.

"Sir, you're required at the Prince's headquarters at Sherborne Hall immediately." The soldier had learned the message word for word; something Candles had insisted on.

"What is it about, man?"

"Sir, you're required at the Prince's head..."

"Alright," Hanson said. It was clear that he was going to get nothing out of the messenger other than the one-line message. Still, it was the summons Hanson had been waiting for. "Dismount and get some beer and something to eat..." But the messenger was wheeling his horse to return, risking his life and that of his horse to do exactly as he had been instructed.

Hanson felt pressure to act likewise; clearly, his attendance was of some importance. But he resisted the urge to speed his horse and took a few minutes to pack two spare sets of clothes. Jane saw him off at the door.

"I don't know how long I'll be. It all depends on the Prince and what he wants of me." On the doorstep he kissed his wife, like any soldier going to war.

Only, so far, this had not been a war at all; just a war of nerves as Orange's growing army moved around the West Country, picking up support like a stone gathers moss. How different to Monmouth three years earlier. Yet Orange and his wife, Mary, daughter to King James, had no more right to the throne than Monmouth had. They both lacked legitimacy, just in different ways. Yet Orange had gained traction like a pump in a mine, whereas Monmouth had never got the machinery to work properly.

And now he, Colonel Hanson, had been called for. Perhaps there was to be war now, with a battle to resolve everything and restore liberty and religion to the English.

He rode as quickly as he could sensibly with the poor conditions. He had no problem gaining access to the estate. He was simply waved through with saluting soldiers either side of the road.

"We know who you are, sir," the sergeant said in his halting English.

At the front door to the house, a man who introduced himself as Peter Simms was waiting for him.

"Colonel Hanson, it is a pleasure to meet you, sir. Please come this way." Simms led him into the house and up the main stairs, heading, it seemed, straight for the Prince's suite. But Simms walked past the door that gave access to the Prince of Orange, along the corridor and into the new wing. Then there was a winding way, up a flight of stairs, along another corridor and down a flight with several turns right and left. "It's quite a rabbit warren back here," Simms joked.

"Where are we going?"

"To meet Mr Candles, sir."

"Not the Prince?"

"Good Lord, no, sir. He is leaving today anyway, sir."

"Oh." There was nothing more to say. Perhaps Orange had briefed Candles in his rush and Candles was to brief him now.

But this was not to be. Hanson had an irritating forty minutes in Candles' outer office at the back of the house, all the best rooms being taken by the Dutch, it seemed.

"Colonel Hanson, I want you to follow the Earl of Sherborne and report his movements back to me."

"Why, sir?"

"Because I order it, sir!" There it was; a definite Scottish brogue coming through. Despite the disappointment, Hanson felt a surge of satisfaction for his wife's reasoning and deduction.

"I meant, Mr Candles, on whose authority will you have me go on this chase?"

"Why, the authority of the cause, Colonel. Is that not sufficient?"

"Do you have it in writing? You don't?" Why was Candles so

keen to have Henry tracked? *Maybe*, Hanson thought, *I am approaching this the wrong way.*

"Mr Candles, perhaps you had better tell me all about it so that I may better perform the duties placed upon me."

"Of course, Colonel Hanson. Please take a seat and a glass of wine." He rang a bell and Simms appeared, went to the cabinet and pulled out two glasses and a bottle of wine.

He had been listening at the door, thought Hanson. *How else would he know to bring the wine?*

"I will need all known addresses for Parchman, Mr Candles."

"Why for Parchman?"

"Because he is the killer that the Earl has been asked to track down. I will go there and find both Parchman and the Earl."

"We only have the one; a house in Park Street, near the Strand. I followed him there once or twice."

It seemed that he had underestimated Sherborne if he had determined so quickly who the real killer was.

"I'm relying on you, Colonel." It would not do for Sherborne to come over as the hero. "I would go myself except that I have to be by the Prince's side."

The distance from the centre of Sturminster Newton to Great Little is exactly six-and-three-quarter miles. It was almost exactly on the route to Dorchester. Over Okeford Hill and down the other side, past Hedge End Farm; now owned by Lady Merriman as one of her recent purchases. Then a short distance later you arrive in Winterbourne Stickland, just one-and-a-half miles from Great Little, down a seldom used road that headed south towards the ancient mounds of Bulbarrow.

The four in the coach did not stop and, consequently, arrived at Great Little just as dark was descending.

Henry had sent on one of the coachmen on a fast horse, to give notice of their arrival. Consequently, there was a small party to greet them. Tomkins opened the coach door and helped Grace descend. The others were waiting on the steps.

"Lady Roakes, how kind of you to put us up."

"Please call me Alice, and it is a pleasure to accommodate you, My Lord."

"And you must call me Henry. You remember my travelling companions from last time?"

"Of course, I do. Thomas and Matthew Davenport did so much to save us from the fire; as did you, Henry. You are always welcome here. But, shame on you, Henry, for not introducing me to this fine lady."

"My wife, Grace." Grace turned to look at Lady Roakes and all colour fell from her face. She stared at her host for the longest minute; until Henry, feeling the embarrassment keenly, sought to start the conversation again.

"We made excellent progress from…"

"Mrs Beatrice," Grace said. And then Thomas knew her, too. Such a change, such an elevation of elegance, yet underneath it was the same woman.

Grace stared again as if set in a trance the moment she turned and saw her host. Then she gathered her skirts, turned, and made her way back to the coach.

"What is the matter, my dear?" Henry, all embarrassment forgotten, ran after her.

"I can't stay in her house. She's… she's the one who imprisoned Lady Merriman."

"My God." Henry turned back to Lady Roakes, as if expecting to see someone else there altogether; a common criminal to be hauled off in chains, not the graceful and considerate owner of Great Little. The woman he saw on the steps was Lady Roakes, however. Yet she also was transfixed, staring somewhere above the carriage, out to the trees in the mid-distance. Did she think Sir Beatrice would come riding to her rescue?

Henry helped Grace into the coach and then came back to Thomas and Matthew.

"We cannot stay," he said, finality leaving his lips and forming a barrier around him.

"Nor we," said Thomas. "Come, brother." They ducked below Henry's barricade.

Another lady approached the coach. Thomas remembered her as the Duchess of Wiltshire, wandering the burnt-out buildings in a grubby brown dress, assisting those burnt.

Where was her maid, who had featured so much in the after-fire scenes of a few weeks ago?

"Henry, I do not know what is happening such that a happy reunion has soured so much. All I know is that Alice Roakes is a dear friend to me and, because I am fond of you and Grace, it pains me to see such discomfort between you."

"It's a long story; longer than we have time for tonight," replied Henry.

"Then please do not go far tonight, so that we might try and settle matters between us. Please, Henry, do it for one who might have been your wife, had I not been too vain and contemptible for words." It was an honest approach from someone who had always been honest; even as she had ridden roughshod over others, she had been herself.

And Henry agreed not to go far and the carriage left, rattling rudely down the drive as night closed in; the coachmen, looking inordinately proud, clearly taking on their master's and mistress' umbrage.

Yet Henry's anger was a little assuaged by Penelope. There again, his stress was the greatest for he had so much to hide from those dearest to him and so much to do should he want to be in with the prince who would be King.

Later that night, Penelope, accompanied by Sally, both in dark cloaks, went on horseback to the White Horse Inn, where Henry had taken his party. She was armed with an awful lot yet was not seeking war.

She had listened patiently to Alice Roakes and together, she and Sally had distilled it down to its essence. Alice related the facts then, predictably, started on justifications for her poor treatment of Lady Merriman.

"It won't wash, Alice," Penelope said time and time again. "You were bad to that woman, very bad. Why not just admit it?"

"Mr Blake told me to have an open heart and maybe the wrong can be righted. But it was such a fright seeing Grace Sherborne, who had come to me seeking Arkwright, I mean Lady Merriman, back in Bristol in '85."

"Yes, Mr Blake was right. But do not expect forgiveness and jollity from those you hurt. That may take a long time, even forever." Penelope spoke but, even as she talked, she was wondering where her wise words were coming from. She knew nothing of morals and human frailty, had walked on human frailty and broken it like eggshells. "Who am I to talk?" she added but Alice was not listening, lost in her devious past which had suddenly caught up with her.

But, as Penelope rode to the White Horse, she thought she understood Alice quite well. "We are like peas in a pod," she said.

"What was that, Pen?"

"Oh, just that Alice and I are similar. We are reformed rogues suddenly expecting the world to like us when we cared not one jot for the world before."

"This is Sally, my maid." But it was clear to all that Sally was a lot more to Penelope than just a maid, especially when Penelope brought up a chair for Sally to sit at the table with them.

Penelope cleared her throat to begin a speech she had rehearsed over and again during her midnight ride; hence Sally knew it as well as Penelope.

"It's no good," Grace said, breaking into the hesitation. "The woman is evil and that is an end to the matter."

"I think I am a better judge of that," Henry replied.

"Why you, husband? You were recovering from your wound while we searched for Eliza. We found her bound to a sink in the basement of that woman's house in Bristol."

"I repeat, Grace, that I am more qualified to talk of matters concerning Lady Merriman than..."

"How so, husband?" The light from her eyes was blinding in its fierceness. Henry had never seen her so angry before. "Tell me, how so? She is my dear friend, not yours."

"But she is my mother." It came out before he could stop it; sort of slipped out like grain flowing from a tilted sack.

There was absolute silence in their private sitting room above the bar. Motherhood had entered and laid claim; a greater claim than friendship.

Into that silence came the tiny voice of Grace, like a sail struggling to fill out with the littlest piece of wind.

"So, you are not the son of Henry Sherborne?"

"I am; just not legitimate." There it was said to wife and to best friend and to others besides.

"I don't understand."

So, Henry told the whole story of Lady Merriman; teenage lover of the heir to the earldom, driven away by the then Earl, his father, taken to the furthest reaches of Yorkshire to live on a pig farm for daring to lie with his son and for they to have a son themselves.

"And I am that son," he concluded. "My grandfather brought me up as if I were legitimate when my father and stepmother died in a fire at Redwood Castle in Oxfordshire. He did it not out of concern for me but for the line; he could not bear to be the last Earl of Sherborne in the long line that stretches back to the conquest."

"And so, you…?"

"I am a lie. My whole life has been a lie and I am no more the Earl than Sally here is."

Everyone turned to Sally at mention of her name. They noticed she was crying; a soft, gentle, quiet crying with great big tears that rolled down her cheeks as evidence of her sadness.

"What is it, Sal?"

"Nothing, Pen… I mean, Your Grace." But it was something and Penelope insisted.

"It's just that Lady Merriman was held on the farm in Yorkshire against her will and lived, it seems, a tedious but easy life. Then, when she escaped and came back to Bagber Manor, she was kidnapped again and made to work in a laundry in Bristol."

"That is hard work, I'm sure. Have you ever worked in a laundry, Sally? Can you imagine what it is like?" Grace was all fire in defence of Lady Merriman, quite insensitive to the moment.

"Yes."

"I thought as much… oh, you said yes?"

"I was taken from my home in Africa at the age of six. I was taken to a place called Barbados and put to work in the laundry of my master's house. At the age of seven, I worked twelve hours a day at back-breaking tasks. I was quite alone, you understand? Although I did experience kindness from others who had nothing to give but themselves and the joy they made."

"How did you get away?" Penelope asked, taking Sally's hand in hers, forgetting Lady Roakes' wise words of warning about familiarity in front of others.

"The young lady in the house came to Europe and wanted a young maid to show off. She selected me. She died in England three years later and nobody knew what to do with me. Eventually I was sold to Sir John Withers, Penny's… I mean the Duchess's father, and Lady Withers took me under her wing."

"Mother is a kind soul," Penelope said. "I never noticed it before."

"Can I ask you a question, Sally Black?" Thomas asked.

"You may, sir."

"If you were sold to Sir John Withers, you are presumably still his property?"

"Yes, I am. Lady Withers always put about that I was a free woman but it is not the case. I am a slave."

Penelope said nothing. She mused that a kinder person would have drawn out the deed that marked Sally as a slave and torn it up in front of witnesses. She loved Sally dearly but also loved the thought that she owned her.

She would make it right one day.

In the meantime, she was trying to make it right between the Davenports and Lady Roakes but was just causing hopeless splits within the Davenport party. Grace was adamant that she would have nothing to do with Mrs Beatrice, as she called her.

"She lied to me," she said. "She told me that Lady Merriman was dead and all the time she was chained to her sink, working her way through the laundry."

Thomas backed her until it was suggested that he have nothing to do with the re-building of Great Little. Then, faced with the fading chance of resurrecting the building business, he switched to Henry's side and backed cautious involvement with her.

"You've changed your mind just to save your silly business." Grace was livid.

"She is truly remorseful," Penelope tried again but to no avail.

The temperature in their little sitting room rose steadily, literally and metaphorically. The fire roared on one wall, blasting out heat while tempers rose to new heights. It seemed to Penelope a lost cause. She was just about to rise and take Sally back to Great Little when Matthew beat her to standing. He walked across to the window and threw it open.

"Silence," he roared. "This is taking us nowhere." He achieved absolute silence with his tone, so out of character. He leaned on the window frame, drinking in the ice-cold air. He could see the dark hills rising around him; an irregular pattern of shades in black and grey. Outside, the world seemed at sleep, at peace. Was all the anger in the world suddenly inside their little sitting room? Even the bar below was quiet and dark; all drinkers gone home and to bed.

He was shocked beyond belief that Eliza, his Eliza, was Henry's mother, and by all the suffering she had been through. He burned with anger at the thought but took great big gulps of cold air in an attempt to quench the flames within him; just as he had worked to quench the flames at Great Little.

Finally, he turned back to face the storm. But the storm was no longer, blown out by his initial words; a storm to scatter a storm.

"Friends, we have a situation we cannot resolve. We also have Henry's pressing need to go to London in search of Parchman. We need to put our differences to one side and concentrate on the task at hand."

"Who or what is Parchman?" Penelope asked.

To answer this, Matthew came away from the cooling window, crossed the small room to squat in front of Penelope.

"Why, he is the man who killed your husband," Matthew said as tenderly as he could. When he got no reaction, he elaborated. "And Sir Beatrice, and struck down your Sally, too."

"Let me come," she said. And there was no persuading her otherwise.

Chapter 37

Parchman rubbed his hands in glee, then dismissed another of his servants.

"Out of this house this instant," he roared when she dared plead with him.

"Sir, I have nowhere to go and it is dark and raining heavily. I will happily attend to your every need if you will just keep me on."

"Go, Stephens, I have had enough of your miserable existence. Did you stop and think of my needs while you ate my food in my dining room and slept in my bed? This is your doing, Stephens, and you shall live with the consequences."

His words were true. He had come back unexpectedly to find his servants enjoying his wine, his food and his house. He had dismissed three straight away. With Stephens' departure there was only one left. He would get rid of him in the morning and start afresh with a new bunch.

Tired and irritable, he still enjoyed the uproar he had caused.

"Sir?" Stephens was back, curtseying reverently but he noticed the trembling in her. He hoped she would plead a little more; it was rare entertainment to send a young girl out into the streets at night.

"What can it be now?"

"Sir, I am owed back wages. I have not been paid these last four months."

"You desire wages? Madam, I consider that you have drunk and eaten your wages five times over since I went away."

"You left us no money to buy food, sir. How else were we to survive?"

"You could have written to me for money." He had expressly ordered them not to write, suggesting it would be inappropriate and rather liking the air of mystery it added to his mission into Dorset. "Or you could have borrowed a little against my good name." They had tried that but no one would give further credit to Parchman.

"Will you send me out in the dark and cold with no

265

money, sir?"

"I will give you five shillings…"

"Thank you, sir." She moved forward, her hands outstretched like the beggar she was.

"You interrupted me. I will give you five shillings if you will grant me certain favours now." Her hands moved to her hips, a little sway, a look of distaste changed quickly to neutral.

"Thank you, sir," she said again, like the whore she had become.

He had been back in London less than twenty-four hours and had already had two audiences with the King. Things were looking up.

"Do you mean to say, Parchman, that you killed two leading traitors with your bare hands?"

"Yes, Your Majesty. I realised that the Duke of Wiltshire was playing a double game on you, Sire. He directed me to kill Sir Beatrice after he had bungled the matter." Already, the facts had grown into fiction. "Instead of attacking Sir Beatrice, he struck at a poor defenceless serving girl from Africa, disfiguring her greatly, I am told."

"And what happened then?" King James asked. Parchman wanted to ask back how can a man be so gullible and yet be King of three nations and colonies across the world? But he did not for it would have defeated his purpose to anger this King.

"Sire, Wiltshire tried to recruit me against you." More untruths, like chaff rising from the threshing barn. "I played along for the briefest moment to create a plan to deal with the traitor. Then I became judge, jury and executioner."

"Quite remarkable, Parchman; quite remarkable. You are clearly a good man to have around in a crisis and we are in a crisis right now."

This crisis is of your own doing, man. Carpe Diem, carpe diem. Fortune favours the bold. I am the boldest so I shall seize the day.

"Thank you, Your Majesty." He bowed low but his eyes were tilted to watch his monarch's reaction.

"I would have you, Parchman, as one of my bodyguards."

"Sire, I am used to command." Would he understand the

266

hidden demand he was making? He held the King's intelligence to be average, at best.

"Then command my bodyguard, Parchman. I need loyalty above all at times like this."

You need a mind of your own and to stop this panic in its tracks; that is what you need... Your Majesty.

"Thank you, Sire, I am honoured to be so chosen. What shall my title be?"

"What title do you want?"

"I think perhaps... Keeper of the King's Person."

"No more? No knighthood or earldom, even?"

"Sire, I crave nothing more in a title than for others to know my grave responsibilities." It was so easy to impress this man, this King of England, Scotland and Ireland.

"So, Keeper Parchman, how will you defend me and my realm from these traitors?"

And that, thought Parchman as he doled out another meaningless cliché in response, was two very different things in one; he could save the King's person with ease but it meant sacrificing the realm. He would think on it but the dichotomy of the King in person and the King as monarch was already in his head.

Parchman never did dismiss the fifth servant and for good reason, yet nothing to do with the servant in question. King James insisted that Parchman move into Whitehall, to be close to him. It took the dismissal right out of his mind.

"I want you within earshot, Parchman."

"Yes, Sire, within earshot at all times."

He had moved in that day; surprised at the available apartments close to the King's.

"It seems there is not much call for rooms at present," the steward said as he showed the apartment to Parchman.

"I wonder why that would be," Parchman replied, knowing that every day courtiers were leaving Whitehall to join Orange.

"I want soldiers on every door," he issued orders as if he were an army man; spilling them out to all around him. "And a log kept of all who see His Majesty. Do you understand? And

267

I am to approve it each day. No visitors without my say-so."

"Yes, sir," Franshaw was back in London, together with his boss, Cartwright; both trying desperately to pick up the shreds of their careers following the failure to hold Matthew and Thomas Davenport captive in Shaftesbury Jail.

At least, Parchman reflected, *they will do anything for me and that might well come in useful with the plan.*

Matthew had pointed out one salient thing during the evening in the White Horse.

"Does anyone know what Parchman looks like?"

"I saw him when I was a boy but I can't be sure I would recognise him," Henry replied.

"There are two people I know of who can recognise him," Penelope said when no one else spoke up.

"Who?"

"Sally saw him but only for a moment."

"Did I?" asked Sally.

"Yes, my dear. You disturbed Wiltshire letting him into the house."

"That was him? But I cannot be sure I would recognise him were I to see him again. I might, I suppose."

"Who is the other person?" Thomas asked, thinking Sally's memory would be pulled apart by an attorney.

"Why, Lady Roakes, of course."

"No," said Grace immediately, then explained herself. "I will not have that woman come to London with us. I will not sit in the same coach as her."

"That won't be necessary," Matthew said. "There are already too many coming for one coach. We will be six, including Penelope and Sally; Lady Roakes will be the seventh. Our coach will only take four." Matthew had made the assumption that if Penelope came, so would Sally. She looked directly at him, grateful for the inclusion.

This settled it. The original four would go in their carriage while Penelope, Sally and Lady Roakes would go in Penelope's. They would leave in the morning, go hard and hope to be in London within a few days.

"Certainly by the fifteenth, and perhaps even the day before," Thomas said as their meeting broke up and Penelope and Sally buttoned into their cloaks for the ride back to Great Little.

It was close to three o'clock in the morning when the two girls got into their bedrooms. They had to wake Tomkins for admittance and he seemed less than pleased but bade them goodnight for what was left of it.

He was even more displeased to be told by Penelope to be sure to wake Lady Roakes in two hours, as they were leaving at six for London. And she would need a maid to help her dress and pack some clothes and they would all require a good breakfast at half past five.

"Yes, Your Grace," he grimaced and left them with a candle to see their way.

"Is it worth going to bed, Sal?" Penelope asked.

"Let's have a cuddle," Sally replied. "Then you can pack my things while I pack yours. That will make it a little different. Well, look to it then, dearest. The nightgowns will not find themselves."

"Of course not. Sorry, Sal, I was miles away." She was in Barbados with a tiny dark-skinned girl who worked in the laundry. The girl had a deliciously sweet smile that she gave out to anyone who would look her in the eye.

Penelope laid two nightgowns neatly on the bed, thinking how wonderful the white lace would look against that same dark skin.

And it was her skin, for she had the document to prove it.

Chapter 38

Penelope's coach arrived in London on the evening of December 14th. The rain had turned to sleet and it was bitterly cold. They went to Drivers Court, Lady Roakes' London home, and sent the house staff bustling around, preparing rooms and a meal for them.

"My cousin is probably next door," Penelope said, referring to the new Duke being in residence in Wiltshire House. "But I certainly do not want to see him."

"I'll send a runner to the Rose and Crown to see whether the others have arrived," Alice said. There was plenty of room at Drivers Court for all of them but Alice had not suggested they stay, fearing the reaction from Grace, in particular.

The runner returned an hour later. There was no sign of them.

"Do we have an address for Parchman?" Penelope asked as the two ladies entered the dining room. Lady Roakes had arranged for hot soup in a big china cauldron, with bread and cheese and then hard-boiled eggs and cold roast pheasant with apples she had brought from Great Little.

"No, but I am sure we can find it out with a little detection tomorrow." She turned to the footmen. "That will be all for now. We will see you in the morning. Good night." It was the most she had ever said to her servants and they all sensed a trap; not one stirred.

"You may all leave for the evening," she repeated with just a hint of her old sharpness.

"You don't need serving, Lady Roakes?" the most senior spoke up.

"No, you may call Sally, the Dowager Duchess' maid who came with us today. She will serve us. It's about time she earned her keep." Alice was learning that kindness sometimes needed to be wrapped in acerbity, to give it bite. The six servants shuffled out, bowing as if to royalty.

Sally entered a few minutes later, curtseying before realising it was just the two of them, then giving out a little burst of embarrassed laughter.

"Sit down, Sally," said Penelope. "I'll get you some soup." She ladled out a generous bowl, put some crusty bread on a plate and added cheese, bringing it all over to Sally, then poured her some claret without asking whether she wanted any.

"And now you, Alice."

"Quite the domestic, aren't you?" Alice replied.

"Start on your soup, Sal. You don't want it getting cold."

They made a plan that night. It was a plan that might have worked perfectly had Parchman not removed himself to Whitehall.

"He likes having power over people," Alice started as Penelope cut slices of pheasant and passed around the eggs.

"So, we need to put him in a position where he can exert power and then catch him off-guard."

"Good idea, Sally. And it looks like it is going to have to be me that is the bait." Penelope replied.

"Why you?" Sally asked.

"Because, in all likelihood, he will recognise you, and he will certainly recognise Alice. Besides, he may not like dark skin and then it would be a wasted opportunity."

"I have had the pleasure of meeting him on many occasions," Alice confirmed. "He was coming every week or so at the end when…"

"Don't get into that," Penelope interrupted her friend. "There is no need to relive it."

"Thank you, Penelope."

"Whereas he has never met me."

Later on, food all eaten, and onto the second bottle of claret, Sally recapped on the plan they had put together.

"We first need to find where he lives. If he was deeply involved with the government, as we suspect, then he will not live too far from Whitehall."

"Then," Penelope took over, "I need to lure him in his lair, allowing you and Sally time to enter with these two handguns." She went to a satchel on the sideboard and pulled out two gleaming, big pistols, heavy in her small hands.

"Where did you get those from? Put them down, please, Penelope." They wobbled precariously for several seconds before she crashed them down on the sideboard.

"They are in my coach always, in case of attack from robbers. It seems, Alice, that I have broken the marble on the sideboard."

"No matter, Penelope. I'm happy that the guns are no longer in your hands."

"Why are you laughing, Sal?" Penelope asked, turning from her friend to her lover.

"Oh, just the sight of you, Pen, waving those huge guns around like a pirate."

Later that night, in the great big four-poster bed, Sally and Penny played a game of pirates with Penny forced to walk the plank, only being fished out of the shark-infested water at the last minute.

In the morning, after breakfast, Sally left Alice and Penelope on a street corner, walked straight up to the porter's office and knocked on the door.

"What happened to you, lass?" The porter had a round, red face spiked with an almost toothless grin.

"I fell and caught my cheek on the edge of a table, sir." She did a deep curtsey because she wanted something from the porter.

"Where's your mistress?"

"She sent me, sir. She's looking for the house of an important gentleman."

"Well, you won't find any gentlemen here at the palace, my dear." He chortled at his own joke, turning several degrees redder so Sally thought it might be the early stages of a stroke or some such attack.

She responded as planned. And the porter stopped his laughter and looked concerned.

"Don't cry, my little black thing. What's the matter?"

"I'll get beaten, sir, that's the matter. If I don't find Mr Parchman's house and deliver this message, my mistress will surely beat me."

"Parchman you say? Well, that is easy. That particular gentleman lives in a tall, thin house on Park Street, just off the Strand. You can run there in fifteen minutes."

"Thank you, sir." Sally gave another deep curtsey.

"Tell me, girl, who is your mistress?"

But the response was unintelligible as Sally was facing away from the porter and running as she spoke.

Parchman watched this scene with a modicum of interest. From several storeys directly above, in the King's antechamber, all he could see was a dark-haired serving girl seeming to negotiate favours for a fee. Perhaps it was young Stephens, the maid he had dismissed a few days ago, trying to make a living in the real world. But this girl was taller and thinner. She looked slightly familiar but so did a lot of girls.

"Keeper Parchman, you will be ill-advised to ignore your monarch."

"I apologise, Your Majesty. It is just that if I am to guard your person I must examine every face in the crowd, leave no stone unturned in my efforts to ensure your safety. But I am all attention now, Sire."

"Good, my man. You know all is lost, don't you?"

"No, Sire, I do not believe all is lost; not while we live and breathe, Sire."

"I have to leave. I have to leave very soon. If I depart now I will live to fight another day. If I am captured by my son-in-law, he will surely kill me. I must get away now. I must get away to the Queen and the Prince, in France. From there I can plan our next move." Mary of Modena, the queen, had taken their son to France a few days earlier, causing deep stress lines in the character of James Stuart.

Parchman turned back to the pathetic scene being acted out and wished he had sided with a more able man. The old earl, for instance; everything had gone so well when he was in charge.

"Your Majesty, if you are set on going abroad I will take you there and see you safely across the Channel. Then I will return for some unfinished business over here."

"Your presence during my flight is much to be appreciated, sir." James sniffed, remaining haughty even in his despair.

Parchman was about to ask permission to go home for a few minutes for clothes and his sword and dagger but thought better of it. Permission would be denied.

With some people, it was best just to go and seek permission afterwards.

"I won't have it, Sal. The risk is that Parchman will see you and recognise you and then all will be lost."

"We should wait for the others," said Alice, although she was not at all fond of their continued condemnation.

"This is what we shall do," Penelope said, a clear course of action suddenly coming to her. "Alice, you shall go to the Rose and Crown. If they are arrived, bring them to Park Street, where Sally and I shall be."

"What will you do there?"

"We will wait in the shadows until an opportunity comes to us, or else when you and the others arrive."

"I don't want to go," said Alice.

"You have to, Alice. You will definitely be recognised by Parchman here. The most useful thing you can do is go and fetch the others as reinforcements."

"Can't Sally go?"

"My dear, I need Sally here in case… well, just in case. Take heart now. Yes, the Davenports think badly of you but so what? You are another human being with a right to breathe air like they do. You've been a bad girl but you are truly repentant so hold you head high and retain some of that pride you used to show."

Alice Roakes felt no pride as she made her way to the Rose and Crown. For pride is an easy emotion to swallow, this time by fear but it could as easily be several other rival feelings.

And it was not fear for herself. She did not for one moment fear physical action from the Davenports. At worst, they might report her crimes to the magistrates. But this did not frighten her. She was good at disappearing, although she would miss Great Little badly. And if caught she could plead duress in her actions; duress from her first husband, Mr Beatrice, and from Parchman himself. And she could afford the best lawyers.

It was another type of fear altogether; fear that Sir Beatrice would be discovered as Sergeant Roakes, the soldier who had led the rape of Grace Davenport. You cannot bring a dead man to justice but she desperately wanted him to be remembered as a good man rather than the rogue he had been.

No head held high, then, rather anchored to ground level by fear as she saw Henry's coach in the yard and heard Henry exclaim about the precious time wasted with a broken wheel.

"Mrs Beatrice." It was Grace who saw her first. Alice curtseyed.

"My Lady, My Lord, sirs, I bring you urgent news."

"Can it wait until we have eaten and changed?"

"I fear not, sir. I would ask you to follow me to Park Street, just off the Strand, and I can explain on the way."

"How far is that? Thomas asked, his first time in London.

"About half a mile, sir. I just walked it. Penelope and Sally are waiting there for you."

"Then we shall go by coach so as to save time. Boy, don't unharness the horses; they can manage another mile. Run instead for a little food for them and bring us also five pots of ale and a loaf of bread. We will leave directly. Lady Roakes, you may tell us the situation as we travel."

They did set off a few minutes later, Grace a little subdued by the immediate action, not thinking that Lady Roakes was now travelling in her coach after all; something Grace had ruled out categorically. In fact, Lady Roakes was squeezed opposite her so that Thomas and Matthew were uncomfortably perched against the window frames on either side.

Albeit just for half a mile.

Chapter 39

Parchman had always preferred the long way. The Strand was too open and broad for a man like him. He went instead north of the Strand, and wove his way through a network of smaller streets, away from the crumbling mansions of the south side that looked over the Thames. Then, at the easternmost extent of the Strand, under the shadow of the tall tower of St Clement Danes, just completed a few years ago, he crossed the Strand, wound down another short road and onto Park Street; a collection of mid-sized decaying mansions of which his home was the tallest and narrowest.

His route took longer but he usually met no one he recognised. And the fewer people who knew his whereabouts, the better. He also stopped on a whim at a gun shop to arm himself with a fine new handgun, which the owner claimed could hit its target at fifty yards. The boast seemed unlikely but Parchman purchased it anyway.

The two parties left at about the same time but thereafter the time advantage was all the Davenports', or it remained with Parchman, depending on how you see events unfolding.

Was the Davenport party laying a trap for Parchman or Parchman, unwittingly, laying a trap for them?

He saw the coach and stopped a moment. It was parked in the road yet the other houses on Park Street all had short, stubby drives beyond their gates. His did not. That meant either that the occupants were visiting him or planned to surprise him. He took the handgun out of its walnut case and loaded it. Then he moved forward, stuffing it into his waistband.

But instead of using the front door, he went around the back to where the river lapped against a rough wharf that was tumbling down. He tried the back door to his home. It was open so he slipped in.

All was quiet at first. He stood in the back passageway, kitchens he had never been in on one side, the same with the storerooms on the other. But he knew the passage and where it led to for he had often come in the rear entrance when unsure of who might be waiting for him upstairs. And sometimes just to keep his servants on their toes.

Servants! He had dismissed them all. How then could someone get into the house? He had seen no sign of forced entry.

Then he remembered there was one servant he had forgotten to dismiss. What was his name? Something like Johns or Jones. He moved along the passage towards the front of the house, removed his shoes, and in stockinged feet crept up the stairs to the ground floor. Eyes, ears and nose were all alert, likewise his sixth sense, for anything that might give him a clue as to what was going on.

All three physical senses hit him at once. Strictly, it was the perfume first, wafting down the stairs, followed by a murmur of voices and then a swish of skirts as his head poked up to reach ground-floor level. He had time to consider that smell must travel fastest through the air, followed by sound and then vision, the slowest.

But then he shook himself for he clearly saw Mrs Beatrice straight ahead in the drawing room, back to the open door. She was dressed much more regally than before but he would know that arched, slender neck anywhere; had wanted to touch it often enough. That same neck had leaned over him as he lay in agony, unmoving, on the floor of her house in Bristol, just after her husband had stabbed him in the side. He had searched for her for three years and now, after being so elusive, she had come directly to his own home.

The distance was under twenty yards. The gunsmith had promised accuracy at fifty. He wanted to shoot her so badly.

Three things stopped him, ranging from the practical to the emotional. First, the act of cocking the gun might betray his presence. She would hear it and could move sideways, right or left, to safety. Second, she was talking to others in the room and Parchman dearly wanted to know who else had come to his house without an invitation.

Third, and this is where the emotion comes in, he did not

277

want to shoot her at all. He wanted to stab her as he had been stabbed. He wanted to watch her slide to the floor, disbelief at life cut short painted on her face. He wanted to look into her eyes and for her to realise who it was come back for sweet revenge.

Then she could die and he would be content.

But Parchman needed a plan. His dagger was in his bedroom and it was impossible to go up the main stairs without alerting them. He had to think this through calmly; emotion was his driving force but it could not be his engine. For that he needed cold, hard mechanics. How was he to achieve his objective?

As sometimes happens at moments like this, his objective came to find him. For Mrs Alice Beatrice suddenly turned, shaded her eyes against the glare from the December sun, and saw Parchman staring at her from the top of the basement stairs. She let out a cry, recognition mixed with alarm.

"Don't move a muscle," he said, cocking his gun and levelling it at her in one movement. At least now she would see who her killer was. But he still wanted to use his dagger, the same one that had been turned back on him. There was a neatness about this solution that pleased him enormously; it was definitely worth the extra effort to bring it about.

"How many of you are there? Answer me, woman." He had his wits about him; that much could always be said about Parchman.

"Seven of us." If she had thought harder through the shock, she would have said fewer.

"How many men and women?"

"Four women and three men."

"I want each one to come out, one at a time, men first. The doors are wide enough to ensure my gun will not miss you and you are my first target. Any weapons are to be placed in the hall on the floor. Do you understand? Good. Any funny business and my itchy finger will squeeze down on this little trigger."

Thomas came first.

"Next."

Matthew came second then, on command, it was Henry's turn.

"You?" Parchman gasped. "After all I've done for your grandfather."

Henry stood still, not sure whether Parchman genuinely thought he was a force for good or was playing with him.

"Next."

Grace came next.

"Who are you?"

"The Countess of Sherborne," she replied flatly.

"Ah, you're one of them that took Arkwright away, kidnapped her. I suspect the magistrates will be pleased to hear about that."

"What? Are you mad? It was you..."

"Silence. These are your two brothers? Which one helped you kidnap Arkwright and which one is the rebel traitor spreading sedition with every silky word they emit?"

"I am Thomas. I helped Lady Merriman to escape your vile clutches." Thomas stepped forward as he spoke, covering half the distance between them.

"One step closer and she goes to Hell," Parchman retorted, keeping the gun on Alice. Thomas stopped immediately but did not go back.

"Six steps back, my friend, or she is on her way." He raised his right arm slightly and took aim at Alice, still standing in the drawing room. "Next." Thomas shuffled back a step and a half but left it at that.

Sally came out and, incredibly, he did not recognise her from his assault at Great Little. Perhaps it had been battle-rage clouding his vision so he just saw the enemy and struck out at it. Sally said nothing to him and stood at the back behind Matthew, who was the tallest. She looked like the maid. Parchman thought maybe Jones or Johns had started to find a new household. He would enjoy dismissing her later. He had no need of servants until he got back from abroad.

Penelope came out last; a disdainful look on her face that angered Parchman immediately.

"I'm the Dowager Duchess of Wiltshire. I want to thank you

279

for ridding the world of my husband."

"What? I mean… how do you know who killed your husband?"

"It is common knowledge, Parchman. I expect you to be arrested any day now and hauled off to Dorchester where the hangman is waiting." She had, without knowing, hit on the one thing that terrified him; the thought of a noose waiting patiently for him. The idea of ending his days dangling was his worst nightmare.

He moved his gun from Alice to Penelope, then back again, not sure who to point it at, who to take down. And Thomas, only six paces from him, saw his chance. He jumped just as the gun was between targets and Parchman's eyes had to focus on a different distance. Thomas grabbed Parchman's right hand as the finger closed on the trigger. The din was enormous as the gun went off. Then he knocked Thomas to one side, threw the gun in the air and grabbed the barrel, swung the handle down on Thomas' head so Thomas crumpled to the floor. He turned at the top of the stairs to the basement, ready for his getaway.

But Matthew was almost as fast as Thomas, leaned over the bannisters and held Parchman by the hair, gradually improving his steely grip on him. He was held in a vice and Parchman could kick and scream all he liked but he was going nowhere.

Except to a date with the hangman.

Then the world blew apart. Two resounding crashes of thunder and smoke everywhere. As it cleared, Penelope was rocking on her heels with a spent gun in each hand. She had a strange grin on her face, as if she were a scientist doing an experiment with bubbling liquids and the reaction was not as expected.

One bullet had missed Parchman, just. They could all see the splintered wood on the bannister above his head, yellow exposed wood giving a lie to the mahogany finish. Another inch and it would have smashed his skull in. The second bullet had gone into his left shoulder. Matthew had let go of Parchman out of shock so the wounded man was rolling on the steps, trying to stop the bleeding.

He stopped when Sally ran down the few steps that separated them and pulled off her apron to make a tourniquet and then a sling for his arm. He sat quietly like the wounded captive he was. Thomas was helped to his feet, stood shaking his head as Henry wiped blood from a cut on the skull. All seemed dazed and moving slowly; the thunder of three shots still ringing in their ears, numbing all their senses.

But the show was not over. For as stillness spread, Grace heard a moan from the drawing room behind them. She ran back there, crying, "It's Alice, she's hurt," forgetting her acrimony in her haste to help.

She propped Alice up on a cushion just as she opened her eyes. The first thing she saw was Grace Davenport on the steps of the Bristol home she had grown up in.

"She's not here," Alice said, trying to shake her head and wag her finger; any indication of the negative was acceptable. "I tell you she is gone away. I am sorry, truly sorry."

"Hush now, don't stress yourself."

"The baby, my baby." She tried to rise but several pairs of hands pushed her down.

"Best to rest easy, Alice," Penelope said. "For your sake and for the baby's. There has been too much death and violence recently." When Alice showed no sign of doing as she was told, Penelope added, "Relax, woman, or I'll give you something genuine to worry about."

Alice's wound was not serious, although it was extremely painful, as flesh wounds can be. The bullet had gone clean through her right arm without touching the bone. Grace begged Jones, the only servant in the house, for clean hot water, towels, and a sheet for bandages. Within twenty minutes, Alice was sitting on a sofa drinking tea and wondering what incredible luck had caused her to be wounded by Parchman's stray bullet.

She was in luck because Grace had squeezed her left hand and said nothing. Saying nothing said a lot to Alice Roakes. It was more about the past, her sordid past, than the future. Alice could feel this in the type of squeeze it was.

"We had better get Parchman to the authorities," Thomas said.

"Where is he?" asked Matthew, looking around. "I'm not aware that we put him somewhere else."

They followed a trail of blood down the stairs, doubling back along the basement passage and out of the back door. There was a larger pool outside the back door, as if in the escape Parchman had stopped for half a moment in order to consider the best way to go. There were a few more drops going right. No doubt he had decided to go back around to the front and away along the Strand. The drops merged after that into the mud that was everywhere around the banks of the river.

In groups of two, they searched the Strand for him. Thomas took Penelope's two guns and offered them to Matthew and Henry. Matthew declined, saying he would trust to his above-average height rather than use a firearm, so Thomas kept it for himself. Grace, strangely, elected to stay with Alice in case she had need of help.

For the briefest of moments, Alice, fully conscious now, suspected that Grace meant to finish the job started by Parchman and do away with her as soon as the others were out of the house. But then she remembered the squeeze on her good hand and she relaxed.

And she relaxed even more as Grace, kindness itself, tended to her while the others were out searching for the rogue.

And for once it was not her.

Chapter 40

Parchman had seen his chance and taken it. Those fools were so distracted by a mere flesh wound to the woman he would love to rip apart with the dagger that now lay upstairs in his bedroom.

But at least he had hurt her, if only superficially. She would remember forever what it was like to have a metal object enter your body at speed; to threaten the sinew of life itself.

And now he had a chance to creep away and escape that damnable noose. He kept his eyes glued on to their backs as he twisted slightly and felt for the step below him with his foot. He shifted his weight in absolute silence, not daring to breathe and hoping against hope that no spasm of pain would come to torment him. He could cope with the raging throbbing because it was constant but feared that a sharper sudden pain would cause him to cry out.

He made each step down in similar fashion. Then, standing upright, he stepped into his shoes and made easy work of the thirty-foot back passage. He did stop at the door, as they later deduced. His concentration on non-discovery had been so intense, he had not yet decided which way to go. It took a moment only, with his blood pooling just outside the door.

He would go back the way he came. They would never think to go down the small streets to search for him. Instead, when they found him gone, they would concentrate on the Strand; the straight path back to Whitehall.

And that is exactly what they did. Even when Hanson rode up, they only thought to search the main thoroughfare back to Whitehall.

Back and forth along the Strand until daylight ended, rendering their continued search futile.

Parchman made good progress through the back streets, the hunched pose of his wound made passers-by think him a common drunk. They avoided him, crossing the narrow streets or ducking into a shop to keep away. Parchman was back at

Whitehall thirty minutes after leaving his house. But he did not go and seek the King. Instead, he went in search of a royal surgeon, tracking one down within the hour.

"Can you sort me out?" he asked without bothering with introductions.

"Who are you, sir?"

"Why, I am Parchman, newly appointed Keeper of the King's Person."

"Ah, I've heard about you. Well, more fool you to get wounded within days of starting your new duties."

"This was a private matter. Now can you mend me or do I need to find another surgeon? This wound hurts like the devil."

The surgeon examined him and confirmed what Parchman had suspected; his shoulder had been smashed by the ball. It would mend in time but would be forever weakened.

"You'll have to rely on your other shoulder."

"I can't do that, surgeon, my left side was the recipient of a rather large dagger a few years back."

"Well, you are running out of sides to your body, my man. I really should put this in plaster to have any hope of a good mend."

"I don't have the time for that. Just get the bleeding to stop and give it some support so I can travel. Then give me something for the pain."

The surgeon did as instructed and half an hour later Parchman felt tolerably better. The throbbing was still there, intense at times, but the bleeding had stopped and he could just about use the shoulder for light duties.

"My fee is quite reasonable, sir, just..."

"Send it to my house," Parchman cut him off. "I've got to see the King." And he was gone in search of his monarch.

Only James was nowhere to be found.

There was a note, stiffly stating that he could not wait for his keeper for foes were closing in on every side. It begged Parchman to come on to France as soon as possible for 'we require every loyal person by our side during these troubled times'.

If only James knew, if only he could ascertain, that Parchman owed loyalty only to himself.

There was a note but at first Parchman did not see it for the soldier at the door to the King's apartments stubbornly refused to let him in.

"Sir, I am under strict instructions from His Majesty himself not to let anyone through." It was said with pride, as if this particular soldier had been chosen from the vast ranks awaiting assignment of duties, all others turned over for the honour. He overlooked in his mind that the King had referred to him as 'my man' as he could not recall his name after three years of loyal and consistent service in his private apartments.

"Do you know who I am, sir?"

"You are Keeper Parchman, sir. But orders are orders...,sir."

"I demand to see the King." Without yet discovering the note, Parchman still sought the King.

"And I am ordered not to let you or anybody in, sir." It was the last thing this soldier without a memorable name ever said, other than "Shit," when the thin blade Parchman had stolen from the surgeon's instrument bag sliced through his throat.

"Shit," said Parchman for the action had hurt his shoulder considerably.

He stepped over one more body, entered the private apartment and found the note.

'Parchman, if you find this in time to catch us, we are going by river to catch a ship at Sheerness that is made available to us. Come quickly, my man.'

Parchman wasted no time. He pocketed the note in the King's own hand, thought he would decide later what to do with it, called together the King's guard in the courtyard outside, wrote his own hurried note – which he gave to a messenger – and went in search of the King.

The best way to Sheerness was by the river and Parchman wasted no time organising one of the royal barges, complete with its rowers and a cohort of guards. It was late in the evening; cold, damp and raining. Not a night to be out searching the banks for a fleeing king.

Parchman had time to think as the boat made progress down the river, through the city of London and on with Kent on the right and the Essex flatlands on the left. He tried to panic, letting his imagination run wild with all sorts of horrors and everyone turning against him.

For that was the mindset of the King.

He would be thinking of safety first, which meant secrecy. There would be no fanfare. He had not taken a royal barge; Parchman knew that for there had been a full complement at the moorings when he had picked the fastest one for his own use. Parchman briefly considered how strange that a courageous man in battle could become so terrified of this shadowy enemy who never presented himself for a real fight; Orange simply moved around the country, gathering strength and waiting for James to descend into further panic.

But then he threw it out of his mind; it served no purpose to consider how James Stuart had been before he was King; it was the man now he had to deal with.

He found the King and a tiny collection of followers in a fisherman's cottage in Sheerness. He had been drifting on the open water and the fishermen had not known what to do with him so brought him back to one of their homes, as if in their trawling they had caught a remarkable fish, too fine to chop up into pieces for the market.

"How did you know he was the King?" Parchman asked.

"He told us, sir," came the reply. "He first presented himself as a gentleman looking for an old lady-friend who came from these parts. Said he missed her badly and now that his wife had died he wanted to find her again. I asked him what coin he would give us to make this lady known to him. And he looked sad or angry or something and says, 'I do not carry coin, man, I am your King'."

"It was like he wanted to be known, to be recognised as the King, even though he was fleeing for his life." This was the local fish trader they had collected on their way back with the King. They thought to ask his opinion as he was better travelled than them, having been often to London and once, even, to

286

Southampton, as he told everyone who would listen.

James was sitting at the table in the humble front parlour, an untouched tankard of beer in front of him, four tired supporters leaning against the wall behind him. He had refused their offering of lamb stew.

"Ah, Parchman, at last. Are you come to help me to my wife and child in France? The ship will not wait forever, my man."

He seemed like a child playing a game of make-believe.

"No, sir," he said. "I've come to take you back to Whitehall to wait upon the arrival of the Prince of Orange."

It had been an easy decision, made while being rowed down the Thames that night; the only thing he could do to have hope of retaining any power under the new regime.

For his closeness to James over the last week had convinced him that the man had no future. He would end his days in some pathetic court in exile. Parchman could, if he so chose, join him there, gradually being absorbed into an insignificant part of French society, never able to return to his native land; to the London he had grown to love so much over the last three years. He would have James' gratitude but that was not enough.

He loved power and the exercise of it; that was the all of it. The only way to manage affairs was to bring Orange something of substance and there was nothing more substantial than a monarch, whatever his current temperament and standing.

In the balance of things, it would outweigh the accusations of the Davenports and Sherbornes and Wiltshires, allowing him, in time, to turn the tide back on that whole miserable bunch.

He looked at James now as he finally realised there was no way out but to face Orange in person. He was like a shell without a nut; a promise without intention; words without meaning.

He would turn the King in and help make a new king, and be famous for it.

Chapter 41

Parchman returned a furious James to Whitehall, not trusting his guards so accompanying the King himself on the royal barge. It was a tense time with the long night ending during the slow row up river, adding colour to the scene of the captured King like a painter adding dabs of vivid red and orange to brighten up his near-finished work.

The news was not good for James when they finally tied up at the palace. Exhausted rowers sat motionless, frozen either by exhaustion or reverence for the drama being acted out before them. There was no one in officialdom to meet the King; an unheard-of occurrence. Nobody wanted to be the bearer of the news that the Earl of Rochester had set up a provisional government in the King's absence. The King displayed the type of fury that is best meted out in total silence; expressions marking the anger much better than words.

Yet the strangest thing started to happen as the barge manoeuvred into the pier at Whitehall. An early riser called that here was the King. A few more stopped to look. And someone cheered, taken up by others; at first it was ragged and broken but it gained momentum and became a continuous cry of, "God save the King!" Someone beat a drum, another blasted on a trumpet, and the cries of appreciation mounted as the church bells rang. It became a scene fit for the return of a warrior king bringing his triumphs back home.

For a moment, Parchman thought he had it all wrong, had misjudged the situation completely. Then he looked at the empty pier beside the barge, realised that the London mob could cheer all they liked but a king was no king without support from the ruling classes.

He had made the right decision after all.

Parchman installed James in his private apartment in the palace and then resumed his recently-taken-up duties as Keeper of the King's Person. He allowed no one in other than those bringing food and drink. Parchman expected and hoped for recognition when Orange arrived two days later. Indeed, he was summoned the next evening to an audience. He attended to his dress in great detail, particularly his wounded shoulder. He had never met Orange and wanted to make the best impression.

"What are we to do with you?"

"Well, Sire, perhaps…"

"It was a rhetorical question." William rose from his high-backed chair and walked around the stationary man as if examining the goods. He sniffed, wondering why Candles had spoken of this man as a highly capable operator when he seemed a buffoon. Parchman observed the Prince's disdain and did not have a good feeling about his future. "We would have preferred that my uncle left the country. His presence here is a major embarrassment." Orange's English was as perfect as Parchman's deepening sense of despondency, as if each precise word nailed another beam in the scaffold being built.

"Sire, I thought you would wish to have him captive and…"

"The trouble is, Parchman, that you thought. You should not think, rather should follow orders given to you by those that do the thinking." It was a crushing blow against him, worse than his shoulder wound, which still ached badly despite the attentions of that damned royal surgeon.

Parchman was a survivor; survival was his instinct, and it kicked in now in a borrowed room of the Palace of Whitehall just before ten o'clock on the ice-cold and damp evening of December 19th 1688.

"Sire, I recognise my error and am sorry for it. Is there anything I can do to make amends and to prove that my intentions have only been for the best security of the realm?"

"What did you have in mind?" William belied his previous statement requiring the likes of Parchman not to think.

Parchman had a split second to decide his future. Bringing back James Stuart did not break any laws but unless he elevated his status quickly with Orange, news of his past would spread to the new court and he would be undone. He needed something radical to undo the damage.

That was it! Undo the damage done by bringing James back

to Whitehall.

"Sire, I brought him back so I can arrange for him to flee again."

"With minimal fuss?"

"With no fuss at all, Sire."

William wanted details; meaning Parchman was thinking on his feet for another twenty minutes.

"And what do you require in return, Parchman?" This was working out better than he could have hoped. Could he dare ask for it?

"Sire, I have many enemies due to my loyalty. Loyalty is something hard and fast in me and not easily transferred to a new object. I have now made that transfer to you, Sire, and it will not readily move away." He looked at Orange; saw his eyes flicker in boredom; had to act now. "Sire, I ask two things. First, a position in your staff, where I may prove myself to you and gain promotion over time. Second, immunity from my enemies' accusations against me."

"You have these things from me, Parchman, provided my uncle departs this country before Christmas in as quiet a manner as possible." William scribbled on a piece of paper, signed it and handed it to Parchman. "Go now and make your detailed plans. I do not expect to hear from you in person until you send a message back that you have succeeded."

"Thank you, Sire." He bowed several times as he backed out, thinking what a fool this Orange was not to enquire as to what the accusations were before making up his mind. There was much difference between petty misdemeanour, perhaps with the wife of a courtier on the one hand, and multiple murder on the other. He was guilty of both but was now free of all responsibility.

With the doors closed, he read the document and kissed it.

That single sheet was the answer to all his problems. More so because it would be easy to get James to leave; he would probably even by grateful to Parchman for arranging it.

Indeed, Parchman surpassed his own hopes in arranging for James to leave.

"I have a confession to make to you, Your Majesty," he said, his plans in place. "I thought, quite wrongly, that you had given up and were deserting your country in its hour of need. That is the real reason I insisted you return. However, I have consulted on my actions in escorting you back to your palace and realise I did wrong."

"So you did, Parchman," the King sniffed, forgetting in the superiority of the moment that Parchman had promised to see Orange on the throne.

"I see now, Sire, that those with influence in this nation are temporarily set against your policies and that departure is for the best. That way, you will be able to regroup abroad and return shortly in strength, when the ardour of some of your leading subjects has cooled a little and common sense returns. You are, after all, the rightful King, Your Majesty. I see and hear the high regard your common subjects hold you in and do not doubt your return in triumph."

"Yes, my assessment exactly. But it is no good realising this now, when the time has passed."

"Sire, I can help you like I should have done the first time." Parchman outlined his plans for James' flight, then switched its name from flight to escape because it sounded better.

"You will come with me?"

"I cannot, Sire, not immediately." He thought, *Not in this lifetime will I go with you again.* "Somebody needs to stay here to protect your reputation." That seemed a good response. "But I will come as soon as I can," he lied.

The details were easy to set up for the element of subterfuge was a deceit in itself; those who, logically, should have sought out the fleeing monarch were behind the enterprise and turned away at just the right moments.

James left by boat on the Thames again and was safely in France a few days later.

Parchman sought a meeting with William of Orange the moment the boat returned with the news that James had successfully taken ship for France. Parchman had uncharacteristically given the boat captain a crown to share amongst his crew.

"Did he tip us anything?" they asked when their captain returned to the boat.

"Not a penny, the little miser," he replied, thinking how far the crown would go if kept intact. "But as you've worked hard today, I'll stand you all the first drink down the Queen's Head.

Sixpence spent to gain a crown; sixpence multiplied tenfold made a crown.

He would spend his pint working out whether to play cards or put it on that boxer he saw fight the other day.

"But the Prince told me to come and see him when I had news."

"The Prince is otherwise engaged at present," Simms said in the outer office. "I understand it is urgent, sir. Can I suggest we make an appointment with Mr Candles, who can then advise what best to do?" Simms hoped to be retiring very soon; he had his eye on a manor in the West Country, having been very taken by the area in recent weeks. 500 acres, a decent little house with a welcoming hall and a ready quorum of willing servants to work there. Then he could scour the nearby manor houses for a wife; marry into the ruling class.

"Robert Candles, you say?" Parchman's espionage activities, before they were rudely curtailed by Wiltshire, had highlighted this man often enough. He was said to have run the English delegation at Orange's court in Holland. Things were looking up; in fact, decidedly so.

Yet it was thirty-six hours before Candles could make himself available, tipping the scales from Christmas expected to Christmas actual.

"Merry Christmas," said Candles without imparting any sense of merriness at all.

"And to you, sir." An equal response back, although tinged with a degree of deference for Candles held Parchman's future in his big, hairy hands.

"It seems you messed up badly."

Parchman was just about to reply hotly, wondering whether, in fact, he should have gone to France with James, when Candles continued.

"But then recovered neatly."

"Thank you, sir." Another degree of deference would do no harm.

"I like a man who recovers from a mistake."

"That is kind of you, sir." Two more degrees. How many would he sacrifice before his future was known?

"I have a position for you. Particularly as I understand in your previous role you had a spider's web."

"A spider's web?"

"A network of agents across the country and across Europe, too."

"That is correct, Mr Candles." He would, it seemed, peak at four degrees of fawning; the conversation was swinging his way.

"I have none in this country, other than the agents I sent out to England to weigh up the prospects of invasion. Four were arrested and killed by you."

"I recall, Mr Candles." Much closer to even-terms now. He wanted to add that they had not been effective but decided to hold back on observation right now. "My counter-espionage team were busy at their work for certain."

Let Candles do the talking; expose his weaknesses.

"One then turned on me."

That was a surprise, until Candles mentioned the name.

"Matthew Davenport."

"I have no love for the Davenports, sir." Parchman's use of 'sir' now was as an equal; no deference at all anymore. These two were united in their hatred of the Davenports and Sherbornes.

Parchman quickly related recent events with these two families, giving a slant that Candles knew to be false but chose to believe.

"They broke into your house, you say?"

"I believe so. They attacked me and wounded me in the shoulder. It hurts like the devil."

"What did they take?"

Parchman said he did not know for he had to make his escape while they were preoccupied on the main floor. "I slipped out through the kitchens and ran back to Whitehall to resume my duties. I discovered the King was gone and set off in pursuit."

"The ex-King, you mean." For the idea of the King abdicating through his actions was growing. "Sit down, Parchman. Can I get you anything for the pain in your shoulder? Some fine brandy, perhaps, or, better still, I have some Scotch. I need to talk to you about Ireland."

"Ireland? Why there?" He did not want to escape France just to be sent to Ireland.

"Because if Orange becomes King, it is almost certain that James Stuart will attempt to come back through Ireland. But I do not intend for you to relocate there, sir." He could clearly read Parchman's face well; it took one to know one, he supposed. "Rather that you co-ordinate it from here with some of your agents in the field. You and I will need to visit from time to time but mostly it will be a case of sending out capable agents for various assignments."

"It sounds like an excellent position for me, Mr Candles."

"I thought it would appeal. Now, drink up for this bottle needs finishing and I cannot do it alone."

What a Merry Christmas it had turned out to be after all, springing joy from the depths of gloom.

Epilogue

So much happened in 1689.

The new twin-monarchy of William and Mary, for instance; William III and Mary II. Both were unfortunate names from English history. William the Conqueror had stolen the crown in an invasion, much like William of Orange had done. In between had been William Rufus, a cruel and sadistic man finally killed with an arrow in the New Forest. Mary's predecessor as Queen had been even worse. Bloody Mary, infatuated with her husband, King Philip of Spain, had burned and killed her way through her young Protestant realm. And this first Mary was the only other joint monarch to sit on the English throne, in this case with Philip of Spain.

But they took their tainted names into a new Britain. In February, the Convention Parliament, summoned by William, offered him the Crown. Yet Mary had the greater claim; assuming, of course, that her father, James II, had abdicated. The convenient consensus was that he had; not through a declaration but by his actions in fleeing; twice, in fact. Although the Lords and the Tories took some convincing, preferring a Catholic monarch with an absolute right to a Protestant with a questionable claim.

And this assumed that the stated heir to the throne; the baby prince born in June 1688, was, as rumoured, a changeling, smuggled into the birthing room by a female supporter of James.

This new and double monarchy sat on twin coronations chairs on April 11th in Westminster Abbey, a new chair and new regalia made especially for Mary. But those chairs had two wobbly legs so they might have rocked precariously; the question of abdication was one leg and the changeling prince was the other.

But nobody cared whether the chairs wobbled. Nobody cared that the King did not smile. Nobody cared that they were headed into war. For the nation was Protestant again from head to toe.

It had been a time of toing and froing, with the Convention working through the details. Lords and Commons, Whigs and Tories went this way and that, eventually deciding on abdication, Protestant monarchs for a Protestant country and, most significantly, that all future monarchs would reign within the law. One of the first acts of William as King was to dissolve the Convention and turn it into a new Parliament in order to ratify the decisions the nation had made.

There were other meetings involving twin chairs in 1689. One was brokered by Grace and Thomas and held at the Davenport family home in Sturminster Newton. It happened on a blowy March day; the sort of day that could be the start of spring and the future or the return of winter and the past. Grace brought Lady Merriman from Bagber Manor, while Thomas went to fetch Lady Roakes from Great Little.

They both knew what was happening. Grace and Thomas had decided that this was not a time for surprises. Both ladies had their eyes open as they entered the front parlour, where an open fire blazed, spreading warmth across the elegant room that was hardly ever used.

Alice was there first and Thomas tried to settle her nerves. But all the reassurances he uttered fell like gravel down the side of a quarry, slithering to the ground to join the other landslip. After half a dozen, he switched to general comments about the progress of the building work, ignoring the vague responses he got back in his eagerness to fill the space with sound.

They heard the horses first. Thomas went to the window and said, "They are arrived," then went to stand behind Alice. Was this also an attempt at reassurance or so she could not retreat, maybe escaping out of the side door into the study beyond? With his hands on her arms, he could feel the trembling within her.

It took forever for the two ladies to dismount, for the maid to take their horses around to the small stable at the back of the house, then to return and let them in the front door. Grace, as a Davenport, could have walked straight in but the house seemed more belonging to Thomas and Matthew now and she did not want to infringe, such was the delicate nature of the meeting. In time, Thomas and Alice heard their footsteps clicking on the worn parquet floor their mother had put down when they first moved to this house twenty-five years ago.

Grace came first, saw the fear on Alice's face. Once she had hated this woman for what she had done to Lady Merriman but now she felt raw anger mixed with something else. Her education in Salisbury had not been so comprehensive that it went into names for all the finer emotions. If asked, she would not be able to describe the subtle mix she felt. She just knew it was complicated.

More so because she had been the one to nurse her after the shot went clean through her arm.

And, while there is something cleansing about pain, there is something even more so about tending the pain and bringing a gradual recovery to the patient; seeing a large round hole with jagged edges in a limb and then being first on the scene to help mend it. It gave a sense of ownership, or responsibility, that somehow extended beyond the initial wound.

But right behind Grace came Lady Merriman, not at all sure how she felt. During the ride over she had played a game with herself. Let's call that game 'what if'. It started with what if this woman she was meeting was not Mrs Beatrice at all and was someone else entirely? There would be embarrassed light conversation before someone stood to leave.

Then the game moved to what if she was Mrs Beatrice but was wholly unrepentant? Grace had told her the situation but what if it was a cruel joke and Mrs Beatrice would suddenly claim her back again; she could hear the clink of the chains by the sink, hear the scold of Mrs Beatrice's voice chiding her into working still harder.

Finally, as they crossed the new bridge Thomas had helped build, then climbed the hill to the town, she did a what if we never get there, we just keep on riding forever?

But all the 'what ifs' in the world amount to nothing compared to one tiny dose of reality. And that moment was now.

"It is you," Eliza Merriman said.

"It is me," Alice Roakes replied.

"Come and sit down," Thomas called to them both from behind Alice. He was standing like a second at a duel, ready to jump in to ensure good faith and fair play.

Eliza sat directly opposite Alice in the centre of the room; six feet between them. Grace went over to the window seat behind Eliza, then Thomas, feeling self-conscious standing up, took a rocking chair that creaked on each backward rock but not on the forward ones.

For a moment, nobody said anything. The only sounds were the fire rushing to consume its wooden meal, the distant hum of the town outside and the once-every-two-strokes creak of the rocking chair.

"Why are you here?" Eliza broke the silence, plain-faced, like a Puritan at prayer.

"I wanted to apologise and to see you again."

"Why see me? Why not just keep away?"

But Alice had no way to express the need to face what she had done, to wind it back and try and place salve on chaffed skin and chaffed mind.

"Eliza, Lady Roakes is here to express remorse for what she has done," Grace answered for her. "She cannot wind back the clock but wishes she could. Is that not right, Alice?"

"So, it is Alice now, is it? Don't you know who your friends are, Grace?" Eliza stood up to leave, muttering to herself. "I can't take this. Grace, you told me you had helped to repair her from her physical wound. What about my wounds? Not just the physical ones but the oppression too. For five years I was her slave. I was her slave." As she spoke, she jabbed her finger at Alice, saying slowly "I... was... her... slave," over and over again.

"I would happily turn the crime on its head," Alice said quietly.

"What do you mean?"

"I mean to be your slave, Lady Merr...?

"No, don't ever do that. You live at Great Little, do you not?"

"Yes, Lady Merriman." Even the use of her real name was an act of contrition.

"Make something glorious of that house, of the whole estate, too. Jacob Little's son was my first cousin, his mother being a Merriman. I never knew my cousin. He died before I was born. His parents, my uncle and aunt, were recluses after he was killed during the Civil War." She fell silent for a long time while the winter jasmine knocked against the windowpane and the clouds outside blew on by.

"If you want to make amends, rebuild Great Little to its old glory. Do this for the tenants, for the memory of a great estate, and for me. And, in doing this, you will do it for yourself as well."

Eliza Merriman left then. Grace followed her out, looked back from the doorway with a tender anger that filled Alice's world with hope because tender was the core and wrapped in anger, changed about from half an hour earlier.

Grace was on the way towards forgiveness and even Lady Merriman had laid open a path through the storm.

Alice Roakes sat a long time in the front parlour.

"What were you doing?" Penelope asked her when she got home and told her friend of the meeting. "I would have wanted to get right away."

"I was planning our future, the future of Great Little. Yes, I was feeling for Lady Merriman, feeling for Grace Sherborne, of course I was. But, also, I was thinking, yes, Lady Merriman, I shall do as you say. I shall build up Great Little to be something marvellous and I shall do it by honest labour."

"Amen to that," said Penelope. "Although I've never done a day's labour in my life."

That same front parlour, the very same chairs acted a different play in the hot summer months when sweat trickled down the backs of any who laboured at anything, even with a pen by an open window.

Two men sat upon those chairs and one was Thomas Davenport. They talked a long time and the subject matter was smooth and flowing, for Mr Milligan was talking business with his assistant. It was the type of conversation where diversions happened constantly. They would be discussing the re-building of Great Little, or Thomas' church, or one of the other new projects coming in, when suddenly they would divert to how to produce the best mortar for stone on a raging hot day, or else the particular qualities of a foreman or apprentice with promise.

"You must wonder why I asked myself to lunch with you, Thomas."

"I did," replied Thomas, sort of knowing why; excitement and apprehension rising within him like building two rival Towers of Babel.

"I want you to take over the firm. I am retiring, Thomas."

"But..." But there was no interruption to stop Thomas' response; more that he interrupted himself with a realisation that what he had always hoped for was coming about.

There were some negotiations to go through, of course. It was not a gift of the business but a sale on easy terms; those terms would provide for the Milligans for many years to come.

"You will remain my adviser?" Thomas asked.

"I will while I can."

And, so, they shook on it and the firm became Milligan and Davenport, Builders of Sturminster Newton.

Another meeting involved two matching chairs but in a different location and with different players; this time, also, a cast of just two. The scene is Bagber Manor in April. Matthew had been invited to preach at the makeshift church in the Great Hall. Eliza attended for once, sitting in the back row as if a late arrival. Matthew's sermon dealt with the power of love; how God was love and the absence of love was remedied by turning to God.

Beloved, let us love one another: for love is of God; and every one that loveth is born of God, and knoweth God.

"That was a lovely sermon, Matthew."

Beloved, if God so loved us, we ought also to love one another.

"Thank you, Eliza."

"Will you walk with me, Matthew?"

"I will gladly."

They walked a long time, through the trees to the Divelish,

then along the crooked banks to the Stour itself. They passed the mill, wheel turning regardless of the Sabbath. They talked of many things as the pale but promising sunshine gradually warmed through their coats and into their bones.

They talked of God and family and friendships, of work and of the past, including good times and bad.

Finally, as they returned and branched off to follow the Divelish, there was nothing left to talk about.

Except their future together. So, they walked in silence; each of them holding an unspoken conversation with the other.

Each one saying 'yes' and 'I do' to the other.

Then Lady Merriman broke the silence.

"Follow me," she said in a hoarse whisper, as if she feared being overheard when no one was around. She led him to a weather-beaten summerhouse at the end of a large tract of garden that was deliberately left wild and meadow-like. In the summer house, on chains at either end from the roof beam, hung a double seat in wood with a little ridge to mark the division between the two places.

"I used to sit here with Henry; that is, I mean, Henry's father. All the Sherborne firstborns are called Henry."

"Marry me, will you; I mean, please, because I love you so much." It all came out in a rushed jumble from Matthew. He had grabbed her hand as he spoke and now let go of it again, readying himself for rejection.

"Yes."

"Yes, what?"

"I will marry you, Matthew, and you will make me the happiest person alive."

They kissed as, beyond their faded summer house, the sun turned a corner and slid down the sky.

Book One:

A New Lease On Freedom

1680s England is a disturbed place.

Thomas and Grace Davenport, from a Dorset Presbyterian family, seek their missing friend, Lady Merriman.

The Duke of Monmouth, illegitimate son to the old King, Charles II, lands with a small force in Dorset, seeking to depose his uncle, James II.

"For liberty and religion!" is his cry.

Thomas and Grace are more concerned with tracking down Lady Merriman. They meet the heir to the Earldom of Sherborne, who falls for Grace but a Catholic nobleman cannot marry a Puritan and it seems the match is doomed.

Monmouth is no leader; his following dissipates as he wanders around the West Country.

Thomas and Grace cannot escape the rebellion around them. They are embroiled in war.

Through battle, captivity and deceit, they finally come home in the aftermath of failed rebellion and all that means for Dorset and the whole country.

A must-read for those who love the history and drama of an emerging nation.

The Story Continues

Follow the forging of nations through the fates and fortunes of the Davenport family.

The third book in the series takes us to Ireland, amidst new war and rebellion. Then back to Dorset, to fight corruption on a wholesale basis. Desperate times lead to desperate measures, and these are the most desperate of all.

Politics and religion combine with revenge and hatred to produce a tale in which the Davenports and others struggle for survival but find new friendships, new love, and new opportunity along the way.

All set in a fascinating period of British history, when our modern nations were made.

Lightning Source UK Ltd.
Milton Keynes UK
UKHW012140230519
343218UK00002B/248/P